DEEP WITHIN
A WOMAN'S
HEART

DEEP WITHIN A WOMAN'S HEART

JOANNA JOSLIN

THAMES RIVER PRESS

Deep Within A Woman's Heart

THAMES RIVER PRESS
An imprint of Wimbledon Publishing Company Limited (WPC)
Another imprint of WPC is Anthem Press (www.anthempress.com)
First published in the United Kingdom in 2014 by
THAMES RIVER PRESS
75–76 Blackfriars Road
London SE1 8HA

www.thamesriverpress.com

ISBN 978-1-78308-205-6

This title is also available as an eBook

This book is dedicated to the memory of my great aunt.

Annie Elizabeth Taylor, (1879–1931), was a dedicated headmistress who travelled a great deal, including sailing aboard the RMS Lusitania. Although engaged to an Irish doctor, sadly she never married.

Acknowledgements

My appreciation goes to Angela Glister for her diligence in proof-reading this manuscript and to Wendy Binns for her enthusiastic support.

Grateful thanks must also go to my husband Brian, and to my agent, Darin Jewell, for their encouragement and guidance.

'Every person lives his real, most interesting life under the cover of secrecy.'

Anton Chekov, *Lady with Lapdog*

Chapter One

Friday, May 7th 1915

2.10pm

Everything happened within those eighteen minutes. It began as the torpedo smashed into the ship's hull displacing water and debris into the air; to Captain Turner its explosive impact appeared little more than the heavy slamming of a large door in windswept conditions. Some of the passengers were even oblivious to it. However, the same could not be said for the second explosion. The Lusitania shuddered violently before conceding to her downfall. She began to pitch to starboard, defiantly ploughing her way through the water; her three powerful turbines propelling her at eighteen knots as her bow increasingly subsided, now on course to the bottom of the sea.

The Lusitania had left Pier 54 from New York on May 1st, making this her 202nd transatlantic journey. Any rumoured concerns of dangers from German submarines had been quickly quashed by the knowledge and assurance that the Lusitania's speed would outstrip these threats. The passengers, however, had not been informed that the ship's company had instructed Captain Turner to close down six of the ship's boilers, for reasons of economy. A sense of unease must therefore have pervaded the thoughts of those who worked down in the boiler room, as the stoker's mascot, a black cat named Dowie, had suddenly gone missing. The omens were evident: there for those who believed. Seafaring superstition could never be taken lightly by a true seaman.

The Irish coastline was within view as the panic intensified. Scrambling for survival, passengers searched with desperation for available lifeboats. The tilting of the deck beneath their feet hastened the frenzy of departure. The ship was now sinking quickly and the inability to safely launch the lifeboats only served to fuel the anxiety. As the little boats bashed against the portside, their escapees were littered into the cold sea.

Captain Turner stood there in shock. The Irish shore, although visible in the wake of such tragedy, could not save his passengers and his ship. Rising out into the air, the stern was now most visible. As the funnels collapsed, the boilers exploded and the Lusitania travelled to her resting place, 295 feet below the surface. The time now was 2.28pm: only eighteen minutes following the attack.

The survivors thrashed around looking for anything to hold onto. The ship had disappeared, but there was wreckage and carnage in its wake. Pieces of furniture, deckchairs and bodies appeared on the surface, as though being spewed from the guts of the liner. There was now no segregation for first, second or third class passengers. The living made no distinctions as they struggled to claim anything that floated, wrenching their bodies from the freezing water onto wooden crates, upturned lifeboats and other buoyant remains. Many gripped onto the sides of critically full lifeboats, some by nothing more than an outstretched finger. The only thing that mattered was to remain conscious and to cling to life. One second class passenger, Emily Taylor, in an effort to remain conscious, gripped onto a floating piece of wood and tried to remember her first voyage.

Chapter Two

July 1910

Gripping the handrail with quiet determination, she peered down to the minuscule ant-like figures scurrying alongside the quayside; mixed emotions surged and swelled within her. Emily had never experienced such a powerful concurrence of excitement and trepidation. She glanced around at the fervent gestures of parting and only then did she decide to heartily join in and wave to the crowd below, even though they were all strangers. Far better, she thought, to behave like a seasoned traveller, rather than like a novice on her first voyage.

The Lusitania, at 785 feet, was one of the largest liners in the world and to those ant-like characters on the quayside, appeared truly gigantic and magnificent. Returning the frenzied gestures of waving, the onlookers appreciated that the passengers towering above them occupied an echelon dedicated to high living and luxury. However, the reality was that this floating building segregated passengers according to their ability to pay. First-class travel was secured by millionaires and successful business capitalists; second class by business travellers, teachers and middle-class emigrants; whilst third class hosted the better class of emigrant. Edwardian society existed on such maxims; a place for everything and everyone in their place.

The paper bill posted on the side of Emily's travelling trunk held the wording 'SECOND CABIN BAGGAGE,' ascribing her luggage to the hold and her to the opportunities which second class status afforded. First, Second or Third class, the status of travel was inconsequential to Emily. The qualities that mattered to her were human kindness and integrity: the reasons why she became a teacher.

Emily Taylor was a philanthropic headmistress who genuinely cared for the children in her school. Throughout her career, she had opened their minds to imagination, hope and to the possibility of escaping from the insanitary and dispiriting surroundings which many had been born into. She was the one who planted the seeds of success into their minds, whilst nurturing respect and love in their hearts. She was the one who used her own money to purchase shoes for those who came to school barefoot and she was the one who personally financed the outings that took these children away from their industrial slums.

At thirty years of age, Emily Taylor was a middle class spinster with a heart of gold. As a dutiful and hardworking daughter, her parents were eminently proud of her achievements and had regularly reminded her and those around them of her selfless devotion.

'Never was there such a natural-born teacher.'

'She is one who has responded to a professional calling.'

'Teaching is her life.'

With such accolades Emily was the perfect daughter: accomplished, respected and trustworthy. She was exactly the type of person to represent the family.

As the shoreline of Liverpool increasingly became a distant vision, Emily decided to locate her cabin and acclimatise herself to life on-board.

A Blue Riband winner, the Lusitania was elegance personified, exuding charm and sophistication. The finest oak and cedar woods, felled from some of the most ancient forests in England and France, had been transformed by skilled carpenters to adorn the liner's interior. English country style and French Renaissance styles blended together, furnishing the traveller with a mixture of European splendour, more in keeping with a grand hotel than on a transatlantic liner. The underlying result was that passengers enjoyed a type of ambience normally associated with terra firma architecture and conveniently forgot that they were at sea.

Life on-board also echoed life on land in terms of routine, as a steady flow of passengers made their way to the dining room. Emily was amongst them and, like the others around her, marvelled at the grandeur of the Second Class dining room. She was beginning to wonder what life could possibly be like in the First Class dining room when a waiter motioned to her to follow him to a table with seven diners already seated. A mixture of ages, the adults obligingly nodded and smiled as she took her seat.

A rather stocky, matronly-looking woman was the first to speak.

'Hello my dear. I'm Amelia Davenport. This is my son Jonathan, his wife Beatrice and my twin grandsons, Daniel and David.'

The boys stared goggle-eyed for some time at their new dining companion before blinking in unison. The act rather unnerved Emily, even though she was completely used to being stared at by children.

The woman continued. 'Obviously, identical in looks but would you believe also in nature? We sometimes have a devil of a job to tell them apart. Oh, and let me introduce you to Mr and Mrs Robinson. Recently married, they are on their honeymoon.'

The couple smiled coyly and appeared ill at ease, as if preferring to have a quiet table by themselves. A small silence prevailed as each individual fixed a stare at Emily.

Again the woman intercepted. 'And you are?'

'Sorry, please forgive me, my name is Emily Taylor.'

'Are you travelling alone, my dear?'

'Yes, I am.'

'Well, let's hope not for long. I see you wear no wedding ring. I'm certain there'll be a number of single young men aboard.'

'Mother! Please forgive my mother's impertinence. She is an incurable romantic and thinks everyone is the same.'

The woman may have been incorrigible, but Emily found her nosiness rather refreshing, particularly after experiencing years of everyone assuming that Miss Taylor, a highly respectable teacher, was exempt from ever being interested in the opposite sex. At last, it appeared that there was someone who thought it might just be feasible. As the diners began to immerse themselves in the selection of dishes on the menu, Emily found herself beginning to relax for the first time since leaving home and allowed a wry smile to run across her lips.

It transpired from the ensuing conversation that the Davenports were immigrating to America, to begin a new life abroad. At times, Emily felt that Jonathan Davenport would have happily preferred to have taken leave of his mother in England but she, as an elderly widow, (albeit a robust and occasionally outspoken one) relied upon him and he understood the notion of being a dutiful son. His wife Beatrice obligingly followed his wishes and seemed to accept her mother-in-law with good nature.

'So my dear, may I call you Emily? Tell me, what is the purpose of your journey?'

Amelia's question seemed to instantly irritate Jonathan as he closed his eyes and shook his head in disbelief.

'I'm going to America to attend a family wedding.'

'A wedding! How exciting. Where in America?'

'Long Island,' came the reply.

'You have family in Long Island?' Amelia Davenport's excitement could barely be contained.

'Yes, my aunt, who is my mother's sister, married into a family over there.'

'Which one?'

'My mother has only one sister.'

'No, no, I meant which family?'

'Mother, does it really matter?' Jonathan was clearly finding that his mother's inquisitiveness had gone too far. However, the diners around the table were now all silently waiting for Emily's reply, their eyes avidly fixed upon her.

'The Verholts.' The name alone warranted no further questioning. As descendants of one of the original Dutch families to have moved into the Hudson River valley, the Verholts were seriously wealthy bankers who needed no introduction. For once Amelia Davenport was silent, her mind busily contemplating how this middle class acquaintance would survive the Gold Coast experience.

Chapter Three

Emily Taylor had always prided herself upon being a good judge of character. At the heart of every good school were outstanding teachers and she knew that her staff was of this calibre, because she had chosen and appointed them herself. She ran her school with an unblemished record, as she strove for the very best in her pupils, her colleagues and not least, herself. She would not tolerate her code of decency being broken and anyone who dared to transcend these boundaries could expect appropriate punishment. It was for these very reasons that she felt an overwhelming bout of nauseous disgust weighing heavily in the pit of her stomach.

Why had she deluded those people into believing that she was related to the Verholts, one of the wealthiest families on Long Island? Was it for self-gratification? No. Was it for social standing or the need to impress? No. Was it to break out of the boundaries of convention and confront the unknown? The answer to this was uncertain. That frightened her.

Emily had rarely told a lie in her life and had grown up to be a highly respected member of the local community. But, as with all things in life, a counterbalance had always prevailed. The more that Emily had been hailed as the dutiful daughter, the more wayward and unruly her sister had become. Olivia was her senior by five years and it was of some astonishment that she had ever acquired a sibling. Friends, neighbours and relatives all sympathised with the parents of the strong-willed girl. A miracle had occurred when God had granted them a second child and it seemed to everyone that He had tried to compensate for the first.

Surprisingly, Emily had never experienced resentment from her sister. Olivia may have found Emily's dedication to her studies boring and her aptitude to see the best in everyone annoying, but she had never directed any jealousy towards her younger sister. At least her parents were grateful for that.

Olivia had always been surrounded with such a wide circle of friends that she had never required a close relationship with Emily. As she became older, her friends numbered more males than females and her parents knew that there were no chaperones present to ensure propriety. Their fears for disgrace thankfully never materialised, as Olivia managed to provide some respectability by earning a living as a milliner, an occupation which suited her and she enjoyed, before attracting the attention of a decent young man who had recently proposed to her. It seemed as though the 'worm was at last turning.' Emily just hoped that the same adage could not be said for her. She hoped that when she opened her eyes in the morning, the respectable Miss Taylor would stare back at her in the mirror with reliable conviction.

The next morning at breakfast she found herself alone at the table. None of her dining companions had appeared; their table settings lay undisturbed, and she soon began to question whether they were all refusing to associate with a delusional fraudster. She hated herself for not having made the situation clear. Normally a person of utter clarity, she always avoided ambiguity. In an attempt to see whether her companions were seated elsewhere, she quickly swung around in her seat, narrowly missing a waiter hurriedly passing by.

'I'm sorry, please forgive me. Do you know where my dining companions are?' The waiter shrugged his shoulders and before he could reply a lady passenger on an adjacent table approached Emily.

'I take it you haven't yet heard? The old lady apparently suffered a heart attack during the night.'

Emily tried momentarily to voice a reply but the words failed to materialise. Finally she tried again.

'A heart attack, you say? How is she now?'

'I really don't know. Her cabin is situated next to mine and I just overheard the stewards talking this morning.'

Emily now fully appreciated the agony which her pupils had to endure when waiting outside her office to be reprimanded. Time definitely did stand still. Should she knock or just wait until one of the Davenport family appeared? She didn't want to appear intrusive, but then again she didn't wish to be seen as uncaring. There was a muffled conversation from within the cabin, which good manners and decency prevented her from listening to. The dilemma of the situation had made Emily totally oblivious to the man standing behind her.

In a soft Irish accent he leaned forward and gently whispered into her ear, 'Why don't you knock? I'm certain she'd love to see you.'

Not used to being told what to do, Emily could have viewed the incident as impertinence, but turning to face the owner of the provocative voice, she could do nothing but forgive his intrusion when she saw his eyes, the like of which she had never seen before. The intensity of the rich emerald green dazzled her into staring for longer than was normally acceptable. Not only were the eyes mesmerising, but the smile also ensured that he had the upper hand. His presence had thrown her off course and she didn't know how to react.

'Err, yes, um, I was about to.' Emily had just become as flustered as any of her pupils.

She tapped at the door with caution before being invited in by Mrs Davenport's son and daughter-in-law. Behind them, she saw Amelia Davenport, beaming back to the man standing behind her.

'My saviour,' she said as she outstretched her arms to him. 'Goodness me, what have I done to deserve this?' she said, as she realised that she had more than one visitor. The soft Irish accent again prevailed. 'Short visits are just what the doctor orders.' The tone in which the sentence was delivered promoted a degree of sauciness which Amelia Davenport seized upon.

'Of course doctor, I promise to be a very good girl with you around, or should I say bad girl?' Although the light-hearted banter was proving to be of great medicinal value, the looks upon Jonathan's face indicated embarrassment. The severity of what might have been presumably kept him silent.

Emily, mindful of the doctor's words, comforted the patient with kind words of concern and gratitude. She offered to be of assistance to Jonathan and his wife and then left. Although she had only made their acquaintance the previous evening, and thereby knew them only in passing, the impact of this news had shocked her. Perhaps it made her think of her own elderly parents and the probability of encountering such news again in the future. Or perhaps the shock emanated from other emotions?

Her offer to help was quickly seized upon. With the young boys to occupy during the voyage, the Davenports enlisted Emily to occupy Amelia's need for entertainment. Who better than a headmistress to read the works of Dickens and Hardy? However, even the plight of the poor maid who went to the greenwood and returned a maiden no more in Hardy's *Tess of the d'Urbervilles*, could not compete with Amelia's unrelenting quest to probe for information in real life affairs of the heart. Time and again she interrupted her reader.

'So tell me my dear, you've never been married or engaged?'

'No, never,' came the reply. Again Emily continued, '*The village of Marlott lay amid the north-eastern undulations of …*'

'But the question is would you like to be?'

'It's totally out of the question,' Emily retorted in her school-ma'am voice, becoming increasingly irritated with the interruptions. No one ever stopped Miss Taylor when she was in her stride. '*…the beautiful Vale of Blakemore or Blackmoor…*'

'Have you noticed his eyes? I know if I was a few, well more than a few, years younger, I could certainly be encouraged there.' The comments caused Emily to lose her pace, something which she never did. Momentarily she faltered and then proceeded to continue, pretending that she had not heard the remarks. Although, she knew precisely whom Amelia was describing.

Once again Amelia intercepted her reader. 'Why should marriage be out of the question? A young woman like you would have plenty to offer a prospective husband.'

'Marriage and teaching cannot be combined. If I married I would have to relinquish working with children.'

'But surely you realise that if you don't marry you'll never experience the joy of your own children?' Amelia Davenport had made her point. She had posed a question in Emily's head that had never been raised before.

During the course of the next few days, Emily began to relax a little in the company of Amelia Davenport. Although the woman could be infuriatingly inquisitive, she was also unpretentious and refreshingly honest. She also appeared to care for her young friend. Emily began to eagerly look forward to visiting her and, on occasions, her visit would coincide with that of the ship's doctor.

'Come along in, Emily. I'm sure that Doctor Branigan won't object to your presence.'

Amelia was always eager to invite Emily to stay when the doctor was present. The truth of the matter was that Emily was also keen to be present when Niall Branigan was there. His infectious smile and captivating green eyes were enough to induce any woman, even in good health, to seek out his opinion. That was just the problem, Emily thought: he could have his pick of the ladies. But there was also something which made her believe that this was not the case. Experience in the classroom had taught her that the most flamboyant and outspoken pupils were often the most insecure, labouring behind a façade of witticisms which masked their shyness. Even the green colour of his eyes could symbolise an inexperienced gullible innocence.

The colour green of course could have other connotations, which to Emily's dismay began to preside in her own emotions. Occasionally she would see him exchanging pleasantries with other ladies and, for the first time in her life, she experienced the emotion of jealousy.

Although Amelia was confined to bed and supposedly to rest, she recognised the symptoms.

'Why don't you tell him, my dear?' came the question Emily had been dreading.

'Tell him what?' The two women looked at one another briefly before Amelia shook her head in disbelief.

'Considering that you are a well-educated woman, you really are not very worldly, are you Emily?'

'I'm more aware than you think!' she replied indignantly.

'But are you schooled in the art of seduction?' The question completely threw Emily off balance and made her blush.

'No, I thought not. And yet it is the most basic of all lessons. Emily, I'm going to give you a lesson in life.' The young woman continued to stare in bewilderment at her companion. Momentarily, silence intervened.

'What do you see when you look at me? Just an overweight old woman, who now does not deserve a second glance from the opposite sex! That doesn't even worry me. Do you know why? Because I've lived my life, and what a life it has been!' The emphasis upon the word 'lived' made Emily wonder the nature of Amelia's past. 'These legs here were once showgirl's legs. I've travelled through Europe, entertaining on the stage. I've been wined and dined by Princes, Sultans and Dukes. Not bad for a showgirl. I travelled to Paris, where I met my husband. Would you believe that was in a bordello?' The shocked appearance upon Emily's face was sufficient to interrupt the disclosures.

'Bordello?' voiced Emily; this being the first time that she had ever pronounced the word out loud in her life.

'Yes, bordello, brothel, call it what you will. I was a working girl in the oldest profession on earth!' Amelia began to laugh with amusement whilst her companion looked decidedly more and more uncomfortable.

'My dear, it was only for a very short time. Later I married and then became a respectable wife and mother. Needless to say the experience afforded me a little *Je ne sais quoi*!' Raising her right index finger she lightly patted the side of her nose and nodded with a knowing smile, before leaning forward and adding in a whisper, 'By the way, Jonathan does not know about that little bit of my past. I rather think that it would be best to leave that in the past.' Her companion could not agree more.

Emily had always been told by her parents that you cannot go by appearances alone. Who could have imagined that this inquisitive elderly lady travelling with her family would have had such a raucous past? She had been completely shocked by Amelia's revelations and by the fact that she had willingly disclosed them with a stranger. However distasteful Amelia's past had been, it had also been colourful and memorable, judging by the warm glow those memories had brought to her face. Emily recalled the faces of the elderly ladies in the congregation at her local chapel and realised that these Methodists never wore such blooms of colour in their cheeks. By contrast, theirs were pinched features staring out of dour faces. She knew that her parents would have been disgusted by these thoughts. Still, what they didn't know could not hurt them. She now genuinely looked forward to her next meeting with her tutor and her lesson in life.

The voyage aboard the Lusitania was one which would have far-reaching consequences for Emily. The changes began slowly; persuasive suggestions on Amelia's part made Emily question her own hairstyle, clothing and choice of colour. Fashion had never held much interest for Emily, until now. Her position as a headmistress had always demanded decorum and propriety: namely a high necked blouse and a full-length skirt, which in themselves provided respectable uniformity. Rarely had she deviated from these, even in her limited free time. However, the occasion of a wedding occurring across the Atlantic had persuaded Emily to become indulgent with her choice. Amelia Davenport waited impatiently until Emily tapped hesitantly upon her cabin door.

'Yes, yes, come in.' As Emily entered, the old lady made a concerted effort to sit upright in her bed and make the most of her vantage point. The outfit was completely hidden from view by an outdoor coat.

'Take that off! No one can see you in here. I want to see what you are going to wear for the wedding.'

As Emily removed her coat, Amelia's face wore an unmistakable look of disappointment. The silence was uncharacteristic for Amelia.

'What do you think?' enquired Emily.

'What do I think? I think we had better start again! That's what I think.'

As ever, Amelia was nothing less than frank. The dress was plain and unbecoming. It merely covered her figure without accentuating the slimness of her waist; it lacked intriguing decoration and failed to highlight the promise of what would be underneath it all. Her figure needed to blossom in decided curves above and below. No one would give this creation a second glance.

Emily tried unsuccessfully to put her point of view across: 'But it's the bride that everyone comes to see.'

'There you are wrong, my dear. Many a wedding has given rise to future love affairs. The best thing to do is to enjoy a little shopping trip when we reach New York. If we cannot find anything there, then I doubt we can find anything anywhere! Do you know I am beginning to feel much better today? In fact, I feel ready to undertake a little constitutional along the deck. What do you say?'

Emily made no reply. She had been stunned into silence.

Chapter Four

Daniel and David Davenport were regularly described as 'peas from the same pod.' Nine-year-old twins aboard a transatlantic liner resulted, unsurprisingly, in one thing: trouble. Age gave them swiftness of movement and invariably secured them forgiveness. Misdemeanours were followed by staunch warnings and reprimands from their parents until their large brown saucer-like eyes appeared to offer doleful apologies.

During the four days at sea they had amused themselves with petty indiscretions: hiding behind furniture until unsuspecting passengers became seated and relaxed before being scared with their cries of 'Boo' or imitations of animal sounds. Running away, the perpetrators, once caught, would regularly deny their complicity in the crime, blaming one another. No one could distinguish them apart, including their parents. Jonathan and Beatrice Davenport had considered dressing them differently but it would have been to no avail as they would simply have swopped their clothes to intensify the deception.

They were not bad boys, Emily concluded, but just children who would have benefitted from a firmer approach. She knew that if they had been in her care they would have received a far more disciplined approach. However, even Emily would have been at a loss to secure a suitable punishment for their next escapade. Linked arm in arm, Amelia and Emily walked slowly along the deck. The smell and taste of the salty sea air was always hailed as the best tonic for convalescents. As the sea's breezes blew the ladies' skirts inwards, gentlemen were afforded a slight glimpse of their ankles. Light giggles ensued as many of the female passengers tried unsuccessfully to steer their skirts against the wind. Undaunted, Amelia continued to walk ahead whilst Emily tugged at her skirts to ensure some modicum of decency.

'Good afternoon Miss Taylor. I see you are enjoying the air.' The sentiments were voiced in the unmistakable Irish accent.

'Yes, we are. Thank you.'

'You may find the starboard side a little more sheltered than the port side,' he said laughingly. Emily could easily have blushed but she was too preoccupied with her skirts and the wind currents upon them.

As the wind began to blow with more intensity muffling the audible impact, a skirmish behind them would have gone unnoticed, had it not been for the screaming. Everyone stopped and turned, staring towards the source of the screams. The twin boys were running towards them and at first it appeared that they must be in danger. It quickly became clear that this was not the case as one of them was waving a pistol about in the air. Niall Branigan began to move towards them and flung his arms out in a bid to slow them down.

'Your money or your life,' shouted the one waving the gun about.

'Pay up or we'll shoot,' shouted the other.

As they came closer the doctor began to weave across the deck until he managed to grab the boy armed with the pistol. Wriggling to be free, the captive threw the pistol to his brother who, in an effort to assume precedence and appear menacing, grabbed the handle and pulled the trigger. The doctor and his captive fell to the floor. No one knew whether it was Daniel or David who had fired the shot. Neither did they know if anyone had been hit.

A flesh wound to the arm was not life threatening but the ship's doctor was incapacitated and would need treatment and time for recuperation. Fortunately, New York was beginning to appear on the horizon. The boys would be dealt with severely this time. Of course the question on everyone's lips, not least Jonathan's and Beatrice's, was where had the pistol come from?

The entire incident could have been worse. There had been no fatalities. In the aftermath, Emily suddenly remembered that she had been escorting an invalid on her first venture into the open air. Frantically she began to look around for Amelia, fearful of the consequences that the incident may have led to in a heart attack victim. She ran along the promenade feeling guilty and afraid, until she stopped suddenly outside the Second Class Lounge. Relief filtered through every muscle in her body as she saw Amelia Davenport waving at her from within. The old lady was oblivious to the events.

Amelia had not witnessed anything because as she had continued to walk along the deck, she had turned only once to see Emily talking to Doctor Branigan and had decided to afford them a little privacy and walk on. Feeling pleased with herself, but at the same time a little tired, she had decided to rest in the comfort of the Lounge.

Emily carefully shared the news with her companion but as all the passengers were soon beginning to speak of nothing else, Amelia quickly became inquisitive regarding the source of the weapon.

'Where could my grandsons have found a gun? And a loaded one?' Amelia asked repeatedly.

The same questions were being asked by the authorities, now on-board the Lusitania. Being so close to the shores of America, the Police had boarded the ship and questions were being asked, not least to the twins.

Admitting their guilt of sneaking unnoticed into an open cabin, whilst a maid was undertaking her cleaning duties, had now implicated them as trespassers. Once inside they had hidden under the bunks until they were alone and then they had looked through the occupants' luggage. The sight of the gun had been too much to resist.

'So you just picked it up and then what?' growled the inspector.

'We wanted to be highwaymen,' said one of the boys.

The inspector like everyone else was unable to distinguish between the twins. 'You're Daniel, right?'

'No, David,' came the meek reply.

'Do you two have any idea how serious this is?'

'We are sorry sir, truly we are. We never meant to hurt anyone and...' David began to cry.

'Sir, we only took the gun. We didn't steal those rings and things,' said Daniel.

'Rings and things?' The inspector peered forward with decided interest.

'Tell me more, boys.'

The immediate search of the identified cabin revealed more than the inspector and his team could have ever thought possible. The authorities were relentless in their search. As they meticulously examined the contents of the luggage, the inspector and his team quickly realised the importance of these discoveries. False linings had been applied to the inside of a gent's hat box, a large trunk and even a Belgian crewel lady's handbag. The motive had not been for personal security reasons, but to harbour items which were not meant to be found, at least by anyone other than the new owners. Internal fabric, leather and paper coverings were torn away to reveal a cornucopia of jewellery, silverware, snuffboxes and two small oil canvases removed from their frames. Inspector Jackson and his men had never seen anything quite like it in their lives before; nor had they ever held such treasures in their hands. Even in the absence of experts, they recognised the supreme quality initially captured by the masters who had produced them. Staring back at them were faces in Meissen porcelain adorning two of the snuffboxes, whilst a third silver box held an inscription of its presentation to an English Duke and bore the date of 1838. The policemen picked up the silver spoons, recognised that they had hallmarks and put them down again, unaware that they had just held some of the finest and oldest quality silverware from the late seventeenth century. Luscious red rubies, deep blue sapphires, creamy pearls and dazzling diamonds enticed in their unique expensive settings as brooches, earrings, necklaces and of course, rings. Inspector Jackson held two of the rings in his chubby hands and silently acknowledged that the high spirits of those two boys had led him to all of this. When he had woken up that morning he had little realised what the day would have in store for him. Pensively and hopefully, he thought about promotion and then focussed back upon the rest of the treasure trove.

It was quite clear that the occupants of a second class cabin were unlikely to be the legitimate owners of such valuable items.

Furthermore, even if they were, there would be little requirement for such manner of concealment. Inspector Jackson was satisfied in his own mind that further investigations would yield revelations about the origins of the recovered goods, no doubt the property of some ancient aristocratic family in England.

The important question now was who were the occupants of this cabin? That question was readily answered by the steward: Mr and Mrs Robinson, a quiet couple who apparently were on their honeymoon.

In Jackson's words however, 'the honeymoon had just come to an end.' All that remained to do now was to find the elusive couple. Surely that would not be difficult aboard a ship at sea.

Intensive searches of the ship and questioning of both passengers and crew yielded no clues. The only lead was that the honeymoon couple, Mr and Mrs Robinson, had apparently disappeared without trace. No one had seen them since the first evening when they had dined in the Second Class Dining Room. Emily recalled Amelia introducing them to her and like everyone else had discerned certain reluctance on their part to participate in further conversation. This, along with their absence at further sittings, had been attributed to their preference for a little intimacy. Initially everyone had simply smiled and referred to them as the honeymoon couple.

Inspector Jackson knew only too well that the Atlantic provided a lucrative passage for criminals to escape from England. Sometimes it provided a haven of safety for those wishing to flee the constabulary, the judicial system and the spectre of the gallows, depending upon the severity of the offence. For others it was a passage to a market place where ill-gotten goods could be easily exchanged for financial inducements.

Criminals definitely seemed to be attracted by the lure of the sea and the chance of freedom which it bestowed. The notorious names of Dr Crippen, the wife-murderer and his mistress Ethel Le Neve were still fresh in everyone's minds as the couple who had recently been arrested on-board the SS Montrose in July. Advancements in technology had meant that Dr Crippen had become the first criminal to be captured with the aid of wireless communication. Inspector Jackson recalled that Crippen and his mistress had posed as a 'Mr John Robinson' and his son 'Master Robinson.' The similarity ended there, as the honeymoon Robinsons were still free and had not been arrested, facts which the inspector's superiors would be quick to point out.

Crimes of less notoriety frequently occurred aboard Atlantic passenger vessels and the Lusitania was not without exception. During 1910 in particular, there had been numerous robberies on the ship. There had been complaints from passengers who had been robbed; one voyage alone had witnessed the disappearance of $4,000. The confinement of wealthy passengers over several days at sea was a lure to the light-fingered as an irresistible lucrative trade.

The inspector scratched his head in frustration. He knew that this couple could not have left the Lusitania; it would have been suicidal madness to have jumped ship. Therefore they were still on-board. Every likely place of concealment was checked again but to no avail. He knew he could not keep the passengers on-board indefinitely and grudgingly accepted that the ship would have to berth shortly. He shook his head in desperation as he knew he would have to answer to more senior powers. Those questions: always those questions had to be answered and he knew that he would struggle for the answers. He had recovered a gun and a stash of fine quality items and for once those made him smile. Mr and Mrs Robinson had gone to a great deal of trouble and no doubt expense and would not receive payment for their efforts this time. However, that was the biggest problem. Inspector Jackson knew that unless the police were somehow lucky in apprehending Mr and Mrs Robinson, the latter would no doubt be compensated for their troubles in their next successful operation.

As the great liner docked, the passengers eagerly disembarked. Speculation and hearsay had contributed to a fever pitch of emotions, involving exaggerated accounts of attempted murder, theft and even espionage. Everyone wanted to leave the liner as quickly as they could. The Davenports had already secured temporary lodgings before leaving England and, once settled, intended to find a more permanent home. Jonathan Davenport knew that there was a growing middle-class in America and, with high aspirations, he had decided that he could attain a good position in management or in one of the many service jobs, which in turn would secure his family and himself prominence in the American life.

Amelia, however, had once again infuriated her son with her meddlesome attentions.

'Mother, how can you be so irksome?' Jonathan snapped.

'You call it irksome to offer to help a young woman alone in a strange country?' Amelia continued, 'I only suggested that she might like to stay with us at our lodgings until she leaves for the wedding on Long Island. You said that the house had plenty of rooms.'

'But you could not just be content with that, could you mother? One extra person is not enough for you. I've heard that you've also extended your hospitality to Doctor Branigan. Why he would even contemplate sharing lodgings with the boys who shot him, I cannot imagine.'

Amelia smiled to herself, fully aware of the reason for his acceptance. His injury had incapacitated him and afforded him some leave. Although his left arm was supported in a sling, it would not prevent him from joining them at their lodgings. Upon hearing from Amelia that he would not be their sole guest, he had readily accepted the invitation. The only person who didn't know was Emily herself.

Amelia had not forgotten her pledge to Emily to accompany her on a shopping expedition. She had initiated the suggestion and now intended to fulfil her promise. The season's fashions now favoured looser, lighter styles with far less emphasis upon the full, flouncy elements of previous trends. Women were no longer impeded by the constraints of corsets, tight clothing and padding and trivialised with elaborate decorations. For special occasions the focus of attention lay in the profusion of adornment and creativity of the large floppy hat, offset with a softening display of feathers. The final essential fashion accessory was the ubiquitous parasol.

Always a very reserved and modest person, Emily had failed to show Amelia the hat her sister Olivia, a milliner by trade, had made for her. Far from being discreet, the hat box itself was exceptionally large and had caught Amelia's eye amongst Emily's luggage.

'My dear, let me see your hat,' Amelia asked with excited curiosity.

As the creation was lifted out of its box, Amelia acknowledged how talented Olivia was. Such an oversized piece would be an instant head-turner and an enticement to the opposite sex to introduce themselves to the face which it was framing. The hat alone was enough to indicate how completely different these two sisters were. It was now Amelia's task to imbue Emily with a little more panache.

Taking a hansom cab they quickly arrived at their destination; Amelia having supplied specific directions. Emily had pondered how her friend had such knowledge of a place she professed to never having visited before. Little seemed to daunt her; there was always a high degree of worldliness surrounding her which Emily lacked herself. That of course was the catalyst for their friendship.

New York, like many large towns and cities in both America and Britain, was feeling the effects of mass-production in the clothing industry. The advent of the sewing machine and fabric cutting machinery ensured that labour costs could be reduced and shorter time schedules adhered to. Large numbers of immigrant workers, many of whom had escaped pogroms or organised massacres in Russia and Poland, now provided the workforce in the clothing industry.

'Good morning to you both. How may I be of assistance?' enquired the polite and neatly turned out young lady behind the counter.

'My companion requires a special outfit in order to attend a family wedding on Long Island.' Amelia was most particular in her diction, with the emphasis upon the location.

'A wedding on Long Island, well that does call for something special!'

The magic words for the location had completely ensnared the young woman but were now beginning to terrify Emily. She was beginning to consider leaving the shop and make do with the perfectly acceptable outfit that she had brought from England when Amelia astonished her with an unprecedented outburst.

'If this outfit is good, we may have another wedding!'

The sight of Emily in that outfit had been enough to bring tears to Amelia's eyes. American fashion had not only liberated a young woman who had always staunchly abided her parents' advice of Victorian propriety, but had totally transformed the primness of her past into a promise for the future. With that thought in mind, Amelia decided to put the next part of her plan into operation and secure a chaperone; who better than a respected doctor? Emily would have to understand that she was doing him a favour in allowing him to accompany her. It would be seen as a short vacation during his recuperation.

Doctor Branigan had needed no persuasion, especially when he saw Emily in her outfit.

'Miss Taylor! For once I find myself lost for words.'

The dress, featuring a high-waisted Empire line, was simple yet elegant. Neither emphasising the full curves of the bust and the hips, nor the tightened span of the waist, the dress offered freedom of movement, which in itself was a positive inducement for both the woman who wore this alluring style and the man who gazed at it. It held the promise of freedom in every sense of the word.

Amelia's insistence upon a new dress had had a profound indulgence upon Emily's purse. The spending had known no bounds with Amelia. Supported by the shop assistant, Amelia persuaded her friend that the beauty of the dress relied upon the necessary underwear. American women apparently favoured black underwear which Emily found curious to understand and declined to entertain herself. Her mother had always said that undergarments must be plain and white. Coloured or trimmed items denoted the sign of a woman of easy virtue. Emily did however allow Amelia to select some very delicate and rather expensive pieces for her. Having purchased them she later questioned the error of her ways wondering why she had allowed herself to be talked into buying such expensive commodities when the only person to see them would be herself. She also knew that they were the types of garments which her mother must never see.

The colour of the soft grey dress, featuring a glimpse of an under bodice in contrasting dusky pink, worked well with the large oversized hat which her sister Olivia had made for her. A profusion of grey and pink feathers had been used to adorn the creation. New shoes and a matching parasol now completed the outfit. Emily had never spent so much money on herself before. Her strict Wesleyan upbringing had taught her that indulgence was the preserve of others who could be easily led astray. It was definitely a salutary lesson to contemplate.

If Emily was still recoiling from the dilemma of overspending, Amelia's final surprise must have confirmed her worst suspicions of risqué behaviour. On the morning of the wedding, Amelia had booked an early appointment for Emily at a hair and make-up parlour, which she insisted upon paying for herself. This, she declared, was her treat. Emily had never heard of a make-up parlour before, let alone stepped into one.

The face staring back at Emily in the mirror was totally unknown to her. The prim and sombre looking features of the headmistress had dissipated and had been replaced with luscious ruby lips and exceptionally defined eyes which appeared to offer unrestrained insinuations. Her hairstyle was soft and teased with curls which helped to frame her face. Initially alarmed by the stranger peering back at her, Emily saw the reflection of the girl who had just applied her make-up smiling back at her in the mirror.

'Gorgeous. You're going to knock him dead looking like that!'

'Do you think so?' voiced the timid reply from Emily's mouth.

'I know so!'

Emily left the parlour far more confident than she had entered it. She walked out into the sunlight in this cosmopolitan city, head held high agreeing with the girl's sentiments, whatever the meaning of them.

Chapter Five

Long Island was aptly named, being 125 miles in length and only 23 miles across at its widest point. Located in south-eastern New York it had, by the late nineteenth century, become an esteemed and highly valued summer retreat for New York City residents. The North shore in particular attracted the rich and famous and allowed for self-indulging in lavishly spectacular ways. Limitless styles of architecture, influenced by history or geography quickly began to dominate the cliffs overlooking the shoreline. Roman, Norman, Gothic, Tudor, and Georgian styles vied with French chateaux and Mediterranean villas whilst some properties harboured an eclectic fusion of many designs. The only common factor was indisputable wealth. It oozed out of the round tower dominating the thirteenth century Norman manor house with its enclosed cobblestone courtyard, just as much as it did from the classically inspired red ballroom in the Charles II style mansion.

The purveyors of these icons had made their millions in steel, transportation and other industries. As the home of the prominent and wealthy, the Gold Coast was also aptly named.

The opulence of the exteriors was not found wanting inside these mansions. Often furnished with priceless antiques from England as well as the continent, a tour through the numerous rooms would make any visitor feel that their hosts' ancestors had returned from the Great Tour with their antiquities, rather than having recently purchased them. The illusion presented was one of an illustrious past with a hint of mystique.

Accompanied by Doctor Branigan, Emily arrived on Long Island by train before transferring by carriage to a small hamlet in Suffolk County on the North shore, called Cold Spring Harbor. The village itself had had long associations with whaling but since the decline of this trade in the 1860's, a succession of visitors had secured its survival as a favoured resort featuring several hotels. Niall Branigan secured accommodation for himself at one of these local hotels as Emily had arranged to stay with her relatives. The suggestion was agreeably accepted on Emily's part on the principle of respectability.

Presiding by a pond, Saint John's Episcopal Church appeared to be larger than its initial appearance, as its whitened wooden planks were reflected on the water's surface. There they were dappled and appeared to twinkle with the sun's rays. The little wooden tower stood defiantly on top of the structure, having testified against the elements since 1835.

Emily and her companion remained silent for some time, being transfixed by the surrounding beauty of the landscape. Trees, water and the vast expanse of the sky seemed to dominate the eye with the mere exception of a few constructed buildings. Nature was the all-consuming force which demanded recognition and respect. Man could be born, live and die here but nature would exist forever. Wealth paled into insignificance in the shadow of such omnipotence.

Aunt Clarissa had left the shoreline of England behind her whilst Emily was still an infant. For that reason Emily could not remember her mother's sister and accepted that she would possibly have difficulty in recognising her. That would have been the case if it had not been for the fact that Clarissa, although five years senior, closely resembled Emily's mother, in looks and manner. The only difference being that a contented smile upon Clarissa's face had erased a decade of age and left her looking considerably younger than her sister. A small group of people had begun to assemble by the church door. Emily and her companion walked slowly towards them and she found herself being carefully scrutinised by one of the women. The smile on the woman's face widened as Emily introduced herself.

'Excuse me, I'm Emily Taylor and…'

'Of course you are. The accent proves that.'

'The accent?' queried Emily.

'It sure is wonderful to hear someone from the land of my birth,' the woman assured her. 'My little niece is a grown woman.' Emily found herself being enveloped in one of the tightest embraces she had ever been subjected to. Her mother would have never done this; physical contact always had to remain at a minimum.

'Just look at you. I surely would never have believed that my sister would have encouraged you to look like this.' The remark instantly caused Emily to blush. She had forgotten about her appearance, sanctioned by Amelia.

'Oh, I'm afraid I allowed myself to become ...'

'To become beautiful! Fine clothes and a little make up are not trademarks of the devil, you know.' The woman swung round to the assembled party before stating, 'But try telling that to my sister!' The guffaw of laughter made Emily ill at ease.

'Relax girl. You're amongst friends now. We are just so pleased that you could make it. You're going to sit next to me and tell me all about yourself. We have a lot of catching up to do. I hear from your mother that you're a headmistress now and Olivia is a milliner. In fact, I bet you're wearing one of her creations. Am I right?'

The question suddenly made Emily realise that the over-sized hat on her head was also drawing attention to her, as both men and women were staring at her. As Aunt Clarissa invited her into the church to sit with her near the front, she also remembered that her travelling companion was no longer at her side. Turning she saw Niall Branigan sitting at the back of the church. He smiled and winked at her and once again she felt a surge of colour appear in her cheeks.

The American accent was unfamiliar to Emily. As she listened to those around her, she became fascinated by the colloquial conversations and the unusual way that these people inflected their words. Judging by the response of the congregation, Clarissa was inordinately popular in this community, as gregarious smiles and nods were fervently exchanged. Suddenly an air of excited expectation wafted through the aisles heralding the arrival of the bride. Emily had scarcely noticed the nervous young man at the front until he too turned and looked with some relief at his young bride. Uncle Walter proudly walked his daughter down the central aisle before leaving her to stand side by side with her prospective spouse. The wealth of emotion generated in those few moments brought tears to many eyes, not least to Emily's.

Although a stranger by sight, Cousin Charlotte was the reason that Emily had made this transatlantic voyage. She appeared young and slightly tongue-tied upon exchanging their vows, as did her new husband. A simple service in a simple country church held more meaning than sacramental doctrines in a cathedral, as the small but united community sang each hymn with both feeling and vigour. As the married couple walked past their family and friends and out into the sunshine, Emily, without thinking, admitted to herself that if ever she married this would be the type of wedding she would like.

'Emily, shall we join them?' Clarissa's voice quickly broke the daydream and dispelled any lingering thoughts. 'Come along child, you seem to be deep in thought. I hope they are pleasant thoughts,' laughed Clarissa.

Her aunt failed to notice the absence of a reply as the congregation were all now beginning to file out of the church and she herself rushed forward to greet the happy couple. In her haste Clarissa had also failed to notice the other person present without an American accent standing quietly at the back of the church. Niall Branigan waited for the congregation to depart before moving towards Emily and offered her his right uninjured arm to walk with him; an act she readily accepted. As they left the church, she admitted to herself that her thoughts had been pleasant thoughts. In fact, they had been extremely pleasant thoughts but ones which she could never share.

The obligatory photographer alongside a few hearty amateurs captured the events of that day for posterity. Set against the picturesque background of the little whitewashed church and the countryside beyond, these images would show future generations the happiness of their ancestors. Everyone, including Emily and Niall, beamed with happiness.

The large ornamental gates had been opened for their arrival. This was a special occasion which the Verholts were keen to acknowledge.

Normally their staff would enter the grounds of the estate by means of a separate entrance, designed for staff and tradespeople. The Verholts were, however, model employers and although exacting in their expectations of service, were exemplary in their generosity. They had simply insisted that as employees of their household, Charlotte and Benjamin would celebrate their wedding with a reception in their extensive grounds. It would be a wedding present to remember. Walter and Clarissa had of course given undisputed years of loyalty in their service to the Verholts and were still continuing to do so; therefore the proposition had been readily accepted.

The bridal party, their relatives and friends were transported in the time-honoured way from the little church to the sprawling grounds of the Verholt estate, by a succession of horses and carriages. The whole effect created a fairy-tale illusion and seemed so far removed from her life in England that Emily momentarily began to question whether she was dreaming. In fact, the whole journey from her departure at the quayside in Liverpool had been totally unpredictable.

Surrounded by 150 acres of land containing formal gardens, ponds boasting spectacular fountains, a lake and woodlands, the Charles II style mansion was entirely encapsulated in graceful privacy. Wealth maintained such security with infinite contours of hedges, fences, trees, gates, gatehouses and even intersections of private roads.

The wedding party crossed wide terraced areas before filtering down a short series of steps to wide expanses of lawn, where a large white open-sided tented structure had been erected. Little groups of tables and chairs had been carefully positioned under the open structure, in order to shield the occupants from the glare of the afternoon sun. Each table had been carefully laid with linen, cutlery and appropriate glassware. The climate, although exceedingly warm and humid, fortunately received some relief from the afternoon sea breezes blowing inwards from the Atlantic Ocean. These regularly helped to temper the oppressive heat, as well as limit both the frequency and severity of thunderstorms.

As the party became seated a distinct hush descended as all eyes fell upon the approach of a couple of people from the vicinity of the house; the gentleman being a distinguished silver-haired man of around seventy years of age whilst the lady was considerably younger. Both were elegantly attired and, from the reaction of the wedding party, Emily understood that the Verholts were now in their presence.

'Good afternoon, Ladies and Gentlemen. It is our great pleasure to welcome you here to our home and the reception of Benjamin and Charlotte: Mr and Mrs Lee.' A distinctive Dutch accent still pervaded after many years of living in America.

'I must say it sounds good to be able to refer to them as Mr and Mrs Lee.' A ripple of laughter broke out amongst the guests as their hosts smiled and everyone began to relax.

'We have known them for many years. Charlotte indeed grew up here as her parents made their home with us. They have worked for us for so long that we think of them as our friends. My wife and I offer our good wishes to Benjamin and Charlotte. May they have many years of happiness ahead of them. To Benjamin and Charlotte.' Everyone rose to their feet and toasted the happy couple from the recently filled glasses in front of them. Emily, like many present there, had never tasted champagne before, and found herself experiencing an unusual sensation: that of bubbles exploding in the mouth. She coughed and began to feel the same sensation in her nostrils. Embarrassed she tried to suppress any further reaction which only made the situation worse. Mr Verholt remained silent as Niall rose to his feet, asked for some water and using his right arm gently stroked her on the back. Everyone watched as he tenderly applied his care. Aunt Clarissa doubted that Niall Branigan was only a travelling companion and a doctor. With that thought in mind she wondered what her sister would make of that and allowed a wry smile to cross her face.

Clarissa and her younger sister Hannah, the mother of Emily, had been born into a dutiful and exacting family. Allegiance and accordance to the beliefs of the Wesleyan Methodist Chapel were initially tolerated by Clarissa in her childhood but in later years she began to question her elders. The seed of doubt had been planted and atheism was growing in her mind. This was seen as unconventional behaviour and unbecoming in a woman. Persistence made it clear that Clarissa was inciting trouble for herself and showing disrespect for her family. Rebukes had no effect. As she reached adulthood and showed a preference for a drink, her actions went against everything that John Wesley had initially warned against. Meeting Walter Whittaker only compounded the problem, as he enjoyed a gamble but his ideas for his biggest future venture only served to shock the family more.

Clarissa and Walter had been walking out together for a little more than only a year when he proposed marriage. A labourer by trade, his prospects were unremarkable and uninviting to Clarissa's parents, but his genuine affection for their daughter made them concede to the marriage. Sensed as a dreamer by nature, his plans for their married life were seen as little short of disastrous, by everyone except the happy couple.

Dreams of becoming rich had to be confined to the imagination but Walter Whittaker was certain that he could prove to be the exception. A transatlantic journey would deliver them to America and the gateway to wealth. From there they could travel across America and reach those gold fields.

The Cariboo Gold Rush in the Canadian province of British Columbia had attracted numerous pioneers, inducing them to endure crossing the treacherous Rockies with the sustained hope of locating wealth. Gold had been discovered at Horsefly Creek in 1859, with subsequent strikes at Keithley Creek and Antler Horns Lake in 1860. With further strikes at Williams Creek, the rush for gold had begun.

By the 1880s gold was still being discovered and areas such as Upper Libby Creek and Howard Creek were well known gold-panning areas. Walter felt sure that there were still more gold fields to be discovered and he wanted to be there to enjoy that buoyant feeling of free for all. His wife's parents did not share his optimism, as his father-in-law made very clear.

'The journey will be hard, unrelenting and gruelling. Many of those who have gone out have already died from fever, cholera or exhaustion. Once there, many women have been left as widows as their husbands have been killed in mining accidents. The communities they live in co-exist with, I have read, 'soiled doves' or prostitutes. This is no place for a woman and no place for our daughter. We have not raised her to live like this.'

Walter finally accepted that the hazardous hardships would be too much for his wife and agreed to abandon his golden dreams; at least those of prospecting or panning. No one however could take away his dreams of a golden future.

Chapter Six

They arrived on the shores of America in 1885 with the hope that they would begin newly married life in a country boasting promise. Walter had given his word to his in-laws that he would secure a respectable occupation and dutifully look after his new wife. With no job to go to, Walter knew he was taking a risk but that was life. In his mind he knew something would crop up and when it did, he would seize it with both hands. As they prepared to disembark and face a new life in a new country, they little realised how the events of that day would change their lives forever.

As Walter and Clarissa began to leave the quayside, their attention was initially alerted by the high-pitched screams of a woman jostling against the assault of two men. The assailants were rough in appearance and dress and were trying to snatch the woman's bag. Attired in expensive apparel, her refined appearance belied a stubborn streak to retain her belongings. One of the men punched her companion in the stomach, winding him sufficiently to withdraw from the struggle and coil into a painful retreat. Without thinking, Walter ran straight into the fracas and punched the assailant into an unconscious state. The sight of his accomplice lying motionless on the ground was sufficient for the other perpetrator to relinquish his hold on the bag and run away from the scene.

Dutch-born Johan Verholt and his wife Greta owed a debt of gratitude to this young Englishman. He had prevented the stealing of an expensive bag and no doubt equally expensive contents and, truth to be told, had possibly saved their lives. The reward for such bravery had to be appropriate. How more appropriate than secure employment in the Verholt household? Upon learning that this young couple were without employment and a place to live, Johan and Greta Verholt had the perfect solution. Their residence was situated on the north shores of Long Island and had so many rooms to look after that two more servants in their household could easily be found jobs to do.

It seemed that Walter's dream of a golden future had finally begun to materialise.

Twenty five years had now elapsed since that first meeting and the Whittakers owed everything to the kindness of their employers. Clarissa had shown herself to be a highly organised, reliable and thorough maid and as the years passed she achieved the position of housekeeper. Walter had likewise shown his steadfastness of reliability and now was the Verholts' butler. Their daughter Charlotte and her husband Benjamin both worked for these model employers and had met whilst in their employment. This newly married couple knew that they would continue to enjoy full employment and good-quality accommodation on the estate. The added grandeur of the wedding reception, set on the lawns of the property, was further testament to the kindness of their employers in providing this as their wedding gift.

Following the kind words and the toast, the Verholts now withdrew, leaving the wedding party to enjoy a sumptuous wedding breakfast with their friends and family.

As the courses arrived and the wine flowed freely, conversations abounded with a gleeful ease. Emily had now become accustomed to the liquid refreshments being continually poured into her glass by the ever-present waiter. As she looked around she noticed that everyone was happy. Smiles and laughter were evident everywhere that afternoon. Her cousin Charlotte positively glowed, which she attributed to happiness and no doubt to some of the liquid refreshment. With that thought she found herself smiling and as she turned her eyes met those of Niall Branigan's. They shone with such intensity and returned a smile back which held a depth of feeling previously unknown to Emily. She had not noticed that he had been watching her for some time. As she had looked around the gathering, he had looked only at her.

Embarrassed she tried to divert his attention, 'Charlotte and Benjamin make a handsome couple, would you not agree?'

'They do.'

The short reply only added to her embarrassment as she found it difficult to divert his gaze from her face.

'Have you been to many weddings before?' The question had barely left her lips when she realised how ludicrous it appeared. She certainly did not want it to be conceived as an indictment or invitation to anything more.

'Only in Ireland.'

'Of course, you originate from there. Do you manage to return there, I mean with your working commitments?' Emily was beginning to feel flustered. She did not want her questions to be too personal but she felt she needed to show an interest.

'Home is where the heart is. At least that is what I've always been told or led to believe and as my heart is where my body is, that is *home* to me.' His answer only served to puzzle Emily. He knew that and proceeded to firstly wink before grasping her right hand pulling her closer to him, so that he could whisper into her ear, 'At the heart of every good home, I think there should be a good woman.' The releasing of her hand coincided with the appearance of the waiter and the next course.

The refreshing zesty taste of the lemon flavoured water ice was a welcome relief to the palate and the oppressive heat of the afternoon sun. It may have helped to cool down the body temperature but it was questionable whether it would affect the ardour of that moment.

'Have I shocked you, Miss Taylor?' Niall enquired faintly.

'No, certainly not.'

'Good. My bedside manner has always relied upon a little teasing, here and there. It's definitely good for the soul. I am sure you witnessed that with Amelia Davenport. For a moment there however, I thought I'd overstepped the mark, which I wouldn't want to do.' His serious facial expression and contrite manner now seemed completely out of character with his Irish sense of humour.

'I can assure you Doctor Branigan, that you have not shocked me.' Emily was determined to present an outward display of serenity to mask her innermost feelings.

'Niall, please call me Niall.'

'Very well …Niall, but you must call me Emily.' The mutual smiles and subsequent silence were evidence of an agreeable understanding between them.

Contentment abounded on the faces of the guests as the enjoyment of both the drink and the food began to take hold. Some had indulged to such a degree that upon standing they seemed unsteady on their feet whilst others, unable to resist the culinary delights appeared to find that their garments had slightly tightened around their abdomens. The ladies apportioned the blame upon the sweltering sun whilst the gentlemen proceeded to unbutton the lower parts of their jackets and waistcoats for comfort, before swallowing further refreshments. Following the salutations and tributes of the wedding speeches, further encouragement to toast the happy couple resulted in some guests assuming slightly slumped positions before conceding to closing their eyes and snoring. Everyone was in agreement that the wedding celebrations had been splendid and that the Verholts were solely responsible for providing this splendour; none more so than Walter and Clarissa Whittaker, who knew that they owed their employers a debt of gratitude.

As the sun began to wane some of the male guests withdrew into a corner where a series of musical instruments had been deposited. A little band comprising musicians with banjos, violins and guitars along with the accompaniment of a vocalist played together to fill the air with well-known American melodies including, 'Shade of the Old Apple Tree,' 'What you goin' to do when the rent comes 'round?'' and 'Bill Bailey, won't you please come home?' Some guests began to clap, sing or dance whilst others picked up cutlery, such as spoons and began to clatter them together as percussion instruments in time to the music. Some repeatedly hit the tops of tables or chairs whilst others merely tapped their feet but everyone, regardless of musical talent, joined in and appreciated the homespun entertainment.

The beat of the tunes induced men, women and children to gyrate with enthusiasm on the manicured lawns. Holding hands, children and their parents whirled around, spinning both their bodies and their heads until a feeling of dizziness intervened.

The musicians were a varied selection of people; young and old, servants and tradesmen who played together in unison and had but one aim that evening: to ensure everyone enjoyed themselves.

Everyone did enjoy themselves that evening, including Emily and Niall. To onlookers they appeared as a close couple rather than mere acquaintances. They laughed and talked together to the exclusion of those around them. Niall spoke of his time aboard the Lusitania and the quirky patients he had had to deal with, whilst Emily entertained with a series of amusing anecdotes, relating to the naivety of children. The tales were gentle true to life stories, containing neither malice nor condemnation, each one opening a window upon the other one's life. As the conversation continued they seemed oblivious to the replenishment of wine in their glasses, which in turn induced more animated tales and more laughter. Aunt Clarissa was not oblivious to the mutual attraction between them and for this reason resisted approaching them. There would be plenty of time to talk with her niece in the days that followed.

A potent mix of infectious bonhomie and subliminal passion will always lead to chance antics; none more so than when alcohol is present. Upon what seemed to be a sudden whim, Niall rose quickly to his feet and using his right hand reached out and grasped Emily's hand, pulling her also to her feet. The pair giggled as they walked to the area of the lawn which was now being used as a dance floor and began to dance to the rhythm of the music. Both were seemingly unsteady upon their feet, as a result of the wine and, to some degree, their adherence to propriety; an injured arm was proving an obstacle in holding a lady correctly, especially when the lady was intoxicated. She felt his hand upon her back both steadying and drawing her towards him whilst he experienced the soft scent of her perfume and her body beginning to yield towards him. Her head began to tilt in his direction until he could smell the fragrance of her hair and skin close to him. Not a word passed between them as he tightened his supportive hold around her and realised that the drink had taken effect; she was unconscious in his embrace. He smiled to himself as he realised that this was the first time that he had ever held a headmistress like this; indeed it was the first time that he had held a headmistress. A small voice inside told him that it would not be the last.

Chapter Seven

Upon waking Emily slowly opened her eyes and looked around anxiously; nothing was familiar to her. Not the room, not its contents and not the sick feeling behind her eyes. Moving her head only seemed to intensify the feeling. A headache to her was something which occurred with too much written work; her mother had always said eyestrain would lead to the wearing of spectacles. Sometimes a headache preceded her monthly show and made her appear slightly irritable. However she had never experienced a headache like this before. She sank back into the comfort of her pillow, closed her eyes and recalled the grim warnings associated with the consumption of alcohol:

'…Please Miss, I'm hungry. We went to bed without food last night as Mother said Father had taken the wages to the pub.'

'…They say he died a pauper. Drank himself to death.'

'…There is only the workhouse left.'

These were all familiar sayings that Emily had heard from her pupils, their parents and the teachings of the Methodist Chapel which her own parents extolled. She cursed herself for being so foolish and questioned why anyone would be so addicted to a substance that caused so much pain and suffering. When she opened her eyes again the reality of the situation hit her. She had allowed herself to become drunk because she had been enjoying herself, drinking, talking and dancing with a man. The look of disapproval on the faces of her parents loomed into her mind and she instantly resolved to put the incident behind her. She would never touch alcohol again in her life and instead would concentrate upon her vocation of being a respectable headmistress. Thankfully

Aunt Clarissa was not one to communicate regularly with her parents so they would be none the wiser. She reassured herself that everything would soon return back to normal in her life. Treading upon English soil would quickly reinstate the habitual pattern of her normal life.

Sleep once again blocked out the pain of the lingering headache until the click of the door awakened her. As she opened her eyes she saw Aunt Clarissa looking down at her with a benign smile across her face.

'Not feeling too well?'

'I'm fine.' Emily returned a contrived smile but quickly found herself settling for an involuntary grimace.

'Is this the first time that you have had such a pounding headache?'

The silence was sufficient reply. Aunt Clarissa drew up a chair, seated herself and bending slightly forward stroked Emily's forehead.

'Sometimes in life there are times when choices have to be made. These can come about because life may have taken you off course, into uncharted territory. Familiar is safe but it is not always the best option, Emily. Everyone thought that Walter and I were mad leaving England to sail across to America. We had little money, no jobs and nowhere to live. But we did have each other and a burning belief that something good would happen. It certainly did and as a result of that chance meeting with the Verholts, our lives have been turned round. I saw a spark of what could be in you last night. Take that happiness and grab it Emily before it is too late… before you become a dried up old kernel like my sister.'

Contesting this statement would have been futile as Emily's head began to throb. Her aunt left fruit juice, fresh fruit and bread at her side, before departing reminding her that rest would cure the ailment. As Emily closed her eyes she pictured an elderly spinster, grey haired and shrunken in stature and recognised herself in years to come.

Sleeping until the middle of the day was something Emily had never before done in her life. Feeling better, she helped herself to some of the refreshments and having dressed decided to find her aunt.

Leaving her room she found herself in a corridor with steps leading down to a ground floor. As she peered out of the windows she realised that she appeared to be in a small cottage, situated at the back of the Verholt's mansion. There were a small number of these cottages which Emily considered must have been built for the presiding staff on the estate. Judging by the interior the cottage was welcoming, homely and a considerable attribute to have as rented accommodation. The Verholts were certainly forward-looking, model employers.

Emily's appearance coincided with a flurry of activity; she soon found herself being hastily acknowledged by her aunt and uncle before being left alone in the cottage. Within a short space of time her aunt returned and this time the sense of urgency had been replaced with calm relief. She sank into a chair, closed her eyes and stretched out her legs.

'God knows I love my job, but sometimes I just wish they'd give a little more warning.'

'Warning?'

'Yes, warning. On a sudden whim they've taken off to stay with friends in New York. Likely to be gone for two or three days and that always means plenty of clothes and packing. Now they've gone we can all calm down a little, especially after the wedding. How's the head?'

'Clear again.'

'Good. Would you like to take a look around? I'll grant you that you will never have seen anything like it before.'

The design of Suffolk Hall had been influenced by the extravagance of the English Restoration period. Immense wealth had enabled the Verholts to indulge their architectural love of such splendour. Inside, the house paid court to both continental and English styles of furniture and furnishings, including those with a Dutch-cum-French influence. As Emily walked with her Aunt through the numerous rooms she wondered how one family could possess sufficient wealth to own such a house. The Verholts were exceedingly wealthy bankers with a reputation for fine living, dining and entertaining. No doubt many a successful business deal had been agreed within these rooms, where elegant walnut furniture and rich colouring attempted to impress any visitor. Faces from allegorical, Olympian or biblical scenes stared downwards from painted masterpieces on the ceiling.

The rooms were numerous and generous in proportion. Emily listened as Clarissa proudly guided her through the house, stopping occasionally to comment upon an intricate piece of decoration. Although the house dated from the late 1800s, it evoked centuries past, and contained a collection of superb reproductions in terms of furniture, furnishings and decorative work. Contemporary artists had tried to emulate the genius of past masters such as Grinling Gibbons, using lime and fruit woods to depict animals, shells, birds, flowers and fruits in the wood-panelling. Even reproduction pieces such as these were valuable as they entailed complicated entwinements of animal and plant forms and the time afforded to their production would have secured large payments.

However, not everything was reproduction, as Clarissa eagerly pointed out. Tapestries, paintings, mirrors, marble fireplaces and certain pieces of furniture had crossed the Atlantic from their original homes in England and on the continent, to adorn this Long Island mansion. Their presence brought centuries of history and mastery to a relatively new country eager to display them by association. The ensuing implication was that anyone wealthy enough to own them was highly successful: the ultimate maxim for business.

It was not the large pieces of furniture or the ostentatious carvings which commanded Emily's attention the most, but rather the small more personal items. A small round table hosting a collection of framed photographs caught Emily's eye. As she walked towards it, Clarissa began to describe its origins.

'That is simply beautiful. In fact it's one of my favourite pieces. Apparently it belonged to the Verholt's family in Holland. The top has been decorated in marquetry. That is where they use woods of different colours and cut them out before gluing them to the surface and as you can see, the designs of the fruits and flowers decorating this are all made from small pieces of wood. This little table is original. Can you imagine Emily, how old it is?' Clarissa picked up some of the frames so that Emily could see the beauty of the table.

Emily failed to voice a reply as she had ceased to listen to the description of the technique of marquetry. Her eyes continued to stare with disbelief at a photograph in one of the small silver frames still remaining on the table.

'Who is that in the photograph?' The sharpness of Emily's question did not disturb her aunt.

'That is the Verholt's grandson, Mr Christian Verholt.'

Emily remained silent. She had met him only once before. He had been with his wife on his honeymoon; Mr and Mrs Robinson she recalled had however simply disappeared.

Neither the grandeur of the surroundings nor Clarissa's eagerness to impart the provenance of individual pieces of artwork was sufficient to command Emily's attention. The opulence of the house and its contents faded into oblivion as her mind whirled with suppositions. Her preoccupation with these thoughts began to manifest across her face until Clarissa stopped short in a sentence.

'I've overtired you. You must forgive me but seeing all these things every day makes me realise just how lucky we are to work for the Verholts; they have been so good to us. We are so proud to be here. You can understand why, can't you?' Emily smiled and nodded and understood that it was precisely for these reasons that she could not disclose her thoughts with her aunt.

Conveniently feigning tiredness Emily withdrew to her room, supposedly for sleep but sleep was blocked from her reach as reoccurring thoughts flooded into her conscious mind. The seed of doubt in recognition regularly appeared but years of teaching had made her an astute identifier. No one could pull the wool over Miss Taylor's eyes and pretend they were someone else; those pupils who had tried had learned never to attempt any similar tactics in the future. No one except of course for the twins; Daniel and David Davenport had made her feel uneasy as they had stared at her with those indiscriminate large brown saucer-like eyes. Apart from the twins whom even Inspector Jackson could not distinguish between, Emily had always prided herself upon her powers of recognition. Deep in her heart she knew that the face in the photograph was the face she had seen across the dining table on-board the Lusitania.

A faint tap upon her bedroom door suddenly intruded her preoccupation with the mystery. Her aunt's face beamed as she informed Emily that Niall Branigan was downstairs, enquiring about her.

The recognisable green eyes sparkled as their gaze fell upon her. For an instance silence intervened as the smile was traded solely between Niall and Emily. Clarissa experienced a moment of intimacy and withdrew, leaving them alone.

'Your aunt tells me that the effects of last night are taking a while to leave you.' As he spoke his smile intensified, which together with the sentiment made Emily blush.

'Yes, I must admit that my head was a little sore this morning when I awoke. I am not used to alcohol.' Emily was keen to point out that as a respectable headmistress she did not associate with drink.

'I'm just the same. Never touch a drop on duty. My only little tipple is Irish water.'

'You only drink water from Ireland?' The naivety of her question caused him to laugh.

'Irish water is what we call whisky.' His emphasis upon the word, whisky, made Emily smile causing her to look away, presumably with slight embarrassment.

He found the innocence quite refreshing and rather alluring, particularly in an educated woman. She was quite unique and unlike any woman he had ever encountered. Money often bred impossible passengers, especially women who expected a ship's doctor to attend to their every need. Niall had had more than his fair share of encounters; the haughty surrounded with downcast maids could demoralise anyone who would not succumb to their demands; the hypochondriacs whose husbands took little time to spend with them, turned too regularly to the ship's doctor as a bout of seasickness took hold; and finally the wealthy always thought that a good looking man, inferior to their station, could not resist the charms and advances of a rich woman, however young or old she was. Niall was undoubtedly good-looking and a charmer and had used these attributes to maximum effect, within the scope of his bedside manner; however he had never used his charms to bed a passenger; he drew a fine line of decency between himself and the fine ladies.

'I wondered if you would care to come with me for a walk. The air should do you good.'

Emily smiled in recognition. 'I am sure the doctor knows best.'

'I am sure he does.'

Clarissa watched them for some time from her vantage point within the cottage until their diminishing silhouettes became obscured by the numerous bushes and trees. An incurable romantic, she smiled happily at the prospect of this liaison becoming permanent. Momentarily she pictured her sister's face, transfixed with an expression of shock that her daughter Emily would denounce her career for marriage. Her smile deeply intensified with the thought that love was more important than duty; a sentiment she herself had used upon the eve of her own wedding.

The gardens like the house were large, formal and decidedly impressive. 150 acres was sufficient land to host the whims and fancies of any wealthy landholder; a private haven of indulgence was understandably excusable. Horse riding, hunting, shooting, fishing, swimming, golf and tennis were the pursuits of the wealthy and with land to host these, house parties accommodated and entertained the most influential in business and society.

For those appreciative of less arduous pastimes, a simple meander through the gardens could provide stimulation for the senses as well as concealment for assignations. Several individual statues positioned in niches along the south terrace stared down at the couple as they bypassed them. No danger existed with these mute eavesdroppers who sometimes could fall party to financial deals, scandalous gossip and intimate secrets. Ahead of them a formal walkway lined with Tsuga Canadensis, Canadian Hemlock and European lindens extended to a sundial surrounded with mounds of blooming rhododendrons. As they reached the sundial it was possible to see that the shadow of the pointer cast by the sun was directly falling on the 3 o'clock mark.

'What are you thinking about?' Niall enquired.

'I was just considering what time it is in England. It is so strange to think that it must be evening there now.' Emily paused and studied Niall's face for a moment before continuing. 'Do you ever think about home?'

'I once told you before that home is where the heart is.' Moving closer to her he grasped her hand and pressed it to his chest. 'My heart is here Emily. It's beating quickly and that's because you're near me.' As she slightly gasped and began to pull away from him he tightened his hold upon her hand and drawing her closer towards him, until he could once more smell the fragrance of her hair and skin, he kissed her lightly upon the lips. He released his hold and as they parted only their eyes communicated. It was enough for each one to know that they wanted more. The embrace was mutual and demonstrative of strong, unyielding passion. Their arms encircled each others' bodies drawing them together. She grasped his shoulders pulling him down towards her whilst feeling his fingers sliding down her back, lower and lower until they rested upon the contours of her bottom. She gasped again as she experienced previously unknown emotions; seething emotions coursing from her throat down to her stomach which quivered with excitement before transcending further down her body. Only the distant rumblings of a thunderstorm were sufficient to interrupt their passion.

The rain quickly followed, drenching everything blocking its path as it fell from the dark heavily-laden clouds now presiding over Long Island. As their clothing became soaked they anxiously looked around for shelter; the house and buildings seemed too far away but a small summerhouse caught their attention. Safely inside they stood facing one another, watching the final raindrops dripping from their hair. As Emily began to shiver, Niall removed his jacket in customary gallant fashion before wrapping it around her shoulders. He gently guided her to a seat, placing himself closely next to her.

As he spoke he placed his arm around her shoulders, drawing her closer to him.

'The warmth of two bodies together is the best way to stay warm.'

'Is that in the medical books?'

'Of course.' They began to laugh and Niall could not resist the opportunity to plant a light kiss upon her forehead.

'Feeling warmer now?' Emily nodded in response and snuggled up closely to him, like a child in need of a parent's protective embrace.

'Well I don't know where that came from.'

'Do you mean the rain or the affection?' Emily enquired.

'Definitely the rain. I've known about the affection for some time and I think you have too.' As they caught one another's gaze she smiled at him and slowly nodded.

Not a word was exchanged between them for some time as their bodies nestled closely together, their fixed stares directed out beyond the window-panes and the rainstorm beyond; neither one knowing what the other was thinking.

Niall was the first one to break the silence; his usual light-hearted approach was obscured with hesitation.

'Emily, I can't seem to find the words I'm looking for. I'm not normally afflicted with such a problem.' She smiled back with a knowing look.

He rose to his feet and cleared his throat before continuing. 'The only thing to do in such a situation is to speak plainly. Therefore that is exactly what I am going to do. Emily will you marry me?'

Silence once again intervened and as she stared up at him he feared that his proposal was being viewed as impertinent.

'I'm sorry I did not mean to offend, but…'

'Yes Niall, I will marry you. I will.' The repetition and strength of emphasis upon the words 'I will' left Niall with no hesitation that she wanted the marriage as much as he did.

She rose to her feet and into his embrace; holding her closely to him he kissed her with such passion that her head began to feel intoxicated whilst her body experienced spasmodic heights of excitement hitherto unknown to her. The beating of her heart accelerated with each moment of pleasure until she began to feel light-headed and giddy. As their lips finally parted he clasped her to him, steadying her stance. Nestling into the protection of his embrace she quietly mouthed, 'I am so happy' and his arms drew around her even tighter.

They remained there for some time, oblivious to the incessant rain outside. When at last the silence became broken it was with laughter rather than words. Emily suddenly began to shake with uncontrollable laughter. Niall was bewildered by her laughter but slowly found himself infected with her good humour as he too began to smile and laugh.

'Why are you laughing?' Niall repeatedly asked without at first receiving an answer.

Finally she began to take control of the situation until her face wore a slightly more restrained appearance.

'I cannot remember the last time that I laughed so much,' she admitted. The truth was that Emily, the prim but respectable headmistress had never laughed with so much gusto in her life before. A childhood of quite rigid standards of upbringing followed by high expectations of social respectability, had moulded her into a woman now positioned on the pinnacle of a very high pillar of society which condemned fickle attitudes of behaviour.

'I am laughing, Niall, because everyone who knows me, who truly knows me, will not believe what I have just done. I have just agreed to marry a man whom I have only recently met. I know nothing about you or your family and you know nothing about my family or indeed me. Is that not a recipe for disaster everyone will ask? But no it is not, because I truly believe in you and in us. For the first time in my life I have experienced happiness, true happiness and that cannot be bad, can it?'

'There is nothing bad about the way we feel for each other Emily. We're both mature enough to take responsibility for our actions. I am sure that when I meet your parents they will understand. Of course I will seek your father's permission first.' As the words tumbled from his lips they initiated a scene of doom rather than reassurance in Emily's mind.

'That's the problem. My parents expect me to teach instead of marry. I cannot have both. If I marry I must resign my position as a headmistress and as a teacher.'

'But surely your parents would understand. You told me that your sister is engaged to be married. I am sure that they would be delighted to have both their daughters married.'

Emily shook her head with dismay. 'No, that is not the situation. They will be extremely happy to see Olivia married and settled into a respectable marriage but I am supposed to be the one whose true vocation lies in my profession. They provided support whilst I studied and are now proud of my achievements. No, it would be wrong to both upset and disappoint them. I...I cannot marry you...' Tears began to well from her eyes as the celebratory moment had suddenly soured into painful reality.

'You would walk away from a lifetime of happiness for fear of disappointing your parents? Emily, they may have given birth to you but they do not own you. You are mistress of your own destiny and as such you must dictate your own path through life.'

'It is not so easy, believe you me. Here I can pretend to be someone else but when I return home I go back to being Miss Taylor.'

Silence momentarily intervened as they carefully searched for an answer in each other's eyes.

'That is it!' Niall appeared quite animated in his response which also boasted a degree of self-satisfaction.

'What is it?' Emily enquired with quizzical naivety.

'We'll marry in secret. As Mrs Branigan you will be my wife but to everyone else you will be Miss Taylor!'

Chapter Eight

At first it had seemed so simple; the notion of being able to please oneself as well as everyone else. The euphoria of the moment had been heightened by the mutual hedonistic pleasure that always stems from love. However as time lent distance to Niall's suggestion, a turbulence of doubts once more began to visit Emily's mind. How could they live as man and wife but maintain pretence of unmarried status? Deceit and lies, always treacherous and villainous lies, would abound and multiply until the thread of truth became lost and obliterated by sensational scandal.

Each time such thoughts entered her mind, Emily would close her eyes and picture Niall proposing to her in the summerhouse and somehow her anxieties would gradually fade away. He had that reassuring effect upon her which she attributed to his professional medical skills.

They had agreed to keep the secret to themselves; the fewer people involved the less chance of disclosure; they knew they would have to be prepared for the shrewd and watchful eye of Aunt Clarissa. However well-meaning her aunt was, Emily could afford neither a careless slip of the tongue nor the pen to her mother. During the next few days they took the utmost care to meet; their liaisons became more like secret assignations that only the mute statues in the grounds were party to.

Amidst such passionate intrigue lurked an unresolved puzzle. Her own dilemma had not completely erased it from her mind but merely supplanted it. Emily had not forgotten about the photograph that she had seen. Mr Christian Verholt had assumed another identity, that of Mr Robinson, a young man on his honeymoon. The thought made her shiver as she now realised how ugly deception could be. She had to confide in someone and who better than the man she was going to secretly marry.

He listened patiently, allowing her to fully disclose the events on-board the Lusitania including the initial meeting at the dinner table with the Robinsons and later the subsequent discovery of the photograph. He of course had heard about the events surrounding Inspector Jackson's find and of course he had himself borne the brunt of the discovery of the pistol. He allowed her to finish, studying her pensively before replying.

'Perhaps it is just a case of mistaken identity. There was probably something about the man in the photograph that reminded you of this fellow passenger making you think...'

Emily swiftly interrupted him. 'I am absolutely positive that Mr Robinson and Mr Verholt are indeed one and the same. Make no mistake upon that!'

'Very well,' he conceded politely, 'let us just suppose that to be the case...'

'But it is the case!' Emily emphasised vehemently. Niall allowed a passing smile to dart across his face as he was now experiencing the full force of the headmistress's superiority. It rather amused and puzzled him that such a demanding and captivating force could herself be restrained by parental authority.

'Accepting that to be the case, the question then is why anyone as wealthy as a Verholt would become embroiled in theft and smuggling? Christian Verholt has as much need for more money as King Edward VII had for more mistresses.'

The question and statement slightly interrupted Emily's line of thought. 'I don't know. Why do people drive themselves in risky undertakings? Why would anyone want to take part in the Tour de France and face three gruelling weeks cycling? Why does Harry Houdini dangle from a rope wearing handcuffs? Why do people want to walk on a tightrope over the Niagara Falls or go over them in a barrel? Perhaps it is just for the thrill of it, the sense of achievement that these exploits bring. Christian Verholt may have everything that money can buy and perhaps he yearns for excitement, however criminal it is.'

Niall nodded in agreement. The woman in front of him was in truth an enigma; he was attracted to both her genuine naivety and her worldly wisdom. He had never met a female with such qualities before. The moment aroused him; placing a finger across her lips to prevent further disclosures he inclined his head towards hers before kissing her with strength and purpose. She reciprocated with passion and feeling and upon eventually drawing back from him, threw out one final question.

'What should we do about Christian Verholt?'

'Nothing. Absolutely nothing. We have no proof and I think for us and especially your relatives who are employed by the family, it would be best to leave well alone. We now need to concentrate upon our future.'

Emily agreed in principle but she could not stop herself thinking about that photograph.

As they finally took leave of Aunt Clarissa's hospitality their parting was not filled with sadness but rather a degree of hopeful adventure, or so it seemed to their hostess. She had genuinely enjoyed her niece's company and the presence of Niall Branigan. She intuitively knew that the rosy bloom on Emily's cheeks and the twinkle in her eyes had not been solely caused by the air of Long Island. Clarissa also knew that the couple in front of her were deeply in love.

'Just don't leave it too long.' The ambiguous message made Emily and Niall look at one another wondering whether Clarissa was referring to their next visit or to their own nuptial preparations.

'We certainly will not!' Niall quickly replied throwing a wink to Emily which Clarissa did not fail to notice.

Walter, Clarissa and the newly-weds continued to wave until the carriage was out of sight. In her heart Clarissa knew that her niece faced a future of uncertainty and opposition from her family but she also knew from past experience that true affection cannot be severed. As they turned to walk back to their cottage Clarissa slipped her hand into Walter's, kissed him on the cheek and realised that she was a very lucky woman.

The train journey back to New York was completely different to the one out to Long Island. Now they were relaxed and happy and solely mesmerised in one another's company. Sole occupancy of the carriage enabled them to hold hands, kiss and laugh at the least little word uttered by the other. Any fellow passengers were somewhat of an encumbrance but they tolerated them as they tried to furtively touch fingers without being noticed and upon their departure they guffawed at their own antics, having behaved like naughty school children. They continued to giggle long until they reached the Davenports' lodging house, where before entering they agreed to keep their secret to themselves.

Aunt Clarissa and Amelia Davenport were women with not dissimilar points of view. Both had travelled, both possessed fairly liberal views of life and both were extremely perceptive when observing those around them. The difference arose in the handling of such information. Amelia Davenport, unlike Clarissa, had somewhat of a penchant for direct questioning which had regularly infuriated her son, Jonathan.

Amelia listened with great interest as the couple described the wedding, the reception and the Suffolk Hall estate. However her eyes burned with heightened curiosity as Niall left the room and at last she was able to ask the question, the one above everything else that she wanted to know.

'So my dear, have you any news for me?'

'News?' Emily attempted to appear composed but she could feel her heart pumping with more speed and her face began to warm with embarrassment.

'Yes Emily, news of you and Niall. I take it that he's proposed, judging by the way you two keep looking at one another and the blushes in your cheeks.'

Emily felt herself cornered and cast her eyes downwards. Minutes appeared to elapse before she found herself answering in a whispered reply.

'Yes, he has.'

'And? What was your answer?'

'Yes.'

'Oh, my dear this is the best news that I have heard. I am so happy for you both.' Amelia threw her arms around Emily and as the tears ran down her cheeks, she repeated 'I am so happy for you.'

Niall understood how Amelia had prised the information out of Emily; he more than anyone was aware of his former patient's tenacity when dealing with affairs of the heart. He allowed her the indulgence of congratulating them both and then announced that as it was their last night in America, he had booked a special dinner for Emily and himself. Amelia's intuition was sufficiently astute to understand the reason for this. With a knowing look she withdrew leaving them alone.

The restaurant was renowned for serving some of the best seafood dishes in New York. Raw bar oysters and clams, lobster, shrimp, crab, scallop, crayfish and numerous other types of fish were listed in an expensive but extensive menu. The setting was equally as spectacular and must surely have rivalled the first class dining room on the Lusitania. Emily had once remarked that she enjoyed seafood but the extent of her experience was limited and Niall was obviously keen to broaden that experience.

Each course brought a new sensation of tastes which accentuated the natural flavours of the sea and the accompanying wine infused these tastes with decadent indulgence. As her head started to slightly spin Emily began to relax, chat and enjoy the whole scenario. When the waiter produced the dessert menu Niall asked him to return with it later. He smiled across at her before reaching into his pocket to produce a small box and then cleared his throat nervously with a purposeful cough.

'Emily, as we are engaged to be married, it seems only fitting that you wear my ring. Darling, will you do that?'

Not a word passed between them as she shakily accepted the box from his hand. Opening the lid her eyes widened in disbelief as they became transfixed upon the largest emerald ring that she had ever seen.

'Do you like it?'

'Yes it is absolutely beautiful and yes, I will happily wear it.'

Long after he had placed it on the appropriate finger of her left hand she continued to stare at the large oval-shaped green stone, which was surrounded by smaller-sized diamonds. He repeatedly enquired if the size needed altering but she simply shook her head and whispered how perfect a fit it was. As they leaned forward and kissed they suddenly realised that they had attracted attention. Both the customers and the staff offered their verbal congratulations and then compounded it with applause. A bottle of champagne swiftly followed before finally exciting the gathering with its customary popping sound as the cork was removed. For a moment time seemed to stand still as the pair toasted each other, staring deeply across the table amidst the noise of the restaurant.

It was at this point that Niall seemed to relax. The opening of the box had unleashed something within him and he suddenly began to chatter, appearing to want to share his earliest memories with her.

'That ring is very special to me. I vowed that I would only ever give it to a very special person as it holds memories for me, dear memories of two wonderful people.' Emily had never seen Niall like this before. He appeared preoccupied and withdrawn. Moments elapsed before he continued.

'I realise that we have not known one another for very long and thereby have not had the opportunity to find out about each other's respective family. If the truth be known neither of us have said a great deal about the past. In fact I know that I have told you nothing, whereas with you I have had the benefit of meeting your aunt and uncle and cousin. They did indeed make me feel very welcome.' Niall stopped for a brief moment and smiled at Emily before continuing.

'I was given up at birth by my mother's family. That sounds harsh I know, but I don't blame them. She was a young girl from a very poor family in a village, not far from Kilkenny in Southern Ireland. I was illegitimate and the family could not afford to keep me. The delivery was a very difficult one and they were very lucky that a local doctor gave his services for nothing. If it hadn't been for Doctor Branigan I would also have died. Without his kindness I would have ended up in the workhouse. He once told me that following the birth he looked at the squirming little bundle wrapped up in dirty rags and knew that morally he could not let that happen. Why should an innocent, just newly delivered into the world, be condemned to such deprivation? I was indeed the lucky one, there is no disputing that.' Silence once again fell as Niall's mind seemed to be preoccupied and focussed far away. His eyes were moist with emotion.

'What is it Niall?' Emily enquired in a light whisper, reaching across the table to hold his hand.

'Nothing, nothing at all. Just ghosts from the past.'

'You must tell me everything. I want to know everything about you.'

He cleared his throat with a cough and continued. 'I was very fortunate as Doctor Branigan and his wife were childless and they doted upon me. They looked after me and gave me their name and as a result I had a most privileged upbringing. I wanted for nothing, nothing at all except perhaps a brother to play with and share my secrets with. But I cannot complain. It was the Branigans who made me the man I am. They were my mother and father.'

'Presumably you followed in Doctor Branigan's footsteps by studying medicine?'

'Yes. I admired this man so much. He felt that I had the aptitude for the profession and encouraged me.'

'You did not want to become a local doctor in Ireland like Doctor Branigan?'

'Yes initially I did. Whilst I was still a small baby we had moved from Kilkenny to Cork and my father had built up a large and renowned practice. He had been keen for me to work alongside him upon qualifying as a doctor, with the hope of me eventually taking over his practice. However, I lost my mother to tuberculosis and, after only three months, my father too. As you can imagine, losing the two people in the world who had loved and cared for me just made me want to escape from it all. I used to watch the ships sail into the harbour and then sail out again and wonder what was out there. One day I just decided to find out for myself. There was no one left to care for and with the offer of a job I took it.' Niall relaxed back into his chair resembling a man who had just unburdened himself of a great weight from his mind. As Emily remained silent he leaned forward and reached out for her left hand.

'That ring belonged to my mother, Mrs Branigan, and when I look at it, it brings back happy memories of both her and my father. I vowed I would only give it to a woman who was worthy of wearing it. Emily, you are indeed that woman.'

Such heartfelt words made Emily want to cry. They reminded her of some of the most romantic poems that she had ever read. Her heart wanted to burst with grief and at the same time she harboured such pride in her breast that the man in front of her held her in such esteem. She was determined in her heart that she would be a worthy wife to Niall. He deserved her love.

For once they chose not to keep the events of that evening a secret. Their decision was twofold; firstly, it would have been impossible to exclude Amelia from their celebrations as she had a ferreting intuition which would have uncovered the information and secondly, they wanted to share their good news. As soon as they entered the lodging house Amelia appeared and congratulated them.

'How did you know?' Emily enquired.

'Just call it a woman's intuition. Besides which my dear, the twinkle in your eyes is almost as bright as that emerald. Bring it here and let me have a look.'

As the women gazed at the ring Niall stood back and beamed with happiness. He gazed at his fiancée and for the first time in many years felt content knowing that he had someone to love and most importantly, that there was now someone who loved him.

'That is a beautiful ring and she is certainly worth it,' Amelia announced as she looked across to Niall.

'I think so,' answered the soft Irish accent.

'If I'm not mistaken they call it the Emerald Isle do they not? I'm referring to Ireland of course,' Amelia questioned.

'That they do. It is the poetic name for a land rich in green countryside. It is a magical land full of stories about leprechauns, fairies and the power of the shamrock. Being a doctor I don't believe in the supernatural healing powers attributed to the shamrock plant but I do believe in the leprechauns.' Niall's face now wore an impassive look which he was struggling to maintain.

'Why do you believe in leprechauns? 'Emily asked hesitantly.

'Well when you see a rainbow in Ireland you should try and find the end of it and if you do there should be a pot of gold there. However you can never find it.'

'That's because there is no gold there,' Emily answered in her schoolmistress voice.

'That is where you are wrong. You cannot find it because the leprechauns are guarding it!' Niall corrected her. His poker-faced expression had melted away and he was beginning to laugh. The expression on his face had become contagious and soon they were all laughing with amusement.

'My dears, I cannot remember when I have enjoyed an evening so much. I am so very, very happy for you both,' declared Amelia, kissing each of them before she retired to bed.

'I do wish you all the luck in the world.' Amelia's parting words made them both suddenly realise that it would take more than just luck and the leprechauns to allow their dreams to be fulfilled.

Chapter Nine

Their final hours in New York were filled with a degree of both hesitation and longing; the return voyage aboard the Lusitania would ultimately deliver them into an unknown future but conversely, it would also bring them a step nearer to their ultimate future happiness together, wherever that might be.

Niall, as a member of the ship's crew had left early to board the ship leaving Emily some final time with Amelia. The remaining hours in the company of this guardian of human nature would prove to be some of the most important in Emily's life.

'Now my dear, I'm well known for plain speaking and therefore I am going to come straight to the point. When you take leave of one another in Liverpool what is going to happen then?'

Emily appeared initially stunned by the question.

'I don't know, Amelia.'

'Well what we don't want is for all this to come to nothing. I've seen too many romances go sour over time. You must communicate regularly for a start. Ensure Niall has my address and also give me your address and when we become settled in our new home I will write to you. I am sure your parents will see nothing wrong in that. Both you and Niall can correspond with one another through me. I will forward his letters to you, wrapped within my own correspondence to you. Just open the letters in the privacy of your room.'

Emily smiled at the ingenuity of the elderly lady in front of her.

'When the time is right you will marry, make no mistake on that. Now my dear, just because you are only engaged does not mean that you have to be prim and proper.'

'Prim and proper?' Emily repeated the words but had no understanding of their intended meaning.

'Yes, what I mean is, you do not have to wait until your wedding night to give yourself to him. He is the one for you, so it would not be wrong to be with him.'

Emily had thought that Amelia could not embarrass her any further but she quickly coloured in the face. 'It would be morally wrong and against everything that I have been brought up to believe in. My parents would disown me and...'

'They need never know. In fact no one will know except the two of you. Just think Emily in years to come, when you are elderly and grey like me, you can relive your memories and have no regrets. I know that I have no regrets about my life but I would have had if I had not acted upon impulse. That is the key to life. Life is not a rehearsal my dear. Seize the moment and don't be afraid.'

Emily had never met anyone quite like Amelia. For this reason alone she knew that she was going to miss her and was beginning to dread saying goodbye. However, Amelia's next unexpected statement immediately caught Emily's attention.

'I wonder whether Inspector Jackson has caught up with Mr and Mrs Robinson.'

'What made you think of that?' Emily inquired with quiet reservation.

'Oh I don't know my dear. Perhaps it's the thought of you returning on the Lusitania or my talk of engagements, weddings ... they were supposedly on their honeymoon. I remember thinking at the time that they were very withdrawn and the colour now in your cheeks was decidedly absent in hers. There was something wrong about them. There was no love in their eyes. Yes it was a planned operation, a very well thought out one.' For an elderly lady Amelia was extremely astute. As she began to consider the mystery she also noticed how pale Emily's complexion had become. The colour in her cheeks had simply drained away.

'My dear, what is the matter? Come and sit down beside me.'

No amount of persuasion on Emily's part could offer adequate subterfuge for the truth. The more Emily tried to insist that everything was well the more Amelia insisted it was not.

'You cannot fool me my girl. You know something Emily. Come along my dear; two heads are better than one and you know that I am very good at keeping secrets.'

Further resistance would have proved futile. Emily had already tried to discuss the matter with Niall and he had seemed disinterested in it. However in Amelia there was a captive audience and the opportunity to disclose her anxious findings. She kept nothing back, including Niall's advice of not becoming involved.

'I know Niall is right. I certainly do not want to cause any unpleasantness for my Aunt and Uncle, who depend upon the Verholts for their living and their accommodation. Mr and Mrs Verholt have been model employers and I would not like to hurt them. But at the back of my mind lurks the question of whether it is morally right to let crime continue. What makes Christian Verholt take these chances?'

'The thrill of it all! In my time I have met people like him. Just because they come from a wealthy background it does not exclude them from crime and danger. In fact the reverse is true. They become excited by the lure of danger, thinking that they will always outsmart the authorities. Christian Verholt has the breeding and connections to move in the right social settings. He obviously uses that knowledge to shall we say make his mark and acquire attractive treasures from England and the Continent. He then smuggles them back to America where there is a hungry demand for antiques. He simply supplies the demands of the wealthy who can afford to pay for theft and smuggling. Of course he won't be alone in these activities. There will be a network of people involved in these shady dealings.'

Emily was both fascinated and intrigued by Amelia's knowledge of these underworld connections. She now realised that the old lady at her side had had a life of unfathomable experience, including the realms of the unmentionables. She remembered how Amelia had initially shocked her with the mention of working in a brothel. The shock and horror of it all left her as she stared into the old lady's eyes.

'What should I do Amelia? Please tell me what I should do.'

'Nothing! Absolutely nothing. Leave everything to me. I can handle it. Now let us not say goodbye but au revoir, for I know that we will soon see one another again.'

Emily also knew this would be the case. She simply needed Amelia more than anyone else, with the exception of Niall.

As the Lusitania made her way out of New York harbour Emily stared hard at the sprawling metropolis and wondered whether Inspector Jackson would make an arrest. Her thoughts on this matter were immediately interrupted as an arm slid around her waist and a voice, familiar in its soft Irish accent, whispered into her ear: 'Are you daydreaming about the future?' Before Emily could answer, the arm had propelled her around and she suddenly found herself in an embrace and being kissed fully on the lips.

'Miss Taylor, I have wanted to do that for so long. Don't look so shocked. Remember we are engaged to be married!'

Emily smiled to herself at his endearing audacity, as he threw her a wink and continued on his way to tend a seasick passenger. The incident had caused numerous heads to also turn and watch the amorous greeting. Some smiled at her with perhaps a slight embarrassment whilst others looked longingly with envy. Emily turned back to watch the New York skyline diminish into the distance and decided that Amelia's advice should be followed; she would from now on seize any moments that life offered to her.

The days and nights at sea were filled with unexpected moments of pleasure. These occurred when Niall had any spare moments to seek out his fiancée; often he would briefly sit with her in the Second Class Lounge located on the top deck of the aftermost deck house. There the finely crafted wooden columns provided suitable seclusion for intimate conversations. From the Lounge, passengers could step out onto the Promenade and enjoy the fresh and briny sea air blowing across the Atlantic. However love could always counteract the adversity of cold winds and the problems encountered by a Second Class Promenade; the latter being located on the stern could be prone to a covering of soot and debris from the four funnels. Nothing mattered to Niall and Emily except the opportunity of being able to see one another again.

As the final evening drew near, Emily began to feel slightly depressed for she knew that the following day would see a separation to their lives. Her melancholic feelings were compounded with further disappointment when Niall announced that he would not be able to see her that evening; he was obliged to spend his time with the other officers assisting the Captain in his duties as a Cunard Ambassador. This entailed mingling socially with the wealthy in First Class. Emily did not know which was worst; not being able to be with Niall or the thought of rich, beautiful women gaining his attention. These celebrities and aristocrats had influence which could affect the reputation and the future of Cunard.

Retiring to her cabin, she lay down, closed her eyes and reassured herself that Niall had chosen her; she was wearing his ring.

The muffled tap upon her door was repeated again. She awoke, slightly startled by the noise and the fact that she had fallen asleep. Still fully attired she rose, smoothed her skirt and cupped her hands around her hairline to catch any stray hairs in an effort to make herself presentable. As she opened her door he quickly slid inside closing it behind him.

'I did not know whether you would still be awake. What is left of the evening and the night is now for us. Emily, will you come with me?'

'Yes.' She gave no time to thinking about her answer. The confident reply was sufficient.

She would have followed him anywhere with no questions asked; she trusted him implicitly. This part of the ship was unrecognisable to her with its exclusive elegance evident in every affluent and spacious area. On and on they continued, past well-proportioned doorways until they arrived at the largest one of all: this was the entrance to one of the Regal Suites. These two expensive suites were aptly named as they served to satisfy the tastes of the most discerning traveller; each one featured two bedrooms, a bathroom, a parlour, a dining room and a separate pantry. Lavishly furnished, they provided for every indulgence; even the bathroom fixtures were silver-plated.

Once inside Niall, locked the door whilst Emily looked around in anguish. She felt out of place in such an environment, knowing that it was wrong for her to be trespassing. She also knew that it was morally wrong to be alone with a man in a cabin. Drawing back she pulled away from his hold but only until he gripped her hand and pulled her back to face him. He kissed her slowly and deliberately on the lips. Releasing his hold on her, he then walked into one of the bedrooms turned, extending his hand out to her. Standing in silence he waited, waited for her decision. Her heart began to pump quickly and she felt the colour rising in her cheeks. Subconsciously she began to slowly walk towards him; only stopping when she could look closely into his eyes and hear the escalation of his breathing. Now there was anxiety present in his soul instead of Irish charm; that became the catalyst.

He watched as she undid the small pearl buttons down the front of her blouse exposing the soft white flesh of her long, slender neck. Both the action and the exposure began to excite him, even though he had seen a woman's neck and more many times before in medical examinations. This time it was different. Slowly he began to touch and caress her neckline before delicately nuzzling and kissing her throat. The familiar soft scent of her skin stimulated him further, as his fingers began to trace the upper contours of her breasts. Suddenly, she felt his fingers slip between her skin and the broderie anglaise edging at the top of her corset; the action made her slightly gasp in recognition. He stopped in response and gazed at her with tenderness. Momentarily they stared at one another before Emily nodded in agreement.

'Are you sure?' Niall enquired.

A further moment of silence presented itself before Emily replied, 'Never more so.'

As the Lusitania continued to cross the Atlantic that night, Niall knew that he would not be disturbed in an unoccupied suite with the woman whom he loved above everything else. This had to be a special night and although for once in his life he had done something wrong by taking the key for the suite, he instinctively knew that the risk was worth taking. As he made love to Emily he was in no doubt that he would risk anything for her, even his life.

Chapter Ten

The homecoming was exactly how Emily had imagined it to be: charged with an excess of both interest and emotion. Although her parents were normally reserved in their gestures of affection, they did allow themselves a welcoming embrace to a daughter who had recently returned from such an epic voyage. As the questions followed, Charles and Hannah Taylor quickly realised that their daughter's answers were introducing them into a world of the unknown. Travel was indeed a source of wonder to a couple who had never travelled further than the English coast. Accounts of the wedding ceremony and Uncle Walter and Aunt Clarissa's hospitality satisfied their initial inquiries but Emily's references to Long Island, the Suffolk Hall estate, New York and the Lusitania were incomparable to anything they had experienced. The probing interest for these and others was seized upon by Emily's sister, Olivia.

'Are the hemlines higher over there? What about the hats; is it true that they wear more plumage on their heads? How much make-up do the women wear? Are the men as handsome as they say?'

These and many more similar styled questions perpetually left Olivia's mouth prompting her parents to intervene and stem the flood of inappropriate interest.

'Olivia, I very much doubt that Emily will have had either the time or the inclination to notice such things.' Hannah rebuked her in her matter of fact way before adding, 'Emily is a lady whose thoughts focus upon a higher plane of intellect which does not include frivolous fashion and gentlemen.'

Turning to Emily her mother inquired, 'Did you make any agreeable acquaintances?' A slight tinge of colour rose in Emily's cheeks as she mentioned the Davenport family. An elderly widow and her family could not but fail to impress her parents whilst boring her sister. However in Emily's mind the image of Amelia Davenport was synonymous with risqué subjects; fashion and men. Further recollections of Amelia's past including showgirls and bordellos would have impressed Olivia but disgusted her parents.

For that reason and more Emily diverted the conversation to topics related to the home and the proverbial safety of the English weather. It was now her turn to inquire and then to listen. Her mind soon began to wander and as her parents and sister chatted she thought about the one person whose name she had managed not to mention; Niall Branigan.

Returning home to the West Yorkshire woollen mill town of Beckston did not prevent Emily from longing to return abroad. The parting with Niall had been painful and now unable to mention his name, she began to show signs of melancholy. Comparing an overpopulated industrial northern town with the glitz of New York, the glamour and wealth of Long Island and the romance of an Atlantic liner, could only ever result in dissatisfaction. This in turn made Emily feel worse as she had always been an optimist, grateful for the comfortable lifestyle that she had been born into.

Home was a solidly built stone mid-Victorian terrace house, which although not pretentious, held the distinction of being a home suitable for the upper working or lower middle classes. A through terrace house conferred a certain degree of social standing unlike the cramped conditions endured by the lower working classes in back-to-back dwellings or tunnel-back houses. The added attraction of bay windows in the parlour and the main bedroom also decreed that the Taylor family upheld a degree of social rank.

Charles Taylor had never been a wealthy man but as a skilled stonemason he had worked hard all his life and had been blessed with good health, full time employment, and a prudent homemaker. He managed to support his wife, Hannah, and his two daughters, regularly paying the weekly rent on a decent abode. Together Charles and Hannah Taylor had raised their daughters in a respectable neighbourhood and being careful to maintain such a lifestyle they had continually embraced the beliefs of the Wesleyan Chapel; drink was the known curse of the working classes and therefore abstinence prevailed. With years of careful housekeeping their lifetime dreams had finally materialised: a comfortably furnished home, a respectable marriage for their milliner daughter Olivia and their finest achievement, the pride of having a headmistress in the family. All those difficult years of dealing with Olivia now paled into insignificance at the mere thought of Emily's achievements.

Hannah ran her home with ultimate military precision. Acutely aware of the social standing that a headmistress deserved, she ensured that the house lived up to expectation. Secretly she hoped that one day with Emily's financial backing that they would be able to purchase the house that had been home to them for so long. Being a spinster she knew that Emily would have no need to leave the family home and she would remain with them throughout their final years. It was gratifying to know that their support for her in her chosen profession would ultimately support them in years to come.

Although the house was not large, the demands of the daily chores and the constant attention to detail which Hannah expected were beginning to prove too much for her. With a husband and two daughters in employment, it was decided that they could afford to hire a servant, a maid–of–all–work.

Alice Speight was exceptionally lean of frame and small in stature and did not appear physically strong enough to uphold the duties demanded of her. Hannah looked the girl over and would have dismissed her but for the glowing verbal recommendations Emily had provided. Alice had been reared in a very large but poor family and no doubt her lack of height had resulted from malnutrition. She had been a child who had gone to school barefoot and Emily as her teacher had provided shoes for her, at her own expense. She had worked hard at her studies and proved herself capable of conquering inestimable barriers through diligence and hard work. Emily knew that her former pupil would not let her down.

For the first time in her life Alice slept alone in a bed. The attic room had become her bedroom and initially although such privacy was a novelty, in time Alice began to miss the company of her brothers and sisters.

The strict household routine which Hannah had been initiated into by her own mother and had meticulously followed herself was now demanded of Alice. Commencing at 6am each day, Alice soon began to realise that if cleanliness was next to godliness it demanded a great deal of hard work which her own childhood home had never been so subjected to. There were general daily routines, specific daily routines, weekly routines and seasonal routines. Cleaning the kitchen range and lighting it along with all the other fires signalled the start of another day. Dusting, polishing and sweeping, cooking, baking and washing-up became never-ending routines. The laundry days totally sapped Alice's energy and with cracked hands and sore skin she would retire to her bed exhausted but grateful; she knew that she was fortunate to have board and lodgings and a small wage which she could call her own. There were also other incentives in this household for Alice; namely living in close proximity with Emily and Olivia. One she respected for her exemplary standing within the community, having been taught by her she knew first-hand her endearing qualities. It was however the one whose reputation preceded her that interested Alice the most.

At thirty-five years of age, Olivia was rather old to still be a spinster. However she could never be described as an old-maid. Strong-willed and wayward she had never conformed to social propriety. No amount of stern reprimands, dire warnings or physical beatings had been able to persuade her throughout her formative years. As she approached womanhood the real problems only began to manifest themselves; swearing, smoking, drinking and promiscuity. Her preference for married men alarmed and upset her parents without any repercussions for Olivia. It was without doubt most welcome news to Charles and Hannah Taylor when Olivia announced her engagement to an unmarried and decent man.

George Ackroyd had had the misfortune to lose his young wife early in their marriage as a result of a difficult childbirth, leaving him without a wife or dependent offspring. At twenty eight years old and the proprietor of his own grocers store he could have attracted the attention of many young women. However, his late wife had had a particular penchant for hats and had been a regular visitor to the shop where Olivia worked. She had admired the skills of this milliner and it was not long before Olivia was making hats regularly for her new customer. The numbers that were ordered signified how successful her husband's business was. George completely doted upon his young wife and soon was a regular visitor himself, collecting the commissioned pieces in their large and sumptuous hatboxes before transporting them away in his new automobile, a Model T Ford. Olivia would regularly watch him drive away, fascinated by the nickname of it: Tin Lizzie. Charming and attentive Olivia managed to ensnare this young man when he was at his most vulnerable, alone and newly widowed.

She listened intently and showed great interest when he spoke of the Kingston carburettor, 4-cylinder side-valve and the beam-axle suspension. The coy expressions upon her face masked the scheming manipulation building in her mind and unwittingly he found himself proposing marriage to a woman whose past reputation he knew nothing about. Although neither virginal nor virtuous, Olivia had managed to make both her parents and her fiancé very happy.

Charles and Hannah Taylor had worried that their wayward daughter would at best become the mistress of a wealthy but married man. However Olivia was not a social beauty and would never have attracted the attention of the upper echelon. At worst however, she could have entered the salacious surroundings of the stage, in particular the music-hall where drunken audiences would leer at scantily clad females amidst the innuendos of artists such as Marie Lloyd who was the epitome of cheap and cheerful vulgarity. Thankfully, Olivia had never shown any inclination for the stage. Therefore when George Ackroyd asked for their daughter's hand in marriage they very quickly welcomed him into the family.

Agreeable and attentive, George Ackroyd could have had the pick of many young women. Well attired with moderately handsome features he regularly caught the eye of passing females as he drove his Model T Ford along the streets of Beckston. However, George may have been oblivious to their tantalising and youthful smiles but Olivia was not. She soon began to distrust any female in his company, including the exceptionally young Alice Speight.

Good manners, according to George, were the mark of a true gentleman but to his fiancée they were to be lavished exclusively upon her. She expected his attentive care when opening doors, pulling out a chair at the dining table or carrying everything for her. She tolerated his politeness in these areas for Emily, as she knew that a spinster headmistress could never pose a threat but a young maid was a different matter. When Olivia caught her fiancé laughing and talking with the girl she bristled with resentment but when she witnessed him carrying a heavy coal scuttle for her, she decided to devise a plan of retribution.

The opportunity was to present itself within a very short time.

Olivia knew that the best way to teach the girl a lesson was to engineer her dismissal. The easiest way for that was to base it upon an unforgivable act such as theft. To secure the allegation she needed a small but attractive item which could be easily sold or pawned for money. She looked around the house but found nothing suitable until she quietly entered Emily's room. There she looked through the drawers of her dressing-table until she unwittingly came across the small box. The discovery of such an item made her question where Emily could have obtained it from. Holding the ring up to the light, she stared at the large emerald surrounded with diamonds before feeling a pang of resentment that her engagement ring was inferior in both size and quality to the one that she held between her fingers. She smiled as she realised that the ring would be missed and the discovery of it in Alice's room would demand both answers and action, and subsequent dismissal. She also smiled as she realised that Emily would need to do some explaining herself.

It was not difficult for Olivia to creep into Alice's room and hide the ring at the bottom of a linen drawer, where under an enforced search it could easily be discovered. But as Olivia waited for the honeytrap to unfold, impatience began to grow out of the inertia. Emily appeared to show no anxiety in the days that followed and therefore Olivia concluded that she could not have noticed its absence. To determine this she decided to check whether the little box had been moved and once again crept into

Emily's room. Opening the drawer she peeled back the layers of the linens covering the box and was astonished to find that it had been moved from the left to the right side of the drawer. A noise on the stairs alerted her that someone was approaching. Closing the drawer however she suddenly hesitated, stopped and her fingers stretched inside once more. Clasping the box she pulled it out and opened it. She recognised the footsteps on the stairs as those of her sister and knew that she would soon be in the room. Olivia had to think quickly but the sight of the large emerald ring in the box had shocked her.

Opening the door Emily was surprised to find Olivia in her room.

'I hope you don't mind but I needed some writing paper and I thought you might have some,' Olivia exclaimed.

'No of course I do not mind but mother keeps it all in her bureau downstairs.' Turning to face her sister she carefully scrutinised her before enquiring, 'Olivia, are you unwell? I think you look a little pale. Perhaps I should be looking through my drawers for some smelling salts.' The reference to drawers made Olivia feign an excuse to suddenly be elsewhere.

Emily was not one to hold a grudge but she smiled to herself that Olivia's jealousy and meanness had been outwitted. Her sister had always been the other woman on married men's arms and at last she was now beginning to have a taste of how it felt to have to share a man's affections. Not that little, young Alice posed any threats. Trusting and innocent Alice had done nothing wrong, in fact just the reverse. She had been polite and grateful to George Ackroyd for his chivalrous kindness and she had been utterly honest and loyal to her former teacher. She had found the emerald ring by chance when she had needed to find some clean sheets. The ring had been pulled out of its hiding place and had simply tumbled to the floor. Anyone with morals of a low standing would have made a hasty retreat to the pawnbrokers but Alice was determined that she should show it to Miss Taylor.

It was then that Emily realised how faithful this young girl was. Emily identified the ring as one that she had misplaced some time ago and concluded that she must have lost it when folding the sheets. She told Alice that it was only costume jewellery in order to suppress any astonishment that it had not been found until now. Alice had believed her and had certainly not expected a reward of a florin for her troubles. Although the situation had been resolved Emily, understood that Olivia could prove to be an unwelcome adversary; the sooner she married and left the Taylor household, the better. Precautions needed to be taken and the ring was to be the first; it would from now on hang on a chain around her neck underneath her high necked blouses, unseen but never forgotten. She knew that one day it would adorn the ring finger of her left hand but until then discretion had to be observed.

Chapter Eleven

The classrooms with their empty rows of wooden desks were now uncharacteristically silent. It was not that the pupils at St Cuthbert's were poorly behaved but as the school day ended and the children left, the air of intangible but viable energy also departed with them, leaving a definite void in each room. Emily Taylor and her two colleagues were keen to provide an education which stimulated and stretched the minds of all who were seated before them. Reading, writing and arithmetic would always form the basis of the curriculum and the school inspections. Physical education, known as drill, was an important area as a healthy mind could only grow from a healthy body. Observation lessons, nature walks and singing were all conducive to school life. Although Emily gave instruction in all these areas it was the handwork and creative lessons that she believed could capture a child's mind and allow them to make something unique and special. Ledges, window-sills and walls were full of visionary and creative pieces of artwork: clay modelled fruits, chalk drawings of flowers, paper cuttings of flying balloons and toy models of charabancs and carts adorned every available space. The rooms were a flurry of colours and enticement; just the type of place where young minds could develop. The nation had only recently paid its respects to the passing of Edward VII and had shown its true feelings in proverbial black mourning but within these rooms only the enlightenment of colour was allowed to take precedence.

As was customary, Emily had remained at her desk in her small office to complete her daily work. This was something she regularly did following the departure of both her pupils and colleagues. As a headmistress and a dedicated one she fully accepted the rigours of her post. In full concentration she had failed to notice his presence until the momentary click of the door summoned her attention.

'Is it right for an engaged lady to be working so hard?' The words were delivered with a characteristic softness of Irish bonhomie.

'Niall!' For the first time in weeks and months she felt compelled to voice his name out loud rather than merely retain it mutely within her head. As she looked at him she now understood why her work had taken over again; it had become the antidote for his absence.

She had missed his smile, his gentle humour and his touch. As his arms encircled and caressed her tightly corseted wasp-like waist drawing her body to his, she felt the full sensation of passion from his lips. The moment was sufficiently powerful to allow a resurgence of feelings from that night. She recalled how he had touched and kissed every unseen area of her body, his hot sensuous breath and playful fingers arousing every nerve in their reach. She had grasped him to her at the point of intensity and had then lain in his arms afterwards intimately content. That night she had experienced a part of life that she had never known existed and one which she could not ignore.

'Christmas is a fine time for a wedding, wouldn't you agree?' The directness of his question startled her.

'Yes, I presume so,' she replied with a degree of doubt.

'Good. No time like the present! Emily, I want you to be my wife. I want to know that we are there for one another. That is why I have decided to leave the Lusitania and find a practice on land here in England.' The look upon her face was now beginning to trouble him. A moment of silence intervened before he continued. 'I mean to take this one step at a time. We can marry and carry on as we agreed. You can be Miss Taylor at school and in your parents' home but we will both know that we can regularly meet up and spend our holidays and any free time we have as man and wife until you are ready…'

'You mean ready to tell everyone the truth.'

'Well, yes. I promise I will not pressure you into anything.' That was the problem Emily thought; the longer the deception continued, the worse it would be. As painful as it would be she knew that there was only one course of action available.

'I will tell my parents the truth.'

'But if you do that you will also have to relinquish your standing as Headmistress here.' The verbal clarity of the situation did not make it any easier for either of them.

'I understand that. But I do love you and I want to spend my life with you. I don't want to be skulking around trying to snatch a treasured moment here or there with you. That is not what marriage is about. My mind is made up; I will tell them this week.'

Niall was spending his leave at a small local hotel in Beckston. Knowing that he was close to her gave Emily some confidence for the week ahead. She knew that it would be an emotionally challenging time for her but she resolved to remain steadfast in her decision. She was thirty years of age and could not be classed as someone who did not know her own mind. The time was now ripe for all women to stand up for themselves and demand their rights.

As an educated woman, Emily fully appreciated the overdue need for women's emancipation. The telephone and the typewriter had opened the doors to many women seeking employment away from the drudgery of service and there now were even female doctors and dentists. There was increasing support for the women's right to vote. The Women's Social and Political Union founded in 1903 by Emmeline Pankhurst had even supported militant acts. If women had the confidence to riot and break the law risking a spell within prison, surely Emily Taylor could announce to her parents that she was getting married.

The opportunities did arise but events conspired to obstruct the moment of truth. It began with the cursory migraine which her mother often fell martyr to, regularly causing her to withdraw to a quiet and darkened room where she could lay down and rest without being disturbed. Suddenly, from the depths of such despair, Olivia managed to take control and occupy centre stage, by describing the plans for her wedding the following year, in summer 1911. The irony of a white wedding seemed lost upon Olivia, who wanted everyone to know that George Ackroyd was most fortunate in marrying such a chaste bride; although Olivia's age and past reputation would not decree virginal, an expensive white wedding dress just might. As the demands for the perfect wedding evolved the costs were beginning to spiral out of control and Emily for the first time saw a look of fear upon her father's face.

'Perhaps, Olivia, a small quiet but discreet wedding would be best,' her father remarked.

'Best! Best for whom? I haven't got to my age to have to be satisfied with second best, Father. I thought that you would be delighted that I am marrying a respectable man, a man with prospects, a man who can provide for me and take me off your hands. Surely it is not a lot to ask one's parents to do the decent thing and provide for their daughter upon her marriage. I am of course your one and only daughter who will marry. Emily is already married to her profession and has no interest in that part of life.'

Charles Taylor remained silent but Emily perceived a worried man. The expense of the wedding would fall upon the bride's parents and Emily, unlike her sister, realised that finances were now becoming burdensome. The world was indeed changing and successive generations were now demanding more. Those with some education and a sprinkling of social pretension now regarded themselves as superior to artisans and craftsmen like Charles Taylor, a respectable stonemason. Those who could were now securing a footing for themselves within the ranks of the middle class. Although the Taylors did not own their own home, they lived in a desirable area of Beckston and enjoyed the trappings of consumerism and the services of a live-in maid. More warranted more and unfortunately Olivia was oblivious to the fact that her father had reached his limit where spending was concerned.

The discord throughout the household was not conducive to the delivery of Emily's news. She allowed each day to pass, hopeful that an opportunity would present itself, which unfortunately it never did. As her mother regained good health, her father's face began to wear a grey and haggard look which became more intense with time.

She had promised Niall that she would tell her parents before the end of the week. As Emily left school that Friday evening she knew that she had to tell them that evening as she had a special rendezvous with her fiancé; they had planned to discuss the arrangements for their wedding.

Upon opening the door and stepping into the hallway Emily became immediately aware of the unfamiliar. The household always ran with precision; the daily routine of life tracked the seconds and minutes of the household clocks and like a railway station abided to a set timetable of events. That evening there was something different to that routine. Initially there was silence before Emily heard a man's voice followed by the sounds of her mother and sister sobbing. As she climbed the stairs and entered her parents' bedroom she was completely unprepared for the scene in front of her. Her father lying motionless on the bed was surrounded by his grieving wife and daughter and Doctor Lawson. The kind doctor immediately intercepted Emily and tried to offer some comfort with hopeful words.

'I'm afraid that your father has suffered a cerebral embolism and at the moment is unconscious. However, I am hopeful that he will recover consciousness.'

As bad as the news was, Emily was relieved that he was still alive, for the scene in the room as she had entered it had made her suspect otherwise. As she looked across at her mother and sister she knew that she had to be the strong one in this situation. She needed to know the truth, however painful and intimated to the doctor to follow her out of the room onto the landing.

'When will we know the full outcome?'

'It could be within hours.'

'Will he make a full recovery?'

'We can only hope so but he may experience some paralysis. Sometimes in these cases a patient may find that some part of their body, such as the arm or the leg is paralysed or indeed it may affect the whole of one side of the body, including the face. A patient may find that they recover from this paralysis, but some clumsiness and stiffness, particularly of the hand can often be left behind. Every patient is different. We must remember that your father is a strong man, having spent his working life as a stonemason. Let us indeed look on the bright side.' As the doctor allowed a slight smile to grace his face, presumably in an effort to deliver reassurance, Emily felt completely stunned and impassive of emotion, unlike her mother and sister who continued to sob heartily into their lace-edged handkerchiefs. Her mother's outward display of sorrow did not surprise Emily but Olivia's did. For a reckless and strong willed woman who could also be scheming and manipulative, her behaviour seemed out of context.

'Oh Emily, whatever shall we do?' her mother demanded. 'Without your father here to take care of us, I think we will perish.' Each sentence was followed by further demonstrations of grief.

'Well at least I will be one less to worry about when I will shortly have George to provide for me.' The words falling from Olivia's mouth may have been uttered to offer comfort which her mother accepted as she grasped her daughter's arm in recognition, but as they fell upon Emily's ears she instantly detected Olivia's recognisable trait of selfishness.

'We will do as we always do; continue to live as we do. The next few hours will be the deciding factor for father's health. We all need to stay strong and hopeful.' 'Emily you always know what to do,' declared her mother, wiping away the last of her tears. 'We don't need to worry as we always have you here. I am going to remain strong and hopeful and pray for your father.'

'Emily is right. There is nothing more that we can do. It does not need three of us to keep a vigil. Mother, if it is alright with you I should be going to the theatre with George tonight?'

'Yes, yes of course Olivia. Doctor Lawson mentioned that there may not be any change for some time. You must go. I have Emily with me. She will sit with me and keep me company.'

As Olivia disappeared from view, Emily realised that she had to reconcile herself to remaining at home, not just for an evening but for the foreseeable future.

The chimes of the downstairs parlour clock suddenly alerted Emily to the passing of time. She quickly recalled that she had a prior arrangement which she could no longer keep. She had to think quickly and decided that there was only one option; send a message with someone that she could trust. Alice Speight had shown nothing but loyalty to her; the incident with the ring had demonstrated that.

The sealed letter was grasped tightly in her hand as she ran steadily along to the end of the road. She instantly recognised the man standing on the corner from Emily's detailed description; tall and slim in stature and well dressed in appearance, he turned as she continued to stare and approach him.

'Excuse me sir, are you Doctor Branigan?'

'Yes I am,' answered the soft Irish accent.

'I have a letter for you from Miss Taylor.' As she mentioned her name, his eyes instantly shone with verdant intensity before the shine became tinged with a slight disappointment as she handed him the letter.

'Thank you for bringing me this. I hope it has not been of any trouble.'

'Certainly not, sir.'

He waited until she had left before opening the letter. As he read her words he felt so helpless that he could do nothing more than wait, as the rest of the Taylor household was doing. He just wanted to be able to take her in his arms, protect her, reassure her and love her but he knew that everything must now wait. Life was always about the unexpected and no one more than a doctor understood how life hinged upon many factors. Only time would determine how serious Charles Taylor's condition was.

Chapter Twelve

NEW YORK

When Inspector Jackson had first received the anonymous note he had pensively considered that it could only be a hoax, presumably the result of some kind of vendetta possibly resulting from the retaliation of a soured business deal or a wronged husband; money and sex were always the motives. In this he had even allowed himself to add jealousy to the list as the Verholts were seriously wealthy. Who wouldn't be jealous of the only grandchild to the inestimable fortune of the banking empire? Young, blond, good-looking and rich; even the inspector himself experienced a pang of envy.

Therefore, he had initially thrown the note to one side, ever conscious of more pressing cases to solve. But curiosity had reared its head and Sam Jackson decided late one evening that it wouldn't take too much effort to just check the passenger lists of the Lusitania. It would have been too much to hope that the name Verholt made an appearance but when he received the lists something unusual caught his eye. The number of passengers who sailed on the Lusitania on that voyage did not match up with the number booked originally. With further investigation he found that a Mr Robinson in second class had boarded without his wife whilst in third class a Mrs Brown had boarded without her husband, even though each cabin had been booked for two people. A thought began to emerge in his head; what if these two people masqueraded as Mr and Mrs Robinson in second class whilst securing another cabin as a bolthole if needed? Stolen goods could have been spread across both cabins and even though he and his men had retrieved some of the rich pickings, no doubt Mr and Mrs Robinson simply waltzed off the ship with other hidden treasures. This was a set-up operation and one that was no doubt being repeated time and time again. Well planned and methodically undertaken this heist was just one of a continental network of large scale crimes. A wry smile flashed across the inspector's face; if Mr Christian Verholt was part of this, Sam Jackson was the man that would wipe the smug look off his face. Even money couldn't save him from disgrace. That thought was enough to make him laugh; something he hadn't done for a very long time.

Chapter Thirteen

ENGLAND

Everyone agreed that a miracle had occurred as Charles Taylor regained consciousness within the hour. Doctor Lawson had intended for his patient to be nursed at the hospital but having regained consciousness the family persuaded him that he could be safely nursed at home. The truth was that Hannah believed that hospitals posed more of a threat to the sick than remaining in the clean and familiar surroundings of one's own home. The spectre of diphtheria, an acute infectious disease, was sufficient to persuade her to insist that her husband remained in her care. She was old enough to remember the spread of epidemics including typhoid, scarlet fever and diphtheria; even the royal family were not immune as Prince Albert had died of typhoid and Edward VII had even succumbed to an attack, earlier in his life. The recent death in May of Edward VII was still evident in the nation's memory and Hannah anxiously recalled that the cause of his death was bronchitis, another disease which was infectious.

Doctor Lawson agreed to regular visits to the Taylor household. Although his patient had survived he knew as time passed that Charles Taylor would never again have the dexterity and ability to produce the ornate stone carvings which his stone-masonry work demanded. The attack had left a legacy of complete paralysis down the right side of his body. His speech was slurred, he had difficulty walking and he was unable to grasp anything with his right hand. His family however were thankful that at fifty-eight years old he had survived.

Each day Doctor Lawson made his routine visit. Reliable and punctual he served the family well, as he had done for many years.

Agreeable and approachable he was the very epitome of the perfect family doctor, but lately he had begun to accept that his age and agility were becoming decisive bedfellows in future decisions. He often spent time advising others to take life more slowly and now he himself was upon the receiving end. Accordingly he placed a simple advertisement in the Beckston Gazette, received a promising reply, invited the man for interview and offered him a position in the practice. The first anyone knew of this change was when the two men appeared upon the doorstep.

As Alice Speight opened the door, the young man smiled back in recognition. The warmth of his smile and the twinkle of his emerald eyes were sufficiently contagious, prompting Alice to smile back. She remembered where she had seen those eyes before but quizzically wondered how Emily Taylor knew this man. More importantly, she now wondered about the importance of that letter and its contents. Doctor Lawson had deliberately chosen Saturday to introduce his companion, as everyone with the exception of Olivia, who was working, would be at home. Charles Taylor was now sitting up in bed and managed a slightly lop-sided grimace as the two men entered the bedroom. Attempting to raise his hand in further recognition he conceded, with some disappointment, that his paralysed co-ordination would not respond.

As always Doctor Lawson took the opportunity to encourage his patient.

'Good morning; now Charles, don't look so put out. It has only been a matter of days and look at how you have already improved. It is good to see you sitting up. Don't be in too much of a hurry though, especially when you have all these ladies around to look after you.' Doctor Lawson then threw a smile of recognition across to Hannah before adding, 'Good morning Mrs Taylor. How are you and where are your delightful daughters today?' It instantly seemed that the agreeable doctor for some reason was far more agreeable than ever.

'I'm afraid that Olivia is at work and Emily is somewhere in the house. Alice, will you find her and ask her to join us please?' Having sent the girl on an errand, Hannah then focussed her attention upon the stranger standing at the side of Doctor Lawson, prompting the kind doctor to recall the additional reason for his visit.

'Please let me introduce you to my new partner in the practice, Doctor Branigan.'

Alice had lingered sufficiently to overhear his name, which still offered no enlightenment upon his identity. She looked for Emily, firstly tapping lightly upon her bedroom door but receiving no reply she looked in the rooms downstairs and finally found her outside, hanging pillowcases and bed sheets out on the line.

'Miss, you shouldn't be doing that. That's my job,' she quickly rebuked, almost forgetting herself.

'At a time like this, we all work together,' Emily replied softly.

'Thank you Miss. Mrs Taylor has sent me to find you as Doctor Lawson is here.'

'I didn't hear him arrive.'

'They've not long been here Miss.'

'They? Who is with him?'

'Another gentleman.' Alice paused before continuing, 'I believe his name is Doctor Branigan.' Emily stood motionless and stared with disbelief; Alice may have been young in years but she was perceptive enough to discern a moral dilemma on the face of her former headmistress.

Any woman with a weaker spirit would have been forgiven for allowing herself to swoon but Emily's constitution through the years had been shaped through determination and hard work. Taking a deep breath she left Alice with nothing more than a resolute nod of the head.

'Good morning Doctor Lawson,' she said almost brushing aside his companion.

'Good morning Miss Taylor. I am pleased to say that I find your father here in very good spirits.'

'Yes, he is certainly progressing well.' Emily continued to pitch her stalwart gaze between her father and Doctor Lawson. She could almost tangibly feel those emerald eyes burning into her soul and quickly felt a rush of colour rising into her cheeks.

'Emily, Doctor Lawson has brought his new partner to meet us,' her mother intercepted, reminding Doctor Lawson of his formalities.

'Yes, Doctor Branigan here will be joining me in order to make my life a little less hectic. I'm certain that all the young ladies around will no longer require my attention when they can be treated by this fine fellow!' The slap upon his back by his senior partner instantly sealed a bond of approval between the medical men.

'I will be happy to serve both young and old,' voiced the Irish accent. 'Indeed I will be there for anyone who needs me at any time.' With this remark their eyes met for the first time, causing them to linger upon the other's gaze. The penetration of his eyes now conveyed far more than any spoken word.

'That is most comforting to know.' Her composure was fast beginning to disperse and excusing herself she left the room, put on her coat and left the house to take comfort in a walk.

She had experienced many different emotions that morning. Initially, she had been startled by his presence; her composure of the situation had afforded her time for this to grow into anger due to the sheer impertinence of him entering her home, before it finally subsided into tenderness and passion. There had been a moment when jealousy had reared its head, as Doctor Lawson had spoken of all the young ladies who would prefer the presence of his partner, which she knew would be true. The thoughts in her mind were whirling around indiscriminately, blinding her to everything surrounding her. She continued to walk, oblivious to those whom she passed. Since her father had fallen ill, she had taken time off school, the first time in her career, and as familiar faces of neighbours, shopkeepers, colleagues and pupils greeted her enquiring about her father's health, she ignored them with an impassioned preoccupation. She was even indifferent to the local shop windows, proudly showcasing their wares with their wide choice of goods stacked high and their lavish displays complemented with large eye-catching slogans. A fragrant aroma of coffee roasting hung in the air outside the grocers whilst the chemist vied for visual effect with its tall carboys of vibrant coloured liquids but Emily's senses still failed to be impressed or attracted.

The stroll began to quicken in pace; longer strides developed into a purposeful walk and then faster still into a determined trek. On and on she went without direction of thought or indeed thought of direction. Finally she entered the gates of Belle Park and had to adjust her tempo as a chill wind blew against her quite forcibly, causing the lower part of her coat to open slightly before she pulled it back wrapping it around her skirt. The prevailing wind continued to blow through the wide open expanse of parkland and although the leafless autumnal trees and monochrome landscape bore no resemblance to the rich verdant grounds of Suffolk Hall on Long Island, something instantly reminded her of her time there. The act of steering her clothing against the wind even reminded her of that walk along the deck on-board ship. Everything had started with that journey; the Lusitania, Amelia Davenport, Christian Verholt, Long Island and Niall Branigan. If she was going to find the answer to her dilemma she knew she would find it there.

Amelia Davenport had had much more of an effect upon her than she had realised. She had given her the confidence to allow herself to have some fun, something which her respectable upbringing had not found within the confines of biblical text and the encyclopaedia. The time spent in Amelia's company had been very worthwhile. It had opened her eyes to living and given her a very much needed lesson in life.

Emily remained quite oblivious to the passage of time and to any onlookers who merely saw a disorientated woman who was deep in thought. As the hours passed, her determined walk subsided into a stroll and finally halted when she decided to sit down on a lonely seat. There she remained, her thoughts constantly tossing and turning the snippets of advice which Amelia had prescribed. She desperately missed Amelia for there was no one else quite like her. Since returning home she had received but one letter of correspondence from her, informing her that they had moved into a permanent residence, extremely hopeful that she would act as a go-between forwarding letters to Niall and her, and finally inciting Emily to reply quickly, which she duly did. As the chill winds of the afternoon became more intense, Emily continued to sit motionless, unaware of the footsteps that quickened as they approached her.

'Emily!' the voice shouted her name out loud with concern. She looked at him, only at him and failed to see the two figures standing in the background.

'Oh Emily you are chilled to the bone.' In true gentleman-like fashion he removed his coat and placed it around her shoulders, just as he had done before in that summerhouse on Long Island.

'Niall,' was the only word she managed to express before he pressed his warm lips upon hers, wrapping his strong arms around her and drawing her cold body against the warmth of his.

'Remember, pressing two bodies together is the best way to stay warm,' he whispered.

'I do remember,' she answered, casting a smile to him whilst beginning to shiver.

'We need to get you home and warmed. It has taken us some time to find you but a few inquiries here and there proved useful. Your maid Alice was very concerned about you and asked me if I would help find you. She suggested asking George Ackroyd to help as he has a car. He was kind enough to drive us around to find you quickly.' Emily now became aware of Alice and George who were approaching, both looking relieved. She suddenly realised that they must have witnessed the kiss and embrace. There was nothing that she could do about that now. As they strode along she did however admit to herself that she perceived a certain ease between them; there was a definite chemistry present.

George Ackroyd's Tin Lizzie waited patiently to transport them away. Emily and Niall were seated in the back whilst Alice sat next to George in the front; if circumstances had been different it would have appeared to onlookers like two couples enjoying a drive out together.

At first, the driving was very steady but when George moved hand levers under the steering wheel the speed increased, thrilling all the passengers, especially Alice, who squealed with delight.

'What?' questioned George as he looked at his front passenger who seemed speechless with excitement. 'I'm only hurrying to get the patient home quickly!' As they giggled together, Emily knew that she had never seen George look as happy as he did making Alice squeal with delight. She had never witnessed such feelings of contentment upon his face in Olivia's presence.

With that thought, she turned to Niall whose eyes had been watching her throughout the journey; it almost appeared that he was reluctant to let her out of his sight.

'I'm sorry for causing you distress, but seeing you there in my parents' home rather unnerved me; I just needed some time to think things out.'

'And have you?' he asked, his eyes intently searching her face.

'Yes I have.' Appearing far more confident and determined than he had ever seen her, she moved closer to him and whispered into his ear, 'I know what I want for Christmas.'

'And just what might that be?'

'A wedding ring.'

'Well, that can definitely be arranged,' he whispered beaming with delight as he clutched her hand tightly.

Niall made all the arrangements; they were to be married in the neighbouring province of Haxton, a small town situated next to Beckston, as there would be less chance of anyone recognising them there. He decided to rent a room there in order to satisfy any legalities regarding residency within the borough. It would be a small ceremony at a registry office and although they both wished prevailing circumstances could have been different, they reconciled themselves to the fact that small and private imbued a certain feeling of romantic intimacy.

As the weeks passed, Charles Taylor's health improved and he managed to leave his bed and with help descend the stairs and even take some steps outside into the fresh air. His speech remained slurred and his right side weak, causing him to drag his foot whilst his right hand lacked coordination and dexterity, but he was determined that he would give his daughter away at her wedding. Olivia talked of nothing else but her impending nuptials in the summer of 1911, persuading everyone that the event would be the saving of her father.

For Emily, Christmas could not arrive too soon as she looked forward to her own wedding, the day before Christmas Eve. It seemed so unfair that Olivia could bore everyone around her with talk of her wedding arrangements whilst Emily had no one except Niall to share her plans with. On the limited occasions when she managed to steal some time alone with him, it all became worthwhile again. Niall was now lodging with Doctor Lawson who, since the loss of his own wife, had remained in a large house devoid of company. The opportunity to have a new partner to share both his practice and his home with was too good to miss on either side.

The question concerning Emily's wedding outfit was one that she solved easily; she would simply wear the one she wore to the wedding on Long Island. She was being neither unimaginatively practical nor deliberately mercenary, just carefully circumspect in order to avoid unwanted attention from the prying eyes of her mother and sister. A new outfit for Olivia never attracted the questions that one for Emily did. In completion she still had the over-sized hat which Olivia had made for her and some very delicate and expensive pieces of underwear which Amelia had persuaded her to buy whilst staying in New York. She slightly blushed as she realised that she would now no longer be the only person to see them.

The only remaining problem was citing a reason for her absence away from home, one which would necessitate an overnight stay. Eventually, the solution presented itself; an advertisement for Haxton Theatre presenting one of George Bernard Shaw's plays, *Captain Brassbound's Conversion*. A rather unlikely choice for the festive celebrations, this play had originally been published in Shaw's 1901 collection, *Three Plays for Puritans*, together with *Caesar and Cleopatra* and *The Devil's Disciple*. George Bernard Shaw, an Irish dramatist and critic was fundamentally a moralist who believed that the theatre should instruct and improve, rather than merely entertain and make money. Emily knew that a play which acted as a sermon against various kinds of foolishness being disguised as duty and justice, would appeal to her parents' sense of propriety. She also knew that this play or indeed anything by Shaw would not interest Olivia and there would be no danger of her wishing to accompany Emily. The idea of meeting up with an old college friend to do some pre-Christmas shopping in Haxton, followed by a visit to the Theatre and an overnight stay at a small reasonably priced hotel, was sufficient information to satisfy her parents. The nature of the play was indeed sufficient for them to heartily endorse Emily's choice of entertainment, compared with the animated and pleasure-seeking performances which Olivia always sought.

Emily rose early upon the morning of December 23rd having slept fitfully throughout the night. She had already packed her bag, one large enough to hold the oversized hat. If questions arose regarding the large overnight bag, she would merely reply that hopefully she intended to use the space for Christmas shopping; that explanation alone would be sufficient to quell any of Olivia's suspicions.

Descending the stairs she could hear Alice preparing the breakfast, just as she always did. She was happily humming a little tune to herself, oblivious that anyone else was downstairs.

'You sound happy today, Alice.'

She stopped humming and turned around to face Emily. 'I am Miss, I really am.'

'What has caused this?' Emily enquired.

'It's my day off and I'm going to do a bit of Christmas shopping for my family. I love to see the little ones' faces when they open their presents.'

Emily smiled back knowing that Alice was a very generous girl, but soon her smile faded as she realised that the size of Alice's family, consisting of four brothers and three sisters, would not allow generously filled stockings from her meagre wages.

'Alice, why don't you and I go shopping in Beckston together this morning?'

'But Miss, I thought you were going to Haxton today.'

'I am, but having risen early, I can enjoy a double shopping trip.'

The truth of the matter was that Emily wanted everyone close to her to be happy on this particular day. The deception still troubled her conscience; therefore the only way she could placate this morally, was by treating those who deserved a smile being placed on their faces.

Once the breakfast pots had been washed, dried and put away, Alice was free to leave the household. She accompanied Emily into Beckston, chatting and looking around with unparalleled excitement. The shop window displays positively brimmed with festive attraction and promise but Alice was acutely aware of the constraints of her purse. Reluctantly she passed by the expensive stores remembering her mother's advice, that it costs nothing to look. Soon they found themselves outside Alice's favourite shop, the Penny Bazaar, a store she knew would meet the challenge of a long shopping list with limited finances. Once inside, her eyes began to dart about as they lighted upon the systematically laid out rows of enticements. A large assortment of confectionery including stripy humbugs, liquorice, creamy toffees, pear drops, bull's eyes and vibrantly coloured boiled sweets immediately caught her eye. It was certainly true that a penny or two would go far on this counter. Then the real enticements began to prise the pennies from the customers' hands. Rows of thimbles and cotton reels, tin whistles and small tin toys and little dolls with china heads and stuffed bodies, lay there just wanting to be picked up and bought. They all wanted to bring a little happiness to children at Christmas time. Alice would have loved to have bought everything but she knew that her purse had limits. As long as each child had some sweets and a toy, that would suffice. She had carefully planned what she could afford and then opened her purse to pay; the look of astonishment on her face made Emily smile. In addition to her coins she found five separate florins. She knew exactly who had placed them there and when as she had given Emily her purse to hold when she had selected the confectionery. No amount of protestations would convince Emily to take the money back.

'Those coins are doing absolutely no good sitting in your purse,' Emily reminded her with a smile. 'We are not leaving until you have spent them.' The tone of voice was delivered in a characteristic headmistress manner, which uncharacteristically made them each laugh. Now they both darted about the shop picking up yet further presents. When at last they had spent the money, Emily directed Alice who now had her arms full of purchases, out of the Penny Bazaar and back towards the more expensive stores. Flakes of snow were unexpectedly floating steadily downwards from a sky which had changed dramatically within the last hour; although grey and slightly overcast the street scene appeared fresh, clean and unsurprisingly festive.

First they stopped at a small bookshop where Emily purchased several copies of Beatrix Potter's books including *The Tale of Peter Rabbit*, *The Tailor of Gloucester* and the relatively recently published edition of *The Tale of the Flopsy Bunnies*. Then they made their way to a large grocer's store, which was more of an emporium as it stocked a diverse selection of goods. This was George Ackroyd's business and, being a progressive businessman, he had seen the potential for stocking a wide variety of goods under one roof and as such had now become a direct competitor for the Co-operative stores. His Model T Ford was parked proudly outside and was already covered in snow. Inside the store was filled with customers who were eager to secure their provisions for Christmas but George, whilst busy serving and supervising his staff immediately acknowledged their presence with a cheery greeting and his welcoming smile. Emily nodded back in recognition whilst Alice seemed to respond with a coy expression before glancing downwards. Once he had served his customer he quickly came over to Emily and Alice and sporting his usual welcoming smile, commenced to serve them himself.

'Good morning Ladies and how may I be of assistance? Would you care to first take a seat and I will then personally serve you?' He showed them to a row of chairs, where he managed to find two empty seats dotted between other seated customers. Although his smile and relaxed manner belied his astute business acumen, it was understandable why customers, particularly female customers, enjoyed the personal attention from Mr Ackroyd.

Emily ordered a large hamper to be filled with a wide selection of meats, including a goose and a ham as well as a selection of fresh fruits and vegetables, and butter, eggs, tea, cocoa, preserves and cakes. As she handed over a paper with the details of the address it had to be delivered to for Christmas Eve, George smiled and nodded obligingly.

'Leave that with me, and I will ensure that it is delivered in good time.' He then looked thoughtfully at Alice. 'You certainly have been busy shopping, young lady.'

'Yes, Miss Taylor has been helping me before she leaves for Haxton.'

'Haxton? Are you intending going there today?' He uttered the name with a certain amount of disbelief. 'You're not considering taking the train, I trust?' He now directed his attention to Emily.

'Well yes, that is my intention.'

'The line is apparently blocked with a fallen tree and, with the weather as it is, I'm afraid they don't believe that it will be cleared today.'

'But I have to get to Haxton this afternoon.' The urgency in her voice conveyed the imperative nature of the journey.

Leaving the shop with their purchases over-brimming in their arms, they realised that the streets were turning white under fast-falling snowflakes. The sky had suddenly turned dismally grey and it appeared that the snow was falling with haste. They had to get home, but Emily knew that she also had to get to Haxton for an important appointment later in the afternoon.

'Miss Taylor! Wait a moment!' He shouted out her name with clarity across the street, causing numerous heads to turn and stare. George Ackroyd was running across the street trying to remove his long white serving apron whilst trying to put his outside jacket on.

'If it is imperative that you reach Haxton today, please let me drive you there.'

'That is most kind of you, but I cannot take you away from your business, especially when you are so busy. I will find some other way to get there.'

'But you won't! The weather is quickly getting worse. If you need to go, you need to leave now.' Emily knew that George was right and, with some reluctance, agreed to his suggestion. George also insisted that Alice should get into the car as he felt it would be impossible for her to walk home with so much shopping in her arms.

George drove steadily, and quickly reached the Taylors' home. Within minutes Emily had placed her large bag in the car, said her farewells to her parents and George's trusty Tin Lizzie was soon being expertly manoeuvred through the deepening tracks on the roads. Alice had agreed to accompany them, particularly as George had commented that he required as 'much ballast in the car as possible!' His good nature, accompanied with their laughter, still continued to prevail under the difficult conditions which they were facing; conditions which were steadily deteriorating.

The ladies sat in the back, underneath the hood, which did little to prevent the snow from falling on them. Covered with blankets they pulled them around themselves in an effort to stay dry and warm. George was indeed a remarkable man Emily thought, as she watched him steadfastly battle against the driving snow, with little more than a tent-like cape, gauntlet gloves, a pair of goggles and a cloth cap with ear-flaps. She wondered if her sister was truly worthy of such a kind and respectable man. Alice meanwhile gazed with admiration at the man in front of her; she had never known anyone like George Ackroyd.

At the top of the hill they looked down to Haxton, a small northern town which like Beckston sprawled with some irregularity in the vale below. The tallest landmarks were those of factory chimneys and church towers which rose upwards from darkened clusters of buildings surrounding them. This town had been founded on woollen cloth and was home to a large open manufacturers' hall where weavers had for decades sold their lengths of cloth. The town also boasted a macabre reminder of its past as it had witnessed executions from the thirteenth century until the mid-seventeenth century using a form of guillotine; such tales always made the ladies gasp and clutch their throats in response to the grisly details.

Descending into Haxton the inevitable question was raised, 'Where are you staying?'

'At the Crown Hotel,' Emily replied in as much of a nonchalant air as she could manage.

'Very nice,' George added. 'I know it well, having enjoyed many business meetings, including dinners, there. It certainly is the best place to stay.'

As they entered the imposing surroundings of the hotel's foyer they each caught a glimpse of themselves in the heavily gilded mirrors adorning the walls and were shocked by the appearance of their reflections. Wet hair, wet clothing and pale white faces stared back without recognition. The warmth of the foyer was also accentuating the chill in their bones and each one was quickly beginning to shiver.

George suddenly turned and stared at the outside scene through the door. As a grandfather clock chimed one o'clock, he realised that it had taken them more than two hours to drive a distance which should have been manageable in a quarter of that time, under normal weather conditions.

Without speaking to his companions he strode over to the reception desk and enquired,' Do you have two single rooms available for tonight please?'

Emily's heart was already beating loudly before the receptionist had replied.

Chapter Fourteen

NEW YORK – December 23rd
Inspector Jackson always started the morning with the same routine, sitting at his desk with a cup of strong dark coffee. His colleagues knew him well and avoided any conversation with him during that first half hour in the morning when his senses were still dulled, no doubt as a result of too many bourbon-whiskies from the night before. Those along with insufficient sleep caused by slumping uncomfortably in a chair at his apartment or remaining in the one he was now sitting in seemed to make him exceptionally grumpy and unapproachable. He lived alone and cared little for what others thought of him, except where his professional life was concerned. He knew there was not a colleague in New York who could equal his rate of success in apprehending and charging those who deserved conviction. That of course, was the problem he thought as his chubby hands once more fingered the anonymous note. He had never before felt as bewildered and ineffectual as he now did.

He read the words once again, as he had done many times before expecting to find a hidden clue: 'MR ROBINSON, THE MAN YOU ARE SEEKING FROM THE LUSITANIA, IS MR CHRISTIAN VERHOLT FROM LONG ISLAND.'

The words penned in capital letters using ink, were concise and straight to the point and the post mark showed that the note had been posted in New York. In frustration Sam Jackson pounded one of his huge fists down onto his desk causing any items there to shudder under the impact. He was damned if he was going to be beaten by this case.

He leaned back in his chair, gulped down a mouthful of his now cold coffee and began to recall the events on-board the Lusitania. He and his men had searched every part of the ship and interviewed passengers and crew but they had found nothing to assist them. Since receiving the note he had had Christian Verholt constantly followed but the fellow had behaved as a model citizen, dividing his time between New York and Suffolk Hall on Long Island, always in legitimate circumstances. There had been not one jot of questionable behaviour on his part in any way. He just could not pin anything on him at all. Dammit! Jackson thought as he scratched his head in his customary manner when a case was severely provoking him. There had to be a way. Looking down into his coffee cup he began to idly play with the spoon which he always used to heap too many sugars into his coffee with. This may have been shiny but it was only electro-plated, not solid silver as Christian Verholt was used to. *He* certainly had been born with a silver spoon in *his* mouth.

It was at this point that Jackson remembered the silver spoons along with the other treasures that had been found in the Robinsons' cabin on the Lusitania. Some of these items had since been returned to their owners; an aristocratic family in England Jackson recalled as well as a wealthy family in Paris.

The word 'Paris' suddenly made Jackson sit bolt upright. His mind began to whirr with thoughts and suppositions. As a colleague attempted to enter his office with an inquiry Jackson yelled at him to leave him in peace.

He recalled how one of the passengers had described the clothing of Mrs Robinson, being in the style of Parisian fashion. Inspector Jackson, never having been married, had at the time of the interview taken little notice of the elongated descriptions of the slim graceful elegance of the lady's couture. In fact he had found the woman being interviewed rather attention-seeking and in his eyes, a time-waster. Now he wanted to interview her again because her attention to detail might just give him that necessary lead. He knew that he had her address somewhere, particularly as her grandsons had been so instrumental in locating that cabin. Finding her details he slumped back once more into his chair.

Amelia Davenport's eye for detail might just unearth some important treasure. With that thought he smiled and felt that Christmas had just arrived.

Chapter Fifteen

ENGLAND

Emily now fully appreciated the debt of gratitude she owed to her companions, especially George. He had left his store at the busiest time of year to drive her in dangerous conditions so that she could meet a friend and enjoy the shops and the theatre. All of this had been undertaken with a smile and his characteristic good nature. That was what hurt the most, together with the blatant untruth that she was masquerading under.

Having made her decision, she invited them both to her room.

'I am afraid that I have been less than truthful with you; something which neither of you deserve.' The disclosure immediately secured their attention.

'I had to reach Haxton today because at 3pm I am ...' Emily suddenly stopped in mid-sentence. The revelation was proving too difficult to deliver. Neither George nor Alice broke the intense silence but instead allowed her sufficient time to collect her thoughts and continue.

'At 3pm today I am to be ... married.' The sentence was short and to the point and its effect was as predictable as Emily had imagined.

Whilst the smile had left George's face, Alice's held confusion and seemed to dart with joyful bewilderment.

George was the first one to speak. 'Who are you going to marry?'

'Doctor Branigan. Niall Branigan.' The mention of his name was sufficient to place a knowing smile on each of their faces.

'Well, we should have known that, especially after the kiss in the park!' George said laughingly. Although Emily momentarily blushed with slight embarrassment she now was beginning to feel more at ease.

'I am sorry for the deception, but a woman in my position cannot marry.'

'You are no different to any other woman, are you? You have the same emotions and feelings as every other woman, I take it. So why should *you* not be happy?' George's understanding made everything seem so reasonable.

'Because there are expectations, as I am a headmistress and I am also the daughter of my parents.'

'They have two daughters and seem perfectly happy for me to take Olivia in marriage.'

'But it is different for me. There are expectations, which in order to fulfil I should remain a spinster.'

'In order to please everyone else rather than yourself. Emily, do you love Niall?' George was far more pragmatic and vocal than Emily had anticipated.

'Yes.' The simple but heartfelt admission was sufficient.

'Well then, we have less than two hours. Alice, I suggest that you help prepare the bride for her wedding and I will seek out Doctor Branigan, and find out if he requires any assistance. Emily, where might I locate him?'

As Emily peered through the window at the outside snowy scene she appeared rather anxious.

'We had agreed that he would collect me from the hotel at twenty minutes to three; the registry office is only a few minutes' walk away. He has been renting a room in a nearby street in order to satisfy the legalities about residency within the borough. But with the weather as it is, I do hope that he has been able to make his way across from Beckston. I know that he had patients to see this morning.'

George tried to allay any resounding fears by assuring Emily that her groom would be present. In a moment he had disappeared, leaving the two women alone with nothing more than one hour to prepare for the wedding.

Emily quickly began to disrobe as Alice prepared her bath. The novelty of having a separate bathroom equipped with a full-length bath and brass taps which on turning allowed water to flow freely both surprised and delighted hotel visitors. Emily and Alice were no exception, both marvelling at the technological advancement from back-breaking trips of filling the copper hip bath to the simplicity of merely turning a tap. The cast-iron sarcophagus-shaped bath slowly warmed with the heat of the water. Raised above the floor on clawed feet it looked highly inviting as Emily stepped into it and allowed herself the indulgence of sinking down into the relaxing and penetrating warmth of the water. Alice meanwhile unpacked Emily's luggage and laid out the oversized hat and delicate underwear on the large bed before hanging the dress over the edge of the wardrobe door. She had never seen any of these garments before and was excited at the prospect of seeing Emily in them; normally she wore quite conservative and matronly outfits.

Having bathed, Emily allowed the bath to empty, another rare novelty in itself and then proceeded to refill it, insisting that Alice should also indulge in the warmth of the water. Unlike Emily, Alice had no change of clothing with her, as she had not expected to be away from home. The girl was cold and needed a hot bath to restore her body warmth and replace the glow in her rosy cheeks. She quickly bathed and dressed, keenly anxious to assist Emily in her preparations.

First, she brushed Emily's long hair with comforting, regular strokes before pinning it up. Then she helped her into the soft grey dress which now concealed the very delicate, almost gossamer-like undergarments covering Emily's figure. The application of a little make-up and the positioning of the large oversized hat upon her head was enough to complete the transformation.

'What do you think?' The proverbial bride's question made Alice begin to cry.

'Miss, you look beautiful. I never would have thought that you could look like this.'

Emily was slightly perplexed, but considered that there was a compliment somewhere in that statement.

'Thank you Alice, for helping me and for unpacking.' She noticed the package containing the Beatrix Potter books which she had purchased earlier that morning.

'Alice, I was going to give you these when we reached home but in the confusion I had forgotten about them. Will you give them to your brothers and sisters for Christmas from me? I am sure that they will both entertain and help with their reading.'

Once again Alice began to cry. 'Oh Miss, you are so kind. You deserve to be happy and I am sure you will be with Doctor Branigan.'

'I hope so Alice. I am completely going against convention by marrying him. Dishonesty is not a trait I have ever employed before. I should be setting standards not breaking them. You must think badly of me.'

'Never! I could never think anything but the best of you. I am sure that Doctor Branigan thinks the same. You love him and that matters more than anything. It's only wrong to marry someone if you don't really love them.'

A knock at the door interrupted Alice's outburst but Emily suddenly began thinking about her sister Olivia and wondered whether such thoughts were also present in Alice's mind.

Upon opening the door they had expected to see either Niall or George standing there but instead found a maid holding a pile of thick towels; she enquired if she could change the linen, presumably as a result of having heard the constant running of water from the room. The time was now quarter to three and the snow was still continuing to fall. They made their way downstairs and were oblivious to the looks of surprise upon faces watching the elegantly dressed lady who was most noticeable with her oversized hat. Standing in the foyer, pulling their coats around them, they each stared down the street, their eyes willing the next visible silhouettes to be familiar to them.

'It will soon be too late,' Emily lamented. It was now ten minutes to three and once again she was beginning to feel the bitter chill of the northern weather. She sighed and looked downwards, almost accepting the inevitable.

'Look,' Alice shouted, extending a pointed finger into the distance. 'It's them; I just know it's them.'

As Emily once again stared, this time with almost disbelief, she recognised that the two heavily snow-covered figures were those of

Niall and George. Like Alice she too began to find it impossible to stand still. They began to tentatively shuffle along the street taking care not to slip or slide on the uneven surface. As the gap between the couples lessened joyful smiles were exchanged, until they were sufficiently close enough for Emily and Niall to kiss and embrace.

Emily was the first to speak, tears almost making her inaudible. 'I thought you would not make it.'

'Nothing would prevent me from marrying you. Not even being stranded in a snow drift.'

He explained how he had borrowed Doctor Lawson's car but had had to abandon it on the high road from Beckston because of impassable conditions. Continuing on foot he had found the walk quite treacherous and his spirits had only been lifted when he had seen George Ackroyd walking up the hill from Haxton to find him. He truly knew that he had a good friend in George. Emily also knew how loyal a friend she had in Alice. It was therefore without question that such friends would make wonderful witnesses.

Their arrival at Haxton Registry Office coincided with three striking tones from the Town Hall clock. The bride, initially anxious, now looked beautiful and elegant, whilst the groom was bedraggled in clothing that was slowly beginning to drip with the onset of warmth. There was nothing that could spoil their day. They had everything. They had each other.

The ceremony was quickly performed and they were soon man and wife. Alice allowed a tear to trickle down her cheek before George carefully dabbed it away. He had already squeezed her little hand in an affectionate gesture, winked and smiled as the ring was being slipped onto Emily's finger. Now they watched as Niall took his wife in his arms and kissed her. The four friends shook hands, exchanged hugs and expressed their joy to one another before returning to the Crown Hotel where they enjoyed a meal together. The popping of the champagne cork made Alice squeal and, following a few sips, she began to chatter and giggle quite incessantly which George found amusing. The combination of wine with the meal and champagne for the toast proved rather too much for Alice who was not used to alcohol. Retiring early to bed Alice was the first one to leave the table. Emily insisted upon accompanying her to her room, where within minutes Alice had reclined and swiftly fallen asleep on her bed.

Although George had enjoyed their company, he was also mindful that it was time for Niall and Emily to be left alone. Ever the gentleman, he excused himself and left the newly-weds to enjoy each other's company.

The decided look cast mutually between them signalled that it was time for them to also retire. Emily led the way, holding his hand; they walked up the stairs and along the corridor in silence until they reached the room. Stepping inside and closing the door reminded them of that previous occasion when they had entered one of the Regal Suites on-board the Lusitania. As she looked into his eyes, Emily's heart began to quicken, just as it had previously done on that night.

They kissed lightly at first in a teasing but tempting way, faintly brushing each other's lips. With his arms caressing her shoulders, he began to draw her to him with an increasing magnetism which was reluctant to offer any form of release. The feelings were mutual and Emily responded with such vigour of heated emotion that quickly led to Niall searching for the fastenings down the back of her dress. In his haste, he sighed with a certain resonance of impatience as his fingers fumbled to undo the row of small pearl buttons which finally yielded to his perseverance, allowing the soft grey dress to fall unceremoniously to the floor.

Emily stood in silence as Niall drew back and gazed at her feminine form. He had only once before made love to her, but he now ached to do so again; the urge was so reminiscent of that first time. The fine gossamer-like threads of the alluring undergarments barely concealed the swell of her breasts and the rounded contours of her waist, bottom and thighs. Without speaking, he burrowed his head against her neck and kissed the soft white flesh surrounding her throat whilst his fingers lifted and peeled back the slender straps of her top, enabling her breasts to be exposed. As he kissed each one she murmured with delight before he lifted her into his arms and tenderly carried her to the bed. He hastily undressed whilst she removed any remaining undergarments before becoming entwined with passionate intensity. Very soon, the mutual motion of their bodies began to accelerate with an unleashed orgasmic swell before ultimately reaching the pinnacle of excitement.

In the eyes of the Law, they were now married. In the eyes of each other, they were now truly man and wife.

Chapter Sixteen

NEW YORK – December 24th

"There is no time like the present" was an adage which Sam Jackson lived by. If he chose to get up in the middle of the night to pursue a thought or indeed not go to bed at all, that was his prerogative. There was no lady wife to offer her nagging objections. His heavy-laden eyes stared with some derision as they attempted to focus upon the old and shabby but familiar contents in his apartment; he called it an apartment but it was no more than three rented rooms.

It was only five thirty in the morning but his habitual inability to obtain a full night's sleep continually prevented him from sleeping to a more conventional time; a cycle which made him constantly tired, weary and irritable. For once he had even resorted to sleeping in his bed but the pattern remained the same. His great frame rose from the bed and shuffled into another day.

The apartment lacked any feminine charm. Being so close to Christmas it also lacked any festive charm. In fact Sam Jackson hated everything about this time of year, especially the way everyone pretended that they were enjoying themselves. Then a thought occurred to him which premeditated a smile. Today would see him prepare for the promise of a great New Year. He decided he would make an early start as he had plenty to do.

Two and a half hours later he was knocking on the door of a house which offered temporary lodgings. His heart sank when he saw the sign indicating vacancies. A small elderly man opened the door to the address which he held in his hand.

'Do the Davenports still live here?' he asked in his usual no-nonsense way.

'No.' The reply was succinct.

'Do you know where they are now?'

'They moved out to other accommodation, a couple of months back; somewhere on the West Side I think. I believe I have an address.' The old man shuffled away and finally returned. 'Yeah, here it is.' Jackson smirked. He knew the area well, having once lived there as a child himself.

New York had grown rapidly during the nineteenth century. Immigrants initially from Ireland and Germany and then later from Italy and Eastern Europe had poured into a city which had established itself as the central hub of American industry and commerce. Its attraction to those seeking a better life with prospects caused its population to expand quite dramatically, earning itself the title of being the world's largest city by the end of the century.

The majority of these immigrants had found themselves with no option but to live or rather exist in overcrowded clusters in unsavoury tenement buildings whilst earning their living in sweatshop conditions. The sweltering summer heat and the freezing winter temperatures no longer made New York such an attractive prospect to its recently arrived settlers, but for many it was already too late to alter the situation.

Jonathan Davenport had high aspirations for himself and his family and had already decided before leaving England that they were going to join the growing middle classes in America. Astute and highly organised, he wasted little time in securing a decent and reliable management position within the real estate business which now was booming with speculators eager to satisfy the increasing demands for accommodation. Leaving their temporary lodgings they moved to a small but quite respectable house in Greenwich Village, on the west side of Lower Manhattan in New York City. Not quite one of the brownstone houses which monumentally eclipsed it, it was however in a good neighbourhood, a point so important when trying to secure prominence particularly when rearing two growing sons. For Amelia its attraction lay in its bohemian connections: artists, art galleries and theatres.

Sam Jackson used the doorknocker with a sturdy determination before he found himself being stared at by four large, identical, brown, saucer-like eyes which craned around the slightly opened door. Such scrutiny normally unnerved visitors but Jackson was used to the unexpected.

'Daniel and David, I'm right, yes?' Jackson felt quite pleased for remembering their names but inwardly admitted to himself that he still could not tell them apart.

'I'm David and he's Daniel,' came the reply.

The sound of voices in the background made the boys turn, allowing the door to now open fully.

'Who is it boys?' a woman's voice called out.

'That policeman from the ship.' Such a description made the inspector bristle slightly with resentment.

'It's Inspector Jackson. I headed up the investigation on the Lusitania.' Jackson outstretched his hand in a perfunctory way and managed a passing grimace as he shook Beatrice Davenport's hand.

'Good morning Inspector. Please do come in. I'm afraid you find us in relative chaos, with having only recently moved and now trying to prepare for Christmas.' The mention of Christmas was sufficient for Jackson to throw back a look of disdain, as she showed him into the front parlour, a room reserved for guests.

'I take it you have some news for us?' Beatrice enquired with interest.

'No, nothing like that!' he replied in his usual brusque manner. 'I wondered if I might talk with your mother-in-law.'

'Amelia. Yes of course. I'll go and call her.' Beatrice wondered how her mother-in-law could be of any further assistance. She hoped that she had not been, as her husband often described her, meddling in other people's affairs. Therefore she decided it was better not to mention this to her husband when he later returned from work.

'Inspector Jackson!' Amelia positively beamed with delight as her eyes fell upon the robust figure, now standing in their home. 'How lovely to see you.' Jackson once again performed the expected gesture of the necessary handshake.

'May I ask what brings you here?' she enquired with a certain amount of coy meekness.

Jackson found the utter politeness of the English, at best irritating and at worst, nauseating.

'I'm making more enquiries into the incident on the Lusitania.'

For a moment Amelia considered his statement. 'I don't see how I can be of any further assistance.'

'You might not but I will be the judge of that.'

Amelia very quickly realised that her customary charms of flirtatious banter enhanced by feminine expressions were making no impact upon this hardbitten police inspector. Try as she might to succeed in slightly softening the crusty exterior he resolutely refused to be swayed.

'I believe you dined with the Robinsons on-board the Lusitania?'

'Well, we shared a table together. However, they were I recall on their honeymoon and seemed to just want to be by themselves, if you understand what I mean?' Amelia tried once more with a coy smile which again had no impact upon the inspector.

'They were certainly not on their honeymoon as both you and I now know!'

'Quite.' Amelia understood that she could not afford to play games with this man.

'They may have kept themselves to themselves, but that was for a very good reason, as we have since found out. When I interviewed you on the Lusitania you described the woman's clothes as being of Parisian style. What did you mean by that?'

'I only met them once and that was at the dinner table but I do recall thinking how elegant she looked. She was young, dark haired, slim and quite pretty. We were of course only in second class and at the time it struck me how fashionable she looked, especially not being a first class passenger herself. Inspector, I have always enjoyed following the fashion pages of magazines such as Vogue so I have a relatively good understanding of what is in fashion. She was wearing the type of dress which the Parisian designers are producing; a very straight style, which emphasises the waist but makes the rest of the figure look long and straight. Let me say it is a style which does not emphasise a woman's curves.'

The inspector had listened intently and now nodded in recognition.

'Do you think the woman was French?'

'It is difficult to say. She certainly had a continental look about her.'

'Did you hear her speak?'

'No, I don't think I did. Only her husband, I mean the man who was with her spoke and introduced them both as Mr and Mrs Robinson who had recently married and were on their honeymoon.'

'What do you remember about the man?' The question immediately made Amelia's eyes light up with interest.

'Oh, he was young, perhaps twenty-five years old, blond and good looking. He was also smartly dressed.' The description caused a curl of resentment to momentarily pass across Jackson's mouth.

'You heard him speak; where would you say he was from?'

'Oh, it is difficult to say. He was well-spoken, by that I also mean well-educated. At first I did think that he was from England but then something in his pronunciation made me think that he was American. Neither of them seemed to want to engage in conversation so I didn't find out a great deal about them.'

Jackson again nodded in recognition before fumbling in his pocket and pulling out a photograph which he passed to Amelia.

'Is that the man?'

'Yes. Yes it is. Who is he?'

'Heir to one of the wealthiest banking families in America. His name is Christian Verholt.' The mention of his name slightly disturbed Amelia. Conscious that the inspector was scrutinising her expressions for any sign of recognition, she focussed her mind on other things whilst passing back the photograph.

'Ever heard the name before?'

'No. Never.'

'Well that is strange.'

'Why do you say that?' Amelia now searched Jackson's face to try and understand the workings of his mind.

'The Verholt Family now resides on Long Island, at a place called Suffolk Hall. That is where your friend Emily Taylor went to stay. When I say stay, I don't mean at the big house but with her relatives who work for the Verholts.' The revelation was unbelievable to

Amelia who appeared stunned and for once, speechless. She now realised how serious this case was by the considerable amount of investigation which had been undertaken.

Jackson again fumbled in his pocket and this time pulled out a folded piece of paper. He passed it unopened to Amelia.

'Take a look at that.' Amelia's fingers began to tremble. 'Read it out loud.'

'MR ROBINSON, THE MAN YOU ARE SEEKING FROM THE LUSITANIA, IS MR CHRISTIAN VERHOLT FROM LONG ISLAND.'

The colour drained from Amelia's face as she simply handed the note back without speaking.

'Seems familiar?'

'If by that you are asking if I penned that note, the answer is no.'

The degree of integrity in the delivery of that sentence made Jackson certain that she was telling the truth. The degree of intensity for information made Amelia suspicious; not just about the Verholts but about Jackson himself. There was something about him that definitely unnerved her.

Although Amelia had initially promised Emily that she would deal with the revelation about Christian Verholt, she had in fact done nothing. It had at first been easy to assure Emily to leave it in her capable hands but then as time had elapsed, so had the momentum.

Following the inspector's departure, Amelia found she was unable to concentrate upon anything. There was plenty to do in preparing for Christmas; Beatrice was calling for some culinary assistance from the kitchen whilst Daniel and David were chasing one another spiritedly up and down the staircase in their usual raucous style, playing cowboys and Indians. In the midst of such confusion Amelia sank down into one of the parlour chairs and allowed her mind to wander. She glanced across at the Christmas card which she had received from Emily and suddenly began to wonder whether she was looking forward to her Christmas. There had been no news of the great romance and she sighed fearing that that had soured through absence and time. If that thought was bad enough her next one was worse; Jackson might now be contemplating a transatlantic crossing for himself.

With that thought in mind Amelia stood up and walked over to the small writing desk. She pulled out a piece of writing paper from the drawer, sat down and began to write.

Chapter Seventeen

ENGLAND – December 24th

They had woken that morning to a scene of pure serenity; Haxton lying quietly under a deep covering of glistening white snow, its sounds of life muffled within the layers of ice crystals. Blue skies above allowed the sun to shine down unimpeded, bestowing feelings of universal happiness and joy which in turn encouraged shopkeepers and customers alike to exchange their own glad tidings. Christmas Eve had started well; feelings of well-being always assisted consumerism.

No one knew this more than George Ackroyd. His companions also knew that this was the one day in the year when a grocer needed to be behind his counter. They all rose early, breakfasted and quickly found themselves negotiating the rigour of the climb out of Haxton. Positioned not too far from the Pennine backbone, towns such as Haxton and Beckston, only approachable by demanding gradients, tested the steering skills of any driver even in favourable conditions. George drove with both care and determination following the narrow trail until they came upon Doctor Lawson's car which Niall had borrowed and subsequently had had to abandon due to the weather conditions. They all helped to clear the snow from the car and the men dug around the vehicle until it was possible to manoeuvre it out onto the apparent vestige of road. The newly-weds travelled together whilst Alice travelled with George. There was little opportunity for conversation as each person stared ahead and held their breath, dreading what they would find around the next icy bend. With caution, Beckston finally came into view and Emily realised with regret that her honeymoon was now over as the car came to a halt. They had agreed that it was better for Emily to arrive home in George's car. The newly-weds kissed and parted, neither one voicing a word as their eyes glistened with tears. Once seated in George's car, Emily simply removed her engagement and wedding rings and put them into her handbag. Alice watched in silence, her little heart aching with sadness. She remained silent, anxiously wondering if there was anything she could do by improvisation to bring them together.

As the car came to an abrupt halt outside the Taylors' home they each stared at the house, contemplating their own version of the agreed fabricated story of events. Emily made the first move, collecting her bags she walked up the path, head held high and greeted her mother and sister at the opened door.

'Oh Emily, we have been so worried about you. After you left yesterday, the snow began to fall so quickly and we all thought that you would be snowed in for days, didn't we Olivia?' Momentarily Olivia failed to answer as she looked first at Alice and then at George who was gesturing with a wave before driving away.

'Emily, I understood you were going to Haxton by yourself to meet up with an old friend. I hadn't realised that the trip would turn into a cosy overnight adventure for four,' Olivia announced disparagingly. Emily witnessed the jealous look in her face.

'I can assure you that it was anything but cosy, Olivia. George very kindly offered to drive me there, being the *gentleman* that he is.' She leaned closely to Olivia's ear and whispered, 'A trustworthy *gentleman.*' Olivia fell surprisingly silent; Emily knew however that silence did not signify an end to the matter, merely a prolonged day of reckoning.

Luckily, there was no time for explanations and detailed descriptions as there was a great deal to do. The goose had been delivered and required plucking and drawing. That task was designated to Alice by Hannah who oversaw the initial procedure before producing her own filling for the bird of chestnuts with pork and apple stuffing. Once the task had been accomplished Hannah then withdrew to read to her husband. Emily continued to work alongside Alice in the kitchen, cooking and baking seasonal family favourites such as the ubiquitous mince pies and ground rice tarts. Together they worked through the day and once the culinary preparations were in place they cleaned and ensured everything sparkled in readiness. The large Victorian table in the dining-room was prepared with precision by the etiquette demanded in table setting. Then they transformed the house with fresh greenery from the garden; cuttings of laurel, holly and ivy, which they placed around pictures and dotted on top of the mantelpieces. They made paper chains and paper lanterns and hung them to great effect alongside sprigs of mistletoe. With further creativity they produced intricately cut, fringed paper sachets which they appropriately filled with bonbons; these they would use for table decorations and also to adorn the tree.

Meanwhile, Olivia had spent the day in the parlour decorating the Norway spruce with a selection of glass baubles, gold and silver embossed cardboard tree ornaments in the shapes of animals, bells and stars, toys including penny whistles and toy soldiers, dolls and baskets of sweets. She had clipped metal candle holders onto the tree's boughs to hold the candles safely upright. Being a milliner, she possessed nimble fingers and had transformed lengths of thick golden ribbon into splendid bows which she positioned cautiously on the ends of the branches, not too close to the candles. She had also used an assortment of broken necklaces to produce crystal pendants that twinkled on the tree as air currents caused them to shimmer with iridescent reflective colours. With the tree decoration completed, Olivia retired to her room to rest and left Emily and Alice to clear away.

Christmas Eve in the Taylor household had always featured certain traditions. After the arrival of local carol singers, the family gathered around the piano where Emily obligingly played while everyone sang. Charles Taylor had always read an excerpt from *A Christmas Carol* by Charles Dickens, sitting next to a roaring fire in the parlour with his family seated around him. Unable to adequately undertake the family reading this year, Charles had asked George to perform the honour which he had proudly accepted.

The circle of faces listened intently as George read with gusto, making the story come to life. They had heard it many times before but this year it was different; the novelty of having a new narrator was quite evident.

The arrival of Marley's ghost was heralded by three distinctive knocks at the front door; such a coincidence caused a stirring of alarm amongst the ladies. As Alice opened the door she smiled back with both relief and delight at the familiar face in front of her before showing him into the parlour.

'Doctor Branigan! This is a lovely surprise,' remarked Hannah. 'Do come and join us.'

'That is most kind of you. To be honest I have just visited a patient and as I was in the neighbourhood I thought I would call and wish you all seasonal greetings.' Niall had not once dared to look at his new wife.

'Being out on such a cold night you need to warm yourself. Come and sit next to me by the fire.' Olivia slightly moved along the sofa and delicately patted the space next to her until Niall obliged.

'Forgive me. I hope I am not interrupting your evening but…'

'Certainly not! George was only reading. Besides what could be better than entertaining a guest?' Olivia asked with a smirk on her face. 'We really don't know a great deal about you and I'm sure that there must be plenty to tell.'

For a moment Niall appeared to be lost for words and stared hard into the ever-changing flames of the fire. Suddenly, he turned his head and Emily caught the twinkle of the emerald eyes as they fell in her direction before she fleetingly exchanged a smile of endearment. George and Alice were the only ones who witnessed this and understood the emotional transition.

Hannah's interruption, however, was a welcome relief and broke Olivia's train of questioning.

'Doctor Branigan, would you and Doctor Lawson care to join us for Christmas dinner tomorrow?'

'I cannot speak for Doctor Lawson but I would be delighted. Thank you.'

Doctor Branigan obligingly took his leave as the family followed annual tradition and attended the Christmas Eve service at their Methodist Chapel. On Christmas morning they attended morning service before returning home to enjoy their family celebrations. This year Emily enjoyed these services as she thought of spending her first Christmas in the company of her husband. Whilst Alice looked forward to her Christmas in a household which could afford the indulgence of good festive fare, she was also excited about spending the afternoon with her own family, in particular her young brothers and sisters. She longed to watch them opening their presents and see their faces in wide-eyed astonishment; this would make up for the absence of Christmas fare. She even secretly wondered if the Taylors might allow her to take any surplus food home with her. Of course she would not ask but suspected that it may be suggested. If it was she would certainly not turn down the offer.

The Taylors' Christmas dinner could not fail to delight. The goose which had been traditionally stuffed with Hannah's family recipe of chestnuts, pork and apple stuffing was served with apple and bread sauces alongside a selection of vegetables. The flavours complemented the succulent goose and caused the diners to willingly replenish their plates, after being encouraged to do so. When the plum pudding appeared everyone agreed that they had over-indulged but no one declined a portion of the rich Christmas dish. Doctor Lawson and George Ackroyd leaned back in their chairs and with a satisfied look upon their faces agreed that it was the best Christmas dinner they had ever tasted.

'Thank you, gentlemen, but I cannot take the full credit as Alice has been of exceptional help in the kitchen,' Hannah declared. As George smiled and winked at Alice who was now clearing the table before commencing the task of washing-up, Olivia quickly interrupted.

'I want to play some parlour games. Let us leave Alice to get on with her job. What shall we play; Charades, Blind Man's Buff or Queen of Sheba?' Before anyone could reply Olivia had made the decision. 'Doctor Branigan, are you willing to be blindfolded first? We can then spin you around and let you seek a kiss. I will be the first to sit in the chair. I think there is some mistletoe over here.'

It was futile to refuse Olivia's propositions and Niall begrudgingly accepted Olivia's flirtatious behaviour. Emily pitied George and could not help wondering why he still remained engaged to her sister. He was nothing less than an honourable man who did not deserve such treatment.

Retiring to the kitchen Emily picked up a drying cloth and proceeded to help Alice.

'Miss, you shouldn't be doing my job. Please I'll get into trouble.'

'No, you won't Alice. I would simply rather be here drying the dishes than in there witnessing my sister making a fool out of herself and George.' The mention of his name was sufficient to make Alice's little face look troubled.

'What about Doctor Branigan? Wouldn't you rather be with him, Miss?'

'Of course I would,but I just have to be satisfied with the few moments I can have with him, whenever or wherever that happens to be.' Alice declined to answer but as she continued to work through the ceaseless piles of dishes an ingenious thought came into her head.

'Miss, would you like to come and visit my family with me this afternoon? We're not fancy, but you would be made very welcome.'

'I would like that very much, Alice. Thank you.'

They continued to work together through the greasy dishes until all of them were cleaned. As Emily put the crockery and cutlery away she failed to notice that Alice had left the kitchen. Moments later she heard the familiar sound of the front door closing. When she entered the parlour she discovered that Doctor Branigan had already left; he had been called out to attend a patient.

Abject poverty abounded around the country in all towns and cities; this was a fact of which Emily was acutely aware. Through the years she had regularly witnessed children attending school, barefoot, hungry and wearing threadbare, unwashed clothing. She had always tried to counteract these conditions, often purchasing replacement clothes and shoes using her own purse; such philanthropy somehow made the situation easier to bear. Now the meanness of the streets in front of them served as a harsh reminder of the wretched lives that dwelt within them.

Emily had heard tales of overcrowding, but it was not just limited to multiple occupation of rooms; sometimes there would be multiple occupation of beds, where an occupant would be allowed eight hours within the course of twenty-four, which ensured that the bed was never left empty. Outside the yards and courts often unpaved, led to midden privies; these were often shared by several families and seldom cleared. As Emily and Alice walked briskly past each neglected house, Emily could not but wonder whether the Christmas dinners inside consisted of anything more than bread, dripping and tea; the standard diet of these family homes. At least the basket on her arm held a bounty of additional festive fare from the Taylor household. Alice appeared undaunted by the grim surroundings and instead seemed to joyfully skip along the snow-covered streets, her folded arms positively brimming with the presents from the Penny Bazaar.

'Miss, I can't wait to see the little ones' faces when they unwrap these.' Alice's little face was glowing, presumably as a result of the chill wind which was beginning to blow and also from the impending excitement.

'I think it will be a sight worth seeing, Alice. I am certain that you will make their Christmas.'

As Alice slowed her pace and stopped at the modest little house, Emily heard laughter and children's voices echoing from within. These were sounds that were welcome on these streets and suddenly she too wanted to watch them open their presents.

The Speights occupied the front dwelling of a meagre back-to-back house from which Alice's four brothers and three sisters could tumble out of onto the streets to play, when they needed more space. Normally that is where they would have been found but today the whole family remained indoors. Mrs Speight immediately threw her arms around Alice and thanked her for her generosity and thoughtfulness, before gesturing towards the table in the middle of the room, with its unusually ample supply of food.

'You are so good to us Alice; this all arrived yesterday evening. We couldn't believe what was in the hamper; the biggest goose you've ever seen, and a ham twice the size of ordinary ones. We've even had fresh fruits and vegetables, cheeses, eggs, bread and cakes. There was even a huge plum pudding for afters. The little ones couldn't believe it. I truly feel quite la-di-da with the jams, tea and cocoa.'

Alice smiled back at her mother and remained speechless.

'The man who delivered it all was a real gentleman; spoke nicely and didn't have his nose in the air, as most people who don't belong around here do. He even left a stocking for each of the children, filled with sweets, nuts and fruits. Oh, and I must tell you this; he brought it all in his own little car. Alice, thank you. This has been the best Christmas for us.'

The penny finally tumbled in Alice's mind as she realised the identity of the true benefactor.

'Thank you so much, Miss,' she said turning to Emily, with eyes full of gratitude.

Emily simply smiled back, happy that she had been able to give some festive joy to others who deserved it. She also knew that her order of a large hamper had been handsomely supplemented by George Ackroyd; such a kind-hearted man, she thought, was completely wasted upon her sister.

Once Mrs Speight realised who the companion at her daughter's side was, she did everything possible to make her guest welcome. Momentarily the sight of their headmistress had made the children uncharacteristically quiet but as the presents emerged, the spoils of the Penny Bazaar and the magic of the Beatrix Potter tales were sufficient to quell any anxieties regarding expectations of behaviour.

The overcrowded room became an idyllic haven for escapism. Surrounded by the family, Emily began reading the books, bringing to life the animated characters of Peter Rabbit, the Tailor of Gloucester and the Flopsy Bunnies. The children were enchantingly enthralled and the adults amusingly entranced by the make-believe world of the renowned authoress. The cosy setting of a family, who were warm, well-fed and securely entertained, was the little scene which presented itself to anyone outside who might happen to peer in as they passed by.

Standing outside, Doctor Branigan smiled to himself as he viewed the entire framework of domestic bliss surrounding his wife. He had been watching them for the last few minutes, marvelling at how a little kindness could make such a difference. The sudden chill of the December air made him pull the lapels of his thick coat towards him and reminded him of Alice's detailed plan. He moved to the door and clenched his fist in readiness to knock but at the last moment hesitated as though the action had triggered a former memory.

This type of district, along with the type of home and family within were all familiar scenes to a family doctor, but the scene had struck a personal chord within his own heart and delivered a poignant memory; an Irish scene with an Irish family, existing in misery and squalor. To be born into such a world was a struggle from day one and Niall understood that fate had intervened at the time of his birth; he had been the fortunate one.

The door opened without Niall knocking upon it and Alice's little face beamed from within with anticipation, bringing Niall's thoughts back to Beckston and the household before him.

'I thought it was you, Doctor Branigan. Have you been visiting a patient? Please won't you come in and join us?' Alice managed to deliver the conversation with conviction whilst ushering her guest into the overcrowded room. Mr Speight, a quiet man had already found it difficult and if the truth be told, a little uncomfortable entertaining a headmistress but now the prospect of playing host to a doctor seemed improbable, particularly on Christmas Day. He nodded and then withdrew into his chair in the corner. Mrs Speight was just thankful that there was plenty of food for everyone and accordingly invited her guests to indulge. As the room thronged with life, children playing, chattering and laughing, Emily remained perfectly still in the midst of it all and gazed with contentment at her husband.

'This is a surprise seeing you here,' Niall whispered softly into Emily's ear. He displayed his characteristic smile, enhanced with the twinkle of his emerald eyes.

'Yes, a most welcome surprise but I take it not quite a surprise for Alice.'

'No. You are very fortunate there in having a young lady who is both resourceful and discreet. Is that as a result of your teaching?'

'I hardly think so. More a result of her being a romantic, I think!' The sentiment made them both giggle together, causing Alice to smile across at them.

'Thank you Alice, for this,' Emily said quietly.

'Thank you for *all* of this,' said Alice waving her hand across the table full of food. 'You have made our Christmas something special.'

Slightly lost in thought, Emily smiled before remarking, 'Alice, you may also wish to thank someone else. The hamper alone did not provide all of this food or the Christmas stockings for the children. That was George Ackroyd's kindness.'

The mention of his name was sufficient to bring a pronounced bloom of colour to Alice's cheeks.

Chapter Eighteen

As the old year gave way to the start of a new one, 1911 saw further unrest throughout the nation. More than a quarter of the population living in the towns and cities rarely earned sufficient money to buy food and clothing. For these people, the never-ending cycle of illness and sudden death regularly intervened for the want of a doctor's services.

The seed of discontent had already begun to grow in Niall's mind. Although he cherished every moment that he had with Emily and was accepting of their unconventional married life, Niall was becoming more and more alarmed by the lives of those who lived in the unending streets of slums. These were the people who needed his professional expertise but never visited his surgery because they could not afford the fees. Since 1907, the Board of Education had begun to encourage local authorities to give medical inspections to children in elementary schools, but to Niall this was only the tip of the iceberg. He was not alone in his thinking; several social reformers had been pushing the government to operate an insurance system which would cover all those who could not afford to visit a surgery or go to hospital. David Lloyd George, the Chancellor of the Exchequer, had worked with the Liberal Government to introduce old age pensions in 1908 and being a true advocate of social reform, he understood that the country was in need of a social overhaul.

The invitation to the Speight's home on Christmas Day had triggered something buried very deep in Niall's subconscious; he knew that just offering to treat patients for free at the surgery he shared with Doctor Lawson would produce a two-tier system and would further ostracize those he most needed to see. Furthermore, these patients rarely ventured out of their own communities. The solution was there.

One Saturday morning in late January, he met with Emily and walked with her, leading her back into that working class community. His spirits were high and he talked with such passion and excitement, without actually informing her of his plans; she had never seen him like this before. Turning into one of the most dejected and miserable streets in the district, Niall stopped and flung out his arms.

'Look, look around, what do you see?'

For a moment Emily stood silent, her eyes tracing the never-ending line of squalid slums. She knew that some of her pupils came from these streets and her eyes glistened with the memories of past and present children. She had wondered how they had managed to come to school at all and try to concentrate on lessons with little sleep and empty bellies.

'Poverty, misery and hopelessness.' Her answer was both definitive and succinct.

'Opportunity! That is what I see.'

Emily turned and saw the likeness of a man she did not know. He reached for her hand and they walked in silence until they reached a house that appeared derelict and even more squalid-looking than the rest. Producing a key from his pocket, Niall unlocked the door and invited Emily into the dwelling. A strong fusty smell immediately wafted its way into their nostrils, causing them both to cough; dust and damp were decidedly prevalent.

'This is to be my new surgery. In my spare time I am going to offer free advice and treatment to those who need it the most. I have bought the property; it is mine, I should say ours.'

Emily witnessed a vision for the future in his eyes. She was innately proud of him and leaned closer to him.

'Do you think I am mad, Emily?'

She looked deep into his eyes and smiled. 'I think you are truly wonderful. I know where I will be spending my spare time; here beside you, where a good wife should be.' The strength of the kiss was sufficient to seal the deal.

The house was a front house of a row of back-to-backs. It was entered directly from the street, so it possessed neither a garden or a yard outside, nor a hallway inside. There was a downstairs room with a cellar-head, leading by a flight of steps to a cellar. A further flight of steps led upstairs to two rooms, one slightly larger in dimension than the other. The house was small but Niall considered it perfectly proportioned for his needs.

The main priority was to make it useable. Niall first enlisted a small local firm to ensure it was structurally sound; missing and broken roof slates were replaced to eliminate the problem of the damp. It was then decorated throughout with a coating of paint. Niall, Emily and Alice worked tirelessly to ensure that the stone floors were scrubbed and made as clean as possible; the next priority had to be hygiene.

The undertaking and involvement within this project was not to be kept a secret; they decided to inform everyone of their actions. Friends and family donated furniture and Doctor Lawson generously provided medical implements and supplies. The whole venture had both the backing and blessing of the middle-class community. Everyone knew about it, including the Taylor household. Hannah and Charles were immensely proud that Emily had volunteered to help the kind doctor.

'Emily is such a thoughtful person. She just wants to spend her life helping others,' declared her mother. Emily could not help but wonder what she would have said if she had known the entire truth.

At first, the working-class community seemed rather hesitant and sceptical that others wanted to help them. No one attended the first surgery. Alice encouraged her family to spread the word that this was a legitimate undertaking. Gradually the door began to be opened frequently as the genuine cases arrived. Mothers with babies and young children were the first to seek assistance, followed by the elderly and then young unmarried girls who having found themselves pregnant, wrongly thought a doctor might be able to terminate an unwanted baby rather than the grubby backstreet abortionist. These were always the worst cases for Niall as they made him think of his own mother and the situation she must have had to face.

Bed-bugs and head-lice were extremely common and annoying to their hosts as they often prevented people from sleeping properly at night; children in particular would wake up in the morning feeling exhausted and as Emily knew, unable to concentrate upon their lessons. Cases of measles, diphtheria and scarlet fever poured through the door. One of the most dreaded was that of tuberculosis which Niall knew was frequently attributable to poor living conditions and inadequate diets. The suffering that he witnessed was most often due to insufficiency of income but in too many cases it was a result of improvidence; wages were often squandered before they could be used for food and rent.

Any spare time which Emily and Niall had was spent working at the surgery; legitimately, they were now able to be together. The downstairs room was used as a waiting room and the larger upstairs room was the surgery where Niall saw each individual case. Alice assisted whenever possible and George Ackroyd who was also keen to help the cause, donated made-up packs of groceries which Emily gave to the neediest and most deserving cases.

One evening, not long after the venture had just begun, Alice arrived excitedly at the surgery. She thrust an envelope bearing an American stamp into Emily's hand and waited with hopeful expectation that it would be opened immediately. Disappointingly, Emily simply glanced at it and put it into her bag. She had recognised the distinctive handwriting and knew that the contents of the letter would be better read solely in her own company.

That night alone in her room, she opened the envelope and pulled out the two folded pages:

December 24th 1910

My Dear Emily,

I trust I find you well and indeed ready for Christmas. I know that by the time this letter reaches you, both Christmas and the New Year celebrations will have passed. However please accept my sincere best wishes to you and your family for the festive season.

Do please accept my apologies for not corresponding with you earlier. Since you left New York in August, my son Jonathan has secured an enviable management position in the housing or, as it is termed over here, the real estate business. We have now moved into our own home in Greenwich Village, on the west side of New York. Although not large, the house is sufficiently accommodating and comfortable for our needs and for visitors alike. It is in a good neighbourhood and close to theatres and art galleries, which I adore visiting. Emily, you will always be welcome to come and stay with us here.

My dear, I have thought of you a great deal of late and indeed of Doctor Branigan. Your Christmas card made no reference to any developments; I do hope that you will write to me soon with enlightening news.

Today, I received a visit from Inspector Jackson, the man investigating the stolen goods on the Lusitania. He is certainly not a man to be dallied with. He knows that it was Christian Verholt who was implicated. He has received a letter from someone stating that. Emily, such information did not flow from my pen. I did promise you that I would act upon your information but the time was never quite right. He also knows that you visited Suffolk Hall on Long Island, the family home of the Verholts.

Please believe me Emily; I did not mention your name. It was obvious from his manner that he intends to uncover everything to do with this case. I am writing not to unnerve you, but to make you aware that there was something quite unusual about his visit. As your family work for the Verholts, and he also knows that, I thought you should be aware of his investigation.

I look forward to hearing from you soon.

Your good friend and confidante,

Amelia.

Emily found the letter to be quite perplexing. It initially provoked her own conscience, as she had not informed Amelia about her marriage. There had been little free time in her life of late and she promised herself that she would write to Amelia the following day. Without Amelia's initial intervention, there would have been no romance or wedding. She certainly owed her the courtesy of imparting the good news and tried to imagine her reaction when learning of it; the idea made her smile.

But Amelia was certainly an enigma. She had promised to act upon Emily's revelation regarding Christian Verholt and had then proceeded to do nothing about it. Emily felt slightly let down by Amelia, who had established herself as an experienced woman of the world. Surely, someone who had once worked in colourful surroundings, being wined and dined by Princes, Sultans and Dukes, would possess sufficient bravado to act as an informant? The seductive backdrop of Paris began to slowly wane as Emily realised, somewhat reluctantly, how gullible she had been. She had been completely ensnared by Amelia's illusory tales. Far from being annoyed, she actually admired this dowager of make-believe and realised that she would always owe her a debt of gratitude for her happiness. She longed to still see her, for there was no one quite like Amelia.

There was now just one thing on her mind; Inspector Jackson. The thought of his investigation sent a slight shiver tingling down her back. Why had he investigated her movements on Long Island? Why did he seem to know so much about her? And who had informed him of Mr Robinson's true identity? It was clear from Amelia's letter that this investigation would not be laid to rest. Something made her realise that she was now implicated by default.

Emily replied to Amelia's letter the following day. She knew that her own news would make the old lady very happy and within a short time it brought the ecstatic and expected response back from Amelia. But the expectation of a visit from Inspector Jackson failed to materialise. As the weeks and months passed by, Emily immersed herself in her teaching, her home life and, of course, the special voluntary work at the surgery and put all thoughts of the American investigation to the back of her mind. She told no one about the contents of that letter, not even Niall.

The surgery was now well established. Emily had proven to be invaluable as an assistant who could calm down and reassure any distraught patient in the waiting room downstairs, whilst offering such qualities upstairs during the treatment sessions. One evening, after the last patient had gone, Niall took the opportunity to embrace and kiss his wife as he often did. He then led her by the hand to the smaller room upstairs, next to his surgery, pushing open the door to reveal a double bed which seemed to almost fill the limited space.

'I know that it may not be the perfect answer to our married life, but it is at least a start. I thought that you might be able to occasionally stay with me.' The twinkle in the green eyes was more than sufficient inducement.

'I hope so too,' Emily said quietly but eagerly.

The notion of being able to live as man and wife, albeit on a temporary basis and to some degree in moderately stark surroundings, did not deter Emily. On the contrary, it seemed to heighten the enjoyment of the clandestine times that they managed to snatch together.

It was now June and less than a month away from the wedding which everyone could speak of, whether they wanted to or not. Although Olivia enjoyed both planning and spending George's money for the day and for their subsequent marital home, her transient attention still seemed to wander from George to any passing male. Emily had witnessed how she had fawned over Niall during the Christmas celebrations. She could not understand how her sister could treat a man like this; a man who was kinder and younger, as well as being well-established with his own business and home. Equally, she could not understand why George still wanted to marry her sister. She had remained silent for too long but the opportunity suddenly appeared for her to speak out. George had delivered groceries at the surgery to be given to those who needed them. Emily found herself alone with her future brother-in-law for once; there was no time left for ambiguity. She knew that she had to go straight to the heart of the matter.

'Why are you still going to marry Olivia?' The question appeared brutal as it fell from a sister's lips. George's reaction was predictable as he stared in silence at Emily.

'Why choose Olivia? George, you have so much to offer a wife, someone who would love you and be faithful. Olivia is my sister, but she is not the wife for you.'

'I will not go back on my word. I asked her to marry me and I cannot let her down.'

'Even if she makes you miserable? George, I have seen you laugh with Alice but I have never seen you laugh with Olivia. She will never be faithful to you…'

'I will be to her…I promise you that.' He turned, walked to the door and left.

Emily continued to stare out of the window, long after George had driven away in his trusted Tin Lizzie. The man was nothing less than sincere, having been accorded some attention by Olivia when his first wife died; he was going to rigidly stick to his principles of decency and reliability. He neither could nor would break his promise to her, even if he admitted to himself that he would be marrying the wrong woman, a person who only wanted him for financial advancement. Emily prayed for some form of divine intervention to stop the marriage. She had never been truly religious, as her parents were, but nevertheless she prayed with all her might that something would happen to stop George and Olivia's marriage. Little did she realise that prayers can be answered and wishes can come true, whatever the cost.

Five days before the wedding there was an unexpected early-morning knock at the Taylor's door; Alice answered and showed the policeman into the front parlour. Emily heard the news first; George had been involved in an accident.

Olivia had not yet appeared for breakfast even though it was a working-day morning. Emily quietly tapped at her door before entering and found her sister sitting in front of her oak dressing table and its accompanying toilet mirror, deliberating as to which perfume she should wear from the numerous bottles and boxes littered across the surface of the table.

'Ah, Emily, which would you choose – Essence de Fleurs or Sweet Pea?' Two small glass bottles, each containing distinctive floral perfumes were being held at arm's length for Emily to decide upon the crucial decision. She seated herself upon the bed and looked straight into Olivia's eyes.

'Why the mournful face, Emily? I've only asked you to tell me which you think would be the best to wear. It's not a great deal to ask, is it?' As their eyes gazed into each other's, Olivia finally fell silent, seemingly sensing the change of mood in Emily and allowed her to speak.

'Olivia, I am afraid that I have some bad news for you. George has been involved in an accident and has been taken to the hospital.'

Before any further details could be given, Olivia launched into a series of histrionic performances only a gifted thespian could have rivalled. She began by pacing up and down before clutching her throat and then sweeping her forehead with her right hand.

'Oh, my god, is he dead? I will be a widow before being a wife! What will I wear? Black just doesn't suit me. I don't have anything that is black and dowdy. Emily, you'll have to lend me one of your outfits for the funeral.'

The barrage of nonsensical, selfish and insulting remarks would no doubt have continued, had Emily not intervened.

'George is not dead. He is injured but alive.'

'Injured? What do you mean by injured? Where has he been injured? Will he be disfigured? Oh, the thought of a deformity. I just couldn't live with that, with everyone feeling sorry for me. It would be *horrendous*.'

Yes, thought Emily, it would be *horrendous* if George married Olivia, especially after she had earlier witnessed Alice's eyes brimming with watery grief, as the girl had overhead the policeman's news. A man of sincerity like George deserved a partner of equal measure. Olivia was too selfish to think of anyone else but herself. There was not a tear evident in her eyes.

Irrespective of the weather, Beckston Infirmary always appeared grim and foreboding, presumably as a result of it having originally been designed and built to be a workhouse. The word 'Workhouse' above the entrance was a stark reminder and legacy from the stonemason, of its initial purpose. Its dark grey stone walls were intended to repel rather than invite intended inmates. Anyone who entered did so out of necessity instead of desire. The same principle still applied now to the ill and infirm who transgressed through its doors.

George appeared lifeless, as he lay in the hospital bed, oblivious to the perfunctory routine of an overworked medical staff that checked upon his progress. He had survived the accident and the succeeding operation. Now only time would tell if his recovery would be successful.

It had begun like any other day, with George opening his Emporium doors to the customers of Beckston. His staff, immaculate like himself in white jackets and long white aprons, were standing proudly behind the counters, waiting to serve their customers. No one had expected the morning to begin any differently to any other day.

Unexpected shrieks and screams instantly caught their attention. Everyone looked out into the street through the small apertures of light afforded by the crammed shop-window displays. Each worker craned his head towards any visual opening available in the doors and windows, waiting to find out the source of such distress.

George immediately rushed ahead of his colleagues and out into the street, which was beginning to warm with the pleasant June sunshine. As it was still early, there were few people around, with the exception of a woman with two young infants and a small handful of shop assistants who were diligently sweeping-out in front of their shops. The woman was clearly distressed as she had pulled the two children into a nearby doorway and was crouching over them, shielding the pair with her own body. She turned for a moment and fleetingly saw the gentle grey giants career past her.

Although heavy and powerful, Shire horses were draught horses, used for pulling heavy loads such as carts or ploughs, and were traditionally renowned for their gentle plodding nature. A pair of Shires pulling a brewer's dray in order to deliver barrels of beer to local public houses was a common daily sight. However, something had definitely frightened one or both of these horses and as they ran wildly down the street, propelled by the weight and downhill force of the barrels on the dray, they were gathering momentum and increasing the chances of a catastrophe. Further up the street, the driver was running with all his might, shouting out their names, but to no avail.

As they swerved across the road, just inches in front of George, he acted on impulse without hesitation or fear. A sudden flow of adrenaline had given him sufficient agility and stamina to launch himself at the nearest horse. The horses were both large stallions, at least seventeen hands high, and George could do nothing more than cling to the side of one, his left hand grasping the horse-collar and his right hand gripping the loin strap. They continued their unusually fast journey down the street, the cobbles holding no resistance to their ceaseless rampage. In the distance, George could see the town centre and the junction where other roads crossed and with them a collection of horse buses, a motor bus, automobiles, carriages and pedestrians. The town centre was always busier than the traversing byways and no one would be expecting impending carnage.

George's heart began to beat more quickly; he could feel each pounding throbbing against his own chest and the side of the horse as he gripped the harness tightly. Suddenly, he saw a small passageway to the left further down the street and he knew that this was his only chance. Hauling his body as high as he could, he pulled himself up sufficiently to be able to thread his feet into the breeching straps towards the rear of the horse. When the moment was right he thrust his entire weight down onto these straps; throwing his body away from the animal he prayed that he would be able to steer the horses into the passageway. With his bodyweight being diverted outwards the horses began to turn in a haphazard and uncoordinated way, but eventually they did turn. As they did, George found himself being dragged and pummelled against the stone wall. He was now beginning to lose strength and a sudden jerk of the dray caused George to release his left-hand grip. Trying to steady himself, he found that his left hand, arm and shoulder were suddenly thrust against the wall and were then being wrenched backwards before a searing pain shot through his arm; he had failed to notice an old rusty hook jutting out of the stonework, which acted as a blunt knife would, sliding through butter.

Later, George remembered this as the final action before the horses slowed down and came to a halt. He could feel nothing and presumed that he had a few broken bones. His white jacket was filthy and soaked in blood. As he tried to climb down from his hold on the harness, he felt faint and realised that his left arm seemed to be hanging, indeed just swinging from his jacket sleeve. That is when he realised that his arm had been partially severed. At that moment he lost consciousness.

When George opened his eyes, the unfamiliar scene disturbed him; his mind was telling him that he needed to serve his customers but his shop had drastically altered. Instead of the counters, he found beds and patients, and his staff in their white aprons, had been replaced by nurses. A haze quickly fell over his eyes and obliterated his memory and once again he lapsed into unconsciousness.

His visitors came and went, without George ever knowing that they had been there. They knew that George had had to have his left arm amputated, as the few sinews holding it could neither sustain nor save the arm. On their second visit, Emily, Niall and Alice encouragingly beamed with happiness as George opened his eyes and threw back a welcoming smile, as they approached him. His three friends stood around his bed, eager to offer their salutations.

'Hello stranger! It's wonderful to see that grin again,' remarked Niall.

'Yes, George, it is truly marvellous to see you with a smile on your face.' Emily then reached out and gripped George's right hand in a reassuring manner.

Alice appeared nervous and almost stumbled over her words: 'I am so happy that you are … all right.' Her eyes began to moisten and tears dribbled down her cheeks as she avoided looking at the empty sleeve, hanging loosely from his left shoulder. George, however, stared at the hollow tube.

'Yes, I may be armless but I am alive!' He had instantly lightened the moment, at his own expense, and as they all smiled with some recognition at the joke, Alice giggled slightly before her tears returned.

'You're quite the hero, George. Your actions saved Beckston. You have spared lives and that is something to be enormously proud of. There are not many men who would have been as brave as you were.' Niall's words made George cast his eyes downwards but everyone knew that they were looking at a very special person.

Their visit had uplifted his spirits but now he was beginning to tire. As they said their goodbyes and turned to leave, his final question caught them off guard: 'How is Olivia?'

'She is well and sends her love. She is sorry that she could not visit you today, but she has a great deal of orders to fulfil at the shop.' As Emily spoke, she tried to make light of the situation but in her heart she knew that she was lying. Olivia had visited George but once, when he was unconscious. She had found the whole experience of visiting a hospital so distressing that she vowed she would never go again.

George made no further comment. He simply gazed at Emily; she wondered whether he could sense Olivia's disinterest in him, as her sister had made no mention of her fiancé since that visit.

Chapter Nineteen

Olivia had lost no time in establishing a new life for herself; indeed it had commenced prior to the accident. As she spoke of postponing the wedding, Emily knew that it was merely a euphemism for abandoning the venture. Olivia did not normally consider the feelings of others, but perhaps even she could not be so callous as to directly inform an injured man in hospital, that she no longer wanted to marry him, especially when he was being hailed as a hero.

The enticement of marriage to a younger man, who was an entrepreneur and a car owner, had initially been the lure. However, George was a decent man and that was the problem; Olivia had grown bored of conventional happiness and now craved excitement; the danger of the chase, particularly when the hunter was rich and married, would always add additional arousal to any relationship.

It was true that Olivia had been jealous when George had been in Alice's company, but now she had forgotten those feelings. She longed to tease and dally with new conquests and was still wondering why her attractions had not ensnared the handsome Doctor Branigan at Christmas. Unperturbed, she decided that he must be too preoccupied with his work and decided to move on. The fact that she was engaged to be married presented her with absolutely no moral dilemma.

Her work as a milliner provided her with the opportunity to meet with exactly the type of man she craved; unscrupulous, rich and married. Many such men would use the enticement of an expensive hat to cull favour with a mistress or a wronged wife. A relationship with such a man enabled her to have her cake and eat it. She could enjoy the indulgence of being a mistress whilst still retaining her independence, but when she grew tired of the arrangement, she could without obligation seek a replacement. Any objections would be quickly quashed with the threat of a letter to the duped wife.

Olivia soon returned to her old way of life, giving no thought to the wishes of her parents, her sister or her fiancé.

Men came and went, and with each conquest Olivia blatantly secured a collection of trinkets, dependent upon the gentleman's wealth; jewellery, clothes, footwear, bottles of perfume and even a gramophone. Coupled with these, were the trips to the seaside, theatres, restaurants and the obligatory hotel rooms.

Emily and her parents were extremely concerned about Olivia's promiscuous lifestyle. A complete gulf existed between the chapel and the hotel room. At thirty-six years old, Olivia was old enough to do as she pleased, even if it displeased those around her.

'Emily, it is none of your business where I go and with whom.'

'Don't you ever think about our parents and of course, George?'

'*You* can play the doting daughter. Being the headmistress, you do that very well. As for George, I would think that he's forgotten me. I've certainly forgotten him.'

Emily studied her sister's face, searching for a flicker of remorse but sadly found none. She thought about their parents, especially their father and his disappointment in not being able to walk Olivia down the aisle. He had tried so hard, despite the seizure, to walk steadily and had practised relentlessly each day. Then she remembered George, who was being cared for by Niall and Doctor Lawson and the numerous times that he had asked about Olivia.

'Have you no shame, Olivia?'

'The only shame is that I didn't live my life to the full earlier!'

'Can you not think of anyone but yourself? Are you so rotten to the core that you feel nothing for others?'

'In this life you have to look out for yourself. That is all I am doing.'

'Yes Olivia, that is *all* you are doing,' remarked Emily.

The sarcastic delivery was out of context for Emily and briefly seemed to stun Olivia.

'To be honest Emily, I do pity you. You have spent your life being the role model of a daughter, a teacher and now a helper at some God-awful place helping the sick and needy. You might be Miss Perfect but you'll die without ever having had fun. You don't know what it feels like to be with a man. You wouldn't even know what to do. Yes Emily, I do pity you. A wasted life is such a shame.'

It would have been so easy for Emily to confess everything, but Olivia was not a person to confide in. So she remained silent and allowed Olivia to mistakenly think that she had touched a nerve.

Before leaving the parlour, Olivia turned to face her sister, having remembered that she needed to inform her of something important: 'I will be away next weekend as I am going to stay at Harborough Hall at the invitation of Lord Brooke. He has invited both Harold Blake and me to his house party there.'

As the meaning of her words began to slowly sink into Emily's mind, Olivia smiled smugly before leaving her to contemplate the meaning of the word shame.

Harold Blake was the epitome of the self-made man. Originally from a working-class background (his father had worked as an overlooker in the local woollen mills in Beckston), Harold had initially followed the family pattern and entered the realms of the spinning mills. It had not been long before the young boy's talents had been recognised. Always keen to do his best, Harold possessed a most inquisitive mind. As a child who could only attend school in the morning before going to work at the mill in the afternoon, he had a thirst for knowledge and a driven quest to apply it. In his limited spare time he would sketch the machinery which he worked with each day and then develop his own ideas for streamlining the workings of combing and spinning machines. Following years of rejections for his ideas, an inspired entrepreneur from a neighbouring mill recognised his potential and was encouraged to provide the financial backing for the patents. Success did indeed follow and Harold Blake was finally recognised as an inventor by the textile industry.

Wealth now ensured that Harold and his family could enjoy a privileged lifestyle in a large house, complete with servants. In just one generation, the Blakes had made the transition to the highest level of society.

As a person who had begun life in working-class poverty, Harold now enjoyed mixing with a distinct circle of friends who visited the country estates of acquaintances, spending their time hunting, shooting, fishing, playing bridge and occasionally turning a blind eye to indiscretions. At fifty two, Harold Blake was only slightly younger than Charles Taylor, Olivia's father. This was of no consequence because his bank balance, like his waist, was ample and swelling regularly. His wife was now matronly in appearance and rarely accompanied her husband on his jaunts, preferring to ignore the salacious tongues of the gossips. A rich man would often look elsewhere for a younger companion; as long as he did not soil his own doorstep, Mrs Blake chose to be content with her belief of ignorance like many other wives.

Olivia Taylor was not a beautiful young woman, but she did possess spirit and that was something which Harold Blake admired in a woman. Not for him the meek and retiring; he liked a lustful and gregarious female. His past conquests had included actresses and music-hall artists who exuded warmth and earthiness with straight matter-of-fact honesty. When he had stepped into the milliner's shop to purchase a hat for his previous companion, he had left without the hat but instead had a new companion on his arm.

His generosity continued to secure Olivia upon his arm. He could afford the best and even had a chauffeur-driven six-cylinder Rolls-Royce. That alone was sufficient to make Olivia wonder what she had ever seen in George and his Tin Lizzie; poor George, she thought, perhaps he was better suited with a housemaid, such as Alice Speight. After that, George was never given another thought as the prospect of a weekend at Harborough Hall obscured everything else.

Olivia spoke of nothing else. It was impossible for the family to engage in her excitement. If Harold Blake had been younger and not married, it would have helped. But the fact remained that her jilted fiancé was a hero and held everyone's sympathy. Olivia had to be content with disdain and derision; she alone had nurtured such feelings in the hearts of others.

The weekend provided an excuse for a shopping spree, financed entirely by Harold Blake. He knew his money would bring rich returns, and a little investment in a lady's desires would later secure him his own desirable requests.

As the chauffeur-driven Rolls-Royce pulled up outside the Taylors' moderately modest home, Harold Blake stepped out, walked to their front door and returned escorting Olivia who strutted slowly like a peacock with her head held high, framed in an enormous hat. As they proudly seated themselves in the back of the car, the chauffeur struggled with Olivia's luggage. Neither of them cared about the incessant twitching of neighbours' curtains. On the contrary, they seemed to crave the attention, unlike Emily and her parents who silently longed for the whole charade to vanish. Eventually, the car transported the distasteful scenario away and Emily knew that the resistance by her parents to make any further comment was their way of dealing with the problem. No one in the Taylor household spoke about Olivia that weekend; presumably as everyone else was busily engaged doing so.

The best antidote for disappointment or anxiety, according to the Taylor doctrine, had always been hard work. Emily now immersed herself in it; marking work and preparing lessons and later assisting Niall at the surgery. She had decided that she would not feel guilty for allowing herself the indulgent excitement of working with her husband. Lately, she had seen very little of him as he was now busy looking after George Ackroyd, who was currently living at Doctor Lawson's house along with Niall. George was a model patient, considering the horrific scale of his injuries. Experiencing professional medical care at the hands of these doctors, his two friends, George was eagerly learning how to live as an amputee; something he was doing most successfully. No one disputed that the additional treats of freshly baked bread and cakes were also not beneficial to his recovery, especially when they had been both made and delivered by Alice. George always looked forward to her visits; the effects of which were mutually beneficial to both, judging by the smiles upon their faces.

That Saturday evening in late autumn had witnessed a surgery full of patients, just like any other; the only difference being the appearance of one patient. The evening was cold which had caused the man to wrap his coat up around him, concealing his lower face and pull his hat down over his eyes. He was reasonably dressed; the fabric in his coat was not threadbare, therefore he appeared more affluent than the rest of the patients who frequented these premises, but there was something unfamiliar in the style of his dress which made him slightly conspicuous. His sole form of communication had been a cursory nod or shake of the head and then he had contented himself by sitting in the corner of the room, seemingly crouching over in a somewhat uncomfortable way whilst continually fixing his eyes downwards to the floor. He remained there deep in thought and resolute in his solitude. Emily found it difficult not to look at him; initially snatching a momentary glance until she found herself staring long and hard at the concealed figure sitting across the room from her. As she showed the penultimate patient into Niall's surgery upstairs, she returned downstairs to the waiting room.

The room was now empty; the man had simply disappeared. Emily ran to the door and stared out into the dimly lit darkness of the street but found no sign of him. She knew instinctively that there was something strange about his entire demeanour and sudden disappearance. As the final patient departed, Emily quickly shared her reservations with Niall.

He listened carefully to her account, appearing to seriously contemplate his actions before leaving the house alone. Later, he hurriedly returned with the man, whose clothing was even more bundled around him completely concealing his face. His stance of inclining his upper body forward showed that he was at least in discomfort but more probably in severe pain. Niall's own face wore an uncharacteristic grim look which Emily had never witnessed before. As they brushed passed her before ascending the stairs, Niall drew back and said, 'Emily, I want you to go home.' At that precise moment he appeared to pre-empt her forthcoming reaction by raising his hand to check her refusal.

'Please Emily, do as I ask. You must trust me. I need to deal with this situation, with this particular patient, on my own. Now go and I will see you tomorrow.'

Emily slept little that night as the thoughts of the previous evening continually tumbled through her mind causing her imagination to know no bounds; only Niall could provide the answers. At the first light of dawn she dressed, left the house and went back to the surgery. Instinctively, she knew that Niall would have spent the night there; her intuition proved correct as her knocks upon the door quickly caused him to peer with caution at the upstairs window.

As the door opened she could see the strain in his face. Silence prevailed as they looked into one another's eyes before finally embracing, holding each other tightly until a respite of relief permeated through.

Emily was the first to break the silence.

'Niall, I will not press you for answers that you cannot give me. I trust you and love you and…'

'I know that. Oh Emily, there is nothing that I would not do for you. I love you and want to protect you from anything that is bad. You know that, don't you, my darling?' Emily nodded in recognition as he lightly touched her left cheek with his finger before continuing.

'The man that came here last night is someone from the past; indeed he is a fellow with a past who needed my medical help. I could not deny him that. It was the very least that I could do for him. I do not condone his way of life, but I understand the reasons for it.'

'I take it that he has transcended the Law?' The question was enough to make Niall smile with some sympathy.

'Yes, I'm afraid he has, through no initial fault of his own.'

'Is he all right? Did you manage to treat him successfully?'

'Yes, this time, but who knows in the future?'

Emily declined to ask any more questions. An associate from the past made her think about Niall's seafaring life. She had often heard how sailors spent their leave, drowning their sorrows and using their fists. It was obvious that Niall had once looked after one of the crew who had simply tracked him down again for medical attention; however Beckston was a long way from the sea. That thought alone made her curious, but Niall's reluctance to discuss the matter further made her decide to relegate it to the back of her mind. Besides, she knew that upon Olivia's return there would be more pressing problems to deal with. However, her expectations concerning Olivia proved to be completely unfounded.

Olivia and Harold Blake had left in a glory of attention-seeking but they returned in quiet unobtrusiveness. By the lack of detail upon Olivia's part, Emily assumed that the weekend party at Harborough Hall at the invitation of Lord Brooke, had simply outlined how ill-suited Olivia was to upper-class living; she had obviously been out of her depth. Clearly, she must have embarrassed everyone around her, including Harold Blake. His sudden absence in her life seemed to confirm this. And yet, there was something duplicitous about Olivia's behaviour. Instead of retiring humbly into her shell, Emily detected an element of connivance manifesting itself within her sister. Something was building within her; something which would only benefit Olivia; that was her maxim in life. As always, Olivia never failed to disappoint by living up to her reputation.

The bombshell was dropped on New Year's Eve, just before 1912 was heralded in. Only the Taylor family with Alice in attendance were present, making the celebrations a quiet affair. George Ackroyd was still recuperating with Doctors Lawson and Branigan, and all had been in total agreement that an evening in Olivia's company would not be conducive to healing. How fortuitous that feeling had been.

'I have some news for you all,' Olivia announced casually. Everyone stared at her intently, no doubt dreading hearing that she was pregnant.

'I'm going to start a new life in France.' Everyone around the dinner table silently mouthed her last word, not quite comprehending the implications.

Emily was the only one with sufficient courage to enquire further. 'When you say a new life Olivia, you mean that you are going to live there?'

'For someone who is so educated, Emily, you can be terribly dense sometimes.'

'Olivia that is enough!' snapped her mother. 'How dare you speak to Emily in that manner?'

'Olivia, where will you live and, more importantly, *how* will you live?' her father asked quietly.

'Oh that is all settled. I have been offered employment in Paris. I didn't tell you before, but I met a gentleman at Harborough Hall, a good friend of Lord Brooke's, who said that I was perfect for the job. There will be accommodation provided and for once in my life I am going to do what I want to do. No one here can persuade me to do otherwise.' Everyone accepted that anything else would prove futile.

'Olivia, what does the job that you have been offered entail?' Emily asked.

'Oh, I didn't say, did I? Well, as you may know, Paris is not just the capital of France but the capital of Fashion. I am going to have my own salon where I will be the manageress.'

'Who will be backing you in this venture?' Emily refused to be content until the truth was known.

'Augustus Cassel. He is a wealthy businessman of great repute. Apparently, he has made his money by shrewd investments. I overheard him telling Lord Brooke that there is a great deal of money to be made on the Continent. He knows a good investment when he sees it and obviously he could see it in me. I think I will shortly be a very rich woman.' With an evident look of smugness, Olivia left the room and its bewildered diners as a cloud of silence descended.

Emily could not help but feel that there was something not quite right about the situation, but refrained from pressing the matter further, to avoid distressing her parents. She could definitely detect something secretive and undisclosed. She was of course most perceptive in recognising secrecy, having total experience of it herself. However, in her mind she questioned whether Olivia herself was in full possession of all the details; only time would tell.

Chapter Twenty

The start of a New Year traditionally provides a sense of optimism in peoples' hearts, as if fulfilling a premise that a new start will bring about change for the better. Emily very much doubted the validity of this statement as she read the devastating news that the unsinkable White Star liner Titanic had sunk off Newfoundland on its maiden voyage. The number of lives lost on that fateful morning of the fifteenth of April 1912 exceeded fifteen hundred. Emily wondered how many of those people had begun the New Year with hopeful optimism, little aware that their fate was determined when the ship struck the iceberg. A spasmodic shudder coursed through her body as she thought about the dead and their families. She also thought about her own voyage aboard the Lusitania and considered the futility of the final moments, as people struggled to survive the freezing water of the infinite North Atlantic Ocean. The terror of such thoughts made her family problems seem mild in comparison.

As much as she disapproved of her sister's behaviour and wayward lifestyle, Emily still worried about Olivia. She had nonchalantly left the security of her employment and home during January and had headed off for a new start in France, in the company of a stranger whom the Taylor family had not met.

Olivia's arrival in France had coincided with a time of change, inspired by optimism as new technological and medical discoveries abounded. There had been a succession of inventions in electricity, vaccinations against disease, photography and engineering; the wonders of wrought iron and steel were proudly displayed for all to see in the Eiffel Tower and the Grand Palais. A strong cultural scene flourished within this environment, drawing artists and writers alike to visit and then linger in a country which was socially a more accepting place to be.

The designs of Art Nouveau, a movement which had particularly strong links with the Paris Exhibition of 1900, reflected the new century; although modern in appearance, the inspiration actually flowed from earlier sources, including those of Gothic architecture and eighteenth century Rococo, the latter, a style whose origins had originated in France. The complex style was initially inspired by nature and its seasons and had given rise to sinuous flowing lines and forms, which hinted at provocative desire and seemed somewhat to overturn and disrespect tradition.

These changes were all synonymous with the provision of progress, and within peoples' hearts a feeling of optimism was emerging, insisting that anything was now possible.

Emily little doubted that Olivia had begun her New Year with hopeful optimism, in such an appealing country fuelled by the unrestricted convention of Gallic acceptability. Her concerns for her sister, however, centred upon the unknown; she feared that Olivia was drifting into unchartered waters and unprecedented danger.

The family had received only two letters from Olivia since her departure; one informing them how marvellous Paris was, and a later one which indicated that she had settled and that everything was as had been promised. Neither of the letters provided much detail, which was a cause for concern. However, some people were better correspondents than others, as Emily had witnessed with Amelia Davenport. Following the disclosure of her wedding in a letter to her friend, Emily had received a rapturous reply; the news had made Amelia ecstatic in her congratulations. With the exception of a Christmas card, there had then been no further communication. Emily attributed this to the fact that Amelia was an elderly lady and perhaps now a little forgetful.

The commitments of being a headmistress and assisting in her spare time at the surgery continued to occupy Emily's life to the full. At the school there were three classrooms; one for infants, one for the middle class and the largest room which was used to assemble all the children each day, was reserved for the teaching of the oldest children, who were taught by Emily. Each morning the day began in the largest room where everyone would sing a hymn and say a prayer. The children were then dismissed in silence to their appropriate room and desk where they sat in silent rows awaiting firm instructions. Talking was not allowed and anyone who transgressed the boundaries of behaviour would pay the price of humiliation and pain, as they obligingly stood in front of the class and waited with their hand outstretched for the exacting swish of the cane. Following such a spectacle the class would purposefully return to perfecting their art of copperplate writing, by copying out sentences in a copybook, meticulously taking care with their dip pens and ink. Rote learning of the times tables together with the recital of poetry, allowed for a collaborative and less intense form of education. Miss Taylor and her colleagues were respected but, at the same time, they were also liked and even loved by their charges, for the humility and compassion which they displayed. On cold winter days the children looked forward to the hot drinks which their teachers made for them and the opportunity to huddle around the coal fires in the schoolrooms whilst drinking them.

The unexpected arrival of a letter one morning both bewildered and intrigued Emily. She learned from reading it that St Cuthbert's was to receive a very generous donation from a local benefactor, Harold Blake. Emily read and reread the letter several times and was at a loss to understand the reasoning behind the generous gift. Harold Blake was, to her knowledge, a man who enjoyed his wealth and the ensuing women (including Olivia) who had been attracted by it.

The occasion was marked by a special assembly. Mr and Mrs Blake arrived in their chauffeur-driven Rolls Royce, the same car that Olivia had been whisked away in to Harborough Hall. The children obligingly sang hymns, recited poetry and individually read from the bible in order to impress their guests. Following these formalities, Mrs Blake observed the pupils in a lesson whilst Mr Blake joined Emily in her office.

'Well Miss Taylor, my wife and I are most impressed by the conduct of your pupils and their knowledge. Evidently, there is a great deal of excellent teaching in this school. As a self-made local man, I would like to donate two hundred pounds, which I think you will be able to put to good use.' The look of astonishment upon Emily's face momentarily interrupted the conversation.

'Is the sum enough to equip you with sufficient books or indeed anything else that you need?'

'The amount is exceedingly generous. Thank you. I can assure you that it will be used wisely and effectively. May I ask why you have selected St Cuthbert's?' Emily purposefully paused before continuing. 'Is it because …' Harold Blake looked straight into her eyes and immediately sensed the nature of the question.

'I'd be obliged if you didn't mention my association with your sister to my wife. Indeed, it was my wife who suggested your name and the school. Perhaps it has been a salutary lesson for all of us. Let me just say that I have learned the error of my ways and am now a changed man and devoted husband.'

Emily doubted that the transformation would have occurred if Mrs Blake had not insisted upon it. Perhaps after accepting years of philandering, the woman had decided that she would allow no further humiliation in their advancing years. Emily liked the idea that this woman had made her husband donate to the sister of one of his mistresses; the whole affair ironically was charged with poetic justice.

Something inside Emily insisted that she should ask one more question before he left. She knew that she would never get the chance again.

'What sort of a man is Augustus Cassel?' The question slightly startled him.

'I'd never heard of the fellow before meeting him at Lord Brookes. I'll say this for him; he certainly knows how to keep the ladies enthralled. He could live by his wit and charm alone, that one. Never met a fellow like him before; there was something decidedly strange about him.'

'Are you aware that Olivia is now living in Paris, allegedly with the backing of this man? She is supposedly working as a manageress in a fashion salon.' Harold Blake simply shook his head. 'It does not surprise me. Your sister may have accompanied me to Harborough

Hall, but she definitely was beguiled by this fellow and spent the whole time in his company. I should have left her there, but being a gentleman I did the decent thing and brought her home.'

'What was the man like?'

'Oh, mid-twenties I would say. I can't remember much more except that he had the blondest hair that I have ever seen on a man and everyone thought he was handsome; well, the ladies certainly did. He also had an accent. It was faint but there. No doubt that was also an attraction to the women. I would say American; yes, the accent was American.'

The click of the door and the sudden appearance of Mrs Blake curtailed any further disclosures.

The unexpected generosity of the Blakes was not the only unusual event to occur during the spring of 1912. As Emily read about the transatlantic disaster of the Titanic, she was unaware that a visitor from America would soon appear in her life. He had landed on the English shores two months earlier, almost a year later than he had originally intended. Work commitments fuelled by rising crime figures in New York had prohibited Inspector Jackson from leaving. He was known for his cantankerous ways but no one else came anywhere near to his methodical record of apprehending criminals. He moved around New York undeterred by the growing ranks of gang members, crime fighters and underworld figures. These were the men who referred to themselves collectively as brothers, dudes, gangs, mobs and tongs in order to induce solidarity and at the same time, intimidate.

Sam Jackson was the man who could deal with the Sicilian gang leaders and ensure that they were detained behind bars in the notorious Sing Sing prison. The escalating number of executions there were in the electric chair. Jackson himself revelled in the knowledge that his work was responsible for propelling many of these inmates into the place. It was a tough world, a tough city and only a tough inspector could hunt down these criminals. A just form of retribution would make the streets of New York safe to walk on; a stern message was in Jackson's eyes the only way.

Numerous immigrants had flooded into New York and many had brought family feud grievances from their homelands.

The Italians, Irish, Jews and Chinese Triads all had scores to settle, but could instantly disperse when the authorities started calling. New York's Chinatown offered numerous hiding places, amidst its sinuously sprawling labyrinth of streets and passages and Jackson knew more than most, the addictive dens of opportunity where the effects of hallucinogenic drugs and the rush of euphoric opium provided a way out and a refuge for those on the run. Chinatown was run by tongs, who were racketeers of gambling and prostitution, each group trying to muscle in on the others would resort to the persuasive charms of the hatchet men if their requests were denied.

The brutal world that Sam Jackson lived for and worked in seemed very far removed from the charms of Long Island, England and the Continent, and yet his true interest, perhaps one could say, his true vocation or calling was increasingly being governed from these areas. For many years he had read news accounts voraciously, hunting for the mention of the name, always hoping to find something which would discredit it. There had been nothing, nothing at all until he had received that note; he still did not know who had sent it to him but that was inconsequential. The only thing that mattered was that somewhere there was a link with the family name and with crime. At last he had found a skeleton in the Verholt closet and one which was still very much alive. Surely, he thought if he could deal with the Sicilian Mafia and the Chinese Tongs, he could definitely deal with the Verholts. That would certainly prove to be just retribution, in his eyes at least.

Samuel Jackson had always wanted to be a policeman from being a young child. There was no history in the family of anyone being connected with the Police force so it seemed quite surprising at first that the young boy was so adamant about his chosen career. He was a stocky, well-built lad who, with no siblings to play with, always appeared somewhat of a loner. When friends did appear they did not linger as Sam always seemed to exert an authoritative and overbearing manner towards them which consequently made them frightened and withdrawn. With advancing years the same manner coupled with a stern countenance, also repelled any likely female interest and therefore Sam Jackson was destined for a lonely life.

However the Police force and in particular, one individual, was to have a marked effect upon the young man.

Serving as the head of the New York City Police Department from 1880 until 1895, Thomas F. Byrnes was a formidable man who had risen quickly through the ranks. Sam Jackson worked with him, fully admiring and respecting the rates of success that one individual could achieve.

His long and severe questioning of suspects, practised with a combination of both psychological and physical punishments popularised the term, 'the third degree', and was an expression which Byrnes himself used. He collected photographs of criminals which he continually added to in a book which he referred to as the 'Rogues' Gallery.' He also established the 'Mulberry Street Morning Parade'; a line-up of arrested suspects paraded in front of his detectives, whom he hoped would be able to identify such perpetrators and link them with further crimes.

To some his techniques were brutal and decidedly Machiavellian and as a result in 1895, the new president of the New York City Police Commission, Theodore Roosevelt, forced him to resign amidst allegations of corruption. However Sam Jackson never forgot how effective the methods had been and attributed his own rates of success to some of these. It was, after all, a tough world and a tough city which definitely needed a tough inspector to hunt these criminals down.

The Taylor household was accustomed to receiving two types of visitor; firstly, those who delivered a service and secondly, family, friends and acquaintances who visited for social reasons. The former consisted of weekly visits from the fisherman who came from the East Coast of Yorkshire with a barrel of herring, the butcher's boy who came to take the meat order and the delivery boy from Ackroyd's who brought the weekly groceries. The coalman also regularly delivered his bags of coal but less frequent visitors included the travelling knife-sharpener, who appeared with his grinder and sharpened all the knives and scissors and the annual visitor, a chimney-sweep who entertained the local children as they waited with anticipation to see the brush pop out of the top of the chimney-pots.

Therefore, the visitors who appeared on the Taylors' doorstep were generally expected or invited. They were also usually instantly recognisable to the Taylors and to Alice who received them either at the front or the back door, depending upon their business. When Alice opened the front door to one unexpected visitor in the middle of the afternoon, she neither recognised his face nor his accent.

'Does Emily Taylor live here?' The large outline of the man and his brusque manner presented a menacing first impression.

'Yes, she does. May I ask who is enquiring?' Alice was warily polite.

The man momentarily shuffled his feet and seemed to be deep in thought. He found the English to be annoying in their attention to delicate etiquette. He believed in the direct no-nonsense approach.

'Inspector Jackson.'

'Is Miss Taylor expecting you?' Alice enquired.

'I very much doubt it!' A smirk passed over his face and Alice caught a glimpse of badly-stained teeth.

'Miss Taylor is not in at the moment, but if you would care to call back later I will inform her that you have called.'

'I don't do *calling back*,' Jackson snapped. 'I'll wait for her.' He almost seemed to be ready to barge past Alice, as though he was used to getting his own way forcibly, but then he drew back possibly having remembered that he was now in a different country.

'Perhaps you would like to come inside and wait?' Alice reluctantly offered the invitation and Jackson nodded and followed her into the front parlour. There she obligingly offered to take his coat and make him a drink of tea; both of which he curtly refused. To Alice, the man seemed noticeably rude and she could not imagine what business he could have with a lady like Miss Taylor. She knew that it would be another hour or more before Emily would be home and to make matters worse, Mrs Taylor, Emily's mother had been disturbed by his arrival and was now questioning Alice about him. There was only one option available and that was to inform Emily without delay.

The pallor of her face became whiter with the mention of his name. Emily said little as Alice gave her garbled account of the man with the foreign accent. It was not the accent especially that unnerved her but rather his build, severe countenance and abrupt behaviour. Emily listened and then agreed that she would return home directly at the close of school. When she did, she found her mother trying unsuccessfully to make polite conversation with the stranger.

'Ah Emily, Inspector Jackson has been waiting to see you.' Hannah threw a disapproving look at the man before leaving the room, and added, 'I do not know the nature of his business but no doubt he will inform you of that.'

'I am sure he will,' Emily whispered under her breath, taking care to close the door firmly between her and her mother.

'Emily Taylor?' The question lacked any form of warmth or finesse.

'Yes.'

'I'm Inspector Jackson. I headed up the investigation on the Lusitania.' At this point he extended his hand and offered the perfunctory handshake. Emily looked down at the large chubby hand which quickly seemed to engulf her own small, slim hand.

'On your crossing to America you shared a table with some fellow passengers, I believe?'

Emily merely nodded before sitting down.

'The Davenport family and a young couple on their honeymoon, the Robinsons; is that right?'

Again, Emily nodded.

'You struck up quite a friendship with the old lady, Amelia Davenport, I hear. You even stayed with her, before and after your journey to Long Island.'

'I did. Amelia was most kind to me.' Emily was still very wary of the man but she had decided not to be afraid of him. She knew there was no reason to be.

Reaching into the pocket of his coat which he was still wearing, he pulled out a small brown book, flicked through it and took out a photograph.

'This is my Rogues' Gallery.' He suddenly looked pleased with himself as he handed the photograph to Emily. 'Do you recognise him?'

'I'm not certain.' Emily had decided that a safe answer would be best.

'Take another look. Did you not share a dinner table with this man? Blond and good-looking, I'm sure that most women would remember a man like that, even if he was supposedly on his honeymoon!' He allowed a cynical laugh to disturb the silence before bending down to peer over Emily's shoulder.

'I hear you are a headmistress; your mother proudly told me that. Teachers are like the police, they don't forget faces. So, are we looking at Mr Robinson from the Lusitania?'

'Yes.'

'You are positively identifying the man in the photograph as Mr Robinson, the man who mysteriously disappeared with his alleged wife, following our discovery of stolen goods in his cabin?'

'Yes.'

He took the photograph from her and replaced it back into his brown book. 'Thank you Miss Taylor, you have made me a happy man. In my Rogues' Gallery of criminals, I now have a photograph of Mr Christian Verholt. You of course knew that, having stayed at the estate on Long Island. Did you send me this?' He handed Emily a folded piece of paper with the words: 'MR ROBINSON, THE MAN YOU ARE SEEKING FROM THE LUSITANIA, IS MR CHRISTIAN VERHOLT FROM LONG ISLAND.'

She read the note and simply shook her head, passing the paper back to him.

'No Inspector, I did not write this note and I'm afraid that I cannot help you with anything more.'

'But that is where you are wrong. Your sister is now with Mr Verholt as we speak.'

'Olivia?' Emily was stunned and could not manage to say anything else.'

'Yes, Olivia. Shall we talk some more?'

Emily agreed that they needed to talk but she decided that a change of venue was definitely required. She was aware that walls have ears and she wanted to spare her parents the indignity of overhearing further unsavoury news.

'Would you object to a walk, Inspector?'

A momentary look of surprise followed by a slight grunt seemed to be an indication of his agreement.

The late May afternoon air was still remarkably warm and pleasant and they walked for some time before engaging in conversation. As they entered the grounds of Belle Park, Emily was the first to speak.

'My sister Olivia is currently in Paris working as a manageress of a fashion salon. She was offered this job by a gentleman, Augustus Cassel.' Jackson began to smirk.

'Cassel, Robinson, Verholt! The name doesn't matter. It's *him*.'

Emily remained silent. She recalled the words of Harold Blake who had met Augustus Cassel; '... he had the blondest hair that I have ever seen on a man and everyone thought he was handsome.' She knew now that he was in fact describing Mr Robinson as well as Christian Verholt.

'What does such a man want with Olivia?'

'Her part will be to become acquainted with the wealthy by means of the fashion house. She can acquire their names and addresses as likely suspects for robbery or even as unwitting customers willing to pay out for expensive antiques, which have been stolen. It is all down to supply and demand. Verholt sees to both.'

'Inspector, my sister may not be the most virtuous person where morals are concerned, but she is definitely not a criminal.'

'Just gullible, as we all can be.' With this sentiment Jackson offered a weak smile and Emily felt that for once she had seen a fleeting glimpse of something more behind the rough exterior.

Silence once again fell as they continued to walk.

'How did you find out that Olivia is with Christian Verholt?'

'I've been tailing him for some time, trying to pin the criminal down. He is clever, I will give him that, but one day I know I am going to have him! I heard that he was sailing for England; useful contacts provided news of that. It was then just a matter of time before the next one.'

'The next one?'

'Two society burglaries provide plenty of goodies for him to dispose of.'

'Why didn't you apprehend him, especially if you know his format?'

'That's where he is clever, so, so clever. On each occasion when the burglary took place he was elsewhere surrounded by numerous people, no doubt many of them women. All of them could testify to his whereabouts. He has an accomplice but that doesn't make him any more innocent in my eyes. He's as guilty as if he had broken in and stolen the things himself. It is only a matter of time before I have him and then I will enjoy dragging the Verholt name though the dirt as much as I can.' The mere thought of this was enough to make Jackson smile and reveal his neglected and stained teeth.

'What about Olivia? Should I contact her or even go and see her and bring her home? I don't want her to be in danger.' Emily's voice was now beginning to become slightly staccato in its panicked delivery.

'Nothing. You do nothing. I will tell you when the time is right to act. She is not in any danger; well, not at the moment. Just wait. I'll be in touch.' Jackson decided that the meeting was for now at an end. He knew where he could find Emily and informed her that he would be in touch.

As he walked away, Emily's mind was whirring with suppositions and unanswered questions. When he was finally out of sight she wished that she had shown more bravado in asking him questions, including how she could contact him; she had no idea where he was staying or for how long. However, with a man like Jackson, a person waited to be contacted by him; not the other way round.

Meanwhile, the one thing on Jackson's mind as he walked away was the fact that there was something about Emily Taylor that he liked. He had never known himself to have admiration for a woman before, with the sole exception of his mother. It was then that the thought struck him, how alike they were.

Chapter Twenty-One

Samuel Jackson's father had first arrived on the shores of America in the late 1840's, leaving England far behind him; his first priority had been to make money and his second, to find a wife and companion. Like Walter and Clarissa Whittaker who were to make a similar journey forty years later, the hopes of promise in this new country were infinitely too strong to resist. He soon found employment as a lumberjack, felling and preparing the abundant forest timber.

As with countless others, Robert Jackson had long heard of the rumours of the existence of gold in California, but they were just suppositions until a man called James Marshall proved them to be true at Sutter's Sawmill in 1848. Initially those closest to the discovery tried to remain quiet about it, but as word trickled out it became national news, attracting would-be prospectors from around the world. Those seeking gold endured arduous journeys across the mountains and arduous living conditions when they arrived, but the ultimate aim was the same for everyone; they did not intend to stay, but instead just remain long enough to make their money and then return home. Unfortunately very few did so, but Robert Jackson was one of the lucky ones. Like the others he pitched his tent, shouldered his pick and shovel and strode out with his pan in hand to try his fortune at digging for gold. Fortune did not instantly favour him but with fortitude and perseverance he survived the endemic fevers that swept through the camps, endured the back-breaking work along with the frequent disappointment of finding nothing, until he became one of the fortunate ones to find the elixir of life; that shining metal along the banks of the streams.

Robert Jackson had made his money, found himself a good wife and was now the proud father of a son, Samuel. Life it seemed could not get better. The family had settled in New York, on the west side of Lower Manhattan in a large house in Greenwich Village.

The Jacksons invested their money in a saw-mill and were soon employing numerous workers. Everything was going well; in fact it almost appeared that anything which Robert Jackson participated in would lead to gold. As the business prospered Robert was encouraged to expand his business dealings and branch out into the various safe investments heralded by the technological advancements in shipping, the railways and canals. For these he needed to borrow money and did so from a renowned Dutch bank, initially securing his house and then later his business as collateral. Slightly naive and overly ambitious Robert Jackson realised too late that business markets fluctuate, forcing him to default upon his payments. Banks do not operate upon sentimentality and against his pleas for additional time, foreclosed upon the deal, leaving the Jacksons with neither their home nor their business. From that moment onwards, the name Verholt was responsible for all their ensuing bad luck.

Their lives were irrevocably changed in both physical and emotional ways. They moved out of their large fine house and away from the prestigious address to rented rooms in a down at heel area, albeit in the same city but the surroundings were completely foreign to each of them. Louisa Jackson remained the perfect wife and never chastised her husband for his poor decision-making. In some ways that was the hardest thing for her husband to bear; as he slowly watched the life drain from his young, sweet wife who never once complained. Instead Robert began to hate and despise himself until he could bear it no longer and eventually looked elsewhere to discharge his anger. His aggression caused him to drown his sorrows across bars which he could not afford to visit and then lash out at anyone who confronted him. Drunk and disorderly he spent some nights in cells and others mentally and physically abusing anyone that looked his way. The night he returned home and struck his wife was his last one. The following day, sober and remorseful he found a suitable bridge, jumped from it and hung suspended whilst the rope tightened around his neck.

Louisa Jackson had loved her husband deeply and at first everyone assumed that she too would soon go to her grave. However an inner strength and sense of survival made her refuse to succumb to withering away; she was also aware that her young son clung to her for his own survival. For that very reason she accepted the meagre wages which long hours of cleaning and sewing provided, in order to put food on the table and a roof over their heads.

Samuel Jackson instinctively knew that his mother had done everything she could to provide for her son. Often this meant that he wore clothes which were too tight or too big as they had been handed down to him from other families living nearby. It did not concern him that they were well-worn or that everyone knew that he was wearing cast-offs which were often second or third-hand. The fact that no one dared to mock him was sufficient compensation. As work became more plentiful for his mother who earned her daily bread as a cleaner in the early mornings before becoming a seamstress who would work late into the evenings, the boy grew and filled out whilst she ate sparingly, always ensuring that her son had decent portions. As he grew he became stocky and well-built like his father and together with an air of authority he commanded respect, even in the toughest of neighbourhoods. He was a boy who could take care of himself and one whom many assumed would end up on the wrong side of the law, but he did not because of one factor: his mother. She instilled discipline and morality and taught him right from wrong and good from bad. At times she could be a stern disciplinarian and Samuel both respected and loved her for this. No doubt these were the traits that Samuel Jackson could now see fifty years later in Emily Taylor. For a woman to remind him of his mother, she had to be a special person, a very special person indeed.

Chapter Twenty-Two

Emily found herself in the middle of an infinite quandary which continually caused her head to spin with its relentless association of questions; whether to discuss her meeting with Jackson; if so, who to confide in; how much information to divulge; and when and where should the discussion of such delicate material occur? As she pondered over these worries, the most unsettling one frequently reared its head as problems often do when the unexpected takes control; the possibility of further contact with Jackson.

She was not afraid of him but there was something intangible about the man which premeditated feelings of danger to those around him. Amelia Davenport had obviously been touched with the same perception and had communicated this feeling in her last letter.

Although Amelia had been far from being a prolific writer, Emily instinctively knew that she needed to write to her old friend. She may have lived in a slightly make-believe world in her past, but she had had a visit from Jackson and that alone made her a suitable recipient for Emily's news. Sparing little in her account, Emily informed Amelia of everything that had occurred and in so doing she began to feel better for it. The pleasure was transitory as she knew that time was required to bring back a reply, but she had at least unburdened herself to her old confidante.

She also knew that if she could discuss her problems with a fellow passenger that she had not seen for two years, she could surely disclose her anxieties with the one person with whom she shared her biggest secret, her husband, Niall.

In her own mind she had chosen the perfect time; they were alone and snuggled together in their own bed at the surgery. There had been few patients there that evening; presumably the warm touch of May was proving beneficial to everyone's health. Locking the door with hopeful expectation, they had used this special time for themselves, to first make love and then afterwards to lie contentedly in each other's arms.

For some time no words passed between them as Niall gazed upon Emily's face, before pressing his lips tenderly over hers. Finally, he lay back with his head on the pillow and his face showing a smile of pure satisfaction.

'I am so happy Emily. There is nothing that could make me happier.'

'Even though we do not live together in our own home as man and wife?'

'That does not matter. The time we have together is so precious. I wish everyone could experience this joy. George, for one, is someone who deserves to taste such happiness.'

'I agree, but I doubt he will. Life is so unfair. A person like George deserves the best in luck but he seems to attract the opposite.'

'There, I beg to differ, Mrs Branigan. He has a fine constitution and a thirst for life. Did you know that he has now left Doctor Lawson's and returned home to live? He has been most insistent upon the necessity for independence and upon living his life as he used to, including returning to his Emporium. If the mind is strong, anything is possible. Of course, an added attraction is always a bonus in the healing process.'

'An added attraction?'

'I think Alice Speight has been the best tonic for his speedy recovery.' Emily nodded in agreement before Niall once again planted a light kiss upon her lips. They lay together once more without speaking until Niall broke the silence.

'You've been uncharacteristically quiet this evening. You're not feeling unwell?'

'No,' came the succinct reply.

'Is there something troubling you, Emily?'

The silence was a sufficient reply.

'Emily, I am not just a doctor. I am your husband and someone in whom you must confide. What is troubling you? Is it Olivia?'

'I wish it was just Olivia, but the truth is that I do not know what is troubling me and that is the most frightening part.'

Niall listened patiently whilst Emily told him of Jackson's visit and of the connection between her sister and Verholt. She spoke of the criminal actions and dangers that she feared her sister was being drawn into. She also spoke of the unnerving intensity for information which Jackson exuded and of the fact that Amelia Davenport had in her earlier letter conveyed similar opinions about the inspector.

Throughout the entire disclosure Niall had remained silent, allowing Emily to speak freely without interruption. She had allowed everything to tumble from her lips without reservation and as the final words were imparted, it was only then with a modicum of relief that she studied her husband's face for his reaction. The look was one of ambiguity; instead of finding reassurance there was distraction and in the place of surprise, there was a degree of expectation. Neither the gentle Irish bonhomie expression nor the professionally skilled countenance now prevailed; instead a faraway look implicated as a result of the past or present stared with fixation.

'What should I do Niall?'

'Do?' The question seemed to break the intensity of his reverie.

'Regarding Olivia? I dare not mention such implications to our parents. Father is still weakened through his stroke and Mother; well Mother would resort to having one long migraine. No, it is better for them to have no knowledge of this situation. In the meantime...'

'Meet with the inspector and find out all you can. Then we shall determine the best course of action.'

The advice seemed sensible and at least conferred the next course of action, even though it would be down to Jackson to secure the time and the place.

Before Emily left to return home for the night, a question filtered through her mind which she felt compelled to ask:

'Who do *you* think wrote that note which identified Christian Verholt as the man on the Lusitania?'

'Someone who intensely hates the man.'

Emily agreed; she understood how hatred could compel a man to destroy another man, for whatever the reason. She had remembered the look of malice which had appeared on Jackson's face when he had mentioned Verholt's name. The problem was that Emily now recognised the fact that there was someone else who also despised the name. This now placed Verholt in twice the amount of danger and Olivia accordingly, by association.

Time seemed to pass slowly as Emily waited to be contacted. With each successive day the absence of any communication made her increasingly anxious. Inspector Jackson would inevitably need to return to his work in New York and therefore time was of the essence, as indeed it was with Olivia. An air of muted normality had to prevail and Emily consciously ensured that nothing fell from her lips which would arouse suspicion of any kind; she was of course a skilled performer in the art of secrecy. The air of fascination which had initially surrounded the inspector's visit to the Taylors' home had quickly faded in her mother's mind, as Emily had explained that routine enquiries were being conducted as a result of the misappropriation of belongings; the property of the rich held no interest for Hannah Taylor as she simply shrugged her shoulders and with a flick of the hand attributed their loss justifiably to pretentious display. In her eyes an excess of wealth always led to damnation with implicit amounts of the demon drink and fornication; a familiar statement which surprisingly Hannah never described in association with Olivia's lifestyle.

As daily life continued, Emily became increasingly aware of one change in the household; that of Alice Speight. No longer the timid and under-nourished youngster, Alice, at seventeen years old, was now a woman; a fact which George Ackroyd had not failed to notice. Emily knew that Niall's tribute to her encouraging the recovery of his patient was justified. She had provided the drive for him to live with his disability, to return home and be independent and to work at his Emporium. She had also ensured that any painful memories of his engagement to Olivia had been truly eradicated. She had achieved all of these things without knowing that she had done so and that was what endeared George to her; the delicious innocent naivety.

Ironically, he too now wanted to provide the *drive* for her. At first, the mere suggestion of her taking the wheel of his trusted Tin Lizzie appeared absurd.

'Women and machines don't mix,' Alice protested.

'So women should not use sewing machines?'

'No I'm not saying that. But it doesn't seem right to see a woman driving. Well, certainly not a girl like me.'

'Why not you, Alice? You have just as much right to do so as anyone else. I am willing to teach you and in fact you would be doing me a great service.' George had cleverly baited her interest with the one enticement which he knew she would not refuse: his request for help.

Alice blushed and added, 'If you put it like that, I would be willing to help you in any way that I can. That is only if you think I can do it.'

'I know that you can Alice. You just need a little instruction and encouragement. I will provide both of those.'

'In that case, I cannot say no.'

'That is just what I had hoped for.'

George totally lacked any male chauvinistic traits and coaxed his charge with both patience and deserving praise. The engine whilst low-revving was most reliable but at first Alice struggled with the two forward gears which were affected by a clutch or rather a gear change pedal. Then she struggled with the hand levers which were located under the steering wheel; these covered throttle opening and ignition advance and produced changes in the engine speed. There were many occasions when Alice could not help but think that women were more suited to using a sewing machine, but she persisted for George's sake; often she would feel the reassuring grip of his right hand upon her hands and the steering wheel whilst being painfully aware that his left sleeve hung empty and limp at his side. He was a man for whom she would have driven to the ends of the earth, if only she could have steered that far.

Alice's limited free time was spent assisting at the surgery, visiting her family and learning how to drive. She looked forward to each one but the one which she looked forward to the most was also the most challenging: driving the Ford Model T. George also looked forward to the time that they spent together and the sight of the lovely young girl who never complained in her struggle with the gears or the hand levers. He also particularly enjoyed their return journeys when she would be totally oblivious to the wayward wisps of dishevelled hair framing a face of reddened cheeks, watery eyes and a small button-like nose dotted with a smut. It was at times like these that he longed to kiss the unassuming girl sitting next to him, but he always resisted, being ever mindful that to do so would be to take advantage. He was a gentleman and in accordance with his strict business ethics, his personal and moral principles also ensured trust and responsibility. He had a duty to protect this young girl who was employed by the Taylors and he also had a duty to his two dearest friends, Emily and Niall. He did not wish to compromise the trust of any of them; therefore he resisted temptation with stoic determination.

As the summer months passed into autumn days, Alice continued to use her free afternoons to master the complexities of driving with George at her side. Normally, her eyes would remain avidly fixed upon the road but the sudden appearance of the man stepping out from the roadside across her path unnerved her, causing the car to stall. He was somewhat distanced from her but his presence had made her panic; it was not the action of the man that disturbed her as much as his identity. The awkwardly large outline of the figure immediately presented a menacing image; he continued to stand on the road ahead of them but surprisingly did not communicate. George patiently encouraged her to continue their journey. The man stepped back somewhat reluctantly and as they passed him, he smirked and allowed his badly-stained teeth to show as he called out, 'Someone tell that broad she is sitting in the wrong seat!'

George encouraged Alice to continue driving and ignore the remark which they presumed was offensive, no doubt the result of the man having had one too many. However they could still hear the guffaw of his laughter above the noise of the engine as they drove down the road. Alice did not think that he had recognised her, but she definitely knew him and was sure that Emily would remember the ill-mannered foreigner.

As before, the pallor of Emily's face whitened at the mere mention of the man. This time she enquired where Alice and George had specifically seen him. The location, a residential road along the quieter outskirts of Beckston provided no indication of his whereabouts. Emily knew that she would simply have to wait; that thought disturbed her as did the anxiety regarding the length of time which had elapsed since their previous meeting.

The power of the imagination can be so strong and convincing that a person can believe that they are being followed even in daylight, when in fact they are not. Emily allowed herself to be deluded; an unexpected noise or long shadow could possess sufficient potency to be a threat. Niall now accompanied her home from the evening surgery as the daylight hours began to shorten. Although she needed to meet with the inspector again, she feared doing so and was also fearful of any news he might impart about Olivia.

The one place in which she forgot about his existence was whilst teaching in the classroom. Her mind was solely preoccupied with education. The morning had begun like any other, assembling the children in the largest classroom to sing a hymn followed by a prayer. As Emily opened her eyes she immediately saw the unmistakable silhouette of Inspector Jackson, his eyes focussed intensely upon her.

She dismissed her charges as custom decreed in silence, her own heart pounding with such force that she feared everyone around her would hear its erratic and pulsating beat. Her class stood obligingly behind their desks until summoned to sit down and continue their task of perfecting their copperplate writing; every head bowed with precision as the copying commenced.

Emily stepped into the corridor, her eyes continually glancing fleetingly through the windows of the partitioned wall.

'Very impressive!'

'I am sorry?'

'The way they all show respect.'

'There has to be respect for learning to occur.' Emily was most matter of fact in her statement.

'It's just the same in life. You and I are in the same business. When everything is going smoothly, we leave them alone. When not, we dole out the punishments and ensure that they learn their lesson. You could say it's one of life's biggest lessons. Only some of mine get life and sometimes some get something else.' The skin around Jackson's eyes began to wrinkle as he began to laugh uncontrollably.

'Inspector, please remember that this is a school and as such learning is trying to take place. I invite you to show some decorum.'

The words instantly transported him back decades to the poorly furnished rooms with his mother admonishing him over some petty indiscretion. He stood silently and listened as he used to when his mother taught him right from wrong. She was so like his mother, something which he found quite alluring.

The remark had somewhat served as an ice-breaker; Emily no longer felt in trepidation of the man. In fact she sensed that for once she had the upper hand.

'Inspector, as you can see, it is not currently convenient for me to speak freely with you. Could we possibly meet later somewhere?'

'The Black Bull at Seven.'

The matter seemed non-negotiable as Jackson turned and left as abruptly as he had arrived. Emily was left wondering about the chosen location. She knew of its whereabouts and of its reputation but she had never ventured inside. Indeed she had never been inside a public house before. According to her mother, they were dens of iniquity and no self-respecting woman would ever be found inside one; Olivia was always the exception and the unmentionable in such conversations. Members of the Band of Hope, the Salvation Army and the British Women's Total Abstinence Union were also exceptions to her mother's ruling. Whether situated on a drab street corner or on the edge of a village green, the public house was one place where men could escape to, away from their work and womenfolk, allowing their language to flow with uninhibited passion.

Pushing the door open with caution, Emily peered into the darkened interior. Men's faces stared back in surprise as they greedily swallowed their well-earned pints of traditional mild or bitter; both readily on tap from a line of barrels which the landlord busily attended. Inspector Jackson stood amongst the men at the long bar and signalled to Emily to join him. She followed him to the snug bar at the back, where they found a small table, in a corner away from the masses of people who were beginning to gather around the bar. A whisky and a small sherry quickly appeared in front of them.

'I do not drink,' Emily protested.

'I hardly think one glass of sherry will make much difference.' Emily declined to respond as she recalled the effects of drinking too much wine at the wedding on Long Island. At times of celebration she did allow herself the indulgence of a drink, not that this occasion could be classed as a celebration but she felt it might provide a modicum of Dutch courage.

Moderation in all things was a maxim to sensibly live life by, she thought.

'Thank you,' she added as she took a small sip.

'For what; ordering a drink that you don't want? I guessed you looked the type that would enjoy a sherry.'

'The type?' questioned Emily.

'You know; quiet and reserved but with a character of steel that can detect right from wrong. In many ways, you remind me of my mother.'

'Thank you. I take it that that is a compliment.'

'Definitely.'

The man was unfathomable. He possessed a prickly exterior which could be brusque and heavy-handed and at times menacing; she had for some months been dreading his reappearance and yet, now she was sitting across the table from him not knowing how to deal with his unexpected niceties. Somewhere within him there was an Achilles heel which she felt she had momentarily glimpsed but the moment had passed as he vehemently launched into business.

'What shall we drink to; the spoils of Verholt?' He raised his glass and downed the whisky before ordering another one. 'Yes talking of spoils, there have been plenty of those, as I know full well.' The replenished glass reappeared and for some time Jackson stared into the rich amber-coloured liquor. 'Well not for much longer, I can assure you.'

Emily waited instinctively before enquiring. 'Do you have some news?'

'News! News! What do you want to hear?' His manner now was becoming unsettling and slightly intimidating.

'I am worried about my sister, Olivia.'

'No need! She's having the time of her life.'

'Have you seen her?'

'Oh yes. I have been very busy since we last met. I've toured the large houses of England and have discovered what Verholt has helped himself to. I've been to Paris and seen his set-up over there. He and your sister are living well, extremely well. I suppose she hasn't given you or your family a thought since settling there.'

His comment was true enough as there had been little communication from Olivia; a mere three letters since leaving for France.

'There have not been any more burglaries, have there?'

'None recorded. They're probably living off the proceeds of the last ones.'

'This case must be very serious,' Emily exclaimed. 'The fact that you have been away from America for so long certainly indicates its prominence.'

'Umm. It certainly does. Left to the miserly cents and dollars of the New York Police Force I would still be in New York.' Jackson inclined his body forward, smiled and flashed the badly stained teeth. 'I am now retired and, as such, act under my own steam as a private investigator.'

The revelation shocked Emily. 'You are funding this yourself? It must be costing you a lot of money. Why are you doing this?'

'For one reason and one reason only: my mother.'

The conversation had returned full circle and Jackson now seemed quite at ease disclosing the events of his childhood when his life had been turned upside down because of the action of the Verholts' Bank. The name itself was his Achilles heel and, as Emily thought, his nemesis.

Following the appearance of yet another glass of whisky, Emily continued the conversation: 'But surely it was not Christian Verholt who was responsible for your family's downfall?' Jackson scrutinised her scathingly making her feel that she had now dampened the moment of his enjoyment.

'It may not have been *him* in person but *he* is still tarnished with the name. If I can at least have my revenge with one of them, it will bring disgrace to the whole family. Then they may know what it is like to taste shame. God knows, I have lived with the taste of that in my mouth for most of my life; a taste which taints and sours everything. Now it is their turn.'

The effect of drinking too many whiskies was now beginning to show. Accustomed to the sweeter tasting bourbon-whiskies, Sam Jackson had recently begun to appreciate the pleasure which a scotch whisky could bestow. His recent spate of indulgence was causing him now to slump and stare longingly into his empty glass. As he picked it up Emily intervened, fearing that he was about to order another one.

'Do you not think that you have had enough?' came the reprimand. Attempting to stand up Jackson appeared startled by the question before his legs wobbled, causing his great frame to fall back onto his chair. His heavily laden eyes stared back at her, initially with indignation before they began to wrinkle from a sudden bout of laughter.

'Miss, you are something else. No one, neither man nor woman, has ever dared to say something like that to me. You have guts, lady, and I like that. I like that a lot.' He then proceeded to lean over the table to be closer to Emily. She could smell the whisky on his breath as he began to speak. 'The only person to ever speak to me like that would be my mother. You know, you are definitely like her.' For a moment his eyes penetrated her gaze with a fixed preoccupation. Emily could not discern what was going through his mind but she presumed it was being fuelled by memories from his past.

'I think we would both benefit from leaving now.' Emily decided she had to be the one to take command of the situation.

'I've taken a room here so I only have to attempt to get up the stairs,' Jackson laughed jokingly.

Emily was relieved by his remark and rose to her feet in an attempt to leave but his unexpected question made her freeze with alarm.

'How well do you know Niall Branigan?' His tone was once again lucid and in control. She now wondered if the drunken stupor had been a sham to lull her into a false sense of security. Her answer had to be careful and truthful.

'He is a local doctor.' Her answer was precise and truthful.

'Who was also the ship's doctor on the Lusitania. Yes, I know that, but I asked you how well *you* know him.' Emily sat down again. She knew she had to be careful with this man.

'He is a good man and gives of his time freely to help those who need him. He runs a free surgery for the poor and I help him when I can.' Emily could feel her breathing tightening in her chest.

'How much do you know about his past life?'

'Only that he was orphaned and brought up by a doctor and his wife in Ireland.'

'Where in Ireland?'

'He was born in Kilkenny, but the family then moved to Cork. Inspector, I really do not know anything else. Why are you questioning me about Doctor Branigan?'

Jackson straightened his posture and sat upright with his eyes once again fixed upon Emily. Silence fell between them as he appeared to be weighing up the situation.

'I just wanted to know how much you know about your husband.'

Emily was stunned and suddenly felt the blood draining away from her head. The room seemed to swirl around her as she felt weak before losing consciousness.

This time it could not be attributed to the effect of drink; especially one glass of sherry.

Chapter Twenty-Three

The shame of it: a lady becoming unconscious in a public house. Everyone would say that the lady was definitely not a lady. Emily knew that her parents certainly would; that is if they heard the rumour. Although Beckston was a large town word could easily be spread, especially from the mouths of gossips. Emily prayed that such words however would not reach the ears of her parents.

Niall had been called from his surgery by the landlord's son. The large man who had been sitting with the woman who had fainted had asked for Doctor Branigan in person and as the landlord later pointed out, had remained there until the doctor arrived. Emily had regained consciousness before his arrival but could not remember Sam Jackson taking his leave and slipping away. The following day Emily returned to the Black Bull but Jackson had already paid his bill and departed. The landlord recalled that he needed to catch a train and then a ship which was bound for America, following disembarkation on route in Ireland.

The man made her nervous; he was certainly not one to underestimate in any way. He had cleverly manipulated her with psychological ambivalence, making her feel comfortable in his presence with carefully selected niceties, before disarming her with piercing and devastating magnitude. To some degree she could understand his grievance with the Verholt family, but his obsession with any kin bearing the same name was dangerous paranoia.

More worrying than this was the man's interest in Niall and the knowledge that Jackson had spent time investigating their marital status. The only connection Emily and Niall had with the Verholt family was when they had travelled to Long Island to attend a family wedding of Emily's relatives who were employed by them. That was the only connection and hardly worthy of investigation Emily concluded, as she tossed the matter around in her head. She did however question whether it was coincidence that the ship Jackson would be sailing on would dock in Ireland first; she wondered if he would disembark or continue his voyage back to America. However the one piece of certainty was that Jackson would return.

Niall displayed far more attention in her meeting with Jackson, and his probing curiosity caused her to disclose everything to him, including the interest shown by the inspector in his background.

'Why would he ask me how much I know about you? Is there something that I should know?' Emily queried. His silence unnerved her. She had always been aware of his attractive good looks and remembered the feelings of jealousy that she had experienced aboard the Lusitania, when she had seen the attention the ladies paid to him. Even Olivia had flirted with him one Christmas, and although he had never once given her any cause for concern, she found herself asking him a question that she had never expected to voice.

'Is there another woman? Please I would rather you told me the truth than hear it from someone like Jackson.' The silence and the stern look upon his face made her search through her mind for an even more impossible scenario, fuelled by the fact that he had been content to keep their marriage secret: 'Niall, what is it that you are not telling me? Is there another Mrs Branigan? Do you already have a wife in Ireland?'

'No Emily, I do not have another wife. You are the only woman that I have ever been married to. You need to trust me, as I trust you. Our marriage will stand the test of time if we agree to do that. I love you, Emily, with all my heart and you must never forget that.'

As they kissed, Emily knew that she had never experienced such love from another human being. She loved Niall deeply and trusted him, but the doubtful spectre of Sam Jackson still remained at the back of her mind.

A normal life seemed to be an unattainable notion in Emily's mind. As the family prepared for another Christmas, Emily realised that the uncertainty of Olivia's location and the lack of confirmation that she was safe and well, were proving to be upsetting for everyone. She decided that in the New Year she would travel to Paris herself and find Olivia; that at least would help to reassure everyone that Olivia was not in danger. She even wondered if she might persuade her sister to return home. With such thoughts in mind the contents of the unexpected letter appeared almost prophetic:

Greenwich Village,
New York,
America.
4th December 1912

My Dearest Emily,

Please forgive me for not replying sooner to your letter. You must of course by now think badly of me, which is seemingly warranted until the full facts are imparted. The cause, however, is not of my own making and the truth is that I have been completely ignorant in the knowledge of your correspondence to me.

Since Inspector Jackson's visit, I have not been well. It appears that my heart is not quite what it used to be and as a consequence I have experienced some problems with pains in my chest. It has not been a heart attack this time but seemingly my son Jonathan, has instructed my daughter-in-law Beatrice, to cocoon me from any form of excitement in this life, which my dear unfortunately also includes reading your letters. However, my grandsons informed me that they had seen a letter addressed to me and Beatrice, sweet as she is, duly complied when I asked her about it. Jonathan does not resemble his father, his true father in any way. That of course is another story and one which I will tell you some day.

You have had so much to deal with at a time when you should be enjoying your marriage and hopefully considering the start of a family yourselves. I know that things will eventually change for the better for you and for that reason you must be patient. My life has taught me that!

I can appreciate how distressing it has been for you to be visited by Inspector Jackson. The man is averse to the female charm, as I found out myself and therefore all I can advise is for you to be yourself with him; you have nothing to hide from him, as you are not linked to the Verholt name. Stand your ground and refuse to be intimidated. Remember Emily, you have done nothing wrong.

Do not worry unnecessarily about your sister Olivia. She is a little more mature in years and I would think will enjoy her time in Paris. It is a wonderful city to be in; I for one can testify to its attractions.

My dear, if you should ever decide to visit Paris, in order to locate Olivia and need somewhere to retreat to where you will be safe, I am sure that my old friend and associate Françoise *Morel will be only too happy to assist you. She lives in the North of the city in the borough of Montmartre. Her address is 19, Rue Lepic, Montmartre. I lived and worked with her during my time in Paris. I can assure you that you will be safe with her there and she will not ask any questions.*

I do wish you contentment and I know that you will eventually attain the happiness that both you and Niall deserve. Please give my love to Niall.

With very good wishes for Christmas and the New Year.

Your old friend,

Amelia.

Emily smiled as she recalled her time with Amelia and her larger-than-life tales of working in a brothel and being wined and dined by Princes, Sultans and Dukes. She marvelled at the ingenuity of her friend in now producing a name and address of an associate.

The letter had certainly brought welcome relief to Emily; even if it did stray into the land of make-believe. It also reminded Emily of the importance of visiting Paris in order to find her sister; 1913 would be the year to fulfil this dream.

Chapter Twenty-Four

The charms of the Emerald Isle were not wasted upon Sam Jackson. He recalled from his school days that this was a land that was no stranger to troubled history. It was an island of immense possibilities, rich in beauty with verdant and fertile land, and inhabited by one of the most congenial races on earth; but for fifteen hundred years it had lacked happiness, peace and prosperity. As he stepped onto Irish soil he felt a kindred spirit here, being aware of the turmoil and struggle which the island's inhabitants still faced.

He disembarked at Cork, Ireland's second largest port and made his way slowly to Kilkenny. At times frustrated with the seeming lack of urgency compared to New York, Jackson quickly realised that Irish time differed greatly to any other that he had experienced. Life here had a distinct quaintness which spilled over from its abundant myths and legends and what was not achieved one day would be kept for another. The beliefs in the 'little people' had to be taken seriously and life here, like the golden whiskey had to be savoured slowly for full appreciation. Sam Jackson very quickly learned to appreciate Irish whiskey.

The rural landscape occasionally dotted with a solitary whitewashed cottage, at best accessible by a remote track, was the antithesis to New York and its crammed population and frenetic lifestyle. There, crime was understandably widespread as neighbours coveted what was not theirs or collectively in gangs, engineered plans to swindle others of their wealth. That is what happens with a constantly changing society. Here everyone seemed to know everything about their neighbours, however far flung they were and in such communities trust was paramount. Generations of established families may have produced disagreements or even feuds but rarely desires of pure avarice. Of course Jackson knew that the exception to the rule always prevailed and that in such a tightly-knit community tongues could be loosened, especially with an Irish whiskey.

Arriving in Kilkenny, dominated by its large medieval castle, Jackson immediately located his favourite place to gather local facts from; a public house. It was not long before a friendly customer happily accepted free drinks in exchange for information. He seemed only too eager to disclose the desired address; especially one of such notoriety.

Jackson found the small cottage situated on the outskirts of Kilkenny, along the road running through to Thomastown. There was no longer any trace of the Doyle family there, but Jackson had been informed that the current inhabitant, an elderly woman named Aileen O'Donnell, had been their friend and neighbour for many years. No longer accustomed to visitors, the wizened face peered around the door with suspicion. The eyes narrowed as they squinted with marked effort to recognise the large frame of the man standing in front of them.

'Do I know you?' asked the lilting Irish accent.

'No'.

'Didn't think so. Well, what do you want with me?'

'A little of your time and what you know about the Doyle Family.'

'Just what makes you think that I'd be telling the likes of you anything?'

The appearance of the bottle of whiskey however was sufficient incentive for the old woman to invite the stranger into her home.

Even by Jackson's standards of homemaking the interior of the little cottage was old-fashioned, dusty and pervaded by a musty odour; the tell-tale signs spelt out loneliness as a place that no one ever cared to call at, as well as citing the prevalence of poverty where cold and damp could insidiously seep into the bones of the inhabitant.

Aileen O'Donnell greedily grasped the bottle, opened it and took her first swig before following it with another; only then was she ready to talk.

The Doyle family had lived in the cottage for many years and it was here that they had brought their children into the world, a world which was in want of the necessities of life. Bradan and Mary Doyle had given life to four sons and two daughters, having already lost two still-born babies. Their lives were harsh as they struggled to feed and care for them.

As children themselves, Bradan and Mary had known what it was like to starve, having lived through the Great Irish potato famine 1845–1849, where blight had spread furiously across the countryside destroying nearly every potato in the country. These conditions had been followed by the winter of 1846–47 in which successive blizzards had buried homes up to their roofs in snow. Unscrupulous landlords had evicted many tenants from their homes onto the streets and into jail, whilst some tenants were sent to British North America in overcrowded and poorly built sailing ships which became infected with typhus, thereby earning such vessels the name coffin ships. Those who remained in Ireland and clung to life became survivors who would resort to any extreme without reservation; the Doyles were no exception.

Originally it began with petty misdemeanours; pickpocketing and stealing from shops. The Doyles' children became experts in such swift movements with their nimble fingers and slight frames. But the thrill of these crimes, especially when they were not caught, escalated with age and temptation as far away as Dublin into other areas; burglary, extortion, prostitution and finally murder. The family became notorious as each son died, either through retaliation from another criminal or from the hangman's noose. Brendan Doyle and his daughter were ambushed one night by a gang of men who dragged them to the ground from their horse and cart, before slitting their throats and leaving them to die. The perpetrators were never caught and subsequent public interest showed little concern.

Only Mary Doyle and her youngest daughter Ciara survived.

'What happened to Ciara?' Jackson asked.

'She was only a girl herself and in the family way with no man around to help. She had the babies…'

'Babies?' repeated Jackson to ensure no misunderstandings.

'Twins. Surprisingly, one was a healthy baby which she kept but the other was the runt.' The old lady's eyes began to fill with tears as she continued. 'It would have been impossible to have kept both of them. A decision had to be made, as you would with an animal so as to ensure survival. The doctor took the poor little one away.'

The woman became increasingly distressed as she spoke of Ciara's death the following year and the raising of the child. Jackson knew that the old woman in front of him was indeed Mary Doyle who had reinvented herself in the guise of a former friend. She now lived a solitary existence and no one would question her identity. The child had long since grown up and had left for new pastures.

As Jackson walked to the door, he momentarily hesitated and turned to face Mary Doyle.

'How did you afford to pay for a doctor?'

'We had to have a doctor because of the complications with Ciara having two babies. The doctor was a good man and would not take any money from us. There are not many like that.'

'What was his name?'

'Oh, let me see. It's such a long time ago… I remember now. Doctor Branigan, yes, that was his name.'

Chapter Twenty-Five

Christmas was a word usually associated with time being spent with family and friends. The Taylor family accordingly spent their time together, but each member was acutely aware of Olivia's absence. Even with Doctor Lawson, George, Alice and Niall around their table, her wayward and ebullient character was still noticeably absent. Frequently shocking in both her actions and speech, as well as being totally selfish, Olivia was undeniably missed by Emily and her parents. As the New Year brought in 1913, the same thought played upon each of their minds: would they ever see her again?

The appearance of a Christmas card had momentarily satisfied their aspirations of hearing from her, but there had been no forwarding address provided. It had been then that Emily had decided definitely that she would go to Paris and find her sister. That moment along with Jackson's earlier appearance had convinced her of the necessity.

His words, however, were never far from her conscious mind; indeed subconsciously they disturbed her slumber at night, producing nightmares of amplified distortion. She did not want to admit that she feared not only for Olivia, but the unknown was constantly provoking unanswered questions of Niall in her mind. She knew that it was wrong to question him, for to do so would imply a lack of trust in him. They had been through so much together and she knew that her love for him was unequivocal and pure, as his was for her. She accepted that it was the type of love which elicited neither questions nor answers and therefore resigned herself to an acceptance of the known facts. Truth would come with time and patience; the entire undiluted truth. Emily acknowledged that Niall would tell her everything when he was ready to do so. Until then she would wait. Lately she had become very good at waiting; now she found herself waiting for the reappearance of Inspector Jackson whom she intuitively expected to see again soon. Her intuition proved to be uncannily exact.

A heavy snowfall which had lasted for two days during the early part of January had caused many people to remain in their own homes and avoid the bitter conditions. Only those with desperate complaints had ventured out to the surgery for medical assistance. As Emily turned the corner into the familiar street where she regularly spent her free time working with Niall, she instantly turned back to avoid being seen. His large frame made him definably recognisable. Some time elapsed before Emily dared to crane her head around the corner and see which direction Jackson was taking. When she finally looked he had disappeared from view. She did not know where he had gone to but she did know where he had been; she had just witnessed him leaving Niall's surgery.

There were only two patients waiting to be seen and Niall quickly attended to them. Normally good-natured in his friendliness, Niall seemed impatient and preoccupied. Once alone with Emily, he continued to remain uncharacteristically quiet.

It was Emily who eventually broke the silence: 'I saw Inspector Jackson leaving the surgery tonight.' Nothing more than a worried look was exchanged between them.

'I knew that he would return but I did not expect to see him here,' Emily persistently continued.

'That man should not be underestimated,' declared Niall.

'I certainly know that. He unnerves me and always has done but somehow I think he holds the key to solving this business with Olivia and Christian Verholt. Somewhere in all of this I need him to lead me to my sister...'

Uncharacteristically Niall interrupted his wife: 'Leave it to me. I will go to Paris and find Olivia for you. You need have no further dealings with that man. It needs to be sorted, once and for all and now is the time to do that.'

Emily had never seen her husband so vehemently decisive. His manner slightly shocked her and she resigned herself to having to accept his decision.

Later however she began to wonder why Jackson had visited her husband and the nature of his business with him. Whatever that may be had had a profound influence.

As winter began to give way to spring with the celebratory profusion of verdant new life, the necessity of finding Olivia was made more expedient by an unexpected turn of events. Charles Taylor had not enjoyed robust health for some time but he had learned to live with the consequences which the stroke had imposed. His day to day life although slow and steady was decidedly predictable and therefore the morning that he awoke and complained of feeling unwell, Hannah and Emily had no hesitation in sending for Doctor Lawson. As expected, Niall also accompanied their old family doctor but on this occasion no amount of medical intervention could save the patient. Charles Taylor had lost consciousness before their arrival, having suffered a severe stroke and within a short time had died surrounded by those he loved. Hannah's grief was inconsolable as she leaned over her husband and buried her face close to his, her tears trickling down across his cheeks. No one noticed the embrace that Niall gave his wife and her willing acceptance of it. But everyone heard the commotion later as Hannah began to call out her name with increasing fervour until it reached a hysterical pitch: 'Olivia! Where is Olivia? She should be here. I need her. I need her with me. Someone bring her to me…'

Emily little doubted that her mother needed the comfort of both her daughters but she did question how supportive Olivia would be. The fact remained however that Olivia's presence was needed at home; now more than ever. Niall accordingly left for Paris the following day.

Within the week he had returned, but to everyone's disappointment without Olivia. Following exhaustive enquiries, it appeared that Olivia and Monsieur Cassel had recently left Paris to venture upon a Grand European Tour, whatever that entailed. Emily considered that it was simply a euphemism for a burglary shopping spree.

Hannah had her husband laid to rest with full Victorian decorum; his glass hearse was conveyed through Beckston by a pair of black horses who respectfully seemed to bow their heads as they turned ceremoniously and passed through the gates into the cemetery. There his coffin was lowered into the ground to lay in infinite slumber with other members of the Taylor family. His name would soon be added to the marble headstone; a somewhat fitting tribute to a man who had spent his life as a stonemason.

Life now had to continue but Hannah withdrew more and more to her room with increasing migraines. Emily and Alice soon began to notice the lack of purpose in her daily routine. The decline had to be stopped and Emily hoped that Olivia's appearance might help the situation. Once again Niall agreed to journey to France, find Olivia and persuade her to return home.

The summer months of 1913 were passing quickly and Niall's prolonged absence began to make Emily feel lonely and vulnerable; a fact which did not go unnoticed by a fellow teaching colleague. Eleanor Tordoff was a matronly spinster who had dedicated her life to teaching and who had worked with Emily for many years. She was a woman who did not socialise and who rarely spoke about her family or private life. Nevertheless, she had a perceptive understanding of human nature, especially grief and the loss of loved ones. In Emily she detected a need which could be fulfilled and for that very reason startled her headmistress with the unexpected invitation.

At first, Emily was astonished by her suggestion, being initially sceptical and slightly afraid but with time her mind became changed and she agreed to attend the séance.

The clandestine meeting was being held at the home of a friend of Eleanor's who could supposedly contact the dead. Emily had not told anyone about her intended visit, least of all her mother.

As the door opened, a lady in black invited them in with nothing more than a dramatic sweep of the hand. Although outside the evening was still light, the house had been prematurely darkened; curtains drawn across the windows provided privacy as well as the desired atmosphere. The gas lights had been purposefully turned down low to provide a theatrical ambience for the forthcoming events of the evening and the only audible sound was a slight hissing from the burning gas. They followed the dark figure into an equally dimly lit parlour where two men and a woman were already seated expectantly around a circular table. Each person accordingly nodded with a greeting of recognition as Eleanor and Emily sat down. The lady in black took her seat at the table and everyone in customary fashion linked hands to produce an unbroken human circle.

Emily watched as the lady in black began to breathe deeply before bowing her head and then allowing it to roll backwards, her eyes staring with fixation into a darkened corner of the room. The trance medium waited with anticipation, her body ready to convey the messages from the dead. Suddenly her upper body arched backwards and her lips began to quiver.

'Jenny is at peace now.' The words tumbled out and the man and woman sitting opposite Emily smiled at one another, obviously relieved by the message. Further messages continued to be passed, acknowledged from time to time by those around the table, with the exception of Emily. Neither the names nor the messages themselves held any meaning or interest for Emily. She waited hoping that she might hear the name Charles, her father's name, but nothing remotely similar in sound fell from the medium's lips. She had resigned herself to accepting that the night had been a waste of time when a large shadow played tentatively on the wall momentarily. It made her gasp especially as the hissing of the gas also intensified at that precise moment. She looked around the table but no one else seemed to have noticed the darkened form. Now it was gone but the medium seemed to be in discomfort as she began to twist her head from side to side.

'What is it? What message do you have for us?' Tightly gripping the hands of those alongside her the medium began to thrash around with unlimited exertion.

'What do you want?' The woman was now becoming sorely distressed.

A strange voice resounded through the room: 'Olivia can be saved'.

This time it was Emily who felt some relief but before she could comprehend the impact of the message, the messenger provided more: 'Your husband is in danger.' The final burst of words fell from the medium's lips as she slumped backwards with exhaustion: 'The Irish waters will fill with shrouds.'

The purpose for attending the séance had been to find reassurance about the future; it was meant to be a cathartic way of resolving family issues. Instead it had produced far more riddles which Emily could neither ignore nor solve. It was known that many purporting to be mediums were little more than theatrical charlatans but the woman had referred to Olivia by name. It was true that Eleanor Tordoff could have supplied such details relating to Emily's sister but no one in that room knew of the existence of Emily's husband. Furthermore no one knew that he had Irish connections. The message, although garbled, held a sinister warning; one which could not be ignored. Emily decided she could wait no longer and therefore the time had arrived for her to go to Paris; she needed to save both her sister and her husband.

Chapter Twenty-Six

Paris had always seduced visitors with its provocative sensuality; no doubt the result of centuries of juxtaposition. As a country of contrasts, France had inherited its ancestral blood from many diverse conquering nations; all had left a cornucopia of custom and style behind.

At the heart of France stood the beautiful capital city of Paris, originally built upon two islands in the River Seine. No visitor to such a city could remain untouched by the triggers to the senses. Magnificent avenues, boulevards and squares bombarded the eyes with regal splendour. The straight line of the Champs-Elysees connecting the Arc de Triomphe to the Place de la Concorde could never fail to impress. If the sense of sight needed any further enticement, a vision of the glass-panelled Grand Palais bathed in the blue-and-pink glow of the River Seine in the late afternoon would always provide enchantment.

The degree of stimulation to the senses knew no bounds. The lingering aromas of coffee, tobacco, perfume and fresh garlic tantalisingly teased whilst even the cheapest café with its simple tiled floors, marble-topped tables and metal coffee pots easily enticed its customers by the proven reputation of the taste of a dish of bouillabaisse and the ubiquitous carafe of wine. The French were conspicuously proud of their country, their heritage and the plentiful supply and beauty of delicious fresh produce. The abundance of such sensual and colourful pleasures emphasised how different France was compared to England.

Emily stepped into Paris with a certain amount of trepidation and naivety. Neither a novice nor a seasoned traveller, she was aware that her anguish sprang from much deeper concerns than the inability to converse in a foreign language. The long journey over land and water by ferry and train had been tiring and she was now anxious to find accommodation for herself in Paris. A fellow train passenger had recommended a small, family run but reasonably inexpensive place near the Place de Republique. Amidst the haphazard array of squares and avenues, Emily found L'Hotel, and was shown to a small but clean room. Her tiredness soon overwhelmed her and she slept for much of the afternoon. When she finally awoke, she was hungry and began upon an adventure of wandering around the streets and squares of Paris. Although keen to explore, she was also keen to avoid becoming lost and therefore decided not to venture too far. The little tables and chairs from the restaurants had spilled out onto the pavements and were being occupied by Parisians and tourists alike, who seemed to enjoy nothing more than relaxing in the waning sunlight, sipping wine and chatting casually. The whole ethos here was very different to that back in England; these people appeared relaxed but at the same time there was a buoyant and carefree attitude about them which intrigued Emily; almost as much as the foreign language and the animated gesticulations which accompanied it.

As Emily sat at one of the little tables waiting to order her food, she watched those around her with envy. No one except her appeared to be lonely; the realisation saddened her as she realised that Paris was renowned as the city of romance and one which attracted lovers. Niall was somewhere in this large city but unfortunately he was not in her company. She began to wonder where he might be and if he had managed to locate Olivia. More than anything, she needed to find her sister and encourage her to return home to her mother. As the waiter appeared Emily suddenly realised how little appetite she had when she recollected the words of the medium: 'Your husband is in danger.' Instead of enjoying the famed delights of French cuisine, Emily ordered simply and ate bread and cheese for sustenance that evening. With the exception of the waiter she had conversed with no one and quietly made her way back to the hotel. She needed to rest and sleep as she knew that the following days would bring their own demands upon her strength.

The following two days began with hopeful expectation before subsiding with frustration into predictable disillusionment. Struggling with snippets of acquired French phrases, Emily was far from fluent in the language and, although the Parisians were agreeably helpful, no one could unite her with the people she was seeking; names alone were insufficient, making the search futile. Soon it became apparent that Emily needed some form of intervention or perhaps diversion to clear her mind from the anxious suppositions which clouded any form of rational thought.

The sight of Amelia's letter in her bag made her question why she had kept it. Subconsciously she knew why; to affirm or dispel those imaginary tales. Amelia was of course a polished and believable story-teller and yet, the precise address seemed sufficiently convincing to make Emily curious to discover if such a location existed. It was then that she finally decided that a day of sight-seeing would prove to be a welcome diversion.

Situated in the north of Paris, Montmartre appeared strategically as it must have done four hundred years ago, as a little country village perched high on a butte overlooking Paris. The Montmartre hill offered one of the highest vantage points in the city which no doubt had been of significance in attracting artists there for some years since the end of the nineteenth century. Montmartre's narrow, hilly and winding cobbled streets, together with its commanding views of Paris could easily inspire those with an artistic temperament. Renoir, Van Gogh and Gauguin had lived and worked here and now less illustrious artists could be found in the Place du Tertre, Montmartre's village square, a place which had been renowned for the announcement of marriages as well as for the hanging of criminals.

Emily could not fail to be moved by the atmosphere of Montmartre. The area throbbed with life and yet she felt safe here. The imposing silhouette of the Sacre-Coeur was already capturing both peoples' attention and criticism, as artisans worked to finalise the construction of this new church, based on Roman architecture.

Holding the crumpled letter in her hand Emily approached an elderly lady, showing her the address. The garbled directions although difficult to understand were assisted by definite hand gestures. Emily followed the direction pointed out to her and repeating the exercise twice again, found herself at a gateway leading to an imposing three-storey house surrounded by a carefully-tended garden where orange-blossom, nasturtiums, acacia and violets added both fragrance and colour. The gentile looking house was well kept and each of the numerous windows had been framed at the sides with window shutters.

Standing at the door Emily raised her hand and then hesitated. The address evidently existed but that did not guarantee that the person who lived here was Françoise Morel, Amelia's friend. Before Emily could make a decision she heard the door being opened. A young maid smiled back at her with an enquiring smile prompting Emily to speak.

'Bonjour… Pardon…Madam Morel…' Embarrassment had now usurped Emily's linguistic skills in either French or English making them stilted and uncoordinated. The maid simply stared back at Emily without speaking.

The door was gradually opened fully by an elderly well-dressed lady.

'Can I help you? I am Françoise Morel.'

Later, upon reflection, Emily was not able to remember the remaining conversation at the door that afternoon, except for the fact that she knew she had mentioned the name, Amelia Davenport. Following that she recalled being heartily welcomed into the hallway and then into a pleasant, light-filled drawing room where she had been served refreshments.

Although Madam Morel was now an elderly widow, she was still a remarkably beautiful woman. Her slim and graceful figure was complemented equally by a face which could still cause heads to turn. Benefitting from a well-defined bone structure and a smooth skin which were now helping to resist ageing and wrinkles, Françoise Morel must once have been an exquisitely beautiful woman. There was an air about her that indicated breeding and class; she had not just married money, she had been born into it.

Françoise was keen to know about her companion's friendship with Amelia. Emily described how they had met on-board the Lusitania, before Amelia and her family had settled in New York.

Since then they had exchanged correspondence and Amelia had suggested that as Emily was to visit Paris for the first time, she might like to call upon a friend of hers. Nothing further was disclosed.

'Ah, I remember Amelia with true fondness. She was a very good friend to me, at a time when I needed a friend. She introduced me to life, fun and made me see that I did not have to be afraid.' Françoise's tribute to Amelia served only to confuse Emily. The look upon the latter's face momentarily caused Françoise to pause and look closely at her companion's expression.

'You perhaps do not know much about Amelia's early life. Well I was born into a wealthy family and my parents had, how shall I say, plans for me; I was to be married to someone rich whom I did not know and certainly did not love. I ran away from my family and came to Paris. At seventeen years old I was innocent, afraid and starving. I was living and sleeping on the streets. It has to be said that Paris no longer seemed so attractive. Amelia was the one who stopped and asked me my name. She took me to a small café and bought me a meal and then let me stay with her. She was so good to me. I owe my English friend so much.' The ensuing reflective silence demonstrated the depth of friendship which still existed.

'Emily, I shall not ask your reasons for coming to Paris but, if you need sanctuary for whatever reason you are welcome to come and stay here.'

As Emily left the house she began to realise that Françoise Morel had sensed an air of danger surrounding her visitor. The fact that Amelia had given Emily Françoise's name and address indicated the degree of danger. Taking one last look at the gentile residence, Emily instinctively knew that she would return there, soon.

Chapter Twenty-Seven

The visit to Montmartre had not resolved matters; instead, it had merely heightened the prevailing sense of drama, confusion and destiny. Time was passing by swiftly and Emily was only too aware that she had left her mother at home in a vulnerable state with only Alice and George to look after her. The summer holidays would soon be at an end and Emily so far had managed to locate neither her sister nor her husband. She needed clearly some form of luck, but when it arrived she was not prepared for the harbinger of this fortune.

As another day dawned, Emily stepped out onto the sun-filled streets and wandered almost aimlessly passing the famous landmarks. The great avenues and boulevards branched out from the famous squares like arteries but it was often the smaller, secluded ones that were only reachable through tiny back-streets that Emily preferred. A welcome amount of shade was sometimes provided by paulownia trees that also added greenery against the white facades and grey-blue roofs of the buildings flanking these squares.

Emily had spent the day on the left bank of the River Seine. She travelled to Montparnasse, an area of Paris that was reputedly enticing those with intellectual and artistic traits away from Montmartre, the established gathering place for aspiring talent. The attraction of cheap rents at artist communes was sufficient to draw painters, composers, writers, poets, models and sculptors from around the world and enable them to hopefully flourish in mutual creative atmospheres.

Debates, business dealings and gossip were regularly exchanged in meeting places, such as the Café du Dome. Opened in 1898 it was known as the Anglo–American café due to the global nationality of its customers. Its walls, like those of other cafés in the area, were covered by the drawings of artists unable to pay their bills with cash. The understanding café proprietors merely displayed these works of art until the artist procured a sale and acquired some money; frequently however the walls were increasingly covered by yet further creations.

Emily took a seat at one of the small round tables outside on the pavement and watched in amazement as groups of people conversed passionately whilst studying the artistic works. The more affluent looking ones were obviously the dealers and art connoisseurs who were keen to identify aspiring talent and make a profit. At the other side of the tables sat the producers of the work, invariably penniless and hungry.

Her attention had clearly been diverted and she had failed to notice his presence. He had been watching her for some time and from her first sighting that morning, he had followed her without her suspicion. Of course he had had a lifetime of practice and was undeniably skilled in his business.

The sun momentarily blinded her as she turned and looked upwards, summoned by the familiar accent.

'I knew Paris would be too good to miss,' he chuckled as he pulled out a chair and promptly sat down without invitation.

'Inspector Jackson!' Emily's heart was beginning to race.

'Well, Lady, what have you found here in Paris?'

Emily merely shook her head in response.

'Just as I expected. Nothing! You need my help, don't you? And of course I will need yours. They say no one should be on their own in Paris.' The comment had a certain amount of truth to it but it failed miserably to convince Emily that her companion should be the man facing her.

'Do you know where I can find my sister Olivia or Niall Branigan, my …'

The pause in the sentence was eagerly filled by Sam Jackson.

'…Your husband, I think you were going to say.' Emily merely nodded.

'They say that Paris is for lovers, so I suppose you'll want to find your fellow.' A wry smile momentarily ran across his face as his lips curled with excitement. He stood up pushing his chair away before inclining his head closely towards hers and whispered: 'I'll meet you at the Eiffel Tower at seven o'clock tonight.'

When the waiter came to take the order Sam Jackson had gone, leaving Emily with more to preoccupy her than just the conversations of the nearby artists.

Emily arrived early, allowing herself the indulgence of being the one to be prepared to witness his arrival. At first she waited patiently and then began to slightly pace, looking around and down the various walkways surrounding the four mammoth columns of latticed iron girders. He approached slowly, his undeniably large body girth seemingly increasing in size as he came closer towards her.

'Are you hungry?' His choice of question seemed rather odd.

'Yes, yes I am but I thought we were going to find Niall or Olivia. I need to find them first and then we can eat.'

'Very well, if that is what you want! I just hope you will still have an appetite.' His manner was off-hand but in keeping with his usual character.

Emily dutifully followed as he began to walk away. At first they walked together in silence; his powerful strides no doubt the result of a lifetime of determination in tracking down criminals. A definite air of confidence surrounded him; the antithesis of any aura encircling Emily. Upon approaching the Boulevard St Germain, Jackson stopped suddenly and cast his gaze intently towards the numerous cafés and brasseries situated around them.

'This is where they usually come.'

'They?' Emily questioned the ambiguity of the remark. She did not know whether he was referring to Niall, Olivia or indeed Christian Verholt.

'Yes, *they*, as you will soon find out.'

He motioned towards a café where a group of tables and chairs flanked the front of it and made his way through them to a small obscure corner at the back. About to sit down he suddenly seemed to realise that for once he was not alone and hastily pulled out a chair for his female companion. Emily was slightly shocked by his behaviour which for him seemed to indicate some vestige of softness.

A waiter appeared and took their order for coffee; Emily having already declined the offer of an alcoholic beverage or food. They sat in silence as Jackson's vigilant eyes continued to dart back and forwards along the boulevard. Now Emily realised that she had been strategically seated, with her back towards the avenue.

The silence was broken as Jackson quickly gulped his coffee before asking the unlikely question:

'Do you know the difference between a brasserie and a café?'

'No ... no, I do not.' Emily pondered the question for a moment before taking a sip of her coffee.

'Well, apparently brasseries are run by Alsatians like the one across there. The owner Leonard Lipp could no longer stand to live under the regime of the Kaiser following the French-Prussian war of 1870 and the loss of the Alsace-Lorraine. Cafés however were originally started by Auvergne men. It was their ancestors who came to Paris to sell wood and coal; they also began selling refreshments to make some extra money. They were the ones who started to put the tables outside on the pavements like this one.'

Emily was slightly amused by his knowledge and delivery of such a snippet of cultural information and was beginning to slightly relax when she realised that Jackson's eyes were particularly focussed on something beyond her in the distance. She turned but the moment had passed.

'Did you see something?' she asked.

He nodded. 'I certainly did.'

He allowed a few minutes to pass before settling the bill. In silence they slowly walked across to the Brasserie des Bords du Rhin, a popular eating establishment famed for its Alsatian dishes, in particular its renowned dish of sauerkraut.

Emily instantly recognised her husband. Looking through the large windows, she had no need to enter the brasserie as she saw Niall seated at one of the tables, his back towards her, heavily engaged in conversation with his sole table companion, a young woman. She continued to watch being fixated by the scene in front of her. They were seated closely together, conversing intimately to the exclusion of anyone around them. It was clear that there was a special bond between them.

'I now understand what you meant by *they*,' Emily said, turning her face away and trying unsuccessfully to quell the hot tears that were beginning to run down her cheeks. She began to walk without purpose, being oblivious to everything around her and seemingly blind to any type of road traffic. At that moment she could feel nothing and had not even realised that Sam Jackson had linked his arm through hers, causing her to be guided safely along the Parisian streets.

They walked for some time in order to give distance to the events. Finally they entered another brasserie and took comfort at a corner table. Emily did not hear Sam Jackson's voice. It was only when he lifted a glass of brandy to her lips that the strength and potency of the drink made her cough as she swallowed it.

'They say it will bring the dead back to life,' Jackson remarked.

Emily turned and offered a half-hearted smile before adding, 'I think that may just be true.'

It was at that moment that Emily also warmed to the hardbitten inspector. She realised that he did at least have a heart even if hers had been shattered.

The scene continued to be etched in her mind for some time. Emily remained at the table looking down into her glass of brandy as though she was trying to find a viable explanation. The truth was she knew what she had witnessed; an intimate tryst between her husband and a young attractive, dark haired woman. There had been something remotely familiar about her and slowly the realisation began to unfold. Emily had met her once before in very different surroundings; across a dining table on-board the Lusitania. Then, she had been introduced as Mrs Robinson alongside her husband on their honeymoon. The truth made her gasp as she realised the connection between this woman and Christian Verholt. At first, she babbled with excitement until Jackson took her hand to calm her down.

'Take your time lady, there is no need to rush, no need at all.'

'But what does this all mean?' questioned Emily.

'It means what I hoped it would mean that you have no knowledge of this at all.'

'No knowledge of what?'

'Sure, you now know that the woman with your husband is an accomplice who works with Christian Verholt. They masquerade as newly-weds in order to try and shift their stolen goods from one continent to another. They've been working that scam along with many others for some years. That, of course, is not the only part in which she is involved. She may look cute and ladylike, but that is all a con. She's a Doyle through and through and as violent as any man around.'

'A Doyle?' Emily repeated the name as though she had been expected to know the name.

'Yeah, Doyle. Kerry Doyle. The look on your face tells me everything.'

'For you, I am pleased it does. However, I am completely at a loss to understand anything that you are talking about.'

Sam Jackson smiled, revealing his badly-stained teeth and reached over to momentarily grip Emily's right hand.

'You know, I've always thought you reminded me of my mother and right now you are as much like her as I can ever remember. Niall is certainly a lucky man.'

'Why, because he has a wife and a mistress?' Emily rebuked.

'No because he chose you as his wife. In the case of the other one he had no choice.'

'Inspector, please do not make excuses for him, simply because he is a man.'

'I'm not. She's his sister. To be exact, his twin sister.'

The disclosure, albeit a relief, was somewhat of a conundrum. Niall had never mentioned that he had a sister and certainly not one that was his twin.

Jackson explained his findings from his visit to Ireland. Emily listened and slowly began to understand why the small baby boy who had not been expected to survive had been separated from his sister at birth. She recalled that Niall had spoken of the kindness that Doctor Branigan had shown in taking him into a decent and loving family household and providing him with a name. What she was not aware of was the reputation of the maternal family background. Jackson divulged everything that he had found out about the Doyles' background, including their criminal notoriety in the district. Kerry Doyle, it seemed had grown up and had continued to apply the skills from the family business; burglary, smuggling and violence.

It was a known fact that twins had a special bond, not only from the genes that they had inherited but from the time that they had spent in the womb together. It was to be hoped that in this case the debate which considered the influence of nature as opposed to nurture, would be significantly favoured by the latter. Emily very much hoped that this was the case for Niall.

Chapter Twenty-Eight

Emily opened her eyes the following morning and reflected upon the events of the previous evening. It had been a very strange night, which had seen her emotions capitulate with the acceptance of presumed adultery before being alleviated by the truth; she was now related through marriage to a family of rogues. It instantly made her think of the small brown book which Jackson carried around with him and the collection of photographs in his so-called Rogues' Gallery. The thought almost made her smile as she began to realise that the man she had been so frightened of for so long, also had a tender side to him. Whilst being in the face of adversity she had been one of the few who had witnessed this.

He had definitely tested her; he had waited to see her reaction in order to assess her involvement. From that moment, he had protected her and he was still continuing to do so. Emily's request to find her husband had made Jackson more protective than ever; he was uncertain whether Kerry Doyle knew that she had a sister-in-law, and knowing her past unpredictable feisty reputation, he felt it was better for her to remain ignorant of the fact. Therefore, he promised Emily that he would bring Niall to her alone. As agreed, she waited at the Café du Dome in Montparnasse, the place that she had first been approached by Jackson whilst in Paris. As before, she watched and listened as the artists around her passionately tried to impress and persuade the art dealers to purchase their paintings. This time, however, her attention was not solely concentrated upon the surrounding customers as she frequently glanced beyond them to approaching figures silhouetted by the sun's rays.

At three o'clock in the afternoon a solitary figure appeared; she instantly recognised his walk. As he came closer she saw the unmistakeable dark hair and handsome looks that she had been attracted by. Rising to her feet, she raised her hand and immediately he saw her and began to increase his pace before beginning to gently sprint with energised enthusiasm. The artists around halted their conversations and watched knowingly as the couple kissed and embraced with passionate fervour. It was of course by reputation the city of passion.

There was little need for conversation. Gripping her hand he led her to the first well-appointed small hotel that they could find. Neither of them noticed the grandeur of the Rococo decoration or the magnificent wrought-iron staircase which led them upstairs to a sumptuous bedroom where they could be alone.

As on that night aboard the Lusitania when they had made love for the first time, they needed to search and explore each other's bodies. Then they had kissed slowly and tentatively; now it was with a vehement desire and experienced knowledge of what would surely follow. The unrestrained passion made each one grasp and undo both their own and the other's buttons, releasing and exposing flesh and hair. With nothing more to cover her than the locks of hair which had tumbled down around her shoulders as the remaining hairpins had been pulled out, Emily felt Niall's strong arms encircle her as he lifted her onto the bed. She could feel the softness of his thick jet-black chest hair touching her as he began to move down and kiss her body. She felt his hands cup her breasts and his fingers brush across her nipples before kissing each one. The gesture made her murmur with delight before her emotions escalated with intensity into a mutual climax of indescribable pleasure as she felt them combine intimately together.

Afterwards, they lay cradled in each other's arms. Moments of silence elapsed as they nuzzled together in marital contentment. The emerald colouring of Niall's eyes twinkled with intensity as he continued to smile with happiness, constantly planting light kisses upon Emily's face, causing her to giggle like a young girl. For those brief moments, it seemed that they were immune from conflict and anxiety but they each knew that such utopia could be nothing more than transitory pleasure. Niall explained that his priority was still to find Olivia. However, other extenuating circumstances had come to light.

'Inspector Jackson was the man who made the link between Kerry and Verholt. As Jackson told you, my blood family are literally criminals; Kerry is no exception. As a young man I had been curious to find out about my true lineage. I travelled to Kilkenny and learned that my mother had given birth to twins. Eager to find my sister, I tracked her down in Dublin where she was being held in a cell for pilfering from market stalls. I paid her bail and gave her some money on the understanding that she would become a decent citizen. But it appears that there is too much Doyle blood flowing in her veins. She has continued to rob and cheat her way through life and now works with Christian Verholt. There have been a couple of occasions when she has since sought my help; the last time was at the surgery in Beckston. If you remember I had a patient whom I had to tend to one night, doubled up in pain with a gun-shot flesh wound.' The quizzical look upon Emily's face interrupted Niall's flow.

'I know what you're thinking, Emily, but Kerry is a master of disguise and a mother of invention. She dressed as a man that night with a large tweed overcoat and hat in order to disguise both herself and the wound. She had been shot at following a burglary at a large house. I was able to remove the bullet and patch her up for another time.'

'When I saw her with you in the brasserie I later realised that I had met her once before on the Lusitania,' Emily remarked. 'It was the first night on-board and she and the man who I later found out was Christian Verholt had been introduced as Mr and Mrs Robinson.' Niall knowingly nodded, aware of their connections.

'Yes, I am aware of their partnership, but I can assure you that I played no part with that charade aboard the Lusitania. Jackson, of course, is not a man to be meddled with and it appears that he has his own vendetta for dealing with the Verholts. Emily, you must listen carefully to me. Verholt has plans for something big, very big indeed. If we are cunning we can kill two birds with the same stone; find Olivia and bring Verholt to justice.'

'What about Kerry?'

'She will have to take the consequences; whatever they are. She went her own way at life's crossroad many years ago. My only concern now is to get both you and Olivia away from this place, but we need to be patient and wait for the right moment. Do you trust me, Emily?'

'Yes, of course I do.'

'I now know that Olivia and Verholt have returned to Paris, having been guests at one of the largest estates outside the capital. Your sister is nothing more than just a pawn in the game.'

'The game?' Emily appeared shocked.

'Verholt has installed her as a manageress in a fashion house frequented by the seriously wealthy. She unknowingly establishes connections with the ladies of these households. They are keen to have prior knowledge of the new fashions and their husbands happily become introduced to Augustus Cassel, the wealthy businessman and owner of the fashion business. Regularly invited to house parties, Cassel, or shall we call him Verholt, shrewdly decides whether the place is worth breaking into and what items can be comfortably disposed of. Sometimes, they even burgle to order. That is when Kerry makes her début, always at a time when Verholt is elsewhere with a convenient alibi. According to Jackson, the reason for doing all of this lies within the thrill of not being caught!'

Emily nodded in agreement, as Jackson had already shared some of these facts with her whilst in England. She accepted that her husband had to return to his meetings with Kerry in order to find out more and she promised to wait patiently to hear from either him or Jackson. In the meantime, the writing on the piece of paper which Niall had handed to her was sufficient recompense; it was the address of the Fashion House where Olivia worked.

For more than one hundred and fifty years, Paris had been regarded as the pre-eminent city of fashion. It was during the reign of the Sun King, Louis XIV, at Versailles that sartorial rules ensured that the French aristocracy dressed according to their rank. A multitude of talent was drawn upon from weavers, tailors, dressmakers, embroiderers and milliners who had also begun to provide services to actresses and wealthy courtesans; the supremacy of Parisian fashion had emerged.

Numerous fashion houses had begun to open from the middle of the nineteenth century and were still continuing to do so. The established names including Worth, Poiret, Doucet and Paquin were now being increased by Vionnet, Coco Chanel and others. It was a glamorous industry, as designers could secure the interest and patronage of the monarchy, the seriously wealthy and even the actresses from the Paris Théâtre. Everything was dependent upon connections and promotions. Jeanne Paquin had been instrumental in leading the way by organising the first real fashion shows, which others were now keen to emulate. There was money to be made if one had the means, motive and opportunity; Christian Verholt possessed all of these. He was confident that fashion could be profitable, but he was also confident that crime could provide unrivalled excitement. His money had saved a small financially struggling business and had allowed the passions of the designers to be created by the workforce. He had installed Olivia as the salon manageress. She could be charming when needed and like Coco Chanel had a background as a modiste or milliner.

The Maison d'Elégance was a fitting title for the Parisian Fashion House. Like many houses in France, the business existed behind a simple plain façade which contributed to the contrast of the rich and welcoming interior. Stepping into the small hallway, visitors' eyes were immediately drawn to the magnificent sweeping staircase of stone, marble and intricately designed sinuous curves of wrought iron, which instinctively promised grandeur.

Emily could hear voices from within one of the rooms on the first floor. Remaining still at the top of the staircase, her heart began to beat quickly as she suddenly recognised the familiar voice. A door opened and a woman emerged wearing a tailleur or tailored suit of matching jacket and skirt. Her hair had been cut short in the new fashionable but slightly radical bobbed style, but Emily recognised her instantly.

'Hello Olivia.' Both the greeting and her appearance made Olivia stand and stare at Emily with amazement.

'Emily. What are you doing here?'

'I have come to see you. Olivia, we need to talk.' From deep within Emily had managed to summon up sufficient courage to present unified strength of both her actions and conversation. Usually Olivia was a flippant, overbearing individual but the unexpected presence of her sister had had a calming effect. Coupled with this was the fact that Olivia was now very different; her appearance gave the impression of a professional and seemingly sensible woman. Verholt had obviously had a great influence upon her. Never having properly met him, other than incognito on the Lusitania, Emily wondered how manipulative and cunning he really was.

Olivia led her sister into a room which was furnished with antique-looking furniture, including plush upholstered chairs which reminded Emily of Suffolk Hall, the family home of the Verholts on Long Island. As she sank down into the richness of the thick velvet-covered chair, she little doubted that everything was authentic but wondered whether they had been legitimately bought or just stolen. The thought made her slightly shudder.

Olivia, who had left Emily for a short while, returned with coffee which she proceeded to pour out into small cups before handing one of these to Emily.

'You look well, Olivia.'

'I am, thank you. What about yourself and our parents?' This was the question which Emily had been dreading. The only option was to tell Olivia the truth, however difficult it proved to be. Tears moistened her eyes before being stoically wiped away.

'How is Mother?'

'As you would expect. In fact she is not well herself and wishes to see you.'

'It is impossible for me to come home at the moment. Augustus relies on me so. He has been very good to me. I cannot just leave him when there is so much to do.'

'Even though mother needs you?'

'You don't understand, Emily. There is a very important function next week at which I am expected to be present. Marie Philippe is an influential customer here and regularly provides us with large commissions. Her husband is a most important French industrialist and Augustus will have the opportunity to become acquainted with him, which of course could prove favourable to him in business terms. Following that, I will return home. Surely another week will not make any difference? You do understand Emily, don't you?'

'Of course I do.' Emily fully understood the situation; influential and wealthy necessitated luxuries. She was left in little doubt that there would soon be another burglary but she had not realised just how influential and wealthy the Philippes were.

As Emily left the Maison d'Elégance, she was relieved that she had at last located Olivia and that they would both be travelling home together within the following week. She had agreed to meet her sister for lunch the next day but she knew that night she would be having dinner with Niall. The very notion made her smile with happiness and, for the first time since arriving in Paris, she felt relaxed and content; everything was going well and it seemed that there was nothing which could possibly spoil her pleasure.

They had agreed to meet at a small café not far from her hotel. She had taken time and care to ensure that she looked her best for him. She waited eagerly for Niall to appear and, when he did, her excitement quickly soured into disappointment; alongside him was Sam Jackson.

The momentary silence communicated the disenchantment of the meeting. As Niall's eyes threw a penetratingly sorrowful request for forgiveness across to Emily, Jackson was the first one to speak.

'Don't blame *him,* lady. It was me who invited myself here tonight.' A look of mutual understanding was exchanged between Niall and Emily before Jackson continued.

'I needed to speak with you both. In fact, we needed to get together to pool our information. There's something big about to happen and we have to be ready if we're going to catch them.'

'Why do Niall and I have to be involved? I have found Olivia and I might add she is doing very well for herself. Perhaps Paris has been the making of her.' Emily appeared almost smug in her revelation.

'It may have been the making of her, but like the French Revolution it could be her downfall,' Jackson added before turning his attention to Niall. '… and of course, let's not forget Kerry. She'll never let you forget her. That you can bank on. Turn your back on her once and you'll never do it again. Mark my words.'

Niall initially refrained from speaking; his silence merely compounded the testament of the Doyle family reputation. His eyes stared hard at the inspector before casting their attention upon Emily. Then they appeared to mellow with compassion and suddenly a decision had been reached.

'Very well Jackson, what do you propose? I take it that you have a plan of action for all of us?' As Niall spoke there was more than just a hint of reconciliation in his voice which seemed to make the inspector gleefully animated.

'We have every chance of wrapping this up within the week. You cannot imagine what that means to me,' Jackson chuckled.

Only Emily fully appreciated that success would finalise his life's work and bring to an end the vendetta which had caused so much unhappiness in Jackson's life. It would, in his eyes, be some compensation for the hurt and humiliation his family had experienced. More than anything, it would avenge the suffering of his mother. That in itself was sufficient motivation for Jackson, who was now eager to explain what he wanted each of them to do.

Chapter Twenty-Nine

Both Niall and Emily were instrumental in Jackson's plans. Each knew what was expected of them and had agreed to be compliant. Niall had recently become close to his sister and needed to build upon this bond of trust if he was going to obtain useful information. Kerry was someone who had to be treated with care; one ounce of suspicion on her part would be detrimental to the operation, if not fatal. Emily's task involved becoming acquainted with Olivia's wealthy customer, Madame Marie Philippe and of course her French industrialist husband, Alphonse. By so doing, Emily acknowledged that she would at last meet Augustus Cassel, or rather Christian Verholt.

As agreed, the sisters met the following day and enjoyed a light lunch together. The change in Olivia was remarkable; she appeared to acquiesce to any proposal put before her. Emily enthused with interest as her sister spoke of her work and of the many wealthy clients who provided regular commissions. Perhaps without realising, Olivia's conversation became centred upon the Philippes. The more she spoke of them, the more interest Emily showed and as the wine flowed freely, the more Olivia divulged.

'Of course Alphonse is the businessman, but Marie is actually related way back in history to the Habsburgs; the Austrian family of Marie Antoinette. Her lineage can be traced back to both the Emperor Leopold I as well as Mary Queen of Scots. As you know, Emily, I was never one much for History at school but I find this truly overwhelming. But this is the best bit; the Philippes are hosting a ball next week at their magnificent home to celebrate a special birthday for Marie and I have been invited to attend with Augustus.

The theme is Versailles and the Fashion House has been busy for months producing all the costumes. Can you imagine what it will be like? Oh Emily, I wish you could be there to see it all. I know it is going to be an unforgettable evening.'

Emily smiled and nodded in agreement. She too knew that it would be an unforgettable evening. She also knew that her presence there had to be secured.

Over the course of the next two days, Emily eagerly accepted Olivia's invitation to visit the Maison d'Elégance and witness for herself the artistry employed in the creation of the lavish costumes. Marie Philippe had commissioned numerous costumes for her family and friends and had generously spread the word of the firm's fine reputation to anyone else who had been fortunate enough to receive an invitation to her fiftieth birthday celebrations. As a consequence, the fashion house had been overwhelmed with orders.

The costumes were made in homage to a Queen who upon accession had abstained from wearing unfashionable heavy styles of dress accompanied by thick rouge and stiff curls. Instead, Marie Antoinette had endorsed the talents of Rose Bertin, a leading Parisian couturière of the time, to showcase the provocative robe à la polonaise; a gown which relied upon a bosom-enhancing bodice and a cutaway, draped and swagged overskirt, which was worn over an underskirt or petticoat. To complete the style the head needed to be crowned by a pouf, or elaborate mountain of powdered hair, which was then decorated with veils and plumes and other obscure items.

As the ball was to be held in honour of Marie Philippe, she had been keen to remain faithful in style to her illustrious ancestor and had selected to wear the robe à la polonaise. Some guests had selected the robe à la française or sack-back gown, which featured back pleats that hung loosely from the neckline with a fitted bodice which held the front of the gown closely to the figure.

Amidst such plethora of attention to detail of hooped skirts, side-hoops or panniers, decorative stomachers, and scalloped ruffles and frills adorning necklines and sleeves, there was an immense display of talent of which the Maison d'Elégance could justly be proud. Emily's eyes were bedazzled by both the opulent designs and elaborate fabrics and she soon realised the mastery of the workforce at the fashion house. She also understood why Marie Philippe had taken her custom there.

Historians had often written that Marie Antoinette was not a true beauty; this was in part attributable to her inheritance of the renowned Habsburg jaw, the disdainful Habsburg look and the possession of an aquiline nose. However, she was reputedly an enchantress who could beguile those around her by her own charm and style. Marie Philippe, although not a direct descendent of the last queen of France, bore certain similarities with her. She arrived unexpectedly one morning at the Fashion House with further orders. Her social prominence was sufficient to ensure that any requests would be granted without question. Emily had never before witnessed her sister using such sycophantic adjectives; the strange thing was that the more they were used, the less notice Marie gave to Olivia. Her attention was now focussed upon the stranger in the corner. She appeared to almost glide across the room to Emily, before standing still in front of her. The awkward silence was quickly broken as a warm smile spread across Marie's face.

'Olivia, I believe this lady is your sister, am I correct?'

'Yes, this is Emily,' came the reply.

'Well Emily, it is good that I meet you. Olivia has spoken a great deal about you.'

'Thank you. It is very good to meet you. I know that you are very busy at the moment.'

'Yes, of course, the ball. My husband spoils me. It will be like no other. In fact it will be as it was in the past… before the revolution, of course! Well, Emily, it has been good to meet you.' As she turned to walk away she seemed to hesitate. '…If you would also like to come I am sure that Olivia could get you a costume. You could bring a partner with you, if there is someone.'

'Thank you, that is very kind.'

Following Marie's departure Emily witnessed her sister shrugging her shoulders and raising her hands with abiding submission.

'I don't suppose one more costume will make any difference. However one thing is certain, *you* will not be bringing a partner with you.'

Emily merely smiled at Olivia and wondered how she would eventually react to the whole truth.

The home of a wealthy industrialist, whose wife was related however tenuously to Marie Antoinette, promised to deliver certain expectations. Emily was left in little doubt as they turned through the open country gates, and followed a formal, linear avenue of mature plane trees that the Philippes were seriously wealthy. If further evidence was needed the emergence of the grand eighteenth century building was statement enough. Built over four storeys, the smaller attic windows peering down from the roof with watchful speculation, the house personified elegance and charm rather like its mistress. Situated on the outskirts of Paris to the south west, its position was close enough for business but conveniently sited for indulgent privacy.

As the taxi, a twin-cylinder Renault, came to a halt, Emily waited for her companions to make the first move. Throughout the journey little conversation had occurred between the three of them. Emily and Olivia were almost unrecognisable, not least in their sack-back gowns adorned with frills and ruffles, but also as they were wearing less subtle make-up than normal and in fashion with the period, their heads were each covered with an ostentatious powdered wig. Christian Verholt, or indeed Augustus Cassel, was sitting between the sisters in equally fine period dress of jacket, waistcoat and breeches with an accompanying wig. The blond hair may have been concealed, but the young handsome face was merely enhanced by the sartorial elegance. The man definitely possessed charm; upon being introduced to Emily that evening he had taken her right hand and planted a light kiss upon it before graciously bowing to her without showing any hint of recognition. Presumably the costume, wig and make-up had provided sufficient disguise for Emily. The whole effect had been theatrical as they were all in period dress, but the man certainly had charisma. He also had wealth and no need to dabble with chance and crime; that of course was what made the thrill compelling for him.

A steady queue of taxis and horse-drawn carriages made their way to the torch-lit entrance. Hired servants in red and gold liveried uniform, their heads adorned with small neat wigs, stepped forward and opened the doors of the respective carriage or automobile. Emily found the entire experience surreal as she entered the grand entrance hall and heard her name along with Olivia's and Augustus Cassel's being called out as they were formally introduced to the Philippes. Each guest performed the expected formality of bowing or curtseying before entering a large elongated room, where waiters deftly offered drinks from large silver salvers as a small orchestra played chamber music from Piccinni and Mozart.

The setting was magnificent; the walls, lined in eighteenth century wood panelling displayed numerous oil paintings, ornately carved gilded framed mirrors as well as proudly boasting two considerably large ornamental marble fireplaces. Five large crystal chandeliers twinkled with iridescence, hanging majestically from a richly moulded ceiling. Two sets of double doors, one at either end of the long gallery, were further enhanced by large dominant Corinthian columns. The setting was such that the guests could easily have been transported back to a little more than a century earlier; to Versailles and the court of Louis XVI.

However, daydreaming had to be stringently avoided; Emily needed to be vigilant as her powers of observation would soon be put to the test. It was not long before the Philippes began to mingle with their guests; nor was it long before Marie became captivated with Augustus. She eagerly introduced him to her husband who made polite conversation before leaving to attend to his other guests.

Alphonse Philippe was a deep and diverse individual, well-known for his shrewd business dealings; his reputation was of a man who would not suffer fools gladly. According to Marie, he was a French industrialist whose wealth had enabled him to become a respected, avid art collector. In his youth he had travelled extensively; initially to North America and Canada and later to South America. Whilst in Bolivia and Peru he had explored the mineral mining regions and had spent considerable time in Chile and at the passes between Santiago and Buenos Aires. Those experiences had enabled him to return home to France with extensive botanical, geological and zoological collections. He was also a very keen photographer, having taken pictures of his travels and the people that he had encountered. It appeared that his travels had incited an interest of mankind, perhaps a philanthropic spirit. They had of course made him seriously rich as a result of locating minerals that his industrial business now relied upon. The rewards of that wealth were openly displayed throughout the house and hung around Marie's neck, adorned her fingers and dripped from her ears. The diamond and pearl necklace and earrings that she was wearing were a birthday present from her husband. Having once belonged to Marie Antoinette, their value was inestimable to the onlooker. Emily could easily understand why the Philippes were of interest to Augustus. She just wondered when and where his accomplice, Kerry, would make her debut.

Augustus continued to charm his hostess throughout the evening. She positively glowed with the succession of compliments which fell from his lips, having few linguistic problems with the soft American accent which appeared neither to confuse nor detract in any way. Together they conversed, laughed, danced and consumed food and drink; always in one another's company. Emily suddenly realised that whatever was going to happen was imminent or actually occurring as she watched them together; Marie would be his perfect alibi.

Throughout the evening the Philippe's residence positively resounded with laughter, gaiety and music. Whilst the orchestra continued to play into the small hours of the morning the proliferation of dancers began to dwindle as the consumption of alcohol and tiredness both took effect. The artistic masterpieces around the walls looked down knowingly as if conceding that they had witnessed such scenes numerous times before. Emily was beginning to wonder which would be the designated pieces when Olivia, who had previously abandoned her sister to drink and dancing, approached her anxiously. The effects of the alcohol were quite evident as she began to teeter unsteadily upon her feet having previously bumped into Marie, causing her glass to spill its contents; she was now slurring her words.

'I can...not find Augustus. He seems to have dis...appeared. Have you seen him Em...ily?'

Emily knew precisely where Augustus was; Marie was giving him a tour of the house and showing him the priceless antiques. What was unusual was that his initial reaction to the invitation of the tour had been one of disinterest. He had been happy to admire her diamond and pearl necklace and earrings along with their distinguished provenance but had seemed disinclined to view the celebrated art collections around the house. When they returned he appeared anxious and confused; the antithesis of his earlier charms.

Emily realised that not everything was going to plan. He had not wished to appear too keen to view the treasures and thereby run the risk of being implicated in a planned burglary. That was why he had pretended not to be interested in the very items that he craved to possess. However something was wrong and only Emily could sense it. As they finally took their leave of the Philippe's residence, Emily could not fail to notice that Augustus's face wore a look of disbelief. He sat in the car with his head turned; his eyes continuing to stare in the direction of the house long after it had vanished from view. It was as though his master plan had failed to materialise. It was obvious that his associate Kerry had failed to appear. No crime had taken place and that was the problem.

The repeated tapping upon her door disturbed Emily's slumber. As she opened her eyes she recalled that she had not long been in bed but the sunlight streaming into her room though the open chink of the curtains declared that morning had broken. The knocking upon her door continued; it seemed to have a quiet but determined resonance about it. Wrapping a dressing-gown around her, she unlocked the door and opened it, peering out with caution.

'Niall!' It was the only word that Emily could manage to voice. He followed as she stepped back into the room, quietly closing the door behind them. They embraced and kissed before his arms held her closely to him for some time.

'Emily, I want you to listen to me. You and Olivia must leave. It is no longer safe for you to stay here.'

'Why? What has happened?'

'The Philippe's residence was burgled in the early hours of this morning.'

'What was taken?'

'Jewellery and some papers.'

'No works of art? Monsieur Philippe is a wealthy art collector.' Emily was about to mention the paintings that she had seen when the serious look upon her husband's face stopped her.

'This was not a theft of art; it was an act of reprisal. Marie Philippe had her throat cut.'

'She is dead?' Emily found it incredulous to believe.

'Yes, she is dead. She had opened the safe, removed her jewellery and was about to lock everything away when she was disturbed.'

'Your sister could not have done that. It must have been someone…'

'Someone else? No it was Kerry. She can be insanely jealous. She had been in the house all night. She was one of the hired servants and had witnessed Marie's fascination with Verholt. She is in love with him and that is the problem. He doesn't love her; he merely uses her. Therefore, she is out to destroy him, along with the likes of Jackson.'

'Niall, why can't we all leave together, Olivia, you and I? We can go home and let the authorities, including Jackson, sort this out.'

'I'm afraid I cannot. It is a little more complicated than that. The real purpose of the burglary was not the jewellery or works of art but the papers.'

'Papers?'

'This time Kerry was working for herself. Alphonse Philippe's safe housed something more important in it than just jewellery. It held details of something dangerous and deadly: chemical weapons. Alphonse Philippe has been employing industrial chemists to develop deadly substances which the French Government could use as deterrents or, if the need arose, for warfare. Politically, he is of great importance to the French Government and no doubt agents will be rapidly deployed to ensure that those papers do not fall into the wrong hands. Kerry now has those papers in her possession and the authorities will need someone close to her whom she can trust. That has to be me.'

'This all sounds incredibly dangerous, Niall. What will Kerry do with these papers?'

'No doubt, sell them to the highest bidder. There has and always will be civil unrest and wars. At the moment we are living in unsettled times, Emily, which I think will only become worse. The Balkan wars, the Irish demonstrations against Home Rule and even the worry here in France, as well as at home in England that Germany is becoming too powerful a nation. Life is changing and perhaps not for the better.' Niall's face looked serious and worried; so unlike his usual guise.

'I'll do whatever you want me to do,' Emily said softly but reassuringly.

'Good. Firstly, I need to ensure that you and Olivia are safe. We must hurry. Olivia could be in danger from Kerry. Then, I need to find somewhere safe for you to stay; perhaps for a day or so, until your travelling arrangements can be made. I don't know where to suggest, though.'

'I do.' Emily's instantaneous control of the situation surprised Niall. He fell silent and gazed at her with pride.

'Oh, you do, do you?' Fleetingly the Irish eyes twinkled with a smile.

'Yes. I know of somewhere that we will be safe and there will be no questions asked.'

They kissed briefly and then more passionately; neither one knowing when they would have the opportunity to do so again.

Chapter Thirty

Emily had never visited Olivia's apartment before, but she had remembered that her sister had laughingly joked how she was awakened each morning by the enticing smell of freshly baked bread which wafted continually upwards into her rooms from the bakehouse below. In order to satisfy the French ritual of buying fresh-baked bread, the bakehouse had its own boulangerie which opened directly onto the street. This street was located only two blocks away from the Maison d'Elégance and although it was still early morning, the daily queue was already forming outside the master baker's shop.

Emily and Niall gave instructions to the taxi driver to wait for them, whilst they disappeared from view through an old wooden street door. At the top of the staircase they knocked quietly on the door. Moments passed before they detected any stirring within but eventually they recognised Olivia's voice. The opening of the door allowed a crevice of light to penetrate into the room, whilst Olivia's pale face stared back, her weary eyes trying to fight a severe headache.

'What time is it?' Olivia asked, holding her hands to her forehead.

Emily quickly realised that the task ahead of them was not going to be an easy one.

'Time to get dressed and leave,' Emily said in a commanding manner.

'But I feel sick.' Suddenly beginning to retch, Olivia compliantly allowed the guiding arm to propel her to the washstand, where she proceeded to be violently sick into the basin.

Later she sank down into a chair, exhausted and shivering. It was only then that she recognised Niall.

'Oh God, am I so ill that I need a doctor? I know that I feel that I want to die but...' Olivia hesitated, looking first at Niall and then at her sister.

'What is it? What has happened? Why is he here? It's mother isn't it? I am being punished for all my wickedness. Please say she's not dead. Oh God please not that. I promise I will repent...' Olivia's ramblings continued for some time until she realised that Emily was beginning to quickly pack her case.

'I know that I promised you that I would return home to see Mother after the Philippes' ball, but do we really have to leave just now? I feel absolutely dreadful. Surely one more day cannot make any difference?' Olivia also looked dreadful but Emily and Niall understood that even one more hour could be detrimental.

Time was undoubtedly of the essence as they bundled Olivia into the waiting taxi, before accompanying her on the journey. They ignored her initial protestations of harassment and the indignity of not being allowed time to dress. As the journey continued, Olivia fell asleep and when she awoke she found herself being carried by Niall towards a house that she did not recognise; a large and imposing house with shutters at the windows. The front door was already opened; standing next to Emily was a young maid and a gentile-looking elderly lady. As they approached the door the latter stepped forward and ran her hand softly across Olivia's forehead.

'The poor girl! Please follow Yvette. She will show you to Olivia's room.'

The bedroom was light and airy and a faint breeze outside was gently causing the window netting to sway gracefully against the open windows. The bedding had a fresh smell, reminiscent of a sun-filled garden where the scent of orange-blossom fills the air. Left alone Olivia closed her eyes and relaxed into the soft bedding. Very soon she had drifted into sleep and later when she opened her eyes, both Niall and the taxi had gone.

There were many questions which required answers but with more answers came further questions. Olivia's head began to pound with disbelief at the revelations of the previous night.

'You are mistaken Emily. Augustus is a respectable businessman. He has no need to become involved in crime.'

'Indeed, nor has he as Christian Verholt, heir to one of the wealthiest banking dynasties in the United States. But that is the point, Olivia. He lives for the thrill of it. He uses people just as he has used you.'

'No, you are wrong. For the first time in my life I have met a man who sees potential in me and has given me the chance to prove it.' Emily looked at her sister and realised that the sentiment was true however bitter the pill was to swallow.

'I do agree Olivia but what I have not yet disclosed is that the man is linked not just to burglary but also to murder; Marie Philippe was discovered in the early hours with her throat cut.'

The colour completely drained from Olivia's face as she fainted, falling backwards into the pillows. As Emily began to revive her sister, she knew that further disclosures would need to wait.

Françoise Morel was enjoying the late-afternoon sunshine, wandering amongst the colourful array of pastel and vivid hues which spilled out from the profusion of blooms in her garden. At first Emily drew back; reluctant to disturb Françoise's tranquil musings. A wave signified that she had spotted Emily and intimated for her to join her.

'How is Olivia?'

'She is progressing. Thank you. She has managed some soup and bread and is resting.'

'Bon. I am pleased.' Françoise turned and looked tenderly at Emily, examining her face carefully. 'How are you, Emily?'

'I'm fine. Thank you for allowing us to stay here it is so good …' Françoise immediately interrupted her guest.

'Shush… It is nothing. You and Olivia are welcome to stay here as long as you want. I will ask no questions of you. Come let us walk and enjoy the garden.'

They meandered around the carefully tended garden; Françoise stopping occasionally to stoop down and gently caress a delicate looking flower.

'I have always loved the colours of nature, Emily. I remember my childhood in Provence: the rich golden rows of vineyards in late summer; the sun-baked hills with fields of sunflowers; the image of an old olive tree standing alone in a field of lavender; the smells; the sights - they were just unforgettable. I remember my first love when I look at this flower.' Françoise stopped by a large cluster of marguerites and picked one of the flowers. She began to smile, pulling off the petals one by one whilst saying, 'Je t'aime un peu, beaucoup, passionnément, à la folie... pas du tout.' She stopped and smiled at Emily before continuing, this time in English: 'He loves me, he loves me not, he loves me.' Silence fell as the two women looked at one another; Françoise's eyes clearly showing seniority and depth of wisdom.

'I have seen much in life; love, hate, passion and regret. I know about life. I know about love. I know that you and Niall love each other deeply. Believe in him and trust him. Let him do whatever he has to do. He will come back to you. Never doubt that.'

Françoise seemed to glide away silently, withdrawing into the house leaving her companion alone. Emily remained in the garden for some time, contemplating the conversation. She had failed to realise how discerning a person Françoise Morel was; a woman who had no need to ask questions because she already knew the answers.

By the following morning, Olivia's health appeared to have improved. Although she had consumed a great deal of alcohol at the Philippes and had been drunk, she had never been a practitioner of the Methodist faith, unlike her parents, and was thereby used to the effects of alcohol and the associated hangovers. This time, the symptoms had been totally different to any that she had previously experienced; it was as though her drink had been laced with something. Being of a normally strong constitution, she merely shrugged her shoulders and inferred that Emily was being melodramatic in her suggestions. However, later when Françoise translated the headlines from a Parisian newspaper, she was not so dismissive.

"Two buildings were broken into yesterday in the centre of Paris. One was the Maison d'Elégance, an esteemed Parisian Fashion house. The other, a bakehouse and boulangerie, with apartments above. Both were set on fire and destroyed. It is believed that no one was hurt." Françoise sighed as she put the newspaper down. 'There are terrible things happening. First the murder of Madam Philippe in her own home. Now this.' She looked at Olivia whose pale complexion had turned even paler. 'I am sorry. The news is shocking, n'est pas?'

Olivia nodded in agreement. 'There are no words to describe it.'

Chapter Thirty-One

Jackson was beginning to tire of Paris. For him there was and never had been any romance in the world. He strode past the elegant architecture, failing to be moved by the sense of history which pervaded its streets and squares. The only slight interest to him was when he overheard some excited tourists at a nearby table, talking about the Terror. He listened intently as they sensationalised their guide's information. The executions of the French king, Louis XVI and his queen, Marie Antoinette in 1793, had triggered a gruesome period of French history referred to as the Terror. Thousands of royalists and anti-revolutionaries had been executed at the guillotine; its heavy, sharp blade dropping between the two upright posts, beheading the prisoner to the delight of the watching crowd. The image of people enjoying such a spectacle did not repulse Jackson; it simply made him smile.

The thought made him consider Marie Philippe's murder. Having her throat cut, although grisly was no worse than some of the crimes he had seen committed by the infamous tongs, groups of racketeers in New York. However he now understood how dangerous Kerry Doyle was. For someone who was connected to Marie Antoinette to die from having their throat cut seemed to Jackson to hint of subliminal pertinence. The audacious act had stemmed no doubt from momentary necessity rather than planned execution. In his eyes the girl was definitely gutsy; given another life and gender she would have been tough enough to have become a policeman like himself.

On the night of the Philippes' ball, Jackson had managed to hide in the grounds of the mansion. He had witnessed Kerry arriving earlier in the afternoon, along with other hired servants. His powers of surveillance were inscrutable, having arisen from years of experience. He witnessed Verholt and his female companions arrive and then depart later in the early hours of the following morning. Unfortunately Verholt had failed to return and Jackson therefore could not link him with the murder. Damn the man! Once again Jackson was unable to disgrace and implicate him in the crime.

He so hated the sound of the Verholt name. But for them Jackson and his family would have had a very different life. He remembered his mother and how he had admired her; she had instilled discipline and morality and had taught him right from wrong. Samuel Jackson had respected and loved her and as a young policeman had endeavoured to put those fine principles into practice.

Louisa Jackson had been born a proud woman and following her husband's suicide she had been self-sufficient, enduring long painful hours of cleaning and sewing to take care of her son. When no longer a boy but a young man, Sam had tried to look after his mother financially but her pride had always intervened.

He recalled that night when he had opened her door and stepped inside her meagrely-furnished apartment. He had called out her name but there had been no reply, only noises, groaning sounds which surprisingly were coming from the bedroom. He caught them in the loveless act; a money-making arrangement which allowed his mother to survive. The man, a nameless foreign sailor, quickly fled wishing to remain anonymous, taking care not to look at Jackson who had recoiled in disgust into a corner.

He remembered very little from that moment, except for the sensation of his large chubby hands closing in on her thin neck. She had offered no resistance, resigned to her fate; her eyes looming large as she stared at her son choking the life from her. He believed he had the unquestionable right to punish her, for it had been she who had taught him right from wrong.

He left quickly, taking care not to be seen; the neighbours had frequently witnessed male strangers entering and leaving Louisa's apartment; young, old, drunk, aggressive; any one of them would have fit the profile for an unknown killer. The case was never solved and, although Jackson's associates pitied the man whose mother had been so callously murdered, they also admitted that his steady rise of rank in the police force would at least have made his mother proud of him.

In Jackson's eyes the Verholt dynasty had been responsible for everything that had happened. But for them Jackson and his family would have had a very different life. They were the cause of all Jackson's problems and they needed to be punished.

Jackson's skills were manifold; having always been highly observant and analytical, he had a reputation for gathering crucial evidence. If the groundwork was done, a conviction would easily follow; except in this case. It reminded him of an onion with infinite layers; just when he felt that he could incriminate Verholt, the fellow evaded implication as further factors were revealed. This time Sam Jackson was fully prepared.

He had spent his time gathering information on the key players: Verholt, Kerry Doyle and Alphonse Philippe. His interest in the latter arose as soon as he heard that Verholt was going to a party at his residence. Further enquiries revealed that Alphonse Philippe had influential friends in the French Government who had commissioned him to develop powerful chemical agents involving the use of chlorine and phosgene; pulmonary, lachrymatory and vesicant ones. These were substances which would irritate the respiratory tract, causing coughing and choking; affect the corneal nerves in the eyes causing tears, pain and blindness; and produce chemical burns resulting in painful water blisters on the skin. Such agents were designed to injure and incapacitate the enemy as well as restrict the use of specific areas of terrain. Nations in possession of such deadly substances would hold a position of control if the threat of war arose. More alarmingly they were also strategic tools for nations planning an invasion. Jackson and Niall both understood the dangers associated with them falling into the wrong hands.

The whole affair was layered with infinite danger. To Jackson's mind it was definitely like an onion; peel away one problem and reveal more impenetrable ones enclosing the heart of the trouble. The nearer one came to a solution, the more complex and difficult it became. Jackson's prime motive was to disgrace the Verholt name and attain retribution. However, the magnitude of potential risk which threatened unassuming communities could not be ignored. People's lives could be in danger and for that particular reason, for the sake of humanity, Jackson decided that he would stay close to Niall and Kerry and for once forget about Verholt. And, anyway, the fellow had simply disappeared from Paris.

Jackson's prime motive now was to tail Kerry and those papers which contained the chemical formulae; she was definitely a loose cannon who needed to be kept under control. Hopefully, between them, Niall and Jackson would do just that.

Chapter Thirty-Two

The return train journey was exceeding slow and tiring, even though Emily was accompanied by her sister. Olivia, however, had still not regained her full health; she continued to complain of headaches and appeared to be confused, forgetful, disorientated and drowsy. At times she suffered from throbbing pains in her legs and feet which, made it difficult to walk more than short distances without stumbling. She gave the impression that she was drunk, which Emily knew that she was not. As she fell asleep once more, Emily watched her with concern and wished that Niall was with them. He would have diagnosed the problem and treated her accordingly. However, Emily understood that he needed to remain in France.

The French countryside was stunningly beautiful as it continued to unfurl with incessant attractions; the steam train trundled through fields of newly-turned furrows where the riches of the earth lay exposed in their resplendent shades of brown and ochre, but Emily saw none of it as she thought of her husband. She did not know of his whereabouts or indeed when she would next see him. She anxiously recalled the words of the medium: 'Your husband is in danger.' Tears began to well in her eyes before trickling down her cheeks. She was unaware that Olivia had opened her eyes and had been watching her for some time.

'Why are you crying?' came the inevitable question.

'I don't know,' Emily tried unconvincingly to make light of the situation.

'Those were tears not just of sadness, but of fear.' The sentence astonished Emily; not just because of Olivia's weakened state of health but because it was the most perceptive and profound statement that her sister had ever made.

'There is nothing to concern us now. We are safe and you need to rest.'

Olivia nodded her head in agreement. 'Very well. I am so tired Emily. I wish we were home.' Emily reached across and gripped her sister's limp hand which failed to respond.

'We soon will be. I promise.' Before she had finished the sentence Olivia's heavy-looking eyes had closed and this time she had fallen asleep.

The two women continued to be the sole occupants of their train compartment whilst travelling between Paris and Dieppe. Olivia was asleep for the majority of the journey and Emily contented herself with her thoughts. There was a great deal to think about, not least her worries regarding Niall's safety and Olivia's health. On reflection, Emily now wondered if it would have been more prudent to have remained at Montmartre, but the severity of Olivia's symptoms varied from day to day and she knew that once they reached Beckston, Doctor Lawson would then diagnose and treat her sister. The problem was that Emily had never witnessed symptoms such as these and she was anxious about Olivia. If anything were to happen to her, Emily would definitely hold herself responsible. She repeatedly questioned over and over in her mind why they had left the safe and secure surroundings of Françoise Morel's house; only to find the same answer; they needed to escape from the dangers of being associated with the Philippes.

Françoise Morel's home had been a haven of safety and tranquillity, but the security could have been breached at any time, especially by powerful government agents and, of course, by Kerry Doyle. Such thoughts made Emily shudder. They were also endangering the lives of Françoise and her maid whilst remaining there. This quiet, gentle and dignified lady had already done enough for them. She had kept her promise and had asked no questions. However, just before they left Montmartre, she asked a request of Emily.

'You are a good friend of Amelia's, n'est pas?'

'Yes, as I told you we first met aboard the Lusitania when we travelled to America. Amelia was very kind to me and invited me to stay with her and her family whilst I was in New York.'

'Yes, yes I can understand that. She was always very kind to people. I know that from experience. Emily, do you plan to see her again?' Françoise's question slightly unnerved Emily.

'I very much would like to, but I cannot specify when. Our mother is not well and I need to think about getting Olivia home safely.' The ensuing silence pre-empted Emily to continue. Her inner thoughts voluntarily tumbled from her lips. 'Yes, I do intend to see her and will travel to America again to do so. Meeting Amelia has changed my life. I have become a different person since meeting her.'

'Yes, that is very true. She has an effect upon people. Emily will you take this little box and letter to her please? They once belonged to her, but she left them with me, a long time ago. Please give them to her. She will understand.'

As the train rattled along the tracks, Emily looked down at the small box in her hands. She had already taken the liberty of looking inside and had not been disappointed. The pendant was like no other that she had seen. Hanging from the gold chain was a jewel which possessed all the indicative premiums of its ilk; colour, clarity, cut and carat; it was simply the largest diamond that Emily had ever seen and one which seemed to radiate wealth. Initially, she had been shocked by the discovery of it in her possession but her mind had begun to question how such a piece could have belonged to Amelia. Then, she recalled those tales of Dukes and Sultans and began to wonder if there had been an element of truth in the tales. The letter was a different matter. As much as she would have liked to have opened it and read its contents, she resisted doing so. The letter had never been opened and the envelope simply had the name 'Amelia' written on it.

As Beckston came slowly into view, Emily had never been so glad as to return there. The entire journey had been arduous and fraught with worry and the continuous change of trains and boat travel had merely prolonged the hope of reaching their final destination. There had been times when she had looked across at Olivia only to wonder whether she would survive the journey.

Two familiar faces provided welcome relief as Emily and Olivia stepped onto the platform at Beckston station; Emily had sent an earlier telegram home indicating their planned arrival. The initial happy smiles vanished quickly as a languid-looking Olivia peered at George and Alice, seemingly with no recognition before stumbling feebly into their arms. Now was not the time for niceties and light conversation as they quickly bundled both passengers and luggage into the ever trusty Tin-Lizzie and Alice drove home with as much speed as was possible; George and Alice then promptly disappeared and returned with immediate help.

Doctor Lawson's diagnosis was a shock to everyone except Emily, who began to understand both the motive and means of such a malicious injury. Arsenic poisoning had been a popular murder weapon in the Middle Ages and during the Renaissance, especially within the ruling circles of the Italian nobility, and during the nineteenth century it had earned itself the name of inheritance powder as a means for impatient heirs to attain their inheritance. It was a weapon which could be used stealthily to remove anyone who was a threat. Olivia's working relationship with Augustus Cassel, or rather Verholt, had obviously intensified Kerry's jealousy. Emily realised that it would have been easy for her to have administered the poison by adding it to Olivia's glass before serving her at the Philippe Ball. The thought made Emily realise how fortunate Olivia had been, but it also compounded her fears for Niall's safety. Kerry Doyle was a scheming and manipulative woman, who did not necessarily remain faithful to those she was close to. Love and hatred could blur and intertwine easily in her mind, making revenge justifiable. Niall was unquestionably in danger but Emily knew she had to keep such worries to herself. She now had to dually personify both strength and courage for the sake of her mother and sister.

Doctor Lawson completely emptied Olivia's stomach with an emetic and stomach-syphon before administering freshly prepared ferric oxyhydrate. He then insisted that his patient should be fed on nothing more than milk and a farinaceous diet rich in starchy foods. The draconian measures eventually led to an improvement in Olivia's health and she slowly began to recover. As she did so, her mother's health also improved and the migraines seemed to become less frequent.

As the weeks passed, the Taylor household began to regain a degree of normality, at least to the eyes of the outside world. Emily returned to the daily demands of the school-room, whilst Alice continued to dutifully undertake her domestic chores with nothing less than cheerfulness. The reason for such alacrity lay with the attention George continued to pay her. Their relationship had blossomed and it was now common knowledge that they were stepping-out together. Even the reappearance of Olivia had not dulled their happiness; in fact, merely the reverse. Olivia's recovery had witnessed a new woman in every sense of the word. Where previously there had been malevolence, now there was kindness and contentment. The rebellious daughter had returned tractable and ready for social convention. Perhaps the nearness of death had finally left its indelible mark upon the soul of the near departed. No one knew for certain but everyone agreed that the transformation was a welcome improvement; none more so than Emily.

It definitely seemed that change was looming in the air. Emily recalled how Niall had said that life was changing. He had also said that these were unsettled times which could become worse. As 1914 was heralded in, few could have foreseen the devastating changes and irreversible consequences which the world would have to endure.

Chapter Thirty-Three

For many, the future had long been shadowed in doubt, appearing eerily opaque rather than aglow with transparent promise. A fear of the unknown was beginning to send shivers down the backs of those who had long upheld the established traditions of the status quo. Challenges and tensions were already visibly bubbling to the surface as the suffragettes accelerated their campaigning for the female vote with increasingly violent militant action. Social unrest, rioting and strikes were spreading as miners, dockers and millworkers battled for their rights. The siege of Sidney Street in London had only exacerbated the menacing violence as anarchists had fired back at the police, whilst in Ireland civil war seemed inevitable as the determination for home rule markedly intensified. Life was definitely changing but it was not solely confined to just Great Britain and Ireland.

Since the 1870s the more dominant European nations had contributed to a series of alliances in order to maintain peace and avoid war. Ironically it had been the new German Empire who had feared war, from France in the west and Russia in the east. Europe was now the wealthiest and most powerful region of the world; its supremacy, a result of the affluence created from the technological progress of the Industrial Revolution. However whilst Britain and Germany bathed in the benefits, Russia now a straggler was struggling to survive. Russia was also a country which the rest of Europe feared.

Initially Britain had resisted involvement and maintained neutrality but in 1907 it signed the Triple Entente which ensured that Russia, France and Britain worked together. It had been necessary to do so, as Germany's population had doubled since

1870, its industrial output had heavily increased and it now had an army twice the size of the French one and twelve times the size of Britain's. Germany had also begun to build an immense navy. Britain responded by constructing a formidable collection of battleships called Dreadnought carrying super-sized guns whilst Germany built similar ships. It appeared that the whole of Europe was now poised and ready for the lighting of the touchpaper. However no one could have envisaged the spark that would eventually ignite it.

1914 had begun as one of the most peaceful years to follow decades of crisis. It was a welcome relief but few realised that it was in fact the calm before the storm. In Beckston, life was seemingly continuing as normal; the exception was the absence of Niall. There had been no correspondence from him and Emily was beginning to fear the worst. Following the initial curiosity, people began to speak less frequently of his departure and failure to return; Doctor Lawson had even begun to consider advertising for a replacement. Apart from short, snatched conversational opportunities with Alice and George, Emily had no one else to entrust with her fears. During the day, she managed to preoccupy her mind with her work and her home commitments but at night, when her eyes blocked out the day's events, the spectre of what might be haunted her without mercy. The prospect of a future without Niall was unbearable. With each new day there was however hope that she would receive word of his whereabouts. Even a visit from Jackson would be welcomed.

The weeks and months passed by uneventfully as 1914 became embedded. Olivia regained her strength and returned to her job as a milliner, but her experience of working as a salon manageress had now afforded her some degree of professional ambition. When the opportunity presented itself, she eagerly pursued it. Her employer, an elderly lady, had decided to sell her shop and millinery business, allowing Olivia first refusal. She spoke of her plans and ambitions with heated excitement, impressing everyone with her dedicated motivation, but there was one slight problem; Olivia, a spinster at almost forty years of age, had never considered saving for the future. Until now, there had never been any need to do so; there had always been an abundance of men around to settle the charges. Financial independence was something which Olivia had never before been interested in. She had definitely changed and it seemed that the conversion was likely to be permanent.

All the good ideas would vaporise without the necessary loan. Being a female and lacking a proven record of commercial reliability, Olivia was of little interest to the banks. Her mother had few savings and even Emily lacked the full collateral, but shared collateral would be another matter. The offer to help came from an unexpected source; George Ackroyd was a truly remarkable man. He bore neither resentment nor malice towards his former fiancée. At the close of the agreements between Olivia, Emily and George, he intimated that he then had something to disclose. Hannah Taylor was called into the Taylor's front drawing-room followed by Alice.

Grasping the young girl's hand he drew Alice alongside himself and made the announcement.

'Alice and I are to be married.'

The statement although unexpected was received with genuine enthusiasm by everyone, including Olivia who kissed them both on the cheek.

'I am truly pleased for you both. George, you are a very kind and special person who deserves someone like Alice. I wish you all the best.' Tears were visible in George's eyes as he shook Olivia's hand.

'Thank you for that. It means everything.'

Hannah gave them her blessing and wished them well before Emily clutched them both to her and whispered, 'You each deserve the best and you have that in one another. I am so delighted for you.' As she kissed each one, George whispered into her ear, 'He'll be back soon.' Emily smiled and nodded and swallowed hard, trying to avoid her tears from flowing.

The wedding was small and intimate, just as Emily had imagined it would be. Alice's family swelled the numbers and her younger siblings especially brought gaiety and informality to the gathering. To a stranger, they would have appeared a mismatched couple; his left arm missing, a wide age gap and social standing between them; but on closer inspection anyone could see that the gulf had been eliminated by true affection and love. Nothing else mattered. At least, their love was open and free for everyone to see; not closeted away in the core of the heart.

One day, Emily thought, *one day that will be us*. She just hoped that the day would not be too far away.

As Alice and George exchanged their vows and began to enjoy married happiness, they were unaware of an event occurring far away in Europe which would have devastating consequences for the world. On the morning of 28 June 1914 a couple were being driven through the Bosnian city of Sarajevo. Archduke Franz Ferdinand, heir to the Austro-Hungarian throne, was there with his wife, Sophie, Duchess of Hohenburg, to attend a reception with the Governor of Bosnia. Cheering well-wishers lined the streets to catch a glimpse of the couple in the open-topped car. Secreted amongst the crowds, were three assassins and four accomplices with a mission to assassinate the Archduke. The first attempt, the hurling of a bomb, failed as it hit the car behind the Archduke's, causing injury to the passengers and onlookers. But later, as the driver took a wrong turn, another assassin seized upon the opportunity and shot both the Archduke and his wife dead.

News of this assassination quickly spread through Europe and reached Great Britain, but very few people realised the impact this one event would have upon their lives.

To the people of Beckston such an event had little or no meaning, as it was far away and would not touch their lives. To Emily, it may have been far away but then so was her husband. The news of Austria's declaration of war on Serbia made her more concerned about Niall's safety.

The whole affair was gathering a powerful momentum. When his nephew and heir, Archduke Franz Ferdinand, had been assassinated, the Austro-Hungarian Emperor, Franz Josef I had declared war on Serbia. Such news normally seemed distant, but when Emily read of the family name of the Emperor, everything became more significant. Austria had been ruled by the Habsburg Family since the thirteenth century. Indeed, a large part of central Europe and the Balkans had also been ruled and held together by the Habsburg crown. This was the same powerful family from which Marie Philippe descended.

Emily fully understood the underlying ramifications of this news; she now feared for Niall's life more than ever.

Chapter Thirty-Four

S am Jackson had been discreetly tailing Kerry Doyle and her brother Niall for some time. Following the burglary and murder at the Philippe's home, they had quietly withdrawn from Paris, eventually seeking sanctuary in the Vosges Mountains. They had made their way from Paris to Reims and then on to Nancy. Eventually, they reached the German-held province of Alsace; a region holding testimony to both a turbulent past and present. French in origin, the territory had been claimed by Germany and during the Middle Ages had been carved up into German principalities. In 1648 the land became once again French, before Germany reclaimed it in 1871. It was not surprising that such turmoil of the past had left indelible marks from both nations. Germanic influences were heavily prevalent in the architecture of ornate, timbered houses with their distinctive balconies, leaded windows and window boxes. The French influences had in many ways, like the people, been squeezed out or obliterated. Following the German seizure thousands of Alsatians had left the region, preferring exile in Algeria or elsewhere in France.

It was in this unstable place that Kerry and Niall had now begun to seek refuge. Jackson had been watching them together carefully knowing that Niall was aware of his presence, but that was of no concern to either man. What intrigued him the most was Kerry herself; a twin showing strong physical resemblances to Niall but there the similarity ended. Jackson recalled how he had struggled to identify the Davenport twins but then they had been identical and had shared the same family upbringing.

At thirty-six years old the woman was a raven-haired beauty. She possessed emerald eyes which, unlike Niall's, did not twinkle and tease but stared with menacing effect, like a dominant hunter stalking its prey. Her limbs were agile and powerful and no doubt could be used to outrun any man. Possessing both the physical and mental strength of the male, she was also imbued with the alluring traits of a seductive temptress. She reminded Jackson of a tigress or lioness; proud and attractive, but undeniably wild and dangerous.

Jackson had spent a lifetime in surveillance and had always prided himself upon his mastery of the job; that was until now. He sat at a small village bar one evening watching them together across the road, his eyes following her panther-like walk until she suddenly changed direction and headed towards him. She entered the bar and walked straight to his table before sitting down opposite him. Initially hesitant, Niall accordingly joined them.

'Well then sir, what do you want to know?' The directness of her question took even Jackson by surprise who needed a brief moment before replying.

'What have you got to tell me, lady?'

'Plenty,' came the reply in the Irish accent.

Jackson leaned back, now more comfortable in her company.

'I'm listening, lady, I'm listening.'

Jackson could tell that it was going to be a long night and suggested that an order of drinks would help. Her thirst for alcohol was like no other woman's that he had known. He had known plenty of hookers drinking and plying their trade but she could outdrink any of them. She repeatedly emptied her glass but surprisingly showed no effects of drunkenness.

'How do you know that I'm not here to arrest you?' Jackson enquired.

'Because you've been tailing me for a long time. You're American and I bet that note that I sent to the New York police brought you here.'

'This one?' Jackson unfurled a small piece of paper and handed it to her.

She read the words out: 'MR ROBINSON, THE MAN YOU ARE SEEKING FROM THE LUSITANIA, IS MR CHRISTIAN VERHOLT FROM LONG ISLAND.'

'Yes, that's the one.'

'Why did you send it?' Jackson needed to ask the obligatory question.

'Because I had to. Why do you think I sent it?'

'You're in love with Verholt and he doesn't feel the same way about you. In his eyes, you're just useful.' Jackson's statements made Kerry laugh out loudly.

'You're right on one count, but on the other you have missed the mark altogether.' She leaned across the table and whispered quietly, 'I hate the man. I hate the name. I always have done and I won't rest until I have destroyed both him and the name. Verholt!' She turned away and spat onto the floor in disgust. 'That's what I think about the Verholts!'

The revelation and accompanying gesture were unexpected for both Jackson and Niall; the latter stared at his sister with bewilderment and was the first to air his misunderstanding.

'But I always thought that you were in love with him.'

'Oh, you did, did you? Well brother dear, perhaps I'd better make a few things clear. I have never and nor will I be, ever in love with Verholt. For one thing, contrary to belief, I am the one woman who is not attracted to him, unlike many who fall simpering at his feet. That is not for me and never will be. The reason why I detest both the man and his namesake is because you and I have a share of the Verholt blood in our veins. That of course is all we have!' The disclosure was sufficient to momentarily silence Niall and Jackson.

'What exactly are you suggesting?' queried Niall.

'I'm not suggesting, I'm stating facts. I know that as a young girl waiting on tables in a bar in Kilkenny, Ma must have seemed an easy prospect for a wealthy traveller. He had his fun and then quickly left. Apparently Frederik Verholt, Christian's father, had been a guest of the Butler family at Kilkenny Castle. He had assumed that the local girls, especially the poor and pretty ones, were there for the taking and that is exactly what he did. He took her against her will; no one would believe the word of a serving girl against that of a rich gentleman. He came and went, leaving something in her belly. That is why I hate the name.'

'How can you be so sure that it was a Verholt who was responsible?' questioned Niall.

'Unlike you, I was brought up by the Doyles who all knew who had sired us.'

'But that might be nothing more than hearsay.' Niall was now trying to rationalise the facts.

'It might be, except for this.' Kerry pulled at a hidden chain around her neck until a large gold man's ring hanging from it became visible. She undid the chain, removed the ring and proudly handed it to Niall, who slowly rotated the item between his fingers. The notion of her secretly wearing the ring on a chain around her neck, momentarily reminded him of Emily, whom he knew wore his rings around her own long, sweet neck; a neck that he had so often caressed and kissed. The image immediately transported him to another time and another place; one day soon, he hoped they would be together and live openly as man and wife. He hoped that the day would not be too far away.

The Irish lilt of his sister's voice brought his reverie to an abrupt end.

'She wasn't a Doyle for nothing! In the struggle with him, she managed to remove his ring as a keepsake. To me, it is of course a constant reminder of what I need to do.'

As the gold glinted in the light, Niall could clearly see the imprint of a family crest and the Verholt name inscribed beneath it.

As his mouth dried, Niall began to fervently lick his lips, his mind whirring with a mixture of suppositions and anxiety, as he was only too aware of his sister's potential for revenge.

'What do you intend to do?' The question alone generated terrifying possibilities in Niall's mind.

'Absolutely nothing... for now.' Kerry's answer allowed Niall to audibly exhale a small gasp of filtered relief before Jackson broke it with ham-fisted directness.

'You must have a plan, otherwise why kill Marie Philippe and steal the papers and jewellery?'

'For one reason: power. Never again will I need to dance to Verholt's tune, do his bidding and be grateful for the scraps that he offers. On the evening of the Philippes' ball I was supposed to steal some rare and expensive miniature paintings from the study; Christian had even secured a buyer for them in America. Unknown to him, whilst he had been making plans, I had also made some of my own. Alphonse Philippe had more to offer than just works of art; a few enquiries revealed that his work would secure a handsome ransom.'

'Ransom?' Jackson repeated the word without fully understanding her plan.

'Of course I've considered killing Verholt myself, but that wouldn't give me a great deal of fun for long. This way I can enjoy watching the humiliation of the entire family for a long time; possibly even a lifetime.'

As the evening and the disclosures continued, the two men were stunned into silence; their grave faces becoming even graver whilst reflecting upon the severity of what they were hearing.

Frederik Verholt, the perpetrator of the trouble, had died in a boating accident some years later, leaving a young widow and a young baby son, Christian Verholt. Kerry spoke with little compassion for the young boy, as he was fated to grow up and inherit one of the largest banking dynasties in the world. He was brought up by his grandparents, Johan and Greta Verholt, in sumptuous luxury on the north shores of Long Island. He had wanted for nothing, except parents, as his mother had abandoned him soon after her husband's death and had returned to live in Austria, her homeland. She made no effort to contact him and the Verholts in return made no effort to contact her. Although a poor mother, she had at least performed her duty of providing the heir to the dynasty.

It was only as a grown man that Christian Verholt had learned of the true identity of his mother, an incredibly wealthy woman in her own right because of the Habsburg family connections, and now married comfortably to an equally wealthy and successful French industrialist, Alphonse Philippe.

Christian Verholt had of course wanted to meet his mother, but he could never forget her abandonment of a small helpless baby.

In his quest to secure a meeting, he had decided that the name of Augustus Cassel would attract far less suspicion and attention.

The plan had been for Kerry to secure employment for that evening as a hired servant. Both additional male and female servants were needed and as Kerry had resided for some years in France, she was able to adequately understand and communicate in French. Having secured a temporary appointment, she arrived early that afternoon to undertake the hospitality preparations for the reception. In Verholt's mind she had agreed to perform the burglary during the ball, thereby providing an alibi for him but in her mind she had long ago decided to do things differently.

She hid in the study and waited until the guests, including Verholt, had departed. Her intention had been to wait until Marie or her husband unlocked the safe to deposit Marie's priceless jewellery, as was their strict routine when entertaining. Kerry had purposefully befriended Marie Philippe's personal maid during one of her strolls out on an afternoon off and had discretely elicited important information.

Hiding in the dark, Marie had carefully planned her move; she would wait until the safe was opened and then apply a heavy blow to her victim rendering them unconscious. She had learned from a reliable source, solicited with a certain amount of seduction on her part, that the papers containing the chemical formulae were kept in the house-safe. She would simply take them and, in a final parting gesture to Verholt, she would leave the Verholt crested family ring as evidence of his implication. The scheme was sheer genius, or so she thought.

Kerry had been stationed at a refectory table from which the waiters steadily plied back and forth supplying drinks and returning empty glasses. From this position she had the advantage of watching everyone. At one point, Christian Verholt approached the table himself and winked knowingly at Kerry to signal the start of events. He picked up a glass of wine and later handed it to Marie Philippe. Before he reached her he had however added something to it; Kerry saw him do this. She also saw a woman who had had too much to drink sway into Marie's path causing her to spill much of the wine before it had even been tasted. Greatly apologetic, the inebriated woman insisted upon the swopping of glasses; the latter's newly poured one for the remnant of drink left in Marie's glass.

Kerry made herself scarce and, instead of performing a burglary, she went to the kitchen and washed glasses. She did not see Verholt again that night; it was only later in the early hours of the next morning whilst she waited in the dark study, that she became aware of his presence.

Hiding behind a large chair in front of an elaborate escritoire, she heard the study door open; a chink of light flooding from the hallway enabled her to watch Marie Philippe walk across to a wall-recess lined with books. Removing certain large volumes, she then reached across, repeatedly turned a dial and opened the safe. Kerry's breathing became shallow in an effort to remain undetected. Now was the time for her to stealthily creep up behind Marie who was removing her earrings, render her unconscious with one blow and take the papers, which she so desired.

A sudden noise instantly rooted Kerry to the spot. Remaining hidden she watched the drama unfurl before her.

'Augustus, what are you doing here? I understood that you had left earlier with Olivia and her sister.' Whilst Marie seemed perplexed, she was at the same time slightly flattered that he wished to see her. She had always been a woman who relished sustained interest from the opposite sex. During the evening she had definitely enjoyed his company, especially revelling in the fact that he was considerably younger and extremely good-looking.

'It is time for the truth.' His manner had changed considerably, being now cold and removed.

'The truth?' Her delivery of the word was so very different to his. She managed to inject a mixture of innocent inquiry and teasing provocation but as the look upon his face remained unchanged, she realised that he was no longer playing the flirting game.

'I have been waiting all my life for the truth. Why would a woman abandon her own child? That is what I would like to know.' His face was impassive, his light blue eyes cold and disconcertingly cruel staring out with unwavering fixation.

Marie Philippe remained transfixed. She stared at him almost dazed as if she was in a trance before uttering just one word: 'Christian.'

'Christian *Verholt*. Does it pain you to say the name?'

'It reminds me of my youth. I was very young and a widow, and I did not want to spend my life in mourning. I needed love and to be loved. I knew you would be well-looked after. I am sorry but I did it for the best.'

'You mean the best for you!'

'I cannot deny that I have been fortunate in finding another wealthy man. Yes, I have a good life here but then I am sure, so do you.'

'You have no idea. The fact that I grew up without a father or a mother does not matter to you because I have a rich family. That is the biggest mistake that you have made. Money means nothing to me. I get no pleasure in knowing that one day I will inherit the fortune of one of the biggest banking dynasties in the world. I am simply not interested.'

'You should be grateful. There are many people who would swop places with you. What is it then that you want?'

'Excitement! Doing what I should not do, that is what I crave.' His face suddenly began to grimace as he reached across to her neck and swiftly pulled the diamond and pearl necklace from her; jewels which had once adorned the neck of a fated queen. The action, although unexpected, made Marie gasp in disbelief before prompting her to turn and summon help. In rapid response to her automatic need to scream or shout for help, the sudden glint of steel was the last thing that Marie Philippe saw before she felt the blade slice deep into her neck.

Kerry later explained how Verholt had left as quickly as he had appeared. He had the necklace, still warm from the heat of her body and the accompanying earrings, which he had picked up from the table where she had temporarily placed them. Presumably he was content with the treasures now grasped in his blood-stained hands, as he stepped around the lifeless body, passing by the rare and expensive miniatures which he had initially coveted; the witnesses who required no silencing. Kerry knew that she herself needed to leave quickly and, without wasting the opportunity, emptied the safe until she found what she had originally come for. Later, she remembered that in her haste to depart, she had failed to leave behind her parting gesture to Verholt: the crested family ring. Like the evening itself, it was too late to turn back time. Surely, she thought, Verholt and his family would now be doomed to disaster for their past actions; atonement must be on the horizon.

Niall and Jackson continued to remain silent, not a word passing their lips. Whilst Niall found the episode nauseating, he was also relieved that his sister had not murdered Marie Philippe. Jackson, however, felt just a warm glow inside. At last he had the opportunity to implicate Verholt; a man whom it appeared had even managed to outsmart Jackson's inscrutable powers of surveillance. The man had cunningly returned to the Philippes' house without being noticed. For that alone he needed to ensure that he had the final upper hand; it would be Jackson himself who would have the advantage. He knew that Kerry also intended to use this information herself, for the purpose of blackmail.

Jackson now realised that there was a certain fateful bond between Verholt and himself; he rather liked that. After all, he too understood what it was like for a man to murder his mother.

Chapter Thirty-Five

The assassination of Archduke Franz Ferdinand set into motion a domino effect; it triggered a series of crises which careered throughout Europe and beyond, spreading suspicious aggression and successive disaster, before culminating in full-scale war.

Germany's military advancement into Belgium became the unequivocal precipitate for Britain's reaction: the announcement on Tuesday 4th August 1914 of the declaration of war on Germany.

The new secretary of state for war, Field-Marshall Lord Kitchener, requested that Parliament should authorise the recruitment of half a million soldiers. Army life with the prospect of regular meals and comradeship induced many working-class men to sign up for an adventure, which many glibly believed would 'be over by Christmas'.

As the men left for war the women increasingly filled the gaps left by them, initially in trades such as those of baking, printing and shoemaking but acute shortages saw them also being employed in industrial work.

Initially there were few changes in the Taylor household. Emily continued educating the local Beckston children whilst Olivia worked hard to make a success of her millinery business. Together with their mother Hannah, and former maid Alice who often joined them on an evening, they would sit and knit scarves, balaclavas and pairs of socks which they hoped would provide some modicum of homely comfort to servicemen. Olivia sat alongside them eagerly knitting for the troops, the antithesis of her former self.

Upon her marriage, Alice had reluctantly agreed to relinquish her employment as a maid to the Taylors; having a comfortable home of her own to run, George had insisted that his wife's place was now in her own home. The Taylors had agreed and the three Taylor women had resisted hiring another live-in maid, believing that with the assistance of gadgets such as the pump-action Star vacuum cleaner, they could with part-time help, run their own household, especially with the outbreak of war descending. Patriotic fervour had made everyone want to do their bit for the war. Times were definitely changing but none of them had recognised how drastic these changes would be.

It was Alice with her indomitable energy fuelled by youthfulness and a craving to be useful, who became one of the first to help the war effort. Working as a ticket collector on one of Beckston's newly-introduced trolley buses, Alice was fulfilling a need to help others by maintaining a normal day-to-day life. Although George never referred to his disability and its prohibition to recruitment, it troubled him that he would never be eligible for service. He vowed he would help the war effort in any way that he could and was only too proud of his young wife. He suspected that her ambition to step into men's shoes as a ticket collector would not last for ever and realised that his willingness in having provided driving lessons, would inevitably lead to her actually driving the buses. It was, he felt a small price to pay, when so many around them were giving so much more.

The euphoria of many of the young men, who had eagerly volunteered in the belief that they would be home for Christmas, began to pale significantly. By October 1914 the armies on each side had stopped advancing and were instead digging trenches, signalling the start of a long fight ahead. The conditions for those at the Western Front, the German frontier between Belgium and France, were horrendous; the men had to survive the hazards of living in muddy, flooded trenches, alongside the constant exposure of rain, snow, vermin and disease. Trench foot, body lice, fever and exposure were constant enemies within these battle zones; it was not only the terror of fighting that these men had to fear and endure.

For their families left in Britain, the worry of the unknown was unbearable. Waiting to hear the dreaded news that a cherished one was missing, wounded or had been killed in action was harrowing. Such words confirmed the worst fears signalling the end of hope. For Emily the unknown had existed for so long; it was now considerably more than a year since she had last seen Niall and she had received no correspondence. There was only George and Alice to turn to for words of encouragement but even their reassurance was becoming less frequent with the passing of time. Still wearing his rings on a hidden chain around her neck, she would often touch the outline of them through the fabric of her blouse and recall her wedding day. Alone in bed at night, she would close her eyes and see his face; the smile, the twinkling eyes and sometimes she would hear the soft Irish lilt of his voice in her ears. The next day she knew would be a new day and maybe one that would bring news; good news.

It is a known fact that the best antidote to worry is hard work and Emily had long been an advocate of such medicine. During the day she would work hard at school but she still felt that she wanted to do more for the war effort. Remembering her time working with Niall at the surgery, she decided to volunteer her services as an untrained nurse and began working at Beckston Infirmary during the evenings.

One night, an unexpected visitor made his way to the ward that Emily was working on. It was almost Christmas, but for some of the patients there, the severity of their wounds would prove too great for them to survive until then. As Emily looked pitifully at a young man whose face had been partly shot away, and whose arms and legs had severe wounds to them, she realised how senseless this war was.

'Miss Taylor. You have a visitor.' The young nurse who appeared at her side threw a slight smile at her as she delivered the announcement. Fortunately it was now time for Emily to finish her voluntary shift so she did not feel too awkward in leaving, as she cast one last lingering look at the unfortunate soldier; there was nothing that she could do to make him more comfortable.

He was waiting in a corridor; his large frame as distinctive as ever. On past occasions Emily had always found his unexpected presence disturbing and slightly menacing, but now she perceived an aura of calm and composure. Strangely, for some time she knew that she had been willing his reappearance.

'Good evening, Inspector Jackson.' Even though she knew that he had retired and no longer held rank, she was more comfortable addressing him this way.

'Good evening, Emily.' His informality was a surprise to each of them; in truth he did not know whether to use her maiden or her married name, for reasons known only to himself.

He explained that he had first visited her home where Alice had opened the door; presumably even old habits die hard thought Emily, who knew that the women would have been busily engaged with their knitting. Alice had disclosed where he would find her and he had simply waited, along with a little amber-coloured hospitality in a public house, until he knew that he could see her. Jackson's suggestion of returning to the public house seemed a logical one, for both knew that there would be plenty to discuss.

As they walked together, Emily ached to ask him about Niall but she resisted, waiting patiently and hopefully for some news.

A small sherry and surprisingly, a small whisky appeared; Jackson took only small occasional sips from the whisky, which was so unlike him. Emily likewise took a sip of her sherry, grateful this time for the warm feeling that it gave as it trickled down her throat. It had been a long day and for once she was content to indulge with this fortified wine, especially on a cold night.

He began to disclose his findings; he explained how he had tailed Kerry and Niall, following them from Paris through to the Alsace region; the mention of this area unnerved Emily, as she knew from her knowledge in Geography that the province was German-held and thereby now unstable and unsafe.

Jackson continued, sparing no details. He relayed everything which Kerry had told him in that small village bar; the issues of Verholt's, Niall's and Kerry's parentage, including the existence of the Verholt-crested ring, and the abandonment of Verholt by his mother, who later remarried and became Marie Philippe. He described Kerry's vendetta for revenge, identifying her as the mystery writer of the letter. He explained Verholt's need to attend the ball that evening, assuming the name of Augustus Cassel and his unsuccessful attempt to lace Marie's drink. Emily knew exactly what he had added as it was Olivia who had swayed into Marie, spilling her drink and who had then swopped glasses. Fortunately Marie's glass had had little drink left in it and therefore the potency of the arsenic was thankfully not as dangerous as it might have been. Nevertheless, it was now clear that Verholt had been determined that evening to kill his mother. With a change of circumstances, upon Kerry's part, Verholt had later returned and this time had been successful.

There was a great deal to consider and there were still many unanswered questions.

'The papers that Kerry stole…what exactly has she done with them?' Emily now fully appreciated the dire consequences of them falling into the wrong hands, as the great world powers were now currently battling for supremacy, at any cost. She thought about the likes of the young soldier she had just left. Surely there were already too many evils prevalent without imposing chemical ones.

'I'm not certain what has happened to them. I do know that stealing them will have awakened the interest of many; that you can be sure of.'

'By that I take it you mean they are in danger, not just from Verholt himself, but no doubt the French Government for whom Alphonse Philippe was working, and even the Austrians, as Marie was once of course a Habsburg?' Jackson looked slightly startled at the depth of knowledge that this lady possessed.

'Yes, I'm afraid so.'

'What about Verholt? Do you know where he is at present?' Her question made Jackson stare blankly into his glass.

'Afraid not.'

'Niall told me that Kerry had probably stolen those papers to sell to the highest bidder. In view of what is now occurring, does that include Germany?'

'I believe that was the idea, especially as they had made their way into Alsace. She never actually told me, but I had a gut feeling that she had made a few contacts and intended playing one off against the other. She was playing with the big boys; not a good thing to do when a war begins.'

What unnerved Emily most now, even more than the shocking news that Jackson had already imparted, was his manner; he had never before been so gentle and serene in his delivery. Emily could feel that it was all leading to something more, and that frightened her.

'What is it, Sam? What is it that you are not telling me?'

Jackson stared hard into her eyes, as if trying to reach her soul. Never before had a woman, other than his mother, called him Sam. Emily stared back, little caring that she had transcended boundaries by being personal. Now there was more to concern her, as she saw his eyes glisten with moisture; never before had she seen him display such emotion.

Suddenly, he looked like an old man; tired and worn-down by the gruelling journey of life. For some time he remained silent, just staring into his glass until raising his head he allowed her to see the look of burden which was hanging heavily across his face. He tried a slight smile but it was ineffective in dislodging his pressing trouble.

'I could say nothing…but you deserve more than that. To say nothing would be the easy way out. But for me, I've spent my life looking for the difficult… that's always been the way. You lady have intelligence, and for that reason, you need to know.' His ramblings stopped momentarily whilst he took a gulp of his whisky; Emily watched him do so, her heart beat beginning to race with climatic unease.

'That evening when Kerry disclosed everything to me, was the last time that I saw either of them…alive.' Jackson immediately refrained from continuing as he saw the effect his news was having upon his companion; he regretted that he lacked tactful delivery skills but he had never needed finesse when dealing with criminals. Emily was stunned; any colour present had drained from her face and her complexion was now stone-like.

'Please continue.' Jackson conceded to her directive.

'Very well. I lost touch with them after that evening in late spring. It was as though Kerry wanted to confess everything to me before they gave me the slip. Up until then I had been following them easily but suddenly they just disappeared. I asked around for possible sightings and a few leads took me down through plenty of pretty villages with lots of vineyards and castles. Finally when I arrived at a place called Riquewihr I thought my luck was in; a couple answering their description had recently been seen in the village.' Jackson hesitated, taking one last gulp of his whisky before emptying the glass.

'The following morning the talk was all round the place; two charred bodies had been found in a burned-out automobile, on the road between Riquewihr and the town of Colmar.' Almost before Jackson had finished the last sentence, Emily eagerly interrupted him.

'Could you or anyone else identify them? How do you know it was them? It may just have been a coincidence.'

'This tells me everything. It was found on a chain around her neck.' He pulled the blackened item from his pocket and placed it on the table in front of her. It was a large man's crested ring; the name Verholt became visible as Jackson ran his chubby thumb across it.

Chapter Thirty-Six

At first Emily, refused to accept the possibility of Niall's death; two unrecognisable charred corpses proved nothing and thereby the evidence as such was inadmissible. However, Jackson had continued to make enquiries and found no leads to Niall's whereabouts. Everything about the charred male corpse indicated that Niall together with his sister had perished; whether it was the result of those papers, it seemed no one would ever know.

Jackson did wonder whether Verholt was behind the crime; fire had already been used in Paris to destroy the Maison d'Elégance and the apartment where Olivia had lived. These had the hallmarks of a man wishing to destroy vital evidence. If Verholt had used fire once, he could be the person who had torched that automobile. He had of course already murdered before; a man who could murder his own mother was without doubt, capable of anything.

The unstable conditions which abounded through Europe were, even by Jackson's standards, unsettling. By the time the burned-out car and corpses had been discovered, it was late August 1914 and Europe was increasingly becoming a dangerous place to be. It was then that Jackson decided that the time had arrived for him to depart, with or without Verholt; taking a train and then a boat he knew he needed to make one last stopover before returning to America. For the sake of courtesy, a quality that was usually unacquainted with Jackson, he had made his way to Beckston with the purpose of seeing a lady who was special, simply because she reminded him of his mother.

Having done what was necessary, he then took his leave and left for the shores of America.

Outwardly, Emily now wore a face of stalwart determination but inside she was crumbling with loneliness and despair. Just as she had once ached to tell everyone about her happiness, now she ached to conceal her grief. She even resisted confiding in Alice and George, preferring not to spoil their first Christmas together as a married couple.

She busied herself with her work during the day at St Cuthbert's and at night she spent her time with those who needed her most, the sick and dying. Sometimes she took comfort in thinking that Niall would have been proud of her endeavours; of her need to help others as he himself had done at the surgery. She now gave little thought to herself; instead she wanted to help everyone around her; it seemed that her life was of no consequence as she felt that it was over.

The writing on the envelope was instantly recognisable; it was Christmas Eve and Amelia Davenport's card had arrived just in time, not merely for the festivities but for another reason, as it managed to do something miraculous; it put a smile on Emily's face. The Christmas card featured a young girl coyly hanging up a stocking at the side of a large fireplace, with a blazing fire in the hearth. Inside, Amelia had written; *I hope I've been a good girl for Father Christmas. Have you? Happy Christmas. With all my love, Amelia.* The sentiments were so characteristic of her flamboyance and they immediately transported Emily back to the Lusitania and to Amelia's decidedly shocking outbursts and revelations. It was those recollections which made Emily smile. She carefully slipped the accompanying letter inside into her pocket, preferring to read its contents in the privacy of her own room and placed Amelia's card behind other cards so as not to attract any unwanted attention.

Emily had not received any correspondence from Amelia for two years; the previous letter had accompanied a Christmas card for 1912. In that letter she had provided the name and address of her good friend, Françoise Morel in Paris, whom Emily had initially assumed was one of her larger than life characters in her tales. Now she knew better. She also felt rather embarrassed that she had not replied to her letter. Something else began to trouble her; she still had the diamond pendant in its box and the unopened letter, which

Françoise had trusted her to give to Amelia. Since returning from France she had simply forgotten about their existence. She was displeased with herself as she settled down on the edge of her bed and began to read Amelia's letter:

> Greenwich Village,
> New York,
> America.
> 10th December 1914

My Dearest Emily,

Once again please forgive me for not writing to you. My thoughts, my dear, have often been with both you and Niall. I hope you are at long last enjoying life as a married couple, the way that you deserve to. I understand that life is not easy under the present circumstances. Everyone here, including me, is praying that peace will come soon and put an end to all hostilities. War is a terrible thing when one considers the lives that it destroys.

Please forgive me. I should not be so maudlin. When you have time, please write and send me your news.

My dear, I have some news of my own to impart! As you may recall I had experienced some poor health in the past with chest pains. As a result my son Jonathan and his wife Beatrice took it upon themselves to have me cocooned from life in general. To them all forms of excitement had to be removed from my life. Well as you know, that is not for me!

I now feel better than I have done for some time; in fact I am in rude health. The reason being is that I have found the best medicine for my heart. I have found a man who dotes upon me. Emily, I am in love and about to be married, much to Jonathan's disgust.

Joseph is a wonderful man, my junior by ten years, but of course age does not matter. He is a well-known and respected impresario, based here in the Greenwich Village Theatres. That is how we met as I do love to visit the theatre.

The wedding has been arranged for April 28th next year and we would really appreciate you and Niall being there as our guests if you can possibly arrange the travel.

Please be happy for me. I know that I can rely upon you, Emily.
Your true friend,
Amelia.

The contents of the letter were totally unexpected but the utter quirkiness of the news was refreshing and together with the invitation provided a well-needed source of escapism. To Emily it seemed completely out of the question to be able to sail for America and therefore she instantly dismissed the possibility from her mind. However her conscience continued to remind her that she still had in her possession items which rightfully belonged to Amelia. She had of course given her promise to Françoise that she would deliver them to her friend.

In times of such uncertainty, it was debatable whether postponing something would be the right thing to do. Perhaps one needed to live for the day, for who could determine what the future would bring? With that thought in mind, Emily made her decision.

The impact of the war was felt keenly on British shores when a pair of zeppelins bombed the east coast of England, killing four people in January 1915. These tube-shaped airships consisted of enormous sacks of hydrogen gas held inside skeletons of metal hoops, covered in tough fabric. Their ominous size together with their droning noise signalled their presence, earning them a fearful reputation amongst British civilians who dreaded the omnipotent power of the Germans. Even the gentle lands of Britain were no longer beyond the reach of the German Empire. The Taylor women finally conceded to Emily's wish to sail to New York. Perhaps America would be a safer place to be.

The school church governors at St Cuthbert's peered at Emily with slight derision as she put her request forward for a period of three weeks unpaid leave. Already one of her two colleagues had had to be replaced owing to his decision to enlist. There was the possibility that the school's former retired headmaster would oblige for a limited time as her replacement. Finally they agreed that Miss Taylor was a most diligent and trusted teacher who had suffered the traumas of losing a father, coping with an unwell mother and of course it went without saying, had undergone the anxiety of supporting her sister; their heads nodded knowingly at the mention of Olivia. Following considerable deliberation, her request was granted.

The effects of falling passenger travel across the Atlantic meant that many of the large liners had been laid up during the autumn and winter of 1914-1915. Another reason also existed for their scarcity, protection from the damage of mines. Bookings for passages aboard the Lusitania, although not strong, remained sufficient to retain her in civilian service. Economy measures though had had to be imposed, including the shutting-down of a boiler-room to conserve coal and thereby reduce the crew costs. This had impacted upon her speed, reducing it from over 25 to 21 knots. Nevertheless the Lusitania was the fastest first-class passenger liner at the time in commercial service.

Alice, with George at her side, drove Emily in their trusty Tin-Lizzie to Liverpool where she boarded the Lusitania on the 17th April 1915. This would be the ship's 201st transatlantic voyage before arriving in New York on 24th April. The friends who had insisted upon the drive took leave of their passenger, hoping that the glitz of New York would help to put a hint of colour back into her pale cheeks.

Tired and withdrawn, Emily obligingly performed her parting gesture of waving from the deck. This time she at least had someone to return her gesture, before seeking solace in her cabin. For the first time since hearing the news from Jackson, she could openly feel the pricking and stinging sensation of tears welling in her eyes. As the Lusitania left the shoreline of England behind and by-passed the southern coast of Ireland, Emily could at last do the one thing that she had been unable to do; grieve for her husband in private.

The tears naturally formed a release to the pain which had stayed within her for so long; preferring to tell no one of her news she had refused to be worn down by the agony which gnawed relentlessly inside her. The emotional trigger could have been one of many, but solitude in these surroundings would be both cause and cure.

If Emily was at her lowest ebb at the start of the voyage, a week later the cathartic properties of the sea air had rejuvenated her as the skyline of New York beckoned. This together with the uplifting prospect of seeing Amelia had helped to lighten her mood considerably. The reunion, when it came, did not fail to disappoint.

The elderly lady waiting on the dock side beamed with delight. It was obvious that living in New York had had its influence; Amelia could never have been described as shy or reticent, but now she appeared even more self-confident; the striking make-up accentuated the colouring of her fashionable clothing; the skirt with its very full bell-shaped hemline lying above the ankles and the jacket with wide collars and sloping shoulders, were fully complemented by a small matching toque hat.

'Emily. Over here.' Amelia threw her arm into the air and waved enthusiastically. She began to walk just as enthusiastically towards Emily, followed by a small man in her wake. The two women eagerly embraced before Amelia pulled back, examining her friend's face with some contemplation. She refrained from voicing her thoughts. Only a quiet cough punctured the gap of silence between them.

'My dear, let me introduce my fiancé, Joseph Perlstein.' A short, stocky but well-dressed man stepped forward, smiled and shook Emily's hand.

'I am so pleased to meet you, Emily. Amelia has often spoken of you.'

'I am very pleased to meet you, Mr Perlstein.'

'Please, let's do away with the formalities. Everyone around here calls me Joe.' The infectious smile instantly put Emily at ease, causing her to blush slightly.

Amelia talked incessantly until they reached Joe's vehicle, an open-topped 1913 Moyer Touring car which along with his fiancée was his obvious pride and joy. Seated together comfortably behind Joe, Amelia continued to bombard Emily with her stream of conversation regarding the past, present and future of the couple's relationship. Emily listened whilst Amelia regaled her with their news and occasionally a brief interruption was allowed, as Joe excitedly pointed out a site of interest.

Amelia's personality was as refreshing as the breeze blowing across from the Atlantic. It was here, sitting alongside her friend, that Emily felt the ensnaring cobweb mesh of anxiety, responsibility and despair begin to slacken and afford her some freedom. As they drove to Greenwich Village, situated on the west side of Lower Manhattan, Emily began to relax, smile and nod appropriately as Amelia continued to chatter, seemingly without ever drawing breath. The whole effect, albeit transitory was something Emily had long welcomed; anaesthesia, rendering her insensible to pain.

As a young man full of hope and desire, Joseph Perlstein had, along with countless others, stepped out eagerly onto American soil for two indisputable reasons; freedom and gold. Since the 1860's Jewish immigrants had been flooding North-Eastern America in order to escape Russian anti-Semitism and the pogroms. In a country which promised freedom, hard work could naturally lead to prosperity. Joe Perlstein committed himself to such an ideal, working every hour that he could to survive. The textile industry lacked glamour but it did provide an existence. Joe experienced the hardships of toiling in the garment industry sweatshops where the men undertook the higher-paid work of cutting and pressing whilst the women received less for assembling and finishing garments. Working weeks of sixty-five hours were normal and when the need arose the figure could be as high as seventy-five. Coupled with this, the workers often had to supply their own basic equipment, including needles, thread and even sewing machines. When the long hours made his body ache and his eyes close with exhaustion, Joe remembered how his family had been wiped-out unmercifully; memories which gave him a compelling urge to carry on. That drive had carried him through his life and eventually made him financially secure.

Joe Perlstein was an organiser of men; without a wife and family he managed to save and set up his own workroom, at first employing small numbers of fellow immigrants with reasonable pay. He provided the equipment, secured the business contacts and produced a viable concern whilst offering better working conditions. Slowly, the business allowed him to employ more workers, his good name quickly spreading.

His humanitarian approach had earned him the respect of his workers and at the same time had allowed him to prosper.

With money and a natural ability to organise, Joe had found it easy to gain people's respect. He loved the theatre and although not naturally gifted as a thespian himself, he loved to mingle with people from different backgrounds and cultures. No one knew more about struggle and survival and the fight for human rights than Joe. It was not long however before he became immersed himself with people who had similar points of view. Nor was it long before the artists recognised the credentials of a man who would be happy to organise and finance their concerts and plays. Here in Greenwich Village, social, artistic and political life united in a Utopia of bohemian life. Intellectuals of every kind discussed and debated; proponents of anarchism, atheism, free-thought and socialism. The radicals even extended to the feminine gender, where uncharacteristically bobbed hairstyles and cigarette smoke heralded their presence.

Existing as a natural meeting ground, the medium for their expression was drama. Within the Little Theatre Movement, amateur companies wrote and produced provocative plays, frequently focussing upon social issues enabling new talent to be showcased. Alongside such artistic expression and community spirit, recreations of major theatrical productions were offered as full-length works from Chekhov, Ibsen and Shaw. It was amidst this artistic community that Amelia and Joe had found solace in each other's company.

Amelia had always loved the flamboyance and escapism of the artistic community. In particular she admired the total lack of adherence to conformity, in terms of speech, dress and conduct. Mixing with the artists in Greenwich Village she sensed an immediate connection to these people; instantly becoming a free spirit enveloped in her own hedonistic thoughts; the only sober reflection was regret of lost youth. This she tempered with her private memories; recollections of her own youth, the years spent in Paris which warmed her face with a sunburst of contentment. Now, she mused she was about to be married to one of the kindest and most amicable men in New York. If that could not put a smile on her face, nothing could.

Not everyone was filled with felicitations for the impending nuptials; Amelia's son, Jonathan, constantly voiced his concerns.

'The silly man either thinks the excitement will kill me or that Joe is marrying me for my money. Well, on that score I'm afraid he will be sorely disappointed; being nothing more than a vicar's widow.'

'A vicar's widow? I did not know that ...' Emily hesitated, searching for the correct choice of words.

'That I was once a clergyman's wife. Hard as it is to believe, it is the truth,' declared Amelia.

'Where did you meet him?'

It was at this point that Amelia began to smile. Now alone together in the Greenwich house, Amelia realised that she could share her secret without the fear of being overheard.

'We met in Paris.' Amelia's words were sufficient to totally engage Emily's interest. A pause followed before Amelia continued.

'I was a working girl, full of life and expectation…only that was the problem. I had had too much of a good time. There had been someone … a client, whom I had fallen in love with. I know that was never supposed to happen but it did. He let me down and I later found out that I was pregnant with his child. What could I do? I did not want to be at the mercy of some back-street abortionist. When Arthur appeared it almost seemed as if the Lord had indeed sent him.'

'You married a vicar whilst expecting another man's child?'

'Yes. I married Arthur Davenport. What would you have done?'

'Not that. Oh, Amelia I don't know.'

'No one does until they are in that situation. Arthur was kind and sensitive. We met in a café one afternoon. At first he believed what I told him, that I was a showgirl. But he eventually found out the truth and I thought that he would have nothing more to do with me. Whether he felt it was in his calling to save me, I don't know but he used to wait outside the house until I came out. We would stroll and talk and then one day, out of the blue he proposed. He knew what I did, but still he wanted to marry me.'

'And the baby?'

'You mean, did I tell him? I did try, Emily, but every time he always stopped me in my tracks. We married and began living as husband and wife. When I told him that I was expecting, he smiled and simply said, "This will be our child". He knew Emily, he knew. Somehow by not putting it into words, perhaps it seemed as though it wasn't true. He never questioned whether the child was premature or not. He was a kind and sensitive man. For all my sins Emily, I have been blessed with two good men in my life. That makes me incredibly lucky, don't you think?'

Emily gestured with a nod and a smile but the faraway look in her eyes told Amelia that her companion did not share the same fortune.

'Emily, my dear, please tell me what is in your heart. From seeing you step off the Lusitania I have known that something is wrong. That is partly why I have babbled on in order to take the onus off you. I had not dared to ask you sooner but now we are alone together, tell me what is troubling you. I recognise pain there.'

It was a comfort for Emily to unburden herself. She held nothing back as she recounted the events which she had witnessed in Paris and the later conversation with Jackson. For once Amelia remained silent, her only movement being the placement of a reassuring hand on Emily's arm whilst she spoke; a final embrace provided much needed comfort as Emily sobbed against her friend's shoulder.

'Life seems so unfair, Amelia. I could not openly love him as a wife and now I am unable to mourn him as a widow.'

'Emily, why didn't you write to me sooner, my dear? It is so wrong that you have had to bottle everything up inside you. I may be an old woman on the outside but I have seen most things in life and I do remember what it feels like to be young and in love. You have kept your love, your marriage and now … this secret for far too long.'

The tears continued to provide an outlet of emotion before finally subsiding into quiet sniffs of controlled agitation. Emily finally pulled away from the embrace with some newly-found composure, apologising repeatedly for her behaviour.

'My dear, you have absolutely nothing to apologise for. Remember I was once married to a vicar, so therefore I should be good at providing sustenance for the soul.' As the words fell from Amelia's lips a glint of mischievousness darted across her face, the skin wrinkling around her eyes and lips as the contagious smile almost made Emily smile too.

'That's better, Emily. Sometimes you know, even the Lord can work miracles.'

Neither woman held much faith in such words but Amelia had said them in the hope that they would make Emily feel better. In truth she did not know what to say as words of comfort. She was herself digging deep into her own reserves of reassurance as her mind dominated her thoughts with visions of Emily's disclosures; Niall's death, the discovery of his twin sister, her villainous family background, Christian Verholt, murder, chemical weapons, the Habsburgs; everything had coincided at the most precarious of times; the outbreak of war. Age and wisdom caused a premonition of fear to course through her body. Throughout it all Jackson had been the one link and that thought alone disturbed Amelia. He was she thought, an unpleasant individual, and one who still had scores to settle, whatever those might be.

Chapter Thirty-Seven

Time in New York was passing quickly and Amelia would shortly be married to Joe Perlstein. Before that could occur, Emily needed to keep her promise to Françoise Morel. She did not know why, but her hands were shaking as she gave Amelia the small box and unopened envelope which were both then placed down onto a nearby table. The normally content expression on the old lady's face faded, replaced with an initial look of alarm before finally stabilising into wistful withdrawal. She picked up and opened the box slowly, her eyes lingering upon its contents perhaps for longer than she desired; its appearance no doubt evoking long-lost memories.

'Beautiful, wouldn't you agree?' Amelia asked.

The appearance of the large diamond pendant was so spellbinding that Emily, appearing mesmerised by the refracted colours darting from its facets, seemed almost hypnotised as she nodded silently in agreement.

Suddenly the spell was broken abruptly as Amelia snapped the box shut and attempted to hand it back to Emily who resisted accepting it.

'That was all in the past and should stay in the past. Please take it.'

'Françoise asked me to give you both…'

'Both?' repeated Amelia, interrupting Emily. The old lady's eyes now switched to the forgotten envelope, scanning the name 'Amelia' written clearly on the front. Momentarily she seemed to reach out, hesitate and lightly touch it before resolvedly withdrawing her hand.

'As I said the past is just that.'

'That is not simply costume jewellery. Surely you should wear it or at least consider it as a piece of inheritance for your family, especially your grandsons. Françoise said that it belonged to you.'

'Yes, Jonathan in particular would find that amusing. Of course it will rightfully be his one day; by that I mean it once belonged to his father, or rather his father's family.'

The impact of the disclosure was immediate. Both women remained motionless, their eyes avidly fixed upon those of the other, seemingly without blinking. Emily resisted the obligatory questions, convinced that Amelia would explain in her own time. Instead she picked up the envelope, opened it and withdrawing to a chair, began to read its contents. Her face remained impassive for some time before tears began to well in her eyes. Folding the letter up, she returned it to its envelope and looking up, stared out through the window and beyond. Eventually, she turned and looked at her companion.

'Never doubt yourself or your actions, Emily. We are given life and we do the best that we can with the knowledge at the time. It is easy to look back after the event but at the time, you make a decision and stick by it. That is what I have always done and believed in.'

Silence intervened once more before Amelia continued.

'The diamond pendant was given to me by the son of a Duke; a wealthy family who had made money from the sugar cane industry in southeast Africa. Lord Richard Askhew was a client and I made the mistake of falling in love with him. He showered me with gifts, the most outrageous being this diamond, and took me away on expensive trips but when I became pregnant, naturally he did not want to know about it. As I told you before, Arthur Davenport appeared and proposed marriage. However, just before I left Paris to marry Arthur, I received this letter. I knew at once who it was from; I recognised the writing. I did not want anything to do with him. Françoise told me that I should read the letter but I refused and instead left both the unopened letter and the diamond with her. I told her to sell the necklace and use the money. I should have destroyed the letter but I didn't and now it has come back to haunt me. After all these years of living a decent life it has brought back my secret past.'

'I take it that you never heard from Lord Richard again?'

'Not *from* him, but I did hear *of* him. He decided to join the army and because of his family's connection with South Africa he returned there and was later killed in the first Anglo-Boer war in the Transvaal.' Tears once again began to appear in the old lady's eyes.

'What is the matter, Amelia?'

'The letter. This was the letter that he wrote to me before joining the army and returning to the Transvaal.'

'What of it?'

'He proposed in the letter. He was willing to go against his father as he wanted to marry me and bring up our child. He said that he would join the army and go back to South Africa if I declined to marry him. I sent him to his death, didn't I? I also deprived a father and son of a life together?'

'You did what you considered to be the best at the time, Amelia. You were also fortunate in having a good husband in Arthur.'

'Yes, I cannot dispute that. He was a good man and that makes me feel even guiltier. I loved him Emily, but I was never in love with him. Not as I was with...' Before she could say any more Emily had embraced Amelia, supporting her with understanding and compassion. She wished that she had not brought the box and letter with her and yet she had only fulfilled her promise to Françoise.

'Emily, will you give me your word that you will never tell Jonathan or any of my family about my past?'

'As you said, the past should remain in the past. You have a future to plan for, including a wedding in three days' time.'

Amelia married Joe Perlstein in a civil ceremony in New York City, attended by close family and friends. Joe, who had declined the idea of an elaborate synagogue wedding, wanted his future wife and her family to feel at ease with him. He was such a kind and gentle man who always seemed to put the needs of everyone else before his. Emily genuinely liked Joe and sensed that even Jonathan was beginning to like the man. His wife Beatrice was as always congenial to everyone and the twins David and Daniel, now adolescents, were perfectly agreeable to their grandmother's new husband. Watching them together, Emily became struck by the deep bond which existed between them. Impalpable and inexplicable, the affinity between them had been sorely tested in their formative years when they had goaded one another through countless battles, but now there was a profound unity. Seeing them together made Emily think about Niall and Kerry. Even though they had not grown up together, there remained the existence of an inseparable and protective link between them. She realised why Niall had lost his life; he too was a kind and gentle person who had tried to protect his sister, even if that had resulted in his death.

A small informal reception was later held at the Davenports' home. The guests simply mingled with one another, chatting whilst enjoying their drinks and buffet lunch. The ambience was one of contentment which seemed to gently spread throughout the day. It was exactly the form of celebration which Joe and Amelia had desired; there was little need for extravagance and formality, especially when the rest of the world was tightening its belt through austerity measures.

Emily glanced down at her left hand, focussing upon her wedding and engagement rings. Since leaving Liverpool she had been able to wear *his* rings and today she was more proud than ever to see them on her finger. The light falling upon the large emerald produced a dazzling display of radiance, instantly reminding her of his twinkling emerald green eyes. She remembered the first time she had been dazzled by them, waiting outside Amelia's cabin on the Lusitania. She recalled how they had captivated her attention for a little longer than was acceptable before his smile had intervened to jeopardise any composure remaining. Even the name of the stone itself was an apt reminder of the Emerald Isle, the place of his birth.

Her action did not go unnoticed; Amelia was watching her across the room; the sight made her heart ache with sorrow for a young couple whose lives had been shattered. For once, Amelia could not think of anything to say; no words of comfort would provide consolation. There was nothing that could be done and in three days' time Emily would depart and Amelia began to wonder whether she would ever see her friend again.

Any misgivings Amelia may have had were now deeply defined as she read the newspaper. An advertisement for the fastest and largest steamer in service in the Atlantic first attracted Amelia's eye as she saw the imminent departure date for the Lusitania, Saturday 1st May; a pertinent reminder that time with her friend was quickly passing. But it was the announcement underneath this which held her attention. The Imperial German Embassy had placed an advertisement warning passengers who were intending to cross the Atlantic in ships displaying the flag of Great Britain, or any of her allies, that they were at risk and liable to destruction in the zone of war, the waters around the British Isles. Initially, Amelia had decided not to mention this to Emily but the matter preyed upon her mind so heavily that she decided to show her the warning and persuade her to stay.

It was a risk that Emily ultimately decided she had to take. The school governors at St Cuthbert's had been sympathetic but to request additional absence seemed excessively demanding of their goodwill. A state of war did indeed exist between Germany and Great Britain and now it seemed a war which everyone had expected to be over by Christmas, was likely to continue for some time; no one knew for how long and that was the dilemma. Emily knew she had to return and decided that it was better to sail as planned, rather than delay.

Preparations for the Lusitania's 202nd Atlantic crossing began in earnest long before the appearance of any passengers. A supply of coal to feed the two dozen hungry boilers was laboriously shunted down chutes and into bunkers; an excess of five thousand tons had been supplied. The hold was then filled with loads of copper and brass and heavy packing cases weighted down with dental equipment and machine tools. Culinary provisions were also stored here, including 350,000 lb of beef, bacon and lard, 205 barrels of Connecticut oysters and 25 cases of oil. The comfort of the passengers was paramount, as of course was their safety.

The ship was under the command of William Turner, a Cunard Captain with ample experience. The alarm caused by the announcements in the papers had given Captain Turner no cause for concern. He believed the Germans would not dare to attack a liner as large and as famous as the Lusitania. He also argued that the ship could outrun a submarine even with six of her boilers shut down; the company had instructed Captain Turner to do just that because of the price of coal but the passengers had failed to be informed. Captain Turner however was confident that the Lusitania would carry its 1,959 passengers and crew safely across the Atlantic to Liverpool as it had done many times previously.

Joe and Amelia drove Emily to the docks and accompanied her to Pier 54. The journey had seemed tedious and strained as little conversation had passed between them; each one reluctant to consider the inevitable parting scene. A flurry of excitement was suddenly experienced as heads craned and whispers abounded throughout the assembled parties; Alfred Vanderbilt, the multimillionaire, had just arrived and was boarding the ship. Joe's reaction was simply to turn away with disinterest. Unlike everyone else he still advocated socialist principles; the bedrock of beliefs of the Greenwich community. As the rich and famous continued to arrive, Joe showed no further interest until the noted theatrical impresario Charles Frohman appeared, ever reliant upon his customary cane; the result of a rheumatic knee from a fall some years previous. It was rumoured that he was travelling to London to seek out potential Broadway talent. Joe stared admiringly at the man who had produced over seven hundred plays and who had even promoted playwrights such as J M Barrie. The presence now of such distinguished men on-board the ship appeared to quell any earlier anxiety. Presumably even third class passengers felt reassured that the Lusitania was safe and free from any suspected harm. However both Vanderbilt and Frohman, along with several other American passengers, had received anonymous messages the previous evening warning them not to step aboard. Their decision had been simply to ignore such messages.

Emily's attention was suddenly caught by the arrival of another wealthy man; this time the assembled crowds failed to show any interest, but Emily instantly recognised him. Christian Verholt, for reasons known only to himself, preferred to embark with the least possible commotion. His presence made Emily question his reason for travelling; another robbery or another murder? The thought caused her to shiver and attract Amelia's attention.

'My dear, are you cold?'

'No. I think someone has just walked over my grave.' Emily did not know why she had said this but she was suddenly aware of Amelia's anguished face staring at her.

'What has made you say that?'

'I don't know. Forget that I said it. It is just a foolish saying.'

Long after they had embraced and said their farewells, Amelia looked up at Emily high above them waving frantically from the Lusitania and suddenly sensed a strong feeling of apprehension. She did not know why but she knew that something terrible was going to happen.

Chapter Thirty-Eight

His eyes had lingered on her for some time. Whilst oblivious to his presence, she had caught his attention the moment she had boarded the Lusitania. He had arrived early, being one of the first passengers on-board; he knew he had to be there, waiting. This time he was aware that he could not afford any mistakes, not even one. In his mind, he knew instinctively that this would be his last chance and he sure was not going to waste it. Stepping back, he removed himself from early detection and mingled with anonymity into the assembled crowd on deck as the Lusitania began moving steadily away from Pier 54.

Emily remained on the deck for some time, watching the New York skyline and its definitive landmarks receding into the distance. When there was nothing more than the North Atlantic Ocean to peer out at, she finally filled her lungs with a generous breath of sea air, a measure which both purged and revitalised her emotions, before returning to her cabin. There she rested and took solace in a book before closing her eyes, only to drift into a short slumber. The short sleep revived her and she awoke feeling happier and more secure than she had done for some time. Feeling hungry, she realised that lunch was currently being served. With feelings of contentment and an eager appetite, which she attributed to the effect of the sea air, she made her way to the Second Class dining-room on the Saloon deck which was situated lower down in the ship. There under a ceiling broken with a small dome and a balcony, hungry passengers were enjoying the spoils of a Second Class menu.

Waiting to be seated she instantly recognised his voice with its inimitable inflections swathed in an American accent long before turning around to face him.

'Hello Emily. I didn't expect to see you on this voyage.'

'Inspector Jackson…!' Unsure as to how to address him because of his retirement she decided to still award him his full title. Slightly flustered, she began to chatter unreservedly as though she had to explain herself.

'I am just returning from a wedding in New York. Amelia Davenport, a friend whom I met on a previous journey… has just remarried.' Her sentence briefly faltered as she recalled that Jackson had met Amelia and that had been the result of the occurrences on that first voyage. She also remembered Amelia's dislike of the man in front of her. However she continued: '…And your reason for sailing… if that is not too impertinent?'

'My reason is very different, very different indeed. Let's just call it some unfinished business.' His transitory smile flashed a glimpse of the stained teeth precipitating a sudden malevolent look to loom across his face.

A waiter appeared ready to show them to a table.

'Shall we eat?' Jackson enquired.

Emily nodded doubtfully as she no longer had an appetite.

Jackson failed to mention his name at the table, but Emily knew that her earlier sighting of Verholt was the reason for her companion to be on-board. Reluctantly, she resisted questioning him further, but like many other couples now promenading after lunch they too walked together; suddenly he broke the embargo of the unmentionable name.

'Verholt! He's my unfinished business,' declared Jackson.

Emily turned and faced him.

'Just what do you mean by that?'

'I mean to *have him*.'

'Have him?' Emily repeated his words in ignorance.

He laughed. 'You don't know what I'm talking about, do you? No, I didn't think so. I want his soul. I want him and his family to pay for my family's suffering and for your suffering also. I'm going to take him to *Hell*.'

Emily was now looking at a Jackson that she did not recognise and it disturbed her.

'Please, there has been enough suffering already,' Emily pleaded.

'Don't worry, this time it will be different.'

That was the problem. Emily could not even begin to imagine what Jackson had in mind; the fear of the unknown especially in the subconscious, was always far more terrifying.

The following days at sea were ones of anguish for Emily. In Jackson's presence she could feel slightly more at ease, knowing that he was not sadistically extracting a confession from Verholt at that very moment but she could never quite relax either, for the fear of what he had already done or might be planning to do. Often she would think about Christian Verholt enjoying the decadent splendour of First Class travel; she had overheard envious descriptions of such accommodation. She imagined what it must be like to be present in the Georgian styled lounge with its inlaid mahogany panels, decorative plasterwork and towering green marble fireplaces or in the Queen Anne style smoking room, equipped with mahogany chairs and writing desks amidst a setting of Italian walnut panelling and red furnishings. Wherever he was, he was enjoying the very best alongside the highest echelon of society. Emily also knew that Jackson was sufficiently experienced to keep him under surveillance, even in First Class accommodation. Jackson may have been retired, but his skills of observing others whilst not being noticed himself were still highly proficient.

The day before the Lusitania was due to enter the waters surrounding the Irish shores, Emily had been enjoying the sea air whilst walking alone outside on the deck. She stopped suddenly, gripped the rail tightly and stared out across the water towards the far horizon. She knew that Ireland lay in that direction, but instead of reminiscing over fond memories of Niall she became seized by an unease of dark thoughts. She found it increasingly difficult to breathe and realised that she was experiencing a panic attack; something which had never troubled her before. Gasping for air, she stumbled as she moved away from the rail. Unable to get her breath she felt as though she was about to lose consciousness; an arm quickly swept around her to offer support and reassurance.

'Take it easy Emily,' Jackson advised.

'I will but...'

'Try not to speak.' Leading her to a steamer chair he sat down with her, remaining at her side patiently whilst she recovered.

'I've been watching you for some time. What caused this to happen?'

Emily shook her head. 'I really don't know. I just could not get my breath. At one point I felt as though I was drowning.'

As the colour returned to her face, Jackson began to look less anguished. Although Emily was beginning to feel better physically, she was still troubled emotionally. She did not tell Jackson that at the very moment when her breathing was at its worst, she had been overwhelmingly bombarded by those prophetic words of the medium: 'The Irish waters will fill with shrouds.'

The incident caused Emily to follow Jackson's advice; she retreated to her cabin and rested, only venturing out at mealtimes before taking the decision to retire early for bed.

Jackson was far from ready for slumber. Making his way stealthily to the centre of the ship where the First Class accommodation was situated, he had managed to transgress the class segregations and locate his target. This was not the first time that he had done so; he had frequently watched Verholt and now knew of his precise movements. Tonight as usual, the man had dined alongside other discriminating palates in the salubrious First Class Dining Room before relaxing in the masculine confines of the Smoking Room. There with a cigar and a generous glass of the finest brandy, he had the opportunity to overhear the aristocrats and celebrities discussing stock portfolios. He of course had the credentials himself to join in and discuss such affairs, but having no interest in his family's banking dynasty he preferred to listen to the remarks of others about their own riches.

The evening had been full of entertainment with a private party being thrown by Charles Frohman in his suite, followed later by the ship's concert. Alfred Gwynne Vanderbilt had been present at both, as had many wealthy people, including Verholt.

Jackson knew that tonight Verholt would be unlikely to return to his cabin for some time and therefore there would be ample time to do what he had to do.

Securing entry into Verholt's cabin was not difficult for Jackson. He began to rummage amongst his belongings, little caring for the disarray he was causing; subconsciously he wanted him to know that somebody had been there. Unrelentingly he rifled through expensive clothing, the likes of which he had never known upon his person, grunting with disgust at the thought of their cost. He scanned through personal papers, of which there was nothing even remotely condemning. Frustrated, Jackson banged his fist down on an expensive looking cabinet. He sat down on the bed, scanning around the room for proof. There had to be some incriminating evidence somewhere; there just had to be. Suddenly he realised the door to the en-suite was facing him; an unlikely prospect but one which he recognised as being feasible.

The crocodile skin case, impressed with the personalised gold monogram of CV, held a bewildering set of items which Jackson regarded as pure vanity. Lifting out the ivory backed hair brushes, combs, shaving brush, soap cases and shoe hook, he picked up the cut-throat razor and wondered whether this had been the weapon with which Verholt had despatched his mother. Staring down at the remaining items in the case his hands lingered for a moment over the hammered silver-topped jars and bottles. He had to lift each one out in order to see the contents of them. There was nothing unusual until he saw the last one; instead of toiletries the jar held jewellery. Jackson's chubby hands were totally unsuited for holding diamonds and pearls, but the necklace and earrings which had once graced the necks of beautiful women whose throats had been sliced through, continued to radiate their beauty.

Unceremoniously pushed into Jackson's pocket, the heirlooms now vital evidence were removed from the eminent surroundings of First Class in order to be used as surety for Verholt's descent into Hell.

Chapter Thirty-Nine

Friday May 7th 1915

As the Lusitania approached the southern coast of Ireland the thick fog which had enveloped it was at last beginning to clear. Passengers and crew looked across from the port-side to catch a glimpse of the distant Irish coastline now beginning to emerge on the horizon through the wispy mists above the calm sea. Standing on his bridge Captain Turner was planning the final part of the crossing. During the previous evening he had received a short message from the naval centre at Queenstown on Ireland's southern coast, warning him of the presence of German submarines off the west coast of Ireland.

Captain Turner had decided to maintain his course, providing a smooth crossing for his passengers without subjecting them to the abrupt deviations of a zigzag course which the Admiralty had recommended. Rather than sail down the middle of the sea lane, which would have placed the ship around seventy miles from the coast, Turner planned his course only a dozen miles from the Irish shores, passing close to Brow Head, Galley Head and the Old Head of Kinsale. He did however concede to various precautions; the positioning of additional lookouts, the closure of watertight doors and bulkheads and the swinging out of the lifeboats. The canvas covers of these were removed and their equipment and supplies checked. The windows had already been blacked out and passengers had been asked to avoid outside activities. Captain Turner assured his passengers that all measures were simply precautionary. He knew that if there was any increased likelihood of danger he would be warned by the Admiralty and he would find a protective armed cruiser at the Lusitania's side. With no such warnings or sightings he continued with his responsibility of providing his passengers with a cruise of relaxation and enjoyment.

The repeated knocking at the cabin door finally summoned its opening. Christian Verholt had no opportunity to close the door against the intruder who barged in before locking the door behind him.

'How dare you,' Verholt snapped indignantly.

'Mister, I dare do anything,' Jackson answered defiantly, pushing Verholt back into the centre of the cabin.

'My, what a mess your cabin is in. Looks like you've been burgled. Was anything taken? Well no, don't suppose you've reported it, have you?' Jackson grinned and then began to laugh, displaying the poor dental care of his teeth. Verholt remained silent, his normally immaculate blond hair slightly dishevelled. The cold steel blue eyes stared menacingly back at Jackson for some time.

'What do you want?' asked Verholt begrudgingly.

'Let's make a start with the truth,' came the decisive reply.

The cold eyes continued to scrutinise Jackson; the charm which women normally saw in them had been replaced with callous cruelty. No doubt this was the face which his mother, Marie Philippe, had witnessed just before her death. They did not intimidate Jackson, a man who had experienced looking into the eyes of many of New York's notoriously hardened gang leaders. The eyes may have been trying to engage and divert Jackson's attention but he was not fooled. As Verholt's hand slipped rapidly towards the cut-throat razor lying on a bedside cabinet, Jackson's reflex action was to swiftly punch Verholt hard in the stomach, winding him sufficiently to drop onto his knees and relinquish the razor. Jackson rained his large fist repeatedly into Verholt's face, making the man curl into a defensive ball as he covered his face with his hands. Blood was now gushing from his nose and dripping onto the floor.

For a few moments Jackson had been transported back into the New York cells, where he had always commanded authority before extracting confessions. A rush of adrenaline was welling up inside him; the action had stirred and excited him but he knew that he had to refrain from continuing, as much as he wanted to. The man was of no use dead to him; at least not at the moment.

The kick into his side made Verholt groan with pain.

'Ready to talk yet or do you need more persuading?' Jackson's question elicited no verbal reply but slowly Verholt began to lift up his head. His eyes merely stared back with hateful intensity.

Jackson began to question him about his previous activities and intentions, including his former voyage on the Lusitania. Standing over him he commanded the upper hand. As each answer was given Jackson would deliberate; slowly pacing around Verholt's crumpled body until he reached his decision. A good answer was followed by another question; a bad answer resulted in Jackson's displeasure. It was a simple formula which had repeatedly served Jackson well. He had always been grateful that as a young policeman he had once served under the formidable head of the New York City Police Department, Thomas F. Byrnes. Under his tutorage he had practised 'the third degree,' a combination of both psychological and physical punishments which in his eyes remained unquestionably effective. However distasteful his job appeared to his colleagues, he would always uphold with the argument: a tough world and a tough city needs a tough inspector to hunt down such criminals. It was simply a job and one that he was good at. Being able to also enjoy the job was of course an added bonus. This time it was personal and that alone added an extra thrill.

However reluctant Verholt had been initially to confess, he soon became compliant to the inquisition; the practice being beneficial to both. Jackson did not want to summon unwanted attention from other passengers or stewards and realised that it was better to conduct business with the least amount of noise.

Eventually Verholt began to speak freely and confessed to the murder of his mother which he viewed as little more than retribution for her abandonment of him as a child. He confessed to numerous occasions when he had gained the confidence of wealthy aristocrats only to covet their possessions and arrange for such items to be stolen and then sold to others. Indeed the reason for this voyage was due to the Marie Antoinette necklace and earrings which he had stolen from his own mother; he was about to sell them to a wealthy contact in England. He had a business which supplied on demand; he would seek out the desires of those willing to pay him whilst instigating such theft. Of course he had had a willing accomplice who like himself had a certain reputation.

'You mean Kerry Doyle?' asked Jackson.

Verholt merely nodded.

'Did you also kill *her* and her brother?' demanded Jackson.

'No,' declared Verholt emphatically.

The simple answer was delivered with such conviction. The man had freely confessed to everything else but not to this. For once Jackson refrained from using his fist as doubt was evident even in his mind.

'But you know who did?'

'I'd tried following the double-crossing little bitch; her and her brother. I wasn't going to let her get away with stealing those papers and selling them. I found out that she had formed connections with the Germans and was about to sell the papers to them. I wasn't going to let her get away with that. If I'd had the chance I would have killed her myself. I knew that she held too much on me and I wasn't going to let her destroy me. I'd already torched a couple of places in Paris. But I lost sight of them and with the troubles in Europe I decided to leave for America. The last I heard was that two bodies had been found shot and burned. They didn't die by my hands. Whether it was the Germans or other powers of strength, I cannot say.'

'Powers of strength…what are you talking about?'

'The contents of those papers would have been of interest to a number of countries. Alphonse Philippe was developing chemical warfare for France but any number of governments would have been interested in them. I have even heard that their deaths were killings of reprisal. Even the Habsburgs themselves may have been involved. Nobody knows.'

Jackson shook his head in frustration. Even now when he had the man in front of him, matters still could not be settled. He slid his fingers into his jacket pockets and suddenly he felt the shape of a forgotten object lying there. As he pulled it out, a smile ran swiftly across his face as he held it in front of Verholt's face.

'Does this look familiar?'

'Where did you get that?' asked Verholt staring at his family's crest adorning the ring. His hand reached out to touch it but Jackson denied him any contact.

'Kerry's mother took it from your father's hand when he raped her.'

The effect of those words was as potent and devastating as any punch Jackson could have delivered. The man was instantly silent; appearing punch-drunk and bewildered he seemingly swayed in disbelief. As Jackson looked at him something unexpected began to occur.

An exceptionally loud bang was followed seconds later by another far more amplified and powerful noise, the like of which Jackson could only describe as an explosion. The cabin and its contents were not just swaying but rolling sideways; the ship had immediately begun listing fifteen degrees to starboard causing passengers to be thrown off their feet.

Unforeseen events had now overtaken Jackson's enquiry. Verholt began to scramble to his feet; dazed and shaken he reached out and tried to steady himself against anything that was firmly positioned. Both men made their way to the cabin door, which Jackson unlocked quickly. Soon they were amongst other passengers who were desperately trying to reach the outside deck and the only chance of survival. Around them tortuous noises reverberated; the shattering sounds of breaking glass, tense distorting strains of cracking wood and the eerie ripping and twisting melodic groans of wrenching metal. Beneath their feet they sensed the stricken vibrations of the ship's turbines taking them speedily on their final journey. The Lusitania was now being propelled deeper into the ocean by its three turbines; the forward motion was only accelerating the flooding.

Down in the engine room the forward turbines were frantically disengaged so that the reverse turbines could be used. However the haste of action had not allowed the propellers and their shafts to stop rotating and the turbines were working against one another causing a pressurised build-up of incoming steam. An eruption of steam lines and valves occurred suddenly, resulting in a massive drop of pressure. Captain Turner quickly gave the order for the ship to turn to port and hopefully gain the safety of shallower waters. However one of the steam lines which had burst had been responsible for the ship's steerage which had now resulted in the rudder becoming locked. As her propellers were continuing to push her forward, the Lusitania was plunging ever deeper into the water.

The impact had reinforced to everyone that there was of course a war raging but now they had been drawn into it by a torpedo which had just ripped through the Lusitania.

A new wave of panic emerged as passengers felt the deck increasingly tilting under their feet. Their only chance of survival lay with the lifeboats. On the portside the ship's listing was so severe that the launching of lifeboats there had been so erratic and clumsy that the little boats had been broken apart causing the passengers to be tipped into the sea.

The bow was now below the waves and even the bridge was being washed over with the seawater. Jackson looked around at the frightened faces; he himself immune to the prospects of what lay ahead. There in the crowd his eyes fell upon one figure; she looked solitary even though she was surrounded by many people. He called out her name but she was too far away; the piteous cries around just muffled his call, concealing it from her ears.

Everywhere people were anxiously trying to get near to the lifeboats. Even Alfred Vanderbilt, accompanied by his valet, was helping passengers into the lifeboats. His presence there drew many looks of admiration as he continued to work selflessly. A young woman holding a small baby in her arms had caught his attention as she had been unable to find a life vest. Vanderbilt gave her his own, tying it onto her as she cradled her baby in her arms. Such was the extent of his bravery; a multimillionaire who placed people before himself. The act alone was humbling; even Jackson experienced a fleeting moment of tenderness.

However, that moment vanished as quickly as it had appeared; an escalating commotion of angry voices could be heard in the distance. The remaining lifeboats were now causing a frenzy of anxiety. Jackson could see Emily being pushed and jostled further and further away from the lifeboats; suddenly he used his large frame to surge through the crowds to help her. Just as he became in touching distance of her, he saw Verholt driving himself ever closer to a lifeboat. It was at that moment that Jackson summoned every ounce of stamina that he could muster in his body, launching himself forward in order to grab Verholt by the shoulders and yank him backwards, causing him to stumble and be trampled on by the surrounding crowd. Working hastily he then pulled Emily towards him and thrust her forwards into a lifeboat. Everything had happened so quickly that Emily had not even realised who had pushed her to safety.

As the little boat was lowered, she looked up at Jackson and called out his name, 'Sam.'

He looked down at her and motioned with a simple wave. Somewhere inside he detected a warm sentimental feeling, the type of which he had not experienced since being a young boy cocooned in one of his mother's embraces. He had just done something which would have made his mother very proud of him and that was something which he always craved. The little boat dropped unceremoniously onto the water and Jackson took one last look at Emily. He had managed at last to set her free and he knew that his job was almost completed. He had been indebted to Emily for a long time; she had of course, reminded him of his mother. For that reason alone he would never have allowed any harm to come to her.

The ultimate part of his job now beckoned. He made his way calmly through the ensuing final bursts of panic as the remaining people on-board realised that the ship would soon be completely submerged. Captain Turner stared at the scenes around him in shock; holding onto the rail in front of him for support, he then gazed at the Irish shores as if willing them to come closer.

Jackson found Verholt looking dazed and confused.

'You just cost me a seat,' murmured Verholt.

'Well I've come back for you now.'

The evil glint in Jackson's eyes became disturbing to Verholt who now began to edge away from his tormentor. Suddenly the grasp of his wrist made Verholt look down in horror as he saw Jackson handcuffing them together.

'What the…What are you doing? Are you mad?' Verholt cried out in panic.

Jackson reached into his pocket and once again produced the crested ring.

'Yours, I believe,' Jackson said as he flung it into the sea. 'Don't worry we'll be following it soon.'

Jackson then opened out his large chubby hand and displayed a small key, which he also threw into the sea.

'That was the key for the handcuffs. I'd kept them as a souvenir since leaving the Police; I knew one day they would prove useful. Well, looks as though we're going to be staying together for a long time.' As the words left his lips he began to chuckle with excited anticipation.

'For God's sake!' exclaimed Verholt.

'No good appealing to him. I'm going to take you to *Hell*.'

'Why? What have I done to you?' came the final question.

'The Verholts destroyed my family. It's as simple as that. Well Verholt, our destiny is waiting...'

The bow of the Lusitania hit the bottom of the seabed sending a reverberating shudder throughout the vessel, whilst the stern was raised high into the air; a feature decidedly reminiscent of the sinking of the Titanic, just three years earlier. Captain Turner had climbed up onto the port side of the navigation bridge, determined to be the last person to leave the ship, but suddenly water engulfed the entire bridge, its unabated force sweeping him out into the cold sea. It was only when he was at a great enough distance away from the visible remains of his ship that he could still see human beings on-board. The Lusitania was now on her starboard side, plunging rapidly beneath the huge rolling wave of water which was swallowing her up. Her funnels had collapsed and her boilers had exploded and Captain Turner saw the remaining life on-board being forcefully sucked in before being spewed out. The Lusitania had reached her final destination, only eighteen minutes after the first impact of the torpedo.

Initially its disappearance was covered with a seething mass of foam as the freezing waters became churned with steam and wreckage. Dead bodies popped up to the surface and floated alongside buoyant wooden remains; deck chairs, crates and furniture were being eagerly seized by the grasping hands of bodies thrashing around for survival. Few of the lifeboats had been launched successfully, owing to the listing of the ship and the tendency for the lifeboats to swing inwards; some of those which had, had later been abandoned for fear of being sucked down into the water with the liner's demise.

The little boat which Emily had been in had bounced into the sea upon its launching, causing it to hold water. Around it, survivors in the sea had anxiously grabbed onto its sides pulling it further down into the water, making it impossible to row away from the sinking ship. It soon became obvious that the only way to survive was to jump into the sea and swim away from the sinking Lusitania.

Emily unhooked her skirt and removed it; etiquette was not required now. The other passengers in the boat were beginning to jump into the water. Drawing upon a deep breath, Emily rose to her feet whilst feeling the little boat rocking beneath her and quietly jumped in. The cold was unimaginable and although she had intended to hold her mouth tightly shut, the shock made her gasp and swallow sea water. She panicked as the black water engulfed her. Thrashing around wildly she finally managed to break through the water's surface and gasp for air. Her instinct now was to swim away from the ship; it was disappearing quickly and she knew that there would not be much time. Soon the end arrived; an ignoble one for such a distinguished ship. It was over; the ship had gone and Emily, along with other desperate survivors, searched for anything that would allow them to remain afloat.

Tightly gripping the floating piece of wood, she willed herself to stay conscious. Everywhere Emily looked, there were islands of people holding onto floating remains. She tried conversing with a woman next to her believing that it would help their chance of survival, but the cold reduced the dialogue to curt monosyllabic replies and eventually silence, as the woman slipped away from her wooden crate. Now alone Emily tried to remember her first voyage on-board the Lusitania. She began mouthing the names of those she had met in an effort to remain conscious: 'Amelia Davenport, Jonathan and Beatrice Davenport, Daniel and David Davenport, Christian Verholt, Inspector Jackson...' Hypothermia was now causing her to struggle with any further recollections. Her teeth chattered uncontrollably as she tried again: 'Inspector Jackson, Inspector Jackson...Niall Branigan.' The cold was now so insidious that the mention of the final name was meaningless to her.

Chapter Forty

The final death toll far exceeded any initial estimated speculation of the tragedy. An eclectic mix of naval and civilian vessels, including tugs and trawlers, had plied their way relentlessly from the mainland to the site of the sinking, rescuing survivors and collecting victims before returning to Queenstown harbour; a place already synonymous with tragedy, as this had been the last port of call for the Titanic before it had left for its doom in the North Atlantic, just three years earlier.

The scale of the current tragedy was incomprehensible, especially to the harbour official who had refused to let the vessels land without the necessary paperwork. The continuous arrival of an armada of rescue ships finally pressurised the official to concede to a series of unscheduled landings. The locals stared in horror at the undignified rows of corpses which lay around the waterfront, some having been unceremoniously piled onto the harbour steps; wandering around them, bewildered survivors searched piteously for family and friends. As the sun gradually went down, the hopes of many faded; accepting that anyone left out there in the sea would by now have perished. Some bodies were later washed up on local beaches but many were never recovered. A mass grave was dug for the bodies that could not be identified, of which there were more than 800. The Lusitania had left New York with 1,959 passengers and crew on-board but only 764 had survived.

Captain Turner was one of the survivors, fortunate to have been picked up by a small steamer. Unfortunately, the same fate had not graced either Alfred Vanderbilt or Charles Frohman. The bodies of Jackson and Verholt were never recovered; survivors later told of how they recalled seeing two men handcuffed together just before the boilers had exploded, but afterwards there had been no sightings of them.

The severely injured were taken to Queenstown Hospital, where understaffed doctors and nurses worked tirelessly to retain and repair as many lives as they could. Some patients had broken bones, which could be mended, whilst others were closer to death due to their delicate ages compounded with the alarming effects of hypothermia. Facing difficulty in speaking, they appeared confused and in a stupor, and in some cases, amnesic.

A nurse at the bedside of one unconscious survivor who had been brought in smiled as the woman opened her eyes for the first time.

'Just lie still. You're safe now,' the nurse added reassuringly.

'Where am I?'

'You're in Queenstown Hospital.'

'Where's Niall? Where is he? He should be here…' The anxious demanding questions suddenly stopped as confusion gave way to reality.

'Just lie back and get some rest. We'll talk later.' The soft Irish accent helped to reassure her. It also reminded Emily of *him*. She closed her eyes and realised that she had survived. She also remembered that she had lost her husband long before the sinking of the Lusitania.

When Emily finally opened her eyes for the second time following a period of slumber, the same face as before was smiling down at her.

'Would you like a little soup?'

Emily found herself returning the smile with an eager nod. Oblivious to the time of day, the mention of food had reminded her stomach that she was very hungry. The kind nurse brought her a bowl of soup, which she heartily finished.

'The doctor said you would be hungry. He took a look at you when you were asleep, having examined you earlier when they first brought you in. He knew then that you would be all right. A good doctor is never wrong.'

The nurse's words remained in her mind until she fell asleep again. Upon waking the following morning, Emily struggled to rationally coordinate the images her eyes were sending to her brain. At first, she thought that unconsciousness or even delirium had taken hold, but as she repeatedly blinked she realised that she was entirely conscious and that the face staring down at hers was indeed real. She was in an emotional turmoil; ecstatically happy and yet, there was something not right. In his face there was no recognition, none at all.

'Niall.' It was the only word that she could say and one which caught his attention.

'You're far more on the road to recovery than I thought,' he joked laughingly, before coming closer to her and adding, 'So just how do you know my name?'

It was at that precise moment that Emily felt nauseous as she stared back at the doctor in front of her. A heady mixture of disbelief and bewilderment infiltrated her spirit. Her husband did not know her; the man that she loved, the man that she had believed was dead. The cruel irony was that he was dead to any effect she should have on him.

The emerald green eyes still radiated their verdant light but now there was a fragile far-away look in the gaze. Emily struggled to comprehend the situation; how could two people who had known one another in every way now behave as strangers? The eyes that had once teased and twinkled sensuously in her presence were now impassive. The hands that had once touched her body with tender desire were motionless. The body that she had once known every intimate part of was cold and indifferent to her.

Emily's silence was an indication for him to leave her to rest. As he walked away from her bed, he did cast one look back at his curious patient, only to find her staring at him in a disconcerting way. That fixed look would continue to unsettle him for some time to come.

Sleep was nothing more than a remote possibility for Emily as she tossed and turned over every potential scenario. At first, she considered the effects of the war. She recalled the glazed expressions on the faces of the soldiers she had helped at Beckson Infirmary. Their shell-shocked gazes, trembling convulsions and incoherent speech were very different cases. Niall had no such symptoms; he was as he had always been except with some loss of memory. It appeared, she thought, that he was suffering from amnesia; who or what had caused that Emily could only guess.

The following day she was discharged and allowed to leave the hospital. Niall was not on duty; a fact which troubled her. She dressed herself slowly; her clothing having been donated to the hospital by benevolent locals. The slightly dowdy and ill-fitting garments were at least preferable to those of her own, which had been completely ruined by being immersed in seawater for so long. Everyone had remarked how fortunate she had been in wearing a life vest; without that she would most likely have perished. Emily recalled those final moments in the lifeboat when she had had to make decisions. However uninviting the water was, she had accepted that her only chance of survival would be to enter it. Before removing her skirt she had made one personal gesture; that of removing her wedding and engagements rings and threading them onto a chain around her neck. She had thought that if she was going to die she wanted to keep his rings close to her and not let them slip from her hand into the freezing water. As Emily placed them once again onto her finger she was grateful that she had made that decision.

'Ready to leave?' The soft Irish accent was instantly recognisable. As Emily turned around she saw Niall smiling back at her.

'Yes, I think I am.' She noticed that he was no longer wearing his white doctor's coat and added, 'You're not on duty now, are you?'

'No. I just find it difficult to stay away sometimes.' The eyes began to shine brightly as he coughed hesitantly. 'What will you do now?'

'I don't really know, except that I need to make arrangements to travel back to England. I need to speak to someone from Cunard. I suspect that there will be lots of people doing the same thing.'

'Yes, I am sure you are right, but not today. Queenstown is to pay its last respects to the victims of this tragedy. If you will allow me I would like to walk with you, just to ensure that you are looked after.'

'Thank you. I would like that. I would like that very much.'

The harbour still remained an aftermath of frenzied confusion. Coupled with the emotions of loss, the words on many peoples' lips spoke angrily of blame and avoidable disaster. The fact that the Lusitania had been carrying crates of bullets and shell parts as well as civilian passengers, had made it an outright target. These feelings were at their most sensitive today, Monday May 10th, as family, friends, survivors and locals stood hatless, lining the streets as the carts carried the ninety-two bodies to the cemetery, two miles from Queenstown. The procession trundled through the crooked streets, passing by the closed shops whose blinds had been pulled down as a mark of respect for each body now lying in its cheap coffin. Continuing to follow the undulating country lanes far into the distance, rising and falling between the verdant hills, the long cortège stream finally came to its resting place. The tears that fell were not solely for those that were now being buried but also for the one thousand and more bodies that still remained out there in the Atlantic.

Emily swept her tears away, oblivious to Niall's fixed gaze upon her. When she turned to face him she saw a sad look of loss in his eyes.

'We need to talk.'

'Yes,' was Emily's only reply.

'If it is not too presumptuous, will you come back with me to my house? It is only in Cork.'

'It is not presumptuous. Yes, I would like to do that.'

Niall drove them in his Model T Ford car; the initial sight of it instantly reminded Emily of George's own Tin Lizzie but sadly Niall himself made no reference to it. For much of the journey there was silence between them. It was an awkward silence, the type that ensues when there are many questions to be asked but no perception of how to begin. It was only when the house appeared that Niall spoke.

'The phrase, home is where the heart is, seems a good description of a place, don't you agree?' Emily smiled and nodded, remembering when she had last heard Niall say those words to her. They entered the hallway of the house which seemed to be gloomily steeped in an era of the past, before going into a parlour which more closely resembled a library lined with volumes of books than a place in which to relax or entertain.

'This was my parents' home, the people who loved me and gave me an upbringing. I owe them everything. I longed to be like him. I wanted to become a doctor and at one time there were even two Doctor Branigans; he and I both practising here. They were good people. They were very good to me.' For a moment Niall once again fell silent, as if contemplating the next thread of the conversation.

'Miss Taylor, forgive me but I'm going to speak plainly; have we met before? There is something about you that makes me think that we have. You must think it an exceedingly strange question but there is a very good reason for it. Something happened to me, I don't know quite what, but as a consequence I have lost all memory of a certain part of my life. I can remember growing up here and becoming a doctor. I can remember even going to sea and working as a doctor on the Lusitania.' The mention of the name brought a small amount of colour into Emily's cheeks which Niall sensed as a reaction.

'Did we meet on the Lusitania?' Emily merely nodded in reply.

'There is something more, isn't there?' Niall's eyes now fell to the large oval-shaped emerald and diamond engagement ring on Emily's finger.

'Do you recognise this?' Emily asked tentatively, raising her left hand.

'It's the ring that once belonged to my mother, Mrs Branigan, the lady who raised me. She was a very special woman and I know that I would only have given that ring to someone who was equally as special.'

The bloom in Emily's cheeks now became more pronounced.

'I am the fortunate one because I married an extremely special man.'

Niall suddenly sank down into a nearby chair, clasping his head into his hands. He began to sob; a pitiful sight which drew Emily to him causing her to embrace her husband. The comfort of her arms around him was reassuringly soothing and resulted in him drawing her onto his lap. As he raised his head, their eyes met and their lips, only fractionally apart, moved closer together until each one could sense the soft light touch of the mutually tempting kiss.

Soon the lightness of the touch became consumed with an appetite of greed as the kiss allowed each one to express their emotions. As quickly as the embrace had begun it ended suddenly. Niall drew back; full of remorse and apologies for his action whilst Emily understanding of his reasons, would have liked the experience to have continued. She recognised that it would take time for them to become reacquainted.

It was clear from Niall's conversation that he was fully aware of his upbringing and even of his blood family, the Doyles, including his sister Kerry. He recalled working on the Lusitania but had no memory of meeting Emily, marrying her and living in Beckston. Nor could he recall going to Paris to find Olivia and Kerry. The only recent memory he had was of finding himself on a train to Paris. He remembered confusion, not just prevalent in his own mind but in all those around him, as he later found out with horror, that he had stumbled into a war-torn Europe. The only place that appeared safe to him stemmed from childhood memories; the Emerald Isle was his home.

Epilogue

BECKSTON 1918

Church bells rang out jubilantly throughout Europe on the eleventh hour on 11th November, 1918. Their glorious peals signalling that the fighting had finally ended and the troops were returning home. Once the euphoric celebrations had ended, however, everyone knew that life would never be the same again; more than eight and a half million lives had been lost and twenty-one million soldiers had been wounded. Those who came home were different to the ones who had left; the boys now men, their bodies and spirits weakened and broken by the unforgettable things they had had to witness and endure.

The world was now being attacked by a very different type of killer; an influenza epidemic. The disease had emerged throughout the spring of 1918 in clusters around the world. Even soldiers in the trenches in France had complained of sore throats, headaches and little appetite. By May 1918, the effects of the disease were being felt in Glasgow and within weeks the influenza had reached London; 228,000 people were to die from it in Britain.

As children twined their skipping ropes in school playgrounds, they now sang in time to a new rhyme:

I had a little bird
Its name was Enza
I opened the window,
And in-flu-enza.

The headmaster at St Cuthbert's knew this rhyme well. Previously retired Mr Clarke had originally agreed to cover Emily

Taylor's temporary absence. However, at the time, no one could have foreseen the unlikely events that would occur.

News of the Lusitania's sinking had shocked the Beckston community. Miss Taylor had always been a highly respected and much admired headmistress. Confirmation of her survival was greeted with fervent relief, not least of course by her mother and her sister, Olivia. But it was the next piece of news that was to stun the community and everyone who knew her; Emily Taylor was to return home to England a married woman. As the wife of Doctor Branigan, it was true that she would always hold an esteemed place in the community, but she now had to relinquish her position as a teacher and of course, headmistress of St Cuthbert's.

The Branigans had returned to Beckston in the early summer of 1915; with a war taking place and a lack of suitable candidates, Mr Clarke, who admitted missing his role in educating his pupils, had willingly agreed to remain at the school.

Emily and Niall did not care that they were the centre of speculative talk; on reflection, many were now convinced that the romance had been blossoming for some time. A smile would slide across Emily's lips when she overheard such talk; the period which was being referred to, was of course their early married years. However, now they could live openly as man and wife and for that reason alone their happiness should have been unbridled, but it wasn't.

Although already married, they had received a blessing at a small church in Ireland before returning to England, which had helped to reaffirm their marriage vows. Those early months had once again been like those of a honeymoon period, when a couple delights in getting to know one another. Initially, they returned to the Taylors' home and Niall returned to his practice, working with Doctor Lawson. Everyone was new to him and he had to get to know them. He had tried to enlist, but his memory loss had been to his detriment, and even in offering his medical services at the front he had been turned down. Everyone around him had understood, but to Niall, it was proving a period of inertia. He had fallen in love with Emily but still had no recall of their earlier years together. He had not known of Kerry's death and still had no recollection of his time in Paris or the events which had culminated in his loss of memory. As the time went by, he became frustrated, feeling that he was not contributing to the war effort in any way. He could appreciate how George felt whilst Alice drove the buses; although Niall had recently confirmed her pregnancy which was an absolute source of delight to them both.

The influenza epidemic was now stretching hospital doctors and nurses to breaking point. Hearing of such news, Niall immediately offered his services and obligingly went to London; an area overwhelmed with cases. Although Emily had wished to accompany her husband and offer help, Niall vehemently refused; he knew the illness was highly infectious and would not allow her to be at risk.

The weeks and months seemed to pass slowly and Emily once again felt as though she had lost Niall. She knew that she had to accept his course of action, even though she worried for his health. She returned to Beckston Infirmary and offered her help on the wards working with the wounded; this time accompanied by the generous efforts of her sister, Olivia.

The sight of the telegram made her feel nauseous. She had heard many tales of wives fearing the appearance of such a paper and for that reason alone, she expected the worst. The war was now at an end and the nation was celebrating, but November 1918 had witnessed a second wave of infection; the virus had swept indiscriminately through the celebrations turning them into unexpected wakes. Her hands trembled as she opened the telegram but relief filtered in as her eyes read the message inside. It merely informed her that Niall had been involved in an accident and was in hospital as a patient. He was alive and that was enough.

The following day, she travelled by train to London and went straight to the hospital. A nurse informed her that he had been hit by a car and, although he had sustained head injuries, he was stable and not giving cause for concern. He had been fortunate that the injuries had not been more severe. No doubt the reason for his carelessness when crossing the road could be attributed to overwork and exhaustion. The epidemic had certainly taken its toll of everyone, including the medical staff through sleep deprivation.

Cuts and bruises are repairable, Emily thought, as she looked at Niall who was sleeping. Although she dearly wanted to, she refrained from taking his hand in hers and instead waited quietly at his bedside. When he did awake, the emerald eyes fell upon her face and twinkled with enthusiasm. She returned the smile and for a brief moment had a curious feeling that the old Niall was smiling back at her. There was little need for conversation as his eyes had conveyed everything.

Two days later, Niall was dismissed and the couple travelled back to Beckston. As they boarded the busy train filled with returning troops, Niall appeared to somewhat hesitate, before Emily linked her arm through his reassuringly. She was determined that he would not be returning to the London wards; his work had almost cost him his life.

They found a compartment with two empty seats and sat together holding hands, watching the countryside passing by. The repetitive motion along the tracks was pleasant and calming, seemingly lulling them into slumber.

Emily did not know how long she had been asleep, but when she awoke she was alone in the compartment; Niall was nowhere to be seen and the other passengers had obviously disembarked. Frantically, she ran into the corridor wondering which direction to take, anxious that Niall had already left the train. In a distant carriage she thankfully saw his silhouette and quickly made her way towards it. He was standing by an outer door, his hand hesitant on the handle.

'Niall,' she called out desperately. 'What are you doing?'

Without looking at her he repeated, 'I need to get off this train to save her... I need to get off this train.'

Throwing her arms around him she drew him back and away from danger. They walked back to their compartment and he slumped down exhausted into his seat. Tears began to trickle down his face as he now seemed to be aware of his present surroundings.

'I can remember everything... Emily, I know what happened.'

At first she was apprehensive, but at the same time Emily had willed this moment for so long. She wanted him to be able to remember their earlier years together but such recall, no doubt the result of his head injuries, had also dredged up something alarming.

'I knew if I allowed Kerry to be on her own she would walk straight into danger. That's why I stayed with her. Those papers that she had taken from the Philippes' house were dangerous. She had intended to sell them to a contact in Germany, but it soon became clear that there were a few of them who were double-crossing her; she was of course only a woman in their eyes and therefore an easy target. Soon, we were being pursued by agents from the French Government as well as some others who were representing the Habsburg family.' He then hesitated momentarily before continuing. Emily sensed that the next part would be distressing for him.

'We made our way to a place called Riquewihr in the Alsace region. We knew that we had to keep our heads down as Europe was a dangerous place to be. It was only a matter of time before one of them would find us. I wanted Kerry to return with me to Paris and hand the papers back. I could see the extreme danger we were in. At first, she would hear nothing of it but then suddenly changed her mind. She travelled with me to Strasbourg and boarded a train for Paris. I remember finding an unoccupied compartment and entering it with Kerry behind me. She then said something completely out of context. She told me that I meant a great deal to her and it was for that reason that she could not allow me to remain with her. As I turned to look at her I just remember being struck on the back of my head. When I finally regained consciousness I had reached Paris. I was alone and had only a selective memory. I now know that I owe my life to her. We will probably never know what happened to her after that, or who killed her.' Niall's eyes suddenly began to water.

'However, one thing is certain; she saved my life but I contributed to the loss of hers. I had already substituted the papers with others which were harmless. I burned the details of those chemical formulae which no doubt would have been used by either side for acts of inhumanity. Evil has been prevalent in this war, especially with victims of chemical warfare. As a doctor and a human being, I could not allow further suffering. I did what I thought was best, Emily, in the belief that Kerry would come back with me to Paris.'

'It was her choice,' Emily quietly reminded him.

'Yes, but one which led to her death.'

The details of Kerry's death were never to be solved. The man who died at her side could have been an agent who was also murdered by other government agents or even representatives from the Habsburg dynasty. No one would ever know.

Sometimes Emily felt that this could have been a case for someone relentless in investigative work; someone such as Inspector Jackson. Of course, there was no one like him and there never would be; he truly had been unique. His brusque manners and menacing appearance had proved disconcerting to Emily and others for so long but her final memories of him were glazed in gentleness. His body and that of Verholt's were never recovered. Emily knew that their remains were somewhere out in the Atlantic along with the Lusitania.

They would never be disturbed and neither would certain facts. Emily did eventually discuss with Niall his family connection to the Verholts but he simply shrugged his shoulders with disinterest. As Amelia had said, the past is just that and only the present and the future would hold importance.

Several experiences had also changed Olivia's life. She now looked after her mother at home and also ran a thriving milliner's and draper's shop. Her time helping others at the Beckston Infirmary had changed both her life and her acceptance of others; she had met and married a severely wounded soldier, whose leg injuries had been sustained in the war, forever confining him to a wheelchair. Olivia was no longer the person she had once been; for which everyone was grateful.

Emily and Niall continued to enjoy their special friendship with George and Alice, who by 1920, were a happy and blossoming family with two sons and a daughter. The Branigans also enjoyed visiting Amelia and Joe Perlstein in New York and looked forward to playing host to them in their new home when their friends travelled over to England.

Their marriage was very special and Niall and Emily would have been more than content even if nothing else had occurred in their lives. But something special did occur.

Approaching forty years of age, Emily had not expected to become pregnant. She certainly had not expected to be carrying twins. She gave birth to a boy and a girl and both mother and babies were extremely healthy.

One evening as Niall cradled their daughter in his arms, he looked longingly at her before smiling across at Emily.

'Would you mind if we named her Kerry? I know it may seem strange, especially as she was certainly not a role model, but she was my sister and perhaps if life had been different for her at the start, she would have had a more normal upbringing. Underneath that hard exterior she proved to me that there was an element of softness. Of course I understand if you don't want to...'

'I think that would be a wonderful gesture.'

'Thank you. That means a lot to me. She did save my life and now, being able to look at these two and you, I am immensely grateful for that. But what about the little fellow that you are holding? Shall we name him Charles, after your father? Would you like that?'

'That would also be a lovely gesture but I have another suggestion.' Niall stared at his wife with puzzlement.

'I would like to name him Samuel or rather Sam, in tribute to someone who helped to save my life.'

Niall immediately smiled and nodded in silent approval.

'I think that would be perfect. He also had a hard exterior but there was a definite softness for you there. I am grateful to him for just having you here.'

'Yes, so am I. Without Sam Jackson we may not be together now.'

It was at that precise moment that Emily realised the depth of gratitude she owed to Sam Jackson; a man who had played a large part in shaping their destinies. She knew that, deep within her heart, there was love for him; the man who previously had only been loved by his mother.